GHOSTS OF ONYX

GHOSTS OF ONYX

ERIC NYLUND

BASED ON THE BESTSELLING VIDEO GAME FOR XBOX®

GALLERY BOOKS

New York | London | Toronto | Sydney | New Delhi

G

Gallery Books
An Imprint of Simon & Schuster, Inc.
1230 Avenue of the Americas
New York, NY 10020

First Gallery Books trade paperback edition April 2019

GALLERY BOOKS and colophon are registered trademarks of Simon & Schuster, Inc.

For information about special discounts for bulk purchases, please contact Simon & Schuster Special Sales at 1-866-506-1949 or business@simonandschuster.com.

The Simon & Schuster Speakers Bureau can bring authors to your live event. For more information or to book an event, contact the Simon & Schuster Speakers Bureau at 1-866-248-3049 or visit our website at www.simonspeakers.com.

Manufactured in the United States of America

20 19 18 17 16

Library of Congress Cataloging-in-Publication Data

ISBN 978-1-9821-1167-0
ISBN 978-1-9821-1168-7 (ebook)

For HALO fans everywhere

Linda's medical data winked on a display along with the entire Spartan roster: a long list of every Spartan's current operational status. Only a handful was left, almost every one of them listed as WOUNDED IN ACTION OR MISSING IN ACTION.

"No KIAs?" Dr. Halsey murmured. She touched SPAR-TAN-034's entry. "Sam is listed as missing in action. Why would that be? He died in 2525."

"ONI Section Two Directive Nine-Three-Zero," Cortana replied. "When ONI went public with the Spartan-II program it was decided that reports of Spartan losses could cause a crippling lose of morale. Consequently, any Spartan casualties are listed as MIA or WIA, in order to maintain the illusion that Spartans do not die."

"Spartans never die?" she whispered. Dr. Halsey swiveled out of the contour chair and pushed the monitors out of her way with a sudden violence. "If only that were true."

—*HALO: First Strike*

PROLOGUE

BETA COMPANY'S VICTORY AT PEGASI DELTA

The orbital pod impacted, and metal wrenched and sparked. Inside his cocoon of titanium, lead foil, and stealth ablative coating, SPARTAN-B292 watched black stars explode across his vision, he tasted blood in his mouth, and the last air compressed from his lungs.

Tom's training kicked in: he pulled the pod's twisted frame apart and blinked in the bright blue sunlight.

Something was wrong. 85 Pegasi-914A was supposed to be a faint yellow sun. This was electric blue—boiling plasma blue.

He jumped, rolling to one side as the blast washed over him. The outer layers of his Semi-Powered Infiltration armor boiled and peeled like a bad sunburn.

"Training," his instructor, Lieutenant Commander Ambrose,

— 1 —

had said. *"Your training must become part of your instinct. Drill until it becomes part of your bones."* Tom reacted without thought; a lifetime of training took over.

He raised his MA5K assault rifle and fired along the trajectory of the plasma bolt, making sure to sweep low.

His eyes cleared, and as he automatically reloaded his weapon, he finally saw the surface of Pegasi Delta. It could have been hell: red rocks; orange dust-filled sky; the scars of a dozen impact skids and craters around him; and thirty meters ahead, dark purple splashes of Jackal blood soaking into the sand.

Tom pulled out his sidearm and warily moved to the fallen aliens. There were five with extensive wounds to their lower legs. He shot them each once in their odd angular vulturelike heads, then he knelt, relieved them of their plasma grenades, and stripped off their forearm force shields.

Although Tom wore a full suit of Semi-Powered Infiltration armor (colloquially called "SPI" armor by Section Three technophiles), its hardened plates and photo-reactive panels could only take a few glancing shots before failing. The armor's camouflaging textures sputtered and stabilized, however; and once again blended into the rocky terrain.

Every SPARTAN-III had received extensive training in using the enemy's equipment, so Tom would improvise. He strapped one of the Jackal shields to his forearm. It was excellent protection, as long as you remembered to crouch behind it and cover your legs, a tactic larger UNSC soldiers would have trouble accomplishing.

The display on his faceplate flickered to life, a transparent layer of ghostly green topology. One hundred kilometers overhead, the baseball-sized Stealth Tactical Aerial Reconnaissance Satellite, or STARS, had come online.

A single blinking dot appeared that represented his position. Tom was five kilometers south of the primary target.

He scanned the horizon and saw the Covenant factory city in the distance, looming from the rocky surface like a castle of rust with giant smokestacks and blue plasma coils pulsing deep inside. Beyond the factory lay the lavender shoreline of a toxic sea.

Additional dots appeared on his heads-up screen . . . a dozen, two dozen, and then hundreds. The rest of Beta Company was on-line. Two hundred ninety-one of them. Nine hadn't made it, either dead on reentry or killed from the impact or by Covenant forces before they could get out of the pods.

After the mission, he'd check the roster to see who they'd lost. For now, he stuffed his feelings into a dark corner of his mind.

Tom sighed with relief as he saw the eight *X*s representing the subprowler Black Cat exfiltration craft appear and then fade on his display. That was their only way off this rock after Operation TORPEDO was accomplished.

Text scrolled on his display: "TEAM FOXTROT PROCEED ON VECTOR ZERO EIGHT SIX. PROVIDE FLANKING SUPPORT TO TEAM INDIA."

No reply was necessary. Orders were broadcast from STARS overhead, and any break of radio silence would reveal their position.

Three of the dots on the display winked, and tiny numbers faded into view. B091 was Lucy. B174 was Min. And B004, that was Adam. His friends. Fireteam Foxtrot.

Tom loped forward, found an outcropping of rock, and took cover under it, waiting for them to catch up.

To stay on task, and not get distracted by his racing heartbeat, he reviewed Operation TORPEDO one more time. Pegasi Delta was home to a Covenant refinery. The sea on this tiny world was unusually rich in deuterium and tritium, which they used in their plasma reactors. The factory processed the stuff, and refueled their ships, making this Covenant operation on the edge of UNSC territory a prime target. It allowed the enemy easy access to human space.

There had been previous operations to neutralize the target. UNSC CENTCOM had sent nukes, launched from slipspace, but plutonium emitted an aura of Cherenkov radiation upon reentering normal space, making all the stealth coatings and lead linings useless. The Covenant had easily detected and destroyed them.

There were similarly too many Covenant ships near the moon to send a slow, distantly launched nuke in normal space. Nor was a regular invasion or even the elite Helljumper ODSTs worth the attempt. The UNSC had one chance to take the factory out before the enemy would muster their defenses.

So they were sent.

The three hundred Spartans of Beta Company had been launched seven hours ago into slipspace from the UNSC carrier *All Under Heaven*. They had endured the ride in long-range stealth orbital drop pods, suffered debilitating nausea transitioning unshielded into normal space, and then got parboiled on the fiery ride to the surface of Pegasi Delta.

From the warm welcome given by those five Jackals, Tom knew they'd been detected, but the Covenant might not yet know the size of the breach in their security. He'd have to move quick, take advantage of whatever element of surprise remained, blow the factory, and if possible, the secondary targets of ammunition depots and methane reserves.

They could still do this. They *had* to do it. Destroying that factory would triple the length of the Covenant supply lines to UNSC space. This is exactly what Tom had trained for since he was six years old—years of drills and war games and schooling. But that might not be enough.

He heard the crunch of gravel under a boot. He spun, rifle raised, and saw Lucy.

Every SPARTAN-III looked the same in their Semi-Powered Infiltration armor. The angular shifting camo pattern of the SPI armor was one part legionnaire mail, one part tactical body armor, and one part chameleon. Tom, however, recognized Lucy's short, careful gait.

He made the two-fingers-over-faceplate gesture, the age-old silenced Spartan welcome. She gave him the slightest of nods.

Tom handed her a Jackal shield unit and two plasma grenades. Adam arrived next, and Min ten seconds after that.

When all their appropriated shields were in place, Tom gave Team Foxtrot a series of quick, sharp hand gestures, ordering them to move ahead in a loose arc formation. Stealthy, but fast.

As he stood, thunder rumbled, fire flashed in the sky, and a shadow covered them—and vanished. Two teardrop-shaped Covenant Seraph fighters roared over their hiding spot.

A line of plasma erupted a hundred meters behind them—an inferno that billowed and blossomed straight toward his team.

Tom leapt to one side, activating his Jackal shield, holding it between him and the three-thousand-degree flames that would melt through his SPI armor like butter. The force field flared white from the radiation; his skin on his palms prickled with blisters.

The plasma passed . . . thinned . . . evaporated. The air cooled.

Covenant air support was already in play. That made the situation a hundred times worse.

With a blink, Tom switched his heads-up display from TAC-MAP to TEAMBIO. All members of Team Foxtrot showed sky-rocketing pulses and blood pressures. But they were all still green. All alive. Good.

He sprinted. Stealth was no longer an operational priority.

Getting to the factory where they couldn't be strafed was all that mattered.

Behind him, Lucy, Adam, and Min fell in line, covering the rough ground in long powerful strides at nearly thirty kilometers an hour.

Red ovals appeared on Tom's TACMAP: Covenant Seraphs on another attack run. More than before . . . three . . . six . . . ten.

Tom glanced to either side and saw his comrades, *hundreds* of Spartans running across the broken ground. The dust from their charge filled the air and mingled with the smoke from the last plasma blasts.

Three Spartans lagged behind, turned, and braced, holding M19-B SAM missile launchers. They fired. Missiles streaked into the atmosphere, leaving snaking trails of vapor.

The first bounced off an incoming Seraph's shield; the missile exploded, not damaging the craft, but buffeting it nonetheless into its wingman. Both craft tumbled, lost fifty meters of altitude, and then recovered—but their leading edges scraped the ground, dissipating their weakened shields, and they spun end over end erupting into fiery pinwheels.

The two other missiles struck their targets, overloaded shields, leaving their target Seraphs covered in soot, but otherwise intact. Tom could see the Seraphs wave off their attack runs.

A small victory.

Tom slowed to a trot and watched as the remaining six Seraphs dipped and released their plasma charges, then pulled up, rolled, and vanished in the haze.

Each charge of dropped plasma was a brilliant pinpoint that elongated into a lance of boiling sun-fueled sapphire. When they hit the ground, they exploded and fanned forward, propelled at three hundred kilometers an hour by momentum and thermal expansion.

A wall of flame appeared on Tom's left, and it made the camo panels of his SPI armor shiver blue and white. But he didn't move. He remained transfixed on the other five fires enveloping scores of Spartans.

The plasma slowed, still boiling, and then the clouds cooled and thinned to a dull gray haze, leaving crackling glassed earth and bits of charred bone in its wake.

On his TACMAP, dozens of dots winked off.

Lucy sprinted past Tom. The sight of her snapped him back to action, and he ran.

There'd be time for fear later. And for revenge. When they blew this factory there'd be plenty of time for bloody revenge.

Tom shifted his focus off his TACMAP on his helmet's faceplate and farther ahead to the primary target, now only five hundred meters distant.

From the center of the city-sized factory the blue glow was too intense to stare directly at, casting hard shadows in the web of pipes and the forest of smokestacks. The structure was a kilometer square with towers rising three hundred meters, perfect for snipers.

Tom forced himself to run faster, ahead of Lucy, Adam, and Min, darting from side to side. They understood and mimicked his evasive tactic.

Plasma bolts exploded near his foot. He weaved back and forth through a hailstorm of high-angle trajectories. His suspicions about snipers had been correct.

He dodged, kept running, and squinted ahead at the edge of the factory. His faceplate automatically responded and zoomed to five-times magnification.

There was another threat: shifting luminescent edges of force fields, Jackal shields. And in the shadows, the arrogant eyes of a Covenant Elite in purple armor, staring straight back at him.

Tom skidded to a halt, grabbed the sniper rifle slung on his back, and sighted through the scope. He stilled his labored breathing. A plasma bolt sizzled near his shoulder, crackling the skin of his SPI armor, singeing his flesh, but he ignored the pain, irritated only that the shot had thrown him momentarily off target. He waited for the split second between the beats of his heart, and then squeezed the trigger.

The bullet's momentum spun the Elite around. The articulation of its neck armor exploded off the creature. Tom shot once more, and caught it in the back. A splash of bright blue blood spattered the pipes.

Jackals emerged from the shadows at the periphery of the factory, crawling out behind pipes and plasma tubes.

There were hundreds of them. Thousands.

And they all opened fire

Tom rolled to the ground, flattening himself into a slight depression. Adam, Min, and Lucy dropped, as well, their assault rifles out in front of them, ready to fire.

Plasma bolts and crystal shards crisscrossed over Tom's head—too many to dodge. The enemy didn't have to be able to see them. All they had to do was fill every square centimeter of air with lethal projectiles. His team was pinned, easy picking for those Seraphs on their next pass.

How had the Covenant mustered such a counterresponse so quickly?

If they had been detected earlier, their drop pods would have been vaporized en route. Unless they had had the extreme bad luck to get here when a capital ship had been docked at the factory. On the blind side? Could the STARS overhead have missed something that large?

One of Lieutenant Commander Ambrose's first lessons echoed

in Tom's head: *"Don't rely on technology. Machines are easy to break."*

Tom's COM crackled: "M19 SAMs execute Bravo maneuver, targets painted. All other teams ready to move."

Tom understood: they needed cover. And the only cover was dead ahead in the factory.

From the field six smears of vapor lanced forward to the factory. The M19 SAMs detonated on contact with pipes and plasmas conduits—exploding into clouds of black smoke and blue sparks.

The enemy fire slowed.

That was their opening.

Tom rolled to his feet, and sprinted for the thickest smoke. Team Foxtrot followed.

Every other Spartan on the field charged as well, hundreds of half-camouflaged armored figures, running and firing at the dazed Jackals, appearing as a wave of ghost warriors, half liquid, half shadow, part mirage, part nightmare.

They screamed a battle cry, momentarily drowning the sound of gunfire and explosion.

Tom yelled with them—for the fallen, for his friends, and for the blood of his enemies. The sound was deafening.

Jackals broke ranks, turned to flee, and got shot in the back as their shields turned with them.

But hundreds more held their ground, overlapping shields to form an invulnerable phalanx.

Tom led Team Foxtrot into the smoke-filled shadows of the factory. He found a pipe the size of a redwood dripping condensed water and green coolant and took cover behind it. In the mist he saw Lucy, Adam, and Min take positions behind cover, too. He gave them rapid-fire orders with hand signals: *Move in and kill.*

He spun around, his MA5K rifle leveled—and found himself

face-to-face with a Covenant Elite, its jaw mandibles split in mimicry of an impossibly large human grin. The monster held an energy sword in one hand, and a plasma pistol in the other.

It shot and swung.

Tom sidestepped the deadly arcs of energy, set his foot between the Elite's too-wide stance—pushed and fired at the same time.

The Elite sprawled onto the ground, and Tom tracked his body, spraying rounds into the slit of its helmet. He didn't miss.

Team Foxtrot closed on him, leaving six dead Jackals behind, their bodies snapped like rag dolls.

Behind them on the field came rapid thumps and flashes of heat. Plasma grenades.

Jackals and Elites rushed from their cover in the factory to meet the rest of Beta Company on the field, realizing perhaps it would be suicide to face Spartans in close quarters.

Thousands of Covenant clashed with two hundred Spartans in open combat. Tracer rounds, crystal shards, plasma bolts, and flaring shields made the scene a blur of chaos.

The SPARTAN-IIIs moved with speed and reflexes no Covenant could follow. They dodged, snapped necks and limbs, and with captured energy swords they cut through the enemy until the field ran with rivers of gore and blue blood.

Tom hesitated, torn between moving deeper into the factory complex and executing the mission and running back to help his comrades. You didn't leave your friends behind.

The sky darkened, clouds overhead turning steel gray.

Tom's COM crackled to life: *"Omega three. Execute now! NOW!"*

That stopped him cold. Omega three was the panic code, an order to break and run no matter what the cost.

Why? They were winning.

Tom then saw the clouds move. Only . . . they weren't clouds.

Everything was clear to him now. Why there were so many Covenant here. And why Seraph single ships, craft designed for space combat, were bombing them.

Seven Covenant cruisers sank from the clouds. Over a kilometer long, their bulbous oblong hulls cast shadows over the entire field. If these ships had been parked in formation, refueling over the complex, the STARS might have mistaken such large structures as *part* of the factory.

"We have to help them," Lucy whispered over the TEAM-COM.

"No," Min said, making a short cut motion with his hand. "The Omega order."

"We're not running," Adam broke in.

"No," Tom agreed. "We're not. The order is . . . in error." Despite the environmental controls in his SPI armor, he felt chilled.

Seraph fighters dropped from the cruisers, dozens of them, and gathered into swarms. Darkly luminescent shafts of light appeared from the belly of each cruiser, transport beams, and from them marched hundreds of Elites onto the field.

"But we can't help them either," Tom whispered to his team.

Half of Beta Company turned to face the new threat. Impossible odds, even for Spartans, but they would buy time for the rest of them to find cover.

Finding cover was a futile tactic, though. Seven Covenant cruisers had enough firepower to neutralize even two hundred Spartans. They could pin them down, send in ground reinforcements by the thousands, or if they wanted to, glass the entire moon from orbit.

That left only one option.

"The core," Tom told them. "It's still our mission, and our only effective weapon."

There was a heartbeat pause, and then three green acknowledgment lights winked on his display. His friends knew what he was asking.

Team Foxtrot moved as one, running into the factory at top speed, dodging pipes and supply pods.

A squad of six Elites was ahead, hunkered behind a tangle of ducts.

Tom tossed a handful of concussive grenades to disorient them, but his team kept running. Any delay—even to engage an enemy who could take shots at their backs—might rob them of their one chance.

The surviving Elites recovered and fired.

Adam fell, one hand clutched at the crystal shards that penetrated his armor and punctured his lower spine.

"Go!" Adam cried, waving them off. "I'll hold them."

Tom didn't break stride. Adam knew what had to be done: keep fighting until there was no fight left in him.

The core was a hundred meters ahead. It was impossible to miss, so bright Tom's faceplate automatically polarized to maximum tint, and it was still hard to look at. The core was the size of a ten-story building, pulsing like a huge heart, fed by glowing conduits and steaming coolant pipes, and encrusted with crystalline electronics. It was a marvel of alien engineering, and complex— which hopefully also meant easy to break.

"Main coolant ducts there and there," Tom shouted over TEAMCOM and pointed. "I'll jam the dump valve." He moved to the base of the core.

Lucy's and Min's acknowledgment lights winked.

Tom helmet's display fuzzed with static, then popped and went black. The reactor plasma and its intensely fluctuating electromagnetic field was wreaking havoc with their electronics.

He found the dump valve, a mechanism the size of a Pelican drop-ship, just below the main chamber. He unspooled the thermite-carbon cord and ran it around the valve twice. He then primed and activated the charge. A line of lightning brilliance flared and sizzled through Covenant alloy, fusing the valve into a solid lump.

Tom glanced at Lucy. She set an explosive charge on one of the two main coolant lines that fed the reactor, and then set the timer on the detonator.

Min was setting his timer, too—then vanished in a flash of smoke and thunder. The core flared brighter than the sun. Coolant fumes screamed from twisted pipe and alarms blared.

"No!" Lucy screamed.

She ran past Tom toward the billowing cloud of toxic coolant. He caught her wrist, jerking her to a stop.

"He's gone," Tom said. "EM field must have triggered his charge."

She wrestled out of Tom's grasp.

"We have to get out of here," he told her.

She hesitated, taking one step toward Min.

The support structure groaned and started to melt and sag from the superheating core.

She turned back to Tom, nodded, and they ran out of the chamber—deeper into the factory complex, through a jungle of struts and hissing ducts, and splashing through lakes of leaked, boiling coolant.

The charge Lucy had set went off and silenced the reactor's alarms.

Even with their backs to the reactor, running at a full-out flat sprint, the glare from the core doubled as it reached near super-critical phase. It was too much to endure, even through a polar-ized faceplate, and Tom squinted his eyes nearly shut.

They turned a corner, slid down the railing of angled stairs and onto a catwalk that protruded over a ledge. Five hundred meters below, an ocean churned against rocky cliffs.

They had made it through the factory, out the back side, where massive tubes sucked in the ocean water for processing.

Lucy looked back at the factory and then to Tom. She offered her hand.

He took it.

They jumped.

In free fall, Tom struggled, pumping his legs. Lucy released his hand, and straightened her body. He did the same and then pointed his feet down a split second before he hit the water.

The impact stunned him, then he tasted salt, and choked on water that filled his helmet. He clawed for the surface. The lining of his SPI armor swelled, taking on water, weighing him down.

He broke the surface, paddling as hard as he could with his legs to stay afloat. He clawed at his helmet release and pulled it off.

Next to him, Lucy had her helmet off as well, gasping.

"Look." He nodded to the cliff tops.

From this angle Tom saw the Covenant cruisers over the field. Lances of laser fire rained down from the ships' lateral weapon arrays and blasted his fellow Spartans. Firepower meant for capital ship combat . . . how could anyone survive that?

A new sun appeared. The supercritical core flared and light filled the world. The cruisers rippled, distorted, their alloy skins boiling away in the heat. They disintegrated, bits blasted outward.

The rocky prominence shattered into molten debris.

"Down!" Tom cried.

He and Lucy pushed themselves underwater, diving to escape the overpressure and incinerating blast. His waterlogged armor might now save his life.

Overhead, water flash vaporized. Droplets of liquid rock and metal hissed past him. Heat smothered him . . . and a giant hand grasped and squeezed until all Tom saw was blackness.

Tom lay on the ground panting. They had nearly drowned after the blast, but managed to shed their armor, and finally, exhausted, swam back to the shore, and dragged themselves around the edge of the battlefield and into the hills.

He and Lucy had made it to extraction point six where he had seen one of the stealth exfiltration ships.

No Covenant reinforcements came. They had all been killed when the reactor blew. Operation TORPEDO was a success . . . but it had cost the lives of everyone else in the Beta Company contingent.

All that remained of the factory, the Covenant cruisers, and ground forces of Beta Company was a glass crater four kilometers in diameter. No bones, not even a camo panel from a suit of SPI armor. Gone. Whispers in the wind.

Lucy pulled herself up against the hull of the Black Cat sub-prowler craft, her body trembling. She started to stagger back down the hill.

"Where are you going?"

"Survivors," she whispered and took one uncertain step forward. "Foxtrot. We have to look."

No one had survived. They had checked all the COM frequencies, searched the shoreline, fields, and hills on their long silent hike back. No one else was alive.

Lucy was tiny. Like Tom, she was only twelve years old, but at one point six meters and seventy kilos, Lucy was one of the smallest SPARTAN-IIIs. Without her SPI armor and weapons, and her pale form covered only in modest body sheathing, she looked even smaller.

Tom stood and gently put his arm around her. She trembled violently.

"You're going into shock."

He found a first-aid kit and injected her with the standard postmission antishock medical cocktail.

"Survivors . . ." she whispered.

"There are none," he said. "We have to get out of here. The Black Cat's capacitors will drain in four hours and we won't be able to jump to slipspace."

She turned to him, eyes wide and brimming with tears. "How are you sure we're alive?"

Tom was alive. He was certain. But as he cast one final glance at the crackling fields of Pegasi Delta, he knew *part* of him had died today with Beta Company.

He helped Lucy into the Black Cat prowler and closed the hatch.

The subprowler's engines thrummed to life, then dulled to a whisper. The craft lifted and angled up into the darkening skies.

Lucy's words asking if they were alive would be her last. "Post-traumatic vocal disarticulation," the experts would eventually declare. And although recertified for duty, she would remain silent—either unable, or unwilling, to speak the rest of her life.

In the years to come, Tom would reflect on Lucy's last question every day. "*How are you sure we're alive?*" Something had died for every Spartan that day.

SECTION I

LIEUTENANT AMBROSE

CHAPTER 1

John, SPARTAN-117, despite being encased in a half ton of angular MJOLNIR armor, moved like a shadow through the twilight forest underbrush.

The guard on the perimeter of Base New Hope drew on a cigarette, took a final puff, and tossed the butt.

John lunged, a whisper rustle, and he wrapped his arm around the man's neck, wrenching it up with a *pop.*

The guard's cigarette hit the ground.

Nearby crickets resumed their night song.

John pinged his status to the rest of Blue Team. Four green LED lights winked on his display, indicating the rest of the extended perimeter guards had been neutralized.

The next objective was a delivery gate, the weakest part of the rebel base's defense system. The guardhouse had two men outside, two on the rooftop, and several inside. Past this, however, the base had impressive security even by Spartan standards: motion and seismic sensors, a triple layering of guards, trained dogs, and overhead MAKO-class drones.

John blinked his status light green: the signal to proceed with the next phase.

The setting sun just touched the edge of the horizon when the guards on the roof of the bunker twitched and crumpled. It happened so fast, John wasn't sure which Linda had targeted first. A heartbeat later the two on the ground were dead as well.

John and Kurt ran for the gatehouse.

Kelly sprinted ahead, covering the three hundred meters from the forest in half the time, and leapt to the roof in a single bound. She opened the roof's vent and dropped flash-bang grenades.

Kurt posted outside the door, and swept the aft side for any targets. John waited on the other side of the steel and bulletproof-glass security door, one hand on its handle, one foot braced against the wall.

Inside three muffled thumps sounded.

John pulled, wrenching the door and frame from the steel reinforcing in the wall.

Kurt entered, his M7 submachine gun burping three-round bursts.

John was in a moment later, and assessed the threats in the blink of an eye. There were three guards already down. Behind them, banks of security monitors showed a hundred views of the base.

Seven other men sat at a card table, shaking off the effects of the flash-bangs. They stood with their sidearms halfway out of their holsters.

John calmly shot each man, once in the head.

Nothing moved.

Kelly dropped outside the door, rolled inside, her weapon leveled.

"Security system," John whispered to her and Kurt.

Fred and Linda appeared a moment later, and together they pulled and wedged the heavy door back into its twisted frame.

"All good outside," Fred told them.

Kelly sat before the bank of monitors and pulled out a touch pad, booting the ONI computer infiltration software package.

Kurt tapped on the keyboard, nodding to the sticky note under one monitor. "Password's posted," he said, shaking his head.

"Okay," Kelly muttered. "We can do it the easy way, too. Running monitor-looping protocol, now. I'll get a clean path to the target."

Kurt meanwhile flipped through various camera angles and subsystems on the displays. "No alarms raised," he reported. He paused and watched a group of guards unloading ammunition canisters off a Warthog. One man fumbled and dropped a can; along its side was stenciled: MUTA-AP-09334.

John hadn't ordered a subsystems sweep, though he hadn't specifically forbidden it, either. Kurt's actions could trigger a red flag at the base's command and control.

John had mixed feelings about using SPARTAN-051, Kurt, as Sam's replacement on Blue Team. On the one hand, he was an extremely capable Spartan. Chief Mendez had routinely given him command of Green Team during training exercises, and Kurt had often won when facing John's Blue Team. But on the other hand, he was, for a Spartan, undisciplined. He took time to talk with every Spartan, and even the non-Spartan personnel that trained and supplied them. As a professional soldier in the middle of two wars—one fighting an entrenched rebellion, the other taking on a technologically superior xenophobic alien race—Kurt spent a considerable amount of time and energy making friends.

"Camera system and detectors looped," Kelly announced and made a tiny circle with her index finger. "We have fifteen minutes while dogs and drones are rotated and refueled. So just guards to deal with."

"Move," John told his team.

Kurt hesitated, eyes still fixed on the monitors.

"What?" John asked.

"A funny feeling," Kurt whispered.

This worried John. Everyone had performed flawlessly, and there were no signs the enemy had reacted to their presence. But Kurt had a reputation for sniffing out ambushes. John had been on the receiving end of Kurt's intuition several times during training.

John nodded at the monitor, still devoid of anything but normal activity. "Explain."

"The guards unloading that Warthog," Kurt said. "They look like . . . they're getting ready for something. Security systems and machines can be fooled—or easily rigged to fool," he stated. "People? They're not so easy."

"I understand," John said. "We'll stay sharp, but we have to stick to the schedule. Let's move."

Kurt got up, casting a glance back at the monitor as they exited the gatehouse.

The Spartans melted from shadow to shadow, skirting around a warehouse, under officers' barracks, and finally, at the center of the base, they approached the edge of a warehouse. The building was surrounded by three fences posted with warnings that the gravel yard beyond was mined.

Eight guards patrolled the perimeter. Parked on the side was a modified Warthog; it had been cut in half and a new midsection had been welded in place that looked like it could carry ten men into battle. It would suffice.

John withdrew a tiny rod and pointed it at the building. The radiation counter flickered to a hundred times normal background level for this planet.

That confirmed that their primary target was inside: three FENRIS nuclear warheads.

Recent battles with the Covenant had depleted UNSC stockpiles of fissile materials in this sector to almost nothing. Insurgents had heard of this (which indicated they also had a considerable intelligence capability), and they had contacted the regional CENTCOM to boldly offer a trade. They said they had stolen warheads. They claimed to have people with Borren's Syndrome, and wanted the expertise and medicines only UNSC doctors could provide.

CENTCOM said they'd consider the matter.

They had considered it, and sent in Blue Team to get those warheads, and if presented with the opportunity, they were to target any rebel leaders.

John signaled his team to move out, disperse around the bunker, and take up positions to snipe the guards.

Green acknowledgment lights winked on. Kurt's was last, with a palpable hesitation.

John gave Kurt a short hand wave, and then pointed at the Warthog, indicating that he get the vehicle ready to move.

Kurt nodded.

Kurt's "feeling" that something was wrong was contagious. John didn't like it. He pushed his uncertainties aside. Blue Team was in position.

John unslung his sniper rifle and sighted. He gave the "go" signal and watched as one guard and then another silently fell over. Linda had been quick and efficient as usual.

John gave the go-ahead to move in.

Blue Team eased inside, sweeping the dark corners of the building.

The place was empty, save steel racks cradling three conical warhead casings. John's radiation counter jumped, indicating that they did not hold conventional explosives.

He pointed at Kelly and Fred, to the rack, then to the Warthog outside. They nodded.

Kurt's acknowledgment light winked red.

No Spartan flashed a red light on a mission unless they had a good reason.

"Abort," John said. "Back out. Now."

Dizziness washed over him.

John saw Linda, Fred, and Kelly sink to their knees.

Then blackness swallowed him.

John awoke with a start. Every muscle burned and it felt like someone had hammered his head. This was a good sign: it meant he wasn't dead.

He tensed his muscles against an unyielding pressure.

He blinked to clear his hazy vision and saw he sat propped against a wall, still in the high-security bunker.

The warheads were also still there.

Then John saw a dozen commandos in the warehouse, watching him. They hefted the .30-caliber machine gun, favored by rebel forces. Nicknamed "confetti makers," they were grossly inaccurate, but at point-blank range, it would hardly be a concern.

The rest of Blue Team lay face-first on the concrete floor. Technicians in lab coats crouched over them capturing high-resolution digital video.

John jerked against his inert armor. He had to get to his team. Were they dead?

"No need to struggle," a voice said.

A man with long gray hair stepped in front of John's faceplate. "Or struggle if you want. We've installed neural-inhibitor collars on you and your comrades. UNSC standard issue for dangerous felons." He smiled. "I'd wager without one you could, and would, rip me in half in that miraculous power armor."

John kept his mouth shut.

"Relax," the man said. "I am General Graves."

John recognized the name. Howard Graves was one of the three men believed to be in charge of the united rebel front. It was no coincidence he was here.

"You're suffering from rapid decompression—the bends," he told John. "We used an antigrav plate, old technology that never panned out, but for our purposes, it worked just fine. A focused beam fooled your armor's sensors into thinking you were in a ten-gee environment. It increased internal pressure to save your lives, momentarily rendering you unconscious."

"You engineered this all for us," John said, his voice hoarse.

"You 'Spartans' have put quite a dent in our efforts to liberate the frontier worlds," General Graves said. "Station Jefferson in the Eridanus asteroid belt last year; our destroyer *Origami*; six months ago, our high-explosive manufacturing facility; followed by the incident in Micronesia, and our saboteur cell on Reach. I didn't believe it until I saw the video. All by the same four-man team. Some said 'Blue Team' was a myth." He rapped his knuckle on John's faceplate. "You seem real enough to me."

John struggled, but he might as well have been encased in a mountain of steel. The neural collar neutralized every signal traveling down his spine save the autonomics to his heart and diaphragm.

He had to focus. Did everyone on his team have a collar? Yes. Each Spartan had a thick clamp on the back of their neck, directly over the AI interface port. Graves had excellent intelligence on their equipment.

Wait. John scrutinized his paralyzed team: Kelly, Linda, and Fred. No Kurt.

Graves had said "four-man team." He didn't know about Kurt.

"As you surmised," Graves continued, "this was all for your benefit. We scraped our fissile material together and made sure it was done so sloppily that even your Office of Naval Intelligence saw it happen. We anticipated the miraculous Blue Team would be sent. I am not disappointed that your leaders' minds are still so easily read."

A young commando approached, saluted, and nervously whispered, "Sir, external sensors are off-line."

Graves frowned. "Drag the prisoners out of here. Sound the general alarm. Police those warheads, and tell the liftships to—"

A buzzing sound filled the air. John spied a blur of spinning metal through the doorway. He had a fraction of a second to see it was an eight-armed Asteroidea antipersonnel mine, its pressure trigger jammed with a chunk of gravel—just before it detonated into a ball of thunder.

Metal pinged off John's armor.

Everyone standing in the room doubled over from the concussive force and hail of shrapnel.

Six commandos with multiple cuts and bleeding ears rose, weapons ready, shaking their heads to clear the disorientation.

The modified Warthog that had been parked next to the bunker crashed into the open double doorway.

The entire warehouse shook.

The commandos opened fire, and rushed the doorway.

The Warthog pulled away, then with a squeal, it reversed, and then rammed the doorway again. The corrugated steel walls screeched, buckled, and with a shower of sparks the vehicle wedged its midsection in the building like a pregnant queen termite.

The commandos unloaded their confetti makers, puckering the 'Hog's armor.

The top of the midsection slid open and three more Asteroidea antipersonnel mines arced, whirling like a child's toy—each landing in a corner of the bunker—and exploded.

White-hot metal fragments cut through the commandos like a scythe.

Kurt leapt out and shot the three men still moving. He quickly went to each Spartan and pulled off the collars.

Kelly rolled to her feet. Fred and Linda got up.

Kurt yanked the collar off John's neck. His entire body tingled, but his muscles once again responded to his commands. He flexed his limbs. There was no permanent nerve damage.

"We can forget about stealth now," John said. "Kurt, drive the Warthog. Kelly, Linda, Fred, get those warheads loaded ASAP."

They nodded.

John went to General Graves. A sliver of corrugated steel had lodged in the man's skull.

Unfortunate. Graves had held secrets of the rebels' command and intelligence structure–secrets John had had the barest glimpse of. Their capacities had been greatly underestimated. With the larger Covenant threat looming, John wondered what the rebels would ultimately do. Attack a weakened UNSC as it battled aliens, or fight against humanity's common enemy?

He ignored the larger strategic picture and focused on the tactical, helping Kelly maneuver the last warhead into the Warthog's armored midsection.

Loaded with the bombs and five armored Spartans, the vehicle bottomed its shocks. John climbed into the rear and Kurt drove, and they sluggishly accelerated away from the secure warehouse.

"Best speed to the PZ," John ordered.

Kurt turned on the Warthog's radio. It buzzed with confused chatter.

"Unit One nonresponsive. Gunfire reported. Man down! Tracking APC. Open fire? Confirm—confirm! All units converge. Do it now!"

"Everyone," John shouted, "into the center."

Holes peppered the Warthog, armor-piecing rounds penetrating the side like paper and denting the casings of the warheads.

"Behind the warheads!" Fred told them.

John, Kelly, Fred, and Linda huddled behind the missiles. Nuclear warheads ironically would provide their best defense. Their casings were superhardened, both to contain radiation and hold the fury of a small sun for a split second longer and to boost the thermonuclear yield.

John looked up at the driver's seat. Kurt squeezed himself lower into the seat, presenting the smallest possible target, risking his life to get them all to safety.

The Warthog billowed smoke, but its speed slowly increased to forty kilometers an hour. A sharp rattle came from the engine. A tire shredded and the vehicle swerved right and then left.

Kurt regained control and kept going.

The AP fire slowed and then stopped.

"Brace!" Kurt said and downshifted.

The Warthog barreled through the chain-link and concertina-wire barrier, over gravel fields, and into the forest.

"Road 32-B to the PZ," Kurt said.

"Road" was a creative overstatement. They bounced along, mowing down trees, fishtailing, and spraying mud.

"Drones!" Kurt told them.

"Get the hatch open," John ordered. Kelly and Fred pulled the midsection roof panels apart.

John stuck his head out, and spotted three MAKO-class attack drones jetting toward them, each heavy with a fat missile. One direct hit would take out the Warthog. Even a near miss could destroy an axle.

Linda popped up, her sniper rifle already in hand and eyes on the scope.

John and Linda opened fire.

The lead drone smoked and dropped into the trees. The next drone angled up, bobbing. It released its missile, and banked away. A line of smoke appeared, a tail of fire, and a missile accelerated toward them at a frightening rate.

Linda fired, squeezing off the rounds as fast as the chamber could cycle. The missile started to spin . . . but it was still dead on course.

"PZ three hundred meters," Kelly said, consulting her tablet. "Welcome committee has us in their sights."

"Tell them we have the package," John said, "and we need a hand."

"Roger that," she said.

The missile was two kilometers from them—closing fast.

Ahead, the forest turned into swamp. With a hurricane roar, a UNSC Pelican dropship rose over the treetops and its twin chain guns spat a cloud of depleted uranium slugs at the incoming missile—making it bloom into a flower of fire and smoke.

"Stand by for pickup, Blue Team," the dropship's pilot said

over their COM. "We got incoming single-craft hostiles. So hang tight, and go vacuum protocols."

"Check suit integrity," John ordered. He remembered Sam and how his friend had sacrificed himself, remaining on a Covenant ship under siege because of a breach in his suit. If a single AP round had breached their MJOLNIR, they'd be in a similar jam.

The Warthog, billowing thick black clouds, rattled to a stop.

The Pelican settled over it and clamped tight.

Blue Team came back all green status lights, and John relaxed; he had been holding his breath.

The Pelican lifted the Warthog, laden with Spartans and warheads, into the air.

"Make secure," the pilot said. "Bogies inbound on vector zero seven two."

Acceleration tugged at John, but he stood fast, one hand bracing the nukes, the other against the punctured side of the Warthog.

The clear blue light outside darkened to black and filled with the twinkle of stars.

"Rendezvous with the *Bunker Hill* in fifteen seconds," the Pelican pilot announced. "Prepare for immediate out-system slipspace jump."

Kurt carefully eased out of the driver's seat and into the midsection to join them.

"Nice work," Fred told him. "How did you know it was a trap?"

"It was the guards loading ammunition off the Warthog," Kurt explained. "I saw it at the time, but it didn't register until it was almost too late. Those ammo canisters were marked as armor-piercing rounds. All of them. You wouldn't need that much AP unless you were taking on a few light tanks. . . ."

"Or a squad of Spartans," Linda said, catching on.

"Us," Fred remarked.

Kurt doggedly shook his head. "I should have figured it out sooner. I almost got everyone killed."

"You mean you saved everyone," Kelly said and she butted her shoulder into his.

"If you ever have another funny 'feeling,'" John told him, "tell me, and make me understand."

Kurt nodded.

John wondered about this man's "feelings," his instinctive subconscious awareness of the danger. CPO Mendez had made then all train so hard, lessons in fire-team integration, target prioritization, hand-to-hand combat, and battlefield tactics were part of their hardwired instincts now. But that didn't mean the underlying biological impulses were worthless. Quite the opposite.

John set a hand on Kurt's shoulder, searching for the right words.

Kelly, as usual, articulated the sentiments that John never could. She said, "Welcome to Blue, Spartan. We're going to make a great team."

CHAPTER 2

0500 Hours, October 24, 2531 (Military Calendar) \
Aboard UNSC *Point of No Return,* Interstellar Space,
Sector B-042

Colonel Ackerson ran both hands through his thinning hair, and poured himself a glass of water from the carafe on the table. His hand shook. Ironic that his career in the military had come to this: a secret meeting on a ship that technically didn't exist, about to discuss a project that, if successful, would never surface from the shadows.

Eyes-only classification. Code words. Double deals and back-stabbing.

He longed for earlier days when he held a rifle in his hands, the enemy was easily recognized and dispatched, and Earth was the most powerful, secure center of the universe.

Those times only existed in memory now, and Ackerson had to live in the dark to save what little light remained.

He pushed back from the ebony conference table, and his gaze swept over the room, a five-meter-diameter bubble, bisected by a metal grate floor, with stainless-steel walls brushed to a white reflective sheen. Once sealed, it became a Faraday cage, and no electronic signals could escape.

He hated this place. The white walls and the black table made him feel like he sat inside a giant eye, always under observation.

The "cage," as it was referred to, was contained within a cocoon of ablative insulating layers, and counterelectronics to provide further security, and this ensconced on the most secret ship in the UNSC fleet, *Point of No Return*.

Constructed in parts and then assembled in deep space, *Point of No Return* was the largest prowler-class vessel ever built. The size of a destroyer, she was completely radar-invisible, and when her baffled engines ran below 30 percent she was as dark as interstellar space. *Point of No Return* was the wartime field command and control platform for the UNSC Office of Naval Intelligence, NavSpecWep Section Three.

Very few had actually seen this ship, only a handful had ever been aboard, and fewer than twenty officers in the galaxy had access to the cage.

The white wall sheathed apart and three people walked in, boots clipping across the metal grate.

Rear Admiral Rich entered first. He was only forty, but already gray. He commanded covert operations in Section Three, in charge of every field operation save Dr. Halsey's SPARTAN-II program. He sat on Ackerson's right, glanced at the water, and scowled. He withdrew a gold flask and unstoppered it. The odor of cheap whiskey immediately assailed Ackerson.

Next was Captain Gibson. The man moved like a panther with the low lopping strides indicative of time recently spent in microgravity. He was the field officer in charge of Section Three Black Ops, the hands-on wet-work counterpart to Rear Admiral Rich.

And last, Vice Admiral Parangosky entered.

The doors immediately sheathed close behind her. There were three distinct clicks as locks meshed into place, and then the room fell into an unnatural silence.

Parangosky remained standing and assessed the others; her iron gaze finally pinned Ackerson. "You better have one hell of a reason for dragging us all here through back channels, Colonel."

Parangosky looked fragile and closer to 170 years old than her actual seventy years, but she was in Ackerson's opinion the most dangerous person in the UNSC. She was the real power in ONI. To his knowledge, only one person had ever successfully crossed her and lived.

Colonel Ackerson set four reader tablets on the table. Biometric scanners flashed on the sidebars.

"Please, Admiral," he said, "if you would."

"Very well," she growled and sat. "I'll bite."

"Nothing new with that, Margaret," Admiral Rich muttered.

She shot him a piercing glare, but said nothing.

The three officers scanned the document.

Captain Gibson sighed explosively and pushed the tablet away. "Spartans," he said. "Yes, we're all familiar with their operational record. Very impressive." From the scowl on his face, it was clear "impressed" was not what he was feeling.

"And," Rich commented, "we already know your feelings about this program, Colonel. I hope you did not bring us here to try and once again shut the Spartans down."

"No," Ackerson replied. "Please scroll to page twenty-three, and my purpose will become clear."

They reluctantly examined his report.

Captain Rich's brows shot up. "I've never seen these figures before . . . MJOLNIR suit construction, maintenance staff, and recent upgrades to their microfusion plants. Christ! You could build a new battle group for what Halsey is spending."

Vice Admiral Parangosky did not glace at the figures. "I've seen this before, Colonel. The Spartans are the single most expensive project in our section. They are, however, also the most effective. Come to the point."

"The point is this," Ackerson said. Sweat trickled down his back, but he kept his voice even. If he didn't sell this, Parangosky might roll over him, and he'd find himself busted to sergeant and patrolling some dusty frontier world. Or worse.

"I'm not suggesting that we shut the Spartans down," he continued and gestured broadly with both hands. "On the contrary, we're fighting a war on two fronts: rebels eroding our economic base in the outer colonies; and the Covenant, who, as far as we know, are committed to the total annihilation of humanity." Ackerson straightened and met Gibson's, Rich's, and then Parangosky's gazes. "I'm suggesting we need *more* Spartans."

The smallest flicker of a smile played over Vice Admiral Parangosky's thin lips.

"Crap," Rich muttered. He took a draw from his whiskey flask. "Now I've heard everything."

"What's your angle, Colonel?" Gibson demanded. "You've been on record against Dr. Halsey's SPARTAN-IIs since she started the program."

"I have," Ackerson said. "And I still am." He nodded to the readers. "Screen forty-two please."

They tabbed ahead.

"Here I detail the flaws of Halsey's undeniably 'successful' program," Ackerson said. "High cost, an absurdly small gene-candidate pool, inefficient training methodologies, far too few final units produced—not to mention her dubious ethics of using flash cloning procedures."

Parangosky scrolled ahead. "And you are proposing . . . ah, a SPARTAN-III program?" Her cast-iron expression didn't betray a hint of emotion.

"Consider the SPARTAN-IIs a proof-of-concept prototype," Ackerson explained. "Now it is time to shift into production mode. Make the units better with new technology. Make more of them. And make them cheaper."

"Interesting," she whispered.

He sensed he was getting through to her, so he pressed on.

"The SPARTAN-IIs have one additional feature that makes them undesirable for our purposes," Ackerson said. "A public presence. Although classified top secret, stories have leaked throughout the fleet. Just a myth at this point, but Section Two has plans to disseminate more information, and soon go public with the program."

"What!?" Rich pushed back from the table. "They can't release details of a top-secret—"

"To boost morale," Ackerson explained. "They'll build the legend of the Spartan. If the war goes as projected with the Covenant, we will certainly need drastic measures to maintain confidence among the rank and file."

"That means these Spartans will have to be, what, protected?" Rich asked incredulous. "If they're all dead, that makes a psy-ops campaign kind of moot, don't it?"

"Not necessarily, sir," Gibson remarked. "They can be dead, just not a secret."

"I assume, Colonel," Parangosky said, "that this public

presence issue will *not* be a flaw with your proposed series-three program?"

"Correct, ma'am." Ackerson set his hands on the table and bowed his head. He then looked up. "This was a most difficult conclusion to come to. This new fighting force must be inexpensive, highly efficient, and trained to take on missions that traditionally would never be considered. Not even by Halsey's supermen."

Rich scowled at this and his forehead wrinkled. "Suicide missions."

"High-value targets," Ackerson countered. "Covenant targets. The battles we have won against this enemy have come at unacceptable losses. With their numbers, their superior technology, we have few options against such a force, save extreme tactics."

"He's right," Gibson said. "Spartans have proven their effectiveness on high-risk missions, and although I hate to admit it, they're better than any human team I could assemble. Remove existing UNSC mandates for safety and exfiltration, and we have a shot of slowing the Covenant down. It will give us time to think, plan, and come up with a better way to fight."

Parangosky whispered, "You want to trade *lives* for *time*."

Ackerson paused, carefully weighing his response, then said, "Yes, ma'am. Isn't that the job of a soldier?"

Parangosky stared at him. Ackerson held her gaze.

Rich and Gibson held their collective breath, speechless.

"Is there another option?" Ackerson asked. "How many worlds are now cinders? How many billions of colonists have died? If we save a single planet, gain a few weeks, isn't that worth a handful of men and women?"

"Of course it is," she whispered. "God help us all. Yes, Colonel, yes, it is worth it."

Rich emptied his flask. "I'll reroute funding for this thing through the usual places, no computer records. Too many damned AIs these days."

Gibson said, "I'll make sure you get equipment, DIs, and whatever else you need, Colonel."

"And I know of a perfect staging area to get this off the ground," Parangosky said. She nodded to Rich.

"Onyx?" he said, half question, half statement.

"Do you know of a better place?" she asked. "Section One has made that place a virtual black hole."

Rich sighed and said, "Okay. I'll send you the file on the place, Colonel. You're going to love it there."

Rich's assurances did not at all comfort, but Ackerson kept his mouth shut. He had everything he wanted . . . almost.

"Just one more thing," Ackerson said. "I'll need a SPARTAN-II to help me train these new recruits."

Captain Gibson snorted. "And you're going to ask Dr. Halsey to lend you one?"

"I have a different methodology in mind," he replied.

Parangosky said, "You need a Spartan to train Spartans, of course, but"—her voice lowered—"tread *damned* lightly. This thing goes public, people find out we're making 'disposable heroes,' and morale will plummet across the fleet. Make sure no one in Section Three knows about your SPARTAN-II trainer, or the SPARTAN-IIIs. They're going to have to vanish. Understood?"

"Yes, ma'am."

"And for God's sake," she said, narrowing her eyes to slits, "Catherine Halsey must never know. Her bleeding-heart sympathies for the Spartans have won her too many admirers at CENTCOM. If that woman wasn't so vital to the war we would have had her retired decades ago."

Ackerson nodded.

The three Naval officers thumbed their tablet readers and the files erased. They rose, and without another word, left the cage.

They had never been here.

None of this had ever been discussed.

Alone now, Ackerson reviewed his files and made plans. The first matter of business was already in the works: on-screen appeared the career record of SPARTAN-051.

CHAPTER 3

SPARTAN-051, Kurt, jumped into utter emptiness. It was a hundred-kilometer drop to the moon under his feet. He mentally made the adjustment to the free-floating world of space, and noted that technically there was no "under" or "above" in space—just vectors, masses, and velocities.

He switched on his reverse-angle camera and saw Kelly and Fred jump from the lock of the prowler after him. He knew not to turn his head to look. The motion would make him gyrate out of control. Besides, in the vacuum-enhanced variant of MJOLNIR armor, his mobility was a fraction of normal.

A green status light winked on, confirming they were all on the same vector.

They'd coast for several kilometers before they activated

long-range thruster packs. Although slow, there were two good reasons to be cautious.

First, when their prowler, *Circumference,* had reentered normal space, the NAV Officer had picked up an echo, a partial ship silhouette, prowler class. He had dismissed this as an echo from their reentry to normal space that had bounced off the moon. The NAV Officer had assured them there was nothing to worry about. Still, the anomaly bugged Kurt. In case there *was* another ship, Kurt wanted to be well away before igniting packs. No need to needlessly give away the stealth ship's position.

Second, they had detected an inert COM satellite on the dark side of the moon—something you'd expect if the system was being monitored for a sneak attack. No signal had emitted from the thing. The *Circumference* had jammed, and then fried it with a burst from a pulse laser.

Kurt just made the assumption this simple recon mission would be hot. That way, he'd be happy to be disappointed.

He activated the single-beam laser TEAMCOM system, and said, "ETA to day-night demarcation in five minutes. System check thrusters."

Kurt ran his own diagnostic. They couldn't take any chances with the packs. Designed for long-range deep-space operations, it was one of the riskiest pieces of equipment they'd been trained on. Even with triple redundancy in NAV system and stabilizers, one accident and there was enough compressed tri-amino hydrazine in the double fuel tanks to propel you so far and so fast off course, rescue would be an astronomically remote possibility.

Or as Chief Mendez had put it: *"Start tumbling in this gear, start praying."*

Green status lights winked back at Kurt.

"ETA three minutes," he said.

"Roger," Kelly replied and then she added, "Something wrong?"

"No," Kurt said.

Fred's voice came over the COM: "When you say 'no' like that, you mean 'yes.'"

"Just a feeling," he admitted.

Silence hissed over their linked single-beam COMs.

Kurt watched in his rear-angle display as Kelly and Fred activated their MA5B assault rifles. A data cable linked each rifle to their T-PACK microprocessor to give the proper counterthrust when the weapon fired.

Kurt sighed, momentarily fogging his faceplate. Now they were jumpy, too. But maybe that wasn't a bad thing. Too many things weren't adding up.

There was the echo and the inactive spy satellite. And why had CENTCOM picked them to go on a low-risk recon mission? This was just a simple look to check out reported suspicious activity at a decommissioned USNC shipyard. Sure, a long space walk was a high-risk maneuver . . . but not something you'd send three Spartans on.

"Coming up on the twilight zone," Kurt said. "Go to radio silent."

They drifted toward the razor line that marked night to day on the smooth icy moon. There was no atmosphere, so the transition into the light would be quick, no sparkling sunrise, just a blinding flash of glare.

They crossed into the light. Kurt's faceplate automatically polarized, and they got their first glimpse of the shipyard.

Station Delphi was a floating city of welded scaffolding, cranes, docking pods, tubes, and grappling claws. There were no lights. No thermal emissions. Kurt snapped on his high-def recorder to capture every square meter of the derelict. Whoever had been re-sponsible for the station's decommissioning three years ago had done a sloppy job. There was a halo of debris: spinning steel gird-ers, bolts, and battle plate flashing as it caught and reflected the dull red sunlight from the distant binary stars.

It looked deserted, so Kurt winked his green status light three times—the all-clear to resume single-beam communication.

Fred sent an image over TEAMCOM, the skeletal frame of a partially constructed ship, about three times the size of their prowler. He said, "That TR steel alloy exposed to solar radiation is supposed to turn white."

"It's silver," Kurt replied. "New construction?"

"Check this out," Kelly said.

She uploaded a series of images, capturing at increasing mag-nification a hull-support cradle whose shape suggested the oddly angular structure of a stealth ship. Only this vessel had to be as large as a UNSC destroyer—which was impossible. A large stealth ship was an oxymoron. The bigger the ship, the more radiation leaked, the more thermals, the more stealth-coated surfaces had to be kept in perfect repair so they didn't reflect radar.

"Send that image on a single beam back to the *Circumference*," Kurt ordered.

Kelly's status light went green.

Kurt swept his left hand forward, gathering data on his sensors-encrusted glove. Still no thermals. No, wait, as Station Delphi rotated slowly, a tiny white flare appeared.

"Hot spot," he said, and tagged the region on his display, send-ing coordinates to Fred and Kelly.

Kurt's hand twitched; years of communicating by silent, effi-cient hand signals were something you just didn't unlearn. Talk, even using a single beam, didn't feel right on this mission. One simple wave, however, could send him spinning, and while his T-PACK could compensate, Kurt wanted to continue to stealth without thrusters.

Kelly moved her optics package on the spot, zoomed in, and they all saw a splash of rainbow colors.

Kurt's radiation counter clicked wildly and then went dead. "Broad-spectrum pulse," he reported.

"I've seen one of those before," Fred told them. "They had to repair the Shaw-Fujikawa translight engine on the *Magellan*. It was a risky op. Those things aren't meant to be taken apart once they go active."

Shaw-Fujikawa engines allowed UNSC ships to leave normal space and plow through a dimensional subdomain colloquially known as "Slipstream space." Kurt had received rudimentary training in how it worked. The drive used particle accelerators to rip apart normal space-time by generating micro black holes. Those holes evaporated via Hawking radiation in a nanosecond. The real quantum mechanical "magic" of the drive was how it manipulated those holes in space-time, squeezing a hundred-thousand-ton cruiser into slipspace. The mathematics of how this worked and how a ship reentered normal space was well beyond him. It was, actually, beyond most human geniuses.

Kurt, however, did know this about Shaw-Fujikawa drives: they were dangerous. There was radiation and anecdotal evidence that the normal laws of nature "bent" in close proximity to an active unit.

"Update your mission logs and beam them back to the *Circumference*," Kurt said. "We're going to take a closer look at that thing and confirm it's what Fred thinks it is before we call in HAZMAT."

There was a slight delay before Kelly's and Fred's acknowledgment lights blinked green.

Kurt activated his T-PACK, puffed the thrusters, and angled toward Station Delphi. He tapped the attitude controls, adjusting pitch, roll, and yaw to avoid colliding with the bolts, beams, and tools spinning in the debris field.

As they closed to within one hundred meters of the sputtering, partially disassembled drive coils, his rear-angle camera fuzzed with static.

"Getting interference here," Kurt said. "You two hold position. I'll scout it out."

"Roger," Kelly said. There was an edge of concern in her voice. "Grapple lines ready."

Kurt crept closer and got a glimpse into the heart of the drive: a near-ultraviolet glow that didn't match the thermal output. It wasn't possible for a hole into slipspace to exist for more than a fraction of an instant, but he couldn't help feeling that's exactly what this was . . . and the closer he drifted the more likely he'd get pulled in and forever lost.

But that was just a feeling.

He hesitated.

Kurt altered his direct trajectory and drifted toward a beam thirty meters over the Shaw-Fujikawa engine. The space near the drive rippled like heat waves rising . . . impossible in a hard vacuum.

His heads-up display flickered.

Kelly spoke over the COM, her transmission filled with noise. "Your IFF tag is breaking up. It shows your position in multiple regions. Abort the recon. If your electronics malfunction—"

The COM broke into a hiss of static.

"I've seen enough," Kurt said.

Static answered him.

"I'm heading back."

He tapped his altitude thrusters to spin around. The switch worked, but there was no action from the T-PACK nozzles.

Kurt released the controls. Triple redundancy in the processors or not—if his T-PACK was affected by the nearby radiation, the last thing he wanted to do was give it a command to fire.

He grasped the steel beam, and bracing, he waved back to his team. He couldn't see them out there, but he knew they were watching him. He knew they wouldn't let him down. With Kelly and Fred at his back, he could have been at the edge of hell, and they would have gotten him out.

Of course, with a malfunctioning, partially deconstructed Shaw-Fujikawa drive within spitting distance . . . that might be exactly where he stood.

He spotted motion in the dark, a snaking orange-and-white striped rope and gyrating blob on one end: Kelly's rescue line. Perfect. No worries now.

The steel beam sparked. Kurt reflexively let go, and arcs played across the alloy—radiation inducing a charge.

Every display in his helmet exploded into static. Rows of status lights blinked amber, then all red. Life support, hydraulics, power all fluctuated . . . and failed.

He had to get out of here before that Shaw-Fujikawa translight drive completely shut down his suit.

The basic laws of physics still worked here. Action and reaction. Energy transfer and momentum.

He pushed off the beam, back to Fred and Kelly—hoping to grab the rescue line on his way. If he missed, they would still find him. The only thing he cared about right now was getting away from the source of his suit's malfunction.

He drifted. With his suit shut down, all he could do now was coast. And wait.

Lightning stuck. He was ground zero, and thunder kicked Kurt forward like a rag doll.

He'd absorbed a near-direct grenade explosion once, and it had felt something like this. Only this particular explosion hadn't been *near* him; it had been *on* his armor.

His first thought was sniper fire—an ambush. But then his vision cleared and he saw stars, the dull red binary suns, and Station Delphi whirling around.

His T-PACK had busted a line. He could feel the propellant gushing out . . . even though the tanks had been designed with redundant shutoff valves, and emergency self-sealing foam to prevent such a decompression.

He heard CPO Mendez's voice in his head, again: "*Start tumbling in this gear, start praying.*"

"Mayday," he called out. "Suit malfunction! Mayday!"

Kurt had no idea where he was, where his team was now positioned, or how fast he was rocketing away from them.

Of course, they didn't open radio channels on this mission. Point-to-point single-beam lasers carried their COM signal. Gyrating out of control, any signal that hit a tiny Spartan-sized target in the vast volume of open space would be nothing short of a miracle.

He finally got enough bearings to tap the system override. No response. He hit the harness emergency release. It was jammed.

"I'm okay," he said over the COM. "Life support's minimal, but still functional. Going to deep breathing mode to conserve air and power. I'll ride it out. You should be able to pick up my IFF transponder once I'm clear. Activating rescue beacon now. I'll be okay. I'll be o—"

CHAPTER 4

Addendum \ After-Action Report \
UNSC-Navspecwep Ops, File Ehy-97
Subject: Spartan-051

DURING AFOREMENTIONED OPERATION (SEE ATTACHED MISSION PROFILE) TO INVESTIGATE POSSIBLE REBEL ACTIVITY ON THE DECOMMISSIONED CONSTRUCTION PLATFORM 966A, UNOFFICIALLY NAMED STATION DELPHI, A CATASTROPHIC MALFUNCTION OF A THRUSTER PACK (MODEL 050978, UNIT SERIAL #82.10923.192) OCCURRED.

AT 1000 HOURS, A THRUSTER MALFUNCTION PROPELLED SPARTAN-051 OFF MISSION AND INTO INTERPLANETARY SPACE.

IMMEDIATE RESCUE ATTEMPTS COMMENCED WITH THE ASSISTANCE OF THE UNSC PROWLER CIRCUMFERENCE, JOINED ON 1/13/2535, 1105 HOURS, BY THE UNSC FRIGATE TANNENBERG.

THREE HUNDRED TWENTY-TWO MINUTES AFTER PROJECTED OXYGEN IN SPARTAN-051'S VARIANT-V MJOLNIR SUIT EXPIRED, OPERATION TERMINATED AS NEARBY COVENANT ACTION (SEE ATTACHED

REFERENCES) PROMPTED AN IMMEDIATE CALL TO ACTION OF ALL NEARBY UNSC FORCES.

CAUSE OF THRUSTER MALFUNCTION REMAINS UNKNOWN, PENDING FURTHER INVESTIGATION, BUT IT IS HYPOTHESIZED THAT A PARTIALLY DECOMMISSIONED SHAW-FUJIKAWA TRANSLIGHT ENGINE CORE ON THE PLATFORM AND IN CLOSE PROXIMITY TO SPARTAN-051 AT THE TIME OF THE ACCIDENT MAY HAVE CAUSED A SERIES OF CATASTROPHIC ELECTRICAL MALFUNCTIONS. ANOMALOUS ELECTRICAL ACTIVITY ALSO OBSCURED FURTHER, LATER RESCUE EFFORTS IN THE REGION.

PLATFORM 966A HAS BEEN TAGGED WITH A HAZNAV SATELLITE, PENDING HMAT TEAM DISPATCH (FLEETCOM ORDER D-88934).

SPARTAN-051 STATUS: MISSING IN ACTION.

CHAPTER 5

Kurt woke up in bed, an osmotic IV in his arm, and nearby monitors displaying his vital signs, blood composition, and brain-oxygen saturation levels.

He surmised he was in a hospital, although there was no call button, and no obvious door. There was also a camera mounted in the corner of the ceiling. Kurt felt the familiar subsonic thrum around him, and he relaxed. He was on a spaceship. Although he preferred boot-on-dirt, anywhere was better than hard vacuum.

He lowered the bed's railing, and swung his legs over the edge. Pain lanced up his side. Cracked ribs—he'd had them many times. Bruises covered his pale skin; they were especially livid on his shoulders, stomach, and waist. He checked in the mirror for injuries, and then ran his hand over the long black stubble on his head and face. He was intact . . . but how long had he been unconscious?

The wall slid apart and a balding man entered. Curiously he wore an Army uniform, pinned with the eagle insigne of a colonel. His dark eyes fixed upon Kurt.

"Sir!" Kurt started to stand and salute.

"At ease, soldier," the Colonel said.

Kurt checked his motion. He opened his mouth to correct the Colonel's error, but fell silent. Naval NCOs were never called "soldiers," but in Kurt's experience, officers, Army or otherwise, never appreciated correction unless lives were at stake.

The Colonel's continued stare made Kurt uneasy. In fact, several things contributed to his unease. He was on a UNSC ship, receiving medical care, but how had he gotten here, and why was an Army colonel interested in him?

"I am James Ackerson," the Colonel said. He then did a curious thing: he held out his hand to shake.

This was a rare occurrence. Usually no one wanted to touch a Spartan, let alone shake their hand.

Kurt took Ackerson's hand and gingerly squeezed it.

Ackerson. Kurt knew that name. There had been conversations between Dr. Halsey and Chief Mendez. Ackerson had come up a dozen times, and from their inflection and body language Kurt had surmised he was *not* their friend.

Kurt was aware that everyone in the UNSC had the same basic goal: protecting humanity from all threats. Not everyone, however, agreed on how that mandate should be executed . . . which led to *internal* conflict. Kurt understood this the way he understood basic precepts of a Shaw-Fujikawa translight engine. He grasped the underlying theoretical principles, but the nuances and the actual application of that knowledge remained a mystery to him.

Most likely this colonel was on permanent loan to ONI as a liaison officer. They often recruited civilians, officers from other branches of the military, or anyone they needed to get their job done.

An Army colonel was approximately the same rank as a Navy captain, so while Kurt was wary, he had to be polite, and even take orders from Ackerson as long as they did not conflict with previous orders.

"If you are well enough, get dressed." Colonel Ackerson nodded to the night table on which was a neatly folded uniform.

Kurt stood, removed the osmotic IV patch, and dressed.

"SPARTAN-051, what is your name?" Ackerson asked.

"Kurt, sir."

"Yes, but Kurt what? What is your family name?"

Kurt knew he had had another name, before his training. That, however, was part of a life that seemed more dream than real now. And that other name was just a shadow in his mind, as was the family that had gone along with it. Still, he struggled to remember.

"It doesn't matter," Ackerson said. "For the time being if asked, use the last name . . ." He considered for a moment. "Ambrose."

"Yes, sir."

Kurt buttoned his shirt. The uniform was missing the Spartan patch of an eagle holding a lighting bolt and arrows. It instead had the clasping-hand patch of the UNSC Logistical core. It bore the single pip of a private first class and two combat ribbons for Harvest and Operation TREBUCHET.

"Follow me." Ackerson moved out the open doors into a narrow corridor. He led Kurt through three intersections.

Many Naval officers passed them, but none saluted. They kept to themselves for the most part, eyes down. And while a few nodded to Kurt, no one so much as even glanced at Ackerson.

Kurt's unease at this odd situation grew palpable.

They halted at a pressure door guarded by two marines who

saluted. Kurt crisply returned their salute. Ackerson gave them a casual half-salute gesture.

The Colonel set his hand on a biometric reader and face, retina, and palm were simultaneously scanned.

With a hiss, the door opened.

Kurt and Ackerson stepped into a dimly lit twenty-meter-wide room filled wall to wall with monitors. Spectroscopic signatures, star charts, and Slipstream space pulses strobed across the screens. There were several officers and two holographic AIs consulting with them in whispered tones.

One AI was a gray-robbed figure without a body. A wraith.

The other was a collection of disembodied eyes, mouths, and gesturing hands—what Kurt vaguely recalled from one of Deja's art lessons as an example of cubist art.

Ackerson whisked him across the room and to another door. A second biometric scan and they entered an elevator.

There was downward motion, then a moment of zero-gee free fall, and the sensation of gravity then returned. The doors opened to a catwalk that extended over inky darkness to a blank wall.

The Colonel approached the blank wall, a seam appeared, and then the two sections pulled apart.

"This room is called 'Odin's Eye' by the junior staff," Ackerson said. "You have been temporarily granted a code-word top-secret clearance to enter. Whatever is said inside is similarly classified and you will reveal none of our conversation unless the proper code words are provided. Do you understand?"

"Yes, sir," Kurt replied.

Kurt's instinct, however, was to *not* enter this room. He, in fact, wanted to be anyplace but in that room. But he couldn't refuse.

They entered.

The doors closed behind them; Kurt didn't see the seam.

The room had white concave walls, and Kurt's eyes had a hard time focusing.

"Your classification code word is 'Falcon Forty,'" Ackerson said. "Now, speak freely in here. I certainly will." He gestured to a black circular table in the center of the room and they both sat.

"Sir, where am I? Why am I here?"

His words seemed to evaporate as he spoke them, deadened by the too-still air in this strange room.

"Of course," Ackerson murmured. "Your recovery is not complete. I had been warned of that." He sighed. "We have gone to considerable trouble to extricate you from normal NavSpecWep operations . . . from your recon mission to Station Delphi."

Kurt remembered the explosion on his T-PACK; he blinked and saw for a split second the dizzying blur of stars in his faceplate.

"My team," Kurt said, "are they—"

"Fine," Ackerson replied. "No injuries."

Kurt inhaled, feeling his cracked rib. Not quite no injuries.

Something changed in the Colonel's expression. The dark stare and hardness softened almost an imperceptible fraction.

In a lowered voice, Ackerson said, "Section Three has issued you new orders." He pushed a reader across the table to Kurt.

Kurt thumbed the biometric and the screen warmed. There were code-word classified warnings and then he saw his transfer orders under Colonel Ackerson. The usual fields for assignment location, routing protocols, and record verification were redacted.

"You are now a part of a subsection of Beta-5 Division," Ackerson said, "a top-secret cell within Section Three. All the events at Station Delphi were staged to bring you here in the utmost secrecy for a new mission."

Staging the events at Delphi? Arranged by a subcell of Section

Three? Something seemed wrong in a way Kurt couldn't quite put his finger on.

But part of it made sense now. The partially decommissioned Shaw-Fujikawa drive at Delphi Station was the perfect lure and the ideal excuse for a malfunctioning T-PACK. The sensor echo the *Circumference* had picked up on the in-system jump *was* another prowler, the ship that had picked up Kurt's exhausted body—after he had been propelled on a not-so-random explosive trajectory. Though he resented the manner in which they obtained him, he had to admire the sheer elegance of the extraction plan.

"You have been classified as missing in action," Ackerson said. "Presumed dead."

Something cold contracted in Kurt's stomach. He checked his emotions, though, sensing that in this instance, they might not have been able to help him.

"What is this new mission, sir?"

Ackerson stared at him a moment, then seemed to look through Kurt, past him. "I want you to train the next generation of Spartans."

Kurt blinked, taking in what Ackerson had just said, not quite understanding. "Sir, I was under the impression that Chief Petty Officer Mendez had been reassigned years ago to carry out that mission."

"The effort to train additional SPARTAN-IIs was postponed indefinitely by Dr. Catherine Halsey," Ackerson said. "There were other candidates within the gene pool, but they were out of synch with her age restriction protocols. And with the continuing war, her program funds were . . . diverted."

Kurt had always presumed other Spartans were being trained, that he and his fellows were the first in what would be a long line of Spartans. He'd never considered they might be the first, and the last, of their kind.

Ackerson said, "Mendez will, of course, join you."

"It would be an honor to serve under Chief Mendez," Kurt replied.

One of Ackerson's brows quirked up. "Indeed."

He motioned at Kurt's secure tablet. "Read. New training protocols have been outlined as well as an improved augmentation regime. We've learned much from the unfortunate medical processes Dr. Halsey had at her disposal."

Kurt balled his hands into fists, remembering the pain of the bone grafts—like glass breaking inside his marrow, and the fire that had burned along every nerve as they had been reengineered for enhanced speed.

As he read he started to grasp the opportunities and challenges of this new program. The new bioaugmentations were a quantum leap ahead of those he had received. There were lower projected wash-out rates. There was, however, only a fraction of the original SPARTAN program training time and budget. MJOLNIR armor was to be replaced with something called Semi-Powered Infiltration (SPI) armor systems.

"With these new candidates," Kurt said, "you're trying to do more with less."

Ackerson nodded. "They'll be sent on missions with higher strategic values but correspondingly lower survival probabilities. That's where you come in, Kurt. We need your training as a Spartan, and all your field experience passed along to these candidates. You need to make these Spartans better and train them faster. This program may be the key to our survival in this war."

Kurt scanned the reader again. The new genetic selection protocol expanded the pool of candidates, but there were disturbing references to behavior problems in these less-than-ideal potential Spartans.

But this mission was vital to the war, Kurt sensed that. And there would be CPO Mendez. It would be good to be working under his old teacher again. Could the two of them really train a new generation of Spartans?

"In ten years," Ackerson said, "with your guidance and a little luck, there will be a hundred new Spartans in the war. Employing several of these new Spartans to help train the next classes, there will be thousands within twenty years. With projected improvements in technology, perhaps a hundred thousand new Spartans will be created in thirty years."

A *hundred thousand* Spartans fighting for humanity? The image swam in Kurt's mind. Was that possible?

While Kurt didn't understand all the ramifications, he now understood the importance of the end result. His initial feeling of unease, however, remained. How many of these new Spartans were going to die? He steeled himself. He'd do everything he could to see they had the best training, the best equipment, be the best soldiers humanity had ever produced. Even then, though, would it be enough?

He took a deep breath. "Where do we begin, sir?"

Ackerson said, "New training facilities are being constructed. You will oversee the operation, and simultaneously begin the screening of candidates. I have an ample supply of willing recruits for you." He reached into his pocket and withdrew a tiny box, pushed it across the table to Kurt. "One last thing."

Kurt opened the box. Inside were the single silver bar insignia of a lieutenant junior grade.

"Those are yours now." A faint crease of a smile appeared on Ackerson's face. "I'm not going to have my right-hand man taking orders from NCO drill instructors. You're going to be in charge of the entire show."

SECTION II

SPARTAN-III

CHAPTER 6

===

Kurt watched the incoming Pelicans. The blocky jet-powered craft were so distant they were only specks against the setting sun. He hit the magnification on his faceplate and saw lines of fire tracing their reentry vectors. They would touch down in three minutes.

In the last six months he had developed a training regime tougher than the original SPARTAN program. He had created obstacle courses, firing ranges, classrooms, mess halls, and dormitories from what had been jungle and scrub plain.

He had received every piece of equipment he had requested from NavSpecWep Section Three. Guns, ammunition, dropships, tanks—even samples of Covenant technology and weaponry had appeared as if by sleight of hand.

All personnel were accounted for: six dozen handpicked drill instructors, physical therapists, doctors, nurses, psychologists, and the all-important cooks . . . all here except the most critical person, who was now on the incoming transports: Senior Chief Petty Officer Franklin Mendez.

Mendez had, a dozen years ago, trained Kurt and every other Spartan. He would be invaluable in preparing the new breed of SPARTAN-III, but he wasn't going to be the solution to all Kurt's problems.

After poring over every detail of the new recruits' files, Kurt discovered they didn't match the perfect psychological and genetic markers set in Dr. Halsey's original selection protocols. Colonel Ackerson had warned him they had to draw from a "less statistically robust" group. These recruits wouldn't be anything like himself, John, Kelly, or any of the original SPARTAN-II candidates.

And this would only add to a long list of challenges. With a final target class four times larger than the SPARTAN-IIs', a severely truncated training schedule, and the need for these Spartans in the war increasing every month, Kurt, in fact, expected a disaster.

The Pelican jet transports swooped down on final approach and angled their thrusters. The sod on the parade field rippled like velvet. One by one they gingerly touched down.

Although Kurt's MJOLNIR armor was not designed to bear rank insignia, he nonetheless felt the weight of his new lieutenant's bars. They pressed down on him as if they were a ton each, as if the weight of the entire war and future of humanity rested squarely upon his shoulders.

"Sir?" a voice whispered into his COM.

The voice belonged to the artificial intelligence Eternal Spring. It was officially assigned to the planetary survey team stationed in the northern section of this peninsula.

Kurt wasn't sure why Colonel Ackerson had insisted that Camp Currahee be built next to the facility. He *was* sure, however, there had been a reason.

"Go ahead, Spring."

"Updated details on the candidates available," it said.

"Thanks."

"Thank me after your so-called test, sir." Eternal Spring terminated transmission with a hiss of static that sounded like angry bees.

Cajoled by Section Three brass, Eternal Spring had agreed to devote 9 percent of its runtime to the SPARTAN-III project. The AI was of the "smart" variety, which meant there were no limits on its knowledge capacity or creativity. Despite its occasional theatrics, Kurt was happy for its help.

Kurt blinked and accessed the candidates' data on his heads-up display. Each name had a serial number and linked to background files. There were 497 of them, a collection of four-, five-, and six-year-old children that he somehow had to forge into a fighting force unparalleled in the history of warfare.

The hatch on the nearest Pelican opened with a hiss, and a tall man strode out.

Mendez had aged well. His trim body looked chiseled from ironwood, but the hair was now silver, and there were deep creases around his eyes and a set of ragged scars that ran brow to chin.

"Chief." Kurt resisted the urge to snap to attention as Mendez saluted. As odd as it felt, Kurt was now his commanding officer.

Kurt returned his salute.

"Senior Chief Petty Officer Mendez reporting for duty, sir."

After the SPARTAN-II program, Chief Mendez had, at his request, been reassigned to active duty. He'd fought the Covenant on five worlds, and been awarded two purple hearts.

"You were briefed on the flight?"

"Completely," Mendez said. As he looked Kurt over in his MJOLNIR armor, emotions played over his face: awe, approval, and resolve. "We'll get these new recruits trained, sir."

This was precisely the response Kurt had hoped for. Mendez was a legend among the Spartans. He had tricked, trapped, and tortured them as children. They all hated, and then learned to admire the man. He had taught them how to fight—and how to win.

"Do they let Spartans drink now?" Mendez asked.

"Chief?"

"A bad joke, sir. We might both need one before this day is over," he said. "The new trainees are, well, sir, a little wild. I don't know if either of us is ready for *this*."

Mendez turned to the Pelicans, inhaled, and yelled, "Recruits, fall out!"

Kids streamed off dropship ramps. Hundreds tromped onto the field, screaming, and throwing clumps of sod at one another. After being cooped up for hours, they went wild. A few, however, milled near the ships, dark circles under their eyes, and they huddled tighter. Adult handlers herded them onto the grass.

"You've read *Lord of the Flies,* sir?" Mendez muttered.

"I have," Kurt replied. "But your analogy will not hold. These children will have guidance. They will have discipline. And they have one thing no ordinary children have, not even the SPARTAN-II candidates. Motivation."

Kurt linked to the camp's PA. He cleared his throat and the sound rumbled over the field like thunder.

Nearly five hundred crazed children stopped in their tracks, fell silent, and turned amazed at the giant in the shining emerald armor.

"Attention, recruits," Kurt said and stood akimbo. "I am

Lieutenant Ambrose. You have all endured great hardships to be here. I know each of you has lost your loved ones on Jericho VII, Harvest, and Biko. The Covenant has made orphans of you all."

Every kid stared at him, some with tears now gleaming in their eyes, others with pure burning hatred.

"I am going to give you a chance to learn how to fight, a chance to become the best soldiers the UNSC has ever produced, a chance to destroy the Covenant. I am giving you a chance to be like me: a Spartan."

The kids crowded before him, close . . . but none actually dared to touch the shimmering pale green armor.

"We cannot accept everyone, though," Kurt continued. "There are five hundred of you. We have three hundred training slots. So tonight, Senior Chief Petty Officer Mendez"—he nodded to the Chief—"has devised a way to separate those who truly want this opportunity from those who do not."

Kurt handed him a tablet reader. "Chief?"

To his credit Mendez registered shock for only a split second. He scanned the tablet, frowned, but nodded.

"Yes, sir," he whispered.

Mendez yelled at the children, "You want to be Spartans? Then get back on those ships."

They stood shocked, staring at him.

"No? I guess we found a few washouts. You." He pointed to one child at random. "You. And you."

The chosen kids looked at each other, at the ground, and then shook their heads.

"No?" Mendez said. "Then get on those Pelicans."

They did so, and so did the others, a slow shuffling procession.

"Drill instructors," Mendez said.

Three dozen NCOs snapped to attention.

"You will find Falcon Wing aerial descent units on the field. Load them ASAP and make sure your trainees are properly fitted. Their safe deployment is now *your* responsibility."

The DIs nodded and ran toward the bundled Falcon Wing backpacks.

The Chief turned back to Kurt. "You're going to make them drop?" He raised both eyebrows in surprise. "At night?"

"The Falcons are the safest drop units," Kurt replied.

"With respect, sir, some of them are only four years old."

"Motivation, Chief. If they can do this, they'll be ready for what we have to put them through." Kurt watched the Pelicans fire their jets and scorch the grass. "But just in case," he added, "deploy all dropships to recover the candidates. There may be accidents."

Mendez exhaled deeply. "Yes, sir." He started for the nearest Pelican.

"Chief," Kurt said, "I'm sorry that order had to come from you."

"I understand, sir," Mendez replied. "You're their CO. You have to inspire and command their respect. I'm their drill instructor. I get to be their worst nightmare." He gave Kurt a crooked smile and climbed aboard.

Shane clung to the plastic loops on the side of the Pelican's hull. He stood shoulder to shoulder with the other kids—packed so close that he wouldn't have fallen if he let go. The roar of the Pelican's jets was deafening, but still he could hear his own heart racing in his chest.

This was the end of a journey that had started years ago. He'd heard jets like this when it started, the jets of the light freighter as it rocketed away from Harvest. It had been crowded on that ship, too . . . filled with refugees trying to get as far away, as fast as they could, from the monsters.

Only one in six ships had made it.

Sometimes Shane wished he hadn't lived and seen the monsters burn his family and home.

When the Navy man had come to visit him in the orphanage and asked if Shane wanted to get even with them, he immediately volunteered. No matter what it took, he was going to kill all the Covenant.

They had given him lots of tests, the written kind, blood tests, and then a month-long space trip as the Navy man collected more and more volunteers.

Shane had thought the testing was over when they final got into the Pelicans and came to this new place, but he'd barely touched the ground when they'd been shoved back inside and sent back up into the air.

He'd gotten a glimpse of the one in charge. He wore armor like Shane had seen in fairy tale books: the Green Knight who fought dragons. That's what Shane wanted. He was going to wear armor like that one day and kill all the monsters.

"Check your straps," an old Navy man barked at him and the other kids.

Shane tugged at the black backpack that they'd put on him three minutes ago. It weighed almost as much as him, and the straps had been pulled so tight they cut into his ribs.

"Report any looseness," the man shouted over the roar of the engines.

None of the twenty other kids said anything.

"Recruits, stand by," the man barked. He listened into his headphones and then a green light blinked on a panel near his head. The man punched numbers into a keypad.

The back of the Pelican hissed open, the ramp lowered, and a tornado screamed around Shane. He yelled; so did the other kids. They all pushed and shoved to the front of the Pelican's bay.

The old Navy man stood by the open bay door, unafraid that only a meter to his rear was open sky. He regarded the squirming kids with disgust.

Behind him a dusky orange band marked the edge of the world. Twilight and lengthening shadows slipped over snow-capped mountains.

"You will form a line and jump," the man shouted. "You will count to ten and pull this." He reached up to his left shoulder, grasped the bright red handle there, and made a pretend pull motion. "Some confusion will be normal."

The kids stared at him. No one moved.

"If you cannot do this," the man said, "you cannot be a Spartan. It's your choice."

Shane looked at the other kids. They looked at him.

A girl with pigtails and missing her front teeth stepped forward. "I'll go first, sir," she yelled.

"Good girl," he said. "Go right to the edge; hang on to the guide line."

She took the tiniest baby steps to the edge of the Pelican, then froze. She took three deep breaths and then with a squeak, she jumped. The wind caught her.

She vanished into the dark.

"Next!" the old Navy man said.

All the kids, Shane included, slowly formed a line. He couldn't believe they were doing this. It was nuts.

The next boy got to the edge, looked down, and screamed. He fell backward, and scrambled away. "No!" he said. "No way!"

"Next!" the man called, and didn't give the kid cowering on the deck another glance.

The next boy jumped without even looking. And the next.

Then it was Shane's turn.

He couldn't move his legs.

"Hurry up, loser," the boy behind him said and gave him a shove.

Shane stumbled forward—halting only a half step from the edge. He turned and stopped himself from shoving this kid back. The kid was a head taller than Shane, and his black hair fell into his eyes, making it seem like he was missing his forehead. Shane wasn't afraid of this creep.

He turned back to face the night rushing past him. *This* was what he was afraid of.

Shane's legs filled with freezing concrete. The rushing wind was so loud he couldn't hear anything else anymore, not even his hammering heart.

He couldn't move. He was stuck on the edge. There was no way he could jump.

But now he was so scared he couldn't even turn around and chicken out, either. If he sat down, though, and then slowly inched back—

"Go, dumbass!" The creep kid behind him pushed. Hard.

Shane fell off the ramp and into the night.

He tumbled and screamed until he couldn't breathe.

Shane saw flashes of the dimming sunset, black ground, the white caps of the mountains, and stars.

He threw up.

Some confusion will be normal.

The red handle! He had to grab it. He reached up, but there was nothing there. He clawed at his shoulder until two fingers found purchase. He tugged.

There was a ripping sound and something unraveled from his pack.

Shane jerked straight, his legs whipping after him, and his

teeth snapped together from the sudden bone-jarring deceleration.

The spinning world stopped.

Gasping and blinking away his tears, Shane saw the last bit of amber light fade from the edge of the world, and the stars gently rock back and forth around him.

Overhead the wind whistled and rippled though a black canopy. Ropes connected Shane to this wing, and his hands instinctively grabbed them. As he pulled, the wing turned and angled in that direction.

The sudden motion made him dizzy again, so he let go.

Shane squinted and made out shapes swimming around him: black on black like the bats on Harvest. Those had to be the other kids, gliding like he was.

His face heated as he remembered how he'd chickened out at the last minute in the Pelican . . . in front of everyone. Even that little girl had jumped.

Shane never wanted to be scared like that again. Maybe if he imagined that he was already dead, then there would be nothing to be afraid of. It'd be like he'd died with his parents on Harvest.

He mustered this mental image—dead and nothing to fear—and to test it, he looked down. Past his dangling feet there was a two-centimeter green square. After a moment, he realized it was the field where all the Pelicans had landed. Tiny lines snaked from the field illuminated by tiny firefly pinpoints.

"Nothing to be scared of," he whispered, trying to convince himself.

He forced himself to pull the ropes, angle downward, and speed toward the green field.

Wind whipped through the black silk wing, and tore at Shane's face. He didn't care. He wanted down fast. Maybe if he was the first one down, he'd show everyone that he wasn't scared.

Shane saw tiny people and scorch marks where the Pelicans had burned the grass. And no other parachutes yet. Good. He'd be first, and he'd land right in front of the Green Knight.

Shane hit the ground. His knees pistoned into his chest and knocked the wind out of him.

The black wing caught a breeze, jerked him back on his feet, and dragged him across the grass and dirt. He gasped for air, but he wasn't scared. He was angry that he'd look so stupid having to wrestle with this parachute.

The Falcon Wing hit the fence, and stuck there, fluttering.

Shane got up and unclipped himself from the harness. Something hot trickled down his legs. There was no way he'd been so scared he pissed his pants. With dread, he looked. It was blood. The skin on the back of his legs was raw. He took a tentative step and fire crawled up both thighs.

He laughed. Blood or piss, what did it matter? He'd made it.

"Hey, dumbass. What's so funny?"

Shane turned and saw the kid who had pushed him. He lay on the grass, half tangled in his harness.

Shane marched over to him, ignoring the pain in his legs.

The kid got to one knee and held out his hand to shake. "I'm Rob—"

Shane hit him square in the nose. Blood gushed from the kid's face and he reeled over.

He was going to pay for shoving him. He was the only one who knew that Shane had frozen on the edge and chickened out. He'd have to pay for that, too.

Shane started pounding him with right and left fists.

The kid held up his arms to fend off the blows, but Shane landed a few good ones, skinning his knuckles.

Robert headbutted Shane, and he fell off.

Robert stood, shook off his harness, then, growling, leapt onto Shane.

They rolled on the grass, kicking and punching.

Shane heard a loud snap and he wasn't sure if it was his or Rob's bone breaking; he didn't care, he kept hitting and hitting until blood spilled into his eyes and he couldn't see anymore.

Large hands grabbed Shane and pulled him off. Still swinging, Shane connected with one of the Navy men, bruising the bone over his eye.

The man dropped him.

"Stand down!" barked a voice with godlike authority.

Shane blinked and wiped blood from his eyes. The silver-haired man who had given the order to jump stood between him and the other kid.

The Navy man he'd hit pressed one hand to his swollen eye and said, "Chief, these two were going to kill each other."

"I see that," the old man said. He nodded approvingly at Shane, and then turned to Robert.

Robert ignored the old man and took a step toward Shane with his hands raised.

"I said STAND DOWN!"

Robert dropped his hands and staggered back as if he'd been struck.

"I think you're right, Sergeant," the older Navy man said. "They really might have killed each other." He smiled, only it wasn't a smile. It was more like he was baring his teeth. "Very good. That kind of fight left in them after their first jump? A night jump? My God, I only hope the rest of them are like this."

CHAPTER 7

0000 Hours, July 19, 2532 (Military Calendar) \
Narrow-Band Point-to-Point Transmission:
Origin Unknown; Termination: Section Three, Omega Secure Antenna
Array, UNSC HQ Epsilon Eridani System,
Reach Military Complex

///AUTOMATED REROUTE UNSC SHIP REG-96667
ABY/// FILE ACCESS GRANTED///WORM-PROTOCOL FIREWALL
ENABLED/FILE ERASED///

PLNB TRANSMISSION XX087R-XX
ENCRYPTION CODE: GAMMA
PUBLIC KEY: N/A
FROM: CODE NAME COALMINER
TO: CODE NAME SURGEON
SUBJECT: PROGRESS REPORT/OPERATION HYPODERMIC
CLASSIFICATION: EYES ONLY, CODE-WORD ▮▮▮▮▮

███████ TOP SECRET (SECTION THREE X-RAY DIRECTIVE)

/FILE EXTRACTION-RECONSTITUTION COMPLETE/

/START FILE/

INSTITUTIONAL RECORDS ALTERED AS PER INSTRUCTIONS.

INITIAL CONTACT WITH BASE AI MADE. HELPFUL, BUT I DON'T TRUST IT.

PACKAGES DELIVERED. SELECTION PROCESS STARTED. OPERATION UNDERWAY AND ON SCHEDULE.

CANDIDATES EXHIBIT MARKED AGGRESSION WELL OUT OF BOUNDS OF THE SMITH-KENSINGTON INDEX. AS MUCH WORK TRAINING THEM AS IT IS KEEPING THEM FROM MURDERING EACH OTHER. THEY'RE REAL HELLCATS.

LIEUTENANT CLAIMS ALL UNDER CONTROL. HE HAS A PLAN FOR EVERYTHING. UNSURE WHERE HE'S GETTING THIS CONFIDENCE, BUT I DO BELIEVE HE KNOWS WHAT HE'S DOING. ARE YOU SURPRISED?

/END FILE/

/SCRAMBLE-DESTRUCTION PROCESS ENABLE/

PRESS ENTER TO CONTINUE.

CHAPTER 8

Lieutenant Ambrose and SCPO Mendez had been escorted to this catwalk through a series of corridors and high-security biometric vaults into the bowels of the stealth cruiser *Point of No Return.*

The security officers had then left them standing at attention on the catwalk, and sealed the vaultlike door behind them. Below the metal grating of the catwalk, the shadows swallowed all sound.

Three meters to Kurt's left was a slightly curved white wall. No door. Beyond was Odin's Eye, the high-security conference room where he'd first been told of the SPARTAN-III program by Colonel Ackerson.

"Think this is some Section Three test?" Mendez finally whispered. "Or maybe someone doesn't like getting news about the lousy selection results for the Beta Company candidates?"

"I'm not sure," Kurt replied. "My requested upgrades for the Mark-II SPI armor were over budget."

Mendez raised an eyebrow. "Where did you hear that?"

"The new AI talks a lot."

"'Deep Winter,'" muttered Mendez. "I wonder if AIs pick their own names, or if some officer in Section Three does it."

Kurt was about to offer his opinion when he noticed there now was a door in the curved white wall. Colonel Ackerson stood there. "Gentlemen, join us." Ackerson then retreated into a brightly lit chamber.

Kurt noticed that he hadn't met their eyes. That was always a bad sign.

They entered, and as he crossed the threshold, Kurt felt static crawl over his skin. The concave illuminated walls of the chamber were disorienting. Kurt focused on the center of the half-spherical room, on the black conference table. Two officers sat there, gazing at holographic screens that floated in the air over its surface.

Ackerson waved them closer.

A woman sat with her back to them; opposite her sat a middle-aged gentleman.

The man was gray and balding. The woman appeared older than regs permitted before mandatory retirement. Her osteoporotic slump, slender frail arms, and thinning white hair indicated extreme age.

Kurt froze as he spotted the one- and three-star rank insignia on their collars and snapped off a salute. "Vice Admiral, ma'am," he said. "Rear Admiral, sir."

The Vice Admiral ignored Mendez and scrutinized Kurt. "Sit," she said, "both of you."

Kurt didn't recognize either of these high-ranking officers, and they didn't bother to introduce themselves.

He did as he was ordered, as did Mendez. Even sitting, though, his back was ramrod straight, his chest out, and eyes forward.

"We were reviewing the record of your SPARTAN-IIIs since they went operational nine months ago," she said. "Impressive."

The Rear Admiral gestured at floating holographic panes that contained after-action reports, still shots of battlefields filled with Covenant corpses, and ship damage-assessment profiles. "The insurrection of Mamore," he said "that nasty business at New Constantinople, actions in the Bonanza asteroid belt and the Far-gone colony platforms, and half a dozen other engagements—this reads like the campaign record of a cracking good battalion, not a company of three hundred. Damned impressive."

"That was only a fraction of the SPARTAN-III program potential," Colonel Ackerson said. His eyes stared at some distant point.

"I'm sorry, sir," Kurt said. "'Was'?"

The Vice Admiral stiffened. It was clear that she was not accustomed to her junior officers asking questions.

But Kurt had to. These were his men and women they were talking about. He'd kept his eyes and ears open for news on Alpha Company, and had cultivated intelligence sources outside ONI, Section Three, and Beta-5. Being Commandant of Camp Currahee had its privileges, and he had learned how to use them. He had managed to track his Spartans during the last seven months, until his sources had mysteriously gone silent six days ago. Only the AI Deep Winter had given a clue as to their whereabouts: Operation PROMETHEUS.

"Tell me about the selection process for the next class of SPARTAN-IIIs," the Vice Admiral asked Kurt.

"Ma'am," Kurt said, "we are operating under Colonel Ackerson's expanded selection criteria, but there are not enough age-appropriate genetic matches to meet the larger second-class target number."

"There *are* sufficient genetic matches," Colonel Ackerson corrected. His face was an impassive mask. "What's missing are data to find additional matches. We need to proscribe mandatory genetic screening in the outer colonies. Those untapped populations are—"

"That's the last thing we need in the outer colonies," the Rear Admiral said. "We're just getting a handle on a near civil war. You tell an O.C. they got to register their kids' genes, and they'll all be reaching for their rifles."

The Vice Admiral steepled her withered hands. "Say it is part of a vaccine program. We take a microscopic sample as we inject the children. Inform no one."

The Rear Admiral looked dubious, but offered no further comment.

"Go on, Lieutenant," she said.

"We have identified 375 candidates," Kurt said. "Slightly less than we started with for Alpha Company, but we have learned from our mistakes. We will be able to graduate a much higher percentage this time."

He nodded toward Mendez to give the Chief the credit he richly deserved. Mendez sat completely still and Kurt saw he wore his poker face.

Every instinct Kurt had screamed that something was wrong here.

"But," the Rear Admiral said, "that's nowhere near the one thousand projection for the second wave."

A brief scowl played over Ackerson's lip. "No, sir."

The Vice Admiral set her hands flat on the table and leaned closer to Kurt. "What if we loosen the new genetic selection criteria?"

Kurt took note of the "we" in her question. There was a subtle shift in the power structure at the table. With a single word, the Vice Admiral had made Kurt a part of their group.

"Our new bioaugmentation protocols target a very specific genetic set. Any deviation from that set would geometrically increase the failure rate," Kurt said. The thought of dozens of Spartans being tortured and ultimately crippled as they lay helpless in a medical bay filled him with revulsion. He managed to contain the feeling.

The Vice Admiral raised one threadbare brow. "You've done your homework, Lieutenant."

"However, as our augmentation technology improves," Ackerson said, "one day we will be able to expand the selection parameters, maybe to include the entire general population."

"But not today, Colonel," the Rear Admiral said, and sighed. "So we're back to about three hundred SPARTAN-IIIs. That will have to do then."

Kurt wanted to correct him—three hundred new Spartans *plus* those in Alpha Company.

"Let's move on to the review of Alpha and Operation PRO-METHEUS," the Vice Admiral said, and her face darkened.

Colonel Ackerson cleared his throat. "Operation PROME-THEUS occurred on the Covenant manufacturing site designated as K7-49."

A holographic asteroid materialized drifting over the table, a rock with molten cracks that made a spiderweb pattern over its surface.

"K7-49 was discovered when the prowler *Razor's Edge* managed to attach a telemetry probe on an enemy frigate during the Battle of New Harmony," Ackerson said. "They then followed the craft through slipspace, the first and only time this technology has actually worked, I might add, and they discovered this rock seventeen light-years past the UNSC outer boundary."

The image magnified, revealing midaltitude images of factories on the surface that belched smoke and cinder, and showed that the volcanic fissures were canals of flowing molten metal. A gossamer lattice surrounded the asteroid, tiny lights winked on the filaments, and black specks drifted near.

"Spectral enhancement," the Rear Admiral said, "showed us what they're using all that metal for."

The view shifted closer. The latticework girders were hundred-meter-wide beams, and the black specks appeared to be the bones of whales in orbit over K7-49—a dozen partially constructed Covenant warships.

Kurt had a difficult time believing what he was seeing. So many ships. How large was the Covenant fleet? And only seventeen light-years from the UNSC frontier? It could be nothing less than a prelude to an all-out assault.

"K7-49 is one large orbital shipyard," Ackerson explained. "All the apparent volcanism is artificial, created by these." He tapped his tablet once more. Thirty infrared dots appeared on the surface of the asteroid. "High-output plasma reactors that liquefy metallurgical components, which are refined, shaped, and then transported via gravity beams for final assembly."

"The PROMETHEUS op was a high-risk insertion onto the surface of K7-49," the Rear Admiral explained. "Three hundred Spartans hit dirt at 0700, July 27. Their mission was to disable as many of these reactors as possible—enough so the liquid contents of the facility would solidify and permanently clog their capacity to produce alloy."

Colonel Ackerson then tapped the holographic display. "STARS system and TEAMCAM recorded Alpha Company's process."

A handful of the hot infrared points on the asteroid's surface flared and then cooled to black.

"Initial resistance was light." Ackerson tapped a button and a new window opened.

On this display, Spartans in Semi-Powered Infiltration armor systems moved, their camouflaged patterns shifting imperfectly against the molten metal and black smoke of the factory. Kurt wished his suggested upgrades for the SPI armor's software had been implemented before Alpha had graduated. There was a burp of suppressed submachine gun fire, and a pod of Grunt salve workers fell dead.

"After two days," the Admiral said, "seven rectors were rendered inoperative and a counterforce was finally organized by existing Covenant units."

A new video feed appeared.

The vulturelike Jackals moved in squads through large courtyards, and filed over archways. They were more organized than their Grunt counterparts, and they worked in fire teams, methodically clearing section by section. But Kurt knew his Spartans wouldn't be cornered. *They* would be the hunters.

Thirty Jackals moved into a circular court, where Engineers tended a churning pool of molten steel. The Jackals cleared every hiding spot, and then started to cross, warily scanning the rooftops.

Flagstones exploded and sent the Jackals sprawling. Sniper fire took out the stunned aliens before they could get their shields in place.

"The Covenant counterresponse was neutralized," the Rear Admiral continued, "and over the next three days, Alpha Company destroyed thirteen more reactors."

The large infrared asteroid-wide view changed. Two-thirds of the surface had cooled to dull red.

"But," the Rear Admiral said, "a massive counterforce appeared in orbit and descended to the surface."

Colonel Ackerson opened three more holographic windows:

SPARTAN-IIIs engaged Elites on the ground, trading fire from cover. Banshee fliers swooped down from building tops—two Spartans fired shoulder-launched surface-to-air missiles and stopped the air assault cold.

"On day seven," the Admiral said, "additional Covenant reinforcements arrived."

The video from a helmet camera showed a dozen SPARTAN-IIIs limping and falling on a smoldering landscape of twisted metal. There was no unit cohesion. No two-man teams covering one another. In the heat-blurred background, Elites took up superior positions with good cover.

"By now," the Rear Admiral said, "Eighty-nine percent of the reactors had been destroyed. Sufficient cooling had occurred to permanently shut the operation down. Alpha Company was cut off from their Calypso exfiltration craft."

The window showing the SPARTAN-IIIs tilted sideways as the owner of the helmet cam fell.

Ackerson rotated the holographic display 90 degrees to rectify the image.

Three Spartans remained standing, firing suppressing bursts from their MA5Ks behind a crashed Banshee flier; then they broke from the cover and sprinted—a second before the flier was destroyed by an energy mortar. IFF tags at the bottom of the screen identified these Spartans as Robert, Shane, and, carried between them, Jane. She had been the first candidate to jump that first night of indoctrination.

TEAMBIO appeared in another window. Robert's and Shane's blood pressure was close to the hypertensive limit. Jane's bio signs were flatlined.

Seeing them like this . . . it felt like someone had driven a metal spike into Kurt's chest. A pair of hulking Covenant Hunters blocked the Spartans' retreat. They raised their two-meter-long fuel-rod arm cannons.

Robert unloaded his assault rifle at them, which hardly made the pair flinch as it spanged off their thick armor. Shane switched to his sniper rifle and shot through one Hunter's unarmed midsection, and then pumped two rounds into the other's vulnerable abdomen. They both went down, but still moved, only momentarily incapacitated.

Elite fire teams, meanwhile, popped up on either side and unleashed a volley of needles and plasma shot.

Robert caught a blot of plasma in the stomach—it stuck there, burning through his SPI armor like paper. Screaming, he managed to reload and spray his MA5B on full auto at the Elite who had shot him. TEAMBIO showed his heart in full arrest, but he still grabbed a grenade, pulled the pin, and lobbed it at the enemy fire team . . . and then he fell.

Shane paused to look at Robert and Jane—then turned back to the Elite fire team, and shot in three-round controlled bursts.

More Elites appeared, surrounding the lone Spartan.

Shane's rifle clacked, empty. He pulled out his M6 pistol and continued to fire.

An energy motor detonated like a small sun two meters away.

Shane tumbled through the air, and landed prone, unmoving.

"And that's all we have," Colonel Ackerson stated.

Kurt continued to stare at the screen of static, his heart racing, half expecting the feed to go live again and show Shane gather up Robert and Jane, and together they'd limp off the battlefield, wounded, but alive.

Seven years Kurt had trained them, and grown to respect them. Now they were dead. Their sacrifice had saved countless human lives, and yet Kurt still felt like he'd lost everything. He wanted to look away from the screen, but couldn't.

This was his fault. He had failed them. His training hadn't prepared them. He should have rectified the flaws in their Mark-I PR suits and fixed them faster.

Mendez reached over *and* tapped the Colonel's tablet.

The display mercifully blanked and faded away.

Ackerson shot the Chief a glare, but Mendez ignored him.

"Recent drone recon shows the entire complex cold," the Rear Admiral said. "No more ships will be built at K7-49."

"Just to clarify," Kurt whispered, and then he paused to clear his throat. "There were no survivors of Operation PROMETHEUS?"

"It is regrettable," the Vice Admiral said with the slightest softness now in her voice. "But we would do it again if presented with a similar opportunity, Lieutenant. Such a facility within two weeks' journey of the UNSC outer colonies . . . your Spartans prevented the building of a Covenant armada that would have resulted in nothing less than the massacre of billions. They are heroes."

Ashes. That's all Kurt felt.

He glanced at Mendez. There was no emotion on his face. The man held his pain well.

"I understand, ma'am," Kurt said.

"Good," she said, all trace of pity had now evaporated from her tone. "I've put you in for a promotion. Your Spartans performed well above the program's projected parameters. You are to be commended."

Kurt felt the only thing he deserved was a court-martial, but he said nothing.

"Now I want you to focus and accelerate the training of the Beta Company Spartans," she said. "We have a war to win."

CHAPTER 9

Bullets peppered the dirt near Tom's head. He pushed farther back into the hole, hugging the ground, trying to be as flat as possible.

The irony was Team Foxtrot had done everything by the book. Maybe that was the lesson today: going by the book doesn't always work.

Tom had led them through the forest, evading snipers and patrols of drill instructors waiting to jump them. They made it too easy.

That should have been his first clue. The DIs never made things easy for them.

When they'd come to the open field he'd checked the perimeter. No one had been there. He'd waited, though, and checked and rechecked. DIs in their Mark-II Semi-Powered Infiltration armor were hard to spot even with the thermal imagers in his field binoculars.

Tom had then warily led his team onto the field and toward the pole with a bell. That was the mission: ring the bell. They had had two hours to find and ring the thing to qualify for continued Spartan training.

There were 418 candidates, and only three hundred slots. Not all of them could be Spartans.

His mistake had been leading his entire team into the clear. They'd all been too eager.

It got them ambushed.

Machine-gun fire from the treetops rained down on them. Adam and Min in flanking positions were immediately taken out.

Only Tom and Lucy had made it to the muddy hole. It was just deep enough to keep from getting shot.

"This is crazy," Lucy spat through her mud-covered face. "We gotta do something."

"They have to run out of ammo sooner or later," Tom told her. "Or one of the other teams will show up and get us out of this jam."

"Sure they will," Lucy said. "After *they* ring the bell." She squinted at the trees. "There has to be a way out of this. Automated gun turrets up there. That's why they didn't show up on the thermals."

That's what the Lieutenant was always saying about machines: *"They easily fool the unsuspecting . . . but they're also easy to break."*

The guns wouldn't kill them—but they'd sure as heck stop them cold. With only gray sweat suits and light boots for protection, the stun rounds hit so hard they numbed whatever they hit: legs or arms or God help you if you got nailed in the head or groin or an eye.

"Nuts to this." Lucy rose into a crouching stance.

Tom grabbed her ankle, pulled her down, and punched her in the gut.

Lucy doubled, but she recovered fast—rolled over Tom and got him in a stranglehold.

Tom shrugged out of the lock and held up both hands. "Come on," he said. "Truce. There has to be a way out of this—a way with us not getting shot."

Lucy glared at him, but then said, "What do you have in mind?"

"What is the point of this 'exercise,' Lieutenant?" Deep Winter asked.

The AI holographic projection of an old man took a step toward the bank of monitors and touched the screen showing a boy and a girl pinned by machine-gun fire. A crackle of ice spread over the plastic.

Chief Mendez stood, and swatted at a mosquito, frowning as he glanced back and forth among the two dozen displays in Camp Currahee's control center. The air conditioner had broken, and both Mendez's and Kurt's uniforms were soaked with sweat.

Kurt said, "Our candidates are doing well in their studies?"

Deep Winter turned his glacier-blue gaze to the Lieutenant. "You've have seen my reports. You know they are. Since you announced their grades were a factor in the selection process, they practically kill themselves every night to learn everything before they pass out. Frankly, I don't see—"

"I suggest," Kurt said, "you not worry about seeing the point of my battlefield drills, and focus on keeping the candidates on track with their studies."

What could an AI possibly know what it was like on a real mission? Bullets zinging so close over your head that you didn't so much as hear them but *felt* them pass. Or what it was like to get hit, but still have to keep going, bleeding, because if you didn't everyone on your team would die?

Alpha Company had lost their team cohesion on Operation PROMETHEUS. Kurt vowed that would not happen with Beta Company.

Deep Winter ruffled his cape, and a flurry of illusionary snow swirled about the control room. The AI was likely programmed with human safety protocols, so it was natural for it to be concerned.

"We don't know what they're capable of," Kurt finally told Deep Winter. "Stick with the by-the-book drills and we'll never find out, either. But put them in an impossible situation, and maybe they'll surprise us."

"Short definition of a Spartan," Mendez remarked.

That's what people had said about the SPARTAN-IIs who were the genetic cream of the crop and wore MJOLNIR armor. They *could* do the impossible, and do it alone. The SPARTAN-IIIs, though, would have to work together to survive. Be more family than fire team.

"Still," Deep Winter whispered. "This is cruel. They will break."

"I'd rather break them," Kurt said, "than let them go out into the field without ever experiencing an intractable tactical situation."

"Personally I don't think these kids can be broken," Mendez said more to himself than to Kurt or Deep Winter. His gaze now firmly fixed on Tom and Lucy. "Ten years old and these two have so much grit they scare the bejesus out of even me."

"Look," Deep Winter said. "What are those two doing now?"

Kurt smiled. "I think . . . the impossible."

"Let's go over the plan one more time," Tom said.

Lucy huddled next to him in the mud hole. "Why? You think I'm stupid?"

Tom didn't say anything for a moment, then: "Those turrets are probably using radar to target. So we fool them."

"And if they're using thermals?" Lucy asked.

Tom shrugged. "Then I hope they nail you first."

Lucy grimly nodded and hefted a muddy rock. "So we throw these."

"Into their cone of fire," Tom said. "The small angle will make them hard to track. Maybe tie up their brains for a fraction of a second more."

"Then we run."

"Evasive maneuvers. Try not to step on Adam and Min."

"Got it," Lucy said.

Tom grasped his rock tighter and pumped it once, working up his courage. He and Lucy knocked their fists together.

They stood at the same time—hucked both rocks.

Tom heard gunfire, but didn't pause to look; he ran right, then left, he rolled and tumbled and then sprinted like crazy for the tree line.

He felt the dirt near him exploding with tiny puffs.

Fire cut into his thigh and his leg lost all feeling. He pushed off with his good foot, and landed hard on his stomach in the tall grass by the acacia trees.

Staccato bullets dotted in the ground centimeters from his prone body . . . but missed him. He laughed. He was just inside their minimum angle of fire. Stupid machines.

He rolled over and spotted Lucy, panting and crouched in the grass. Tom waved to her, and then pointed up into the treetops. Lucy gave a thumbs-up signal.

Tom hopped on one leg. Some of the feeling was coming back . . . mostly the feeling of pain. He stomped it out. He couldn't let it slow him down. The drill instructors might show up at any second.

He pulled himself up into the lower branches of one of the acacias that shook with gunfire. He used great care to avoid the spines in the tree's trunk. He climbed up ten meters.

On a platform sat an old M202 XP machine gun hooked up to an automated fire control. It twitched back and forth, waiting for a target to present itself.

Tom reached up and disconnected the wires from the radar array, and then the power supply. The gun froze.

He climbed onto the platform and unscrewed the securing bolts. He pushed the gun off the platform. It made a satisfying thud as it impacted the muddy ground.

Tom climbed down. He grabbed the machine gun, cleared the barrel, and stripped off the remaining autofire control. He test-fired a burst of three rounds into the tree trunk. "Awesome," he said.

Lucy was down from his tree as well, machine gun balanced on her shoulder. She moved onto the field to help Adam and Min get up. "Come on," she said. "We still got a bell to ring."

Adam boosted Tom and then Lucy to make a human ladder, and then Min clambered up and clanged the bell.

Nothing had ever sounded so good.

They all climbed down. "Now for some payback . . ." Tom said. "Adam, Min, take up spotting positions"—he pointed—"in those trees there and there."

They nodded and ran off to the trees.

"You and me and these," Tom told Lucy, patting his machine gun, "will set up there." He pointed to a large boulder. "I'll be there." He nodded to the tall grass on the edge of the field.

"And do what?" she asked.

"Well, we've cleared the field and rung the bell. I figure with the other teams getting here and ringing the bell in record times . . ."

Lucy smiled. "The DIs will come running and gunning."

The DIs at Camp Currahee were a mix of handpicked NCOs, medics, and the washouts from the first Spartan class. The washouts always went out of their way to make the lives of the Beta Spartan trainees hell. Two years ago Team X-ray vanished on a routine exercise up north. A lot of the kids said there were ghosts up there—floating eyes in the jungle—but everyone really knew the DIs had done something and covered it up. ONI even came in and fenced the place off. Called it "Zone 67" and declared it was "absolutely off-limits."

It was time to teach those DIs they couldn't get away with bullying Beta Company.

Min whistled from the treetops.

Teams Romeo and Echo slinked into view. Tom signaled them and explained the plan. Teams Zulu and Lima joined them, and soon two dozen trainees were scattered in the trees and grass, watching and waiting.

It only took fifteen minutes before a whistle sounded at three o'clock. There was a subtle motion in the grass on the edges of the field.

Tom signaled his scouts to fall back while Lucy maneuvered to get a better line. Tom ran in a crouch to intercept.

He spotted three targets, their SPI armor mimicking the grass well, but not well enough to cover the parted grass at their feet. They turned to face Lucy.

Tom fired, spraying at knee level where the armor was weakest.

Three human-shaped outlines crushed the grass, screaming and convulsing as the rubber bullets pelted them.

Lucy joined him and opened fire.

When the screaming stopped, Tom moved in and peeled off their armor, revealing three very dazed DIs.

They had not identified themselves, so by the rules of

engagement they were fair targets. Adam ran up and helped him and Lucy strip the bodies.

"Pistols and MA5Ks, both with stun ammunition," Adam said.

Lucy held up a double handful of grenades, and smiled. "Flash-bangs."

"Now," Tom said, grinning, "this really gets interesting."

The moon had come out and set. The grass was wet with dew and Tom's stomach growled so loud he thought it might give away his position in the dark.

Five waves of DIs had come, and been neutralized by a now armed, armored, and fully equipped Spartan Trainee Defense Team. The instructors were tied up in the middle of the field by the bell. Hostages.

Tom and the other Spartans were working together like they never had before. And they were winning. He was hungry, wet, and cold, but Tom wouldn't have traded places with anyone in the entire galaxy.

He heard a rustle in the tall grass, turned, machine gun aimed waist high.

There was nothing there, and nothing on the thermals, either. He must be getting jumpy.

A hand clamped on his shoulder, while another hand wrenched the machine gun from his grasp.

Chief Mendez stood over him. At his side was Lieutenant Ambrose.

Tom half expected Mendez to shoot him right there.

"I think that's quite enough," Mendez growled.

The Lieutenant knelt beside Tom and whispered, "Good work, son."

CHAPTER 10

Kurt walked the empty corridors of the UNSC *Hopeful* and entered the atrium. Blazing lights overhead mimicked a realistic sun. Air recirculators made the leaves of the small grove of white oaks rustle. He smelled lavender, a scent he hadn't experienced since he was a child.

The most extravagant feature of the *Hopeful,* however, was the ten-meter curving window in the atrium—something utterly unheard of on any other ship in the UNSC fleet.

But then the *Hopeful* was unlike any other ship in the fleet.

Naval officers described her as "the ugliest thing to ever float in zero gee." The ship had been built before there had been major rebel activity in the colonies. A private medical corporation had purchased two scrapped repair stations—each a square kilometer plate of scaffolding, cranes, and cargo trams. These two plates had been connected to make an off-centered "sandwich," and within, a state-of-the-art hospital and research facility had been constructed.

In 2495 the UNSC had commandeered the vessel, added engines, minimal defensive systems, six fusion reactors, and a Shaw-Fujikawa translight system, and transformed the *Hopeful* into the largest mobile battlefield hospital in history.

While most Naval officers agreed she was unsightly, every enlisted Marine Kurt had ever spoken with declared her the most beautiful thing they had ever seen.

The *Hopeful* had taken on mythical proportions with the men and women who had to fight and die on the front lines. She had been damaged, but had survived, eighteen major Naval battles with rebel forces and four encounters with the Covenant. The ship's staff and technology had a reputation of saving lives, in many cases literally bringing the dead back to life.

Today the ship had been parked in interstellar space—essentially the middle of nowhere—by order of Vice Admiral Parangosky. And while the thousands of critically ill patients could not be evacuated, the eight decks surrounding docking cluster Bravo had been cleared of all personnel while ONI moved in their equipment and staff. The SPARTAN-III program had to remain under a cloak of absolute secrecy.

Kurt wished the *Hopeful* lived up to her reputation because today the lives of his Spartan potentials were at stake.

His candidates had had to endure so much in the last year. To accelerate the program's timetable, puberty had been artificially induced. Human-growth hormone as well as cartilage, muscle, and bone supplements had been introduced into their diet, and the children had metamorphosed into near-adult stature within nine months.

They had become clumsy in their new, larger bodies, and had struggled to relearn how to run, shoot, jump, and fight.

And today, they'd face their most dangerous test. They would either become irreparably disfigured, die, or be transformed into Spartans.

No, that wasn't right. While these kids didn't have the heightened speed or strength of a Spartan, they already had the commitment, drive, and spirit. They already were Spartans.

Kurt heard boots clicking down the corridor, then muffled steps crossing the atrium lawn.

"Lieutenant, sir?"

A young man and woman approached with the long loping gaits of people who had spent much time in microgravity. They wore standard Naval uniforms bearing the stripes of a petty officer second class. Both had close-cropped black hair and dark eyes.

Kurt had had to pull a few strings to keep the Beta Company survivors of Pegasi Delta with him. Colonel Ackerson had wanted Tom for his own private operations. And ever-silent Lucy had narrowly avoided an unfit-for-duty classification and permanent reassignment to ONI psych branch for "evaluation."

He'd had to appeal to Vice Admiral Parangosky, claiming he needed Spartans to train Spartans.

Over Ackerson's objections, she had agreed.

The result: Tom and Lucy had become Kurt's right and left hands over these last years, and Gamma Company were the finest Spartans ever.

Tom and Lucy spent so much of their time in their SPI armor, it took Kurt a moment to recognizes his attachés. Their armor, along with the rest of Gamma Company's Semi-Powered Infiltration suits, was being refitted with new photo-reactive coatings to boost their camouflaging properties. There were other experimental refits—gel ballistic layers, upgraded software suites, and other functions—that would hopefully be working within a year's time.

Tom and Lucy snapped off simultaneous salutes.

Kurt retuned the salute. "Report."

"The candidates are ready to board, sir," Tom said.

Kurt got up and the three of them walked back down the corridor and into docking cluster Bravo. It was the size of a small canyon with the capacity to cycle a fleet of dropships simultaneously through its massive air-lock system. There was ample space for triage and trams that could whisk an entire company of wounded soldiers to emergency surgical faculties.

Air locks screamed and there was a sudden gust of fresh air. Dozens of bay doors parted and Pelicans rolled into the bay on steam-powered beds.

The Pelicans' rear ramps lowered and the Spartan candidates filed out in orderly rows.

Kurt had briefed them about the procedures. They'd be sedated and injected with chemical cocktails and surgically altered to give them the strength of three normal soldiers, decrease their neural reaction time, and enhance their durability.

It was the final step in their transformation to Spartans.

It was graduation day.

He'd briefed them on the risks, too. He had shown them the archived videos of the results of the bioaugmentation phase of the SPARTAN-II program, how more than half of those candidates had washed out—either dying from the procedure or becoming so badly deformed they couldn't stand.

This would not happen to the SPARTAN-IIIs with the new medical protocols, but Kurt had wanted one final test.

Not one of the 330 candidates had opted out of the program. Kurt had had to petition Colonel Ackerson for thirty extra slots for this final phase. He simply didn't have it in him to randomly cut thirty—when every last one of them was willing and ready to fight. Ackerson had gladly granted his request.

Kurt stood and saluted as the line of candidates passed him.

They marched by, returning his salute, heads held high, and chests out. On average only twelve years old, they looked closer to fifteen with the sculpted musculature of Olympic athletes; many had hard-won scars; and all had an ineffable, confident air about them.

They were warriors. Kurt had never felt so proud.

The last candidate lingered, and then halted before him. It was Ash, serial number G099, leader of Team Saber. He was one of the fiercest, smartest, and best leaders in the class. His wavy brown hair was slightly over regulation length, but Kurt was inclined to let it slide, today of all days.

Ash snapped off a precise salute. "Sir, Spartan candidate G099 requesting permission to speak, sir."

"Granted," Kurt said, and finished his protracted salute.

"Sir, I . . ." Ash's voice cracked.

Many of the boys had problems with their vocal cords, still recovering from the rapidly induced puberty.

"I just wanted to let you know," Ash continued, "what an honor it's been to train under you, Chief Mendez, and Petty Officers Tom and Lucy. If I don't make it today, I wanted you to know that I wouldn't have done anything differently, sir."

"The honor has been mine," Kurt said. He held out his hand.

Ash stared at it a moment, and then he grasped Kurt's hand, clasped it firmly, and they shook.

"I'll see you on the other side," Kurt said.

Ash nodded and left, catching up to the rest of the candidates. Tom and Lucy both nodded their approvals.

"They're ready," Kurt whispered. He looked away so he wouldn't have to meet their gazes. "I hope *we* are. We're taking a hell of a risk."

Kurt, Tom, and Lucy stopped at a staff conference room, now an improvised ONI command and control center. Medical technicians in blue lab coats watched 330 video monitors and bio-sign sets. Tom spoke to one of the techs while Kurt's gaze flicked from monitor to monitor.

He then went down to the open surgical arena. It had four hundred sections—each partitioned by semiopaque plastic curtaining, and each fitting with a sterile-field generator that blazed with its characteristic orange light overhead.

Kurt entered one unit and found SPARTAN-G122, Holly, there.

The partitioned area was crammed full of machines. There were stands with bio monitors. Several intravenous and osmotic patches connected her to a chemo-therapeutic infuser, loaded with a collection of liquid-filled vials that would keep Holly in a semisedated state while it delivered a cocktail of drugs over the next week. There was a crash cart and portable ventilator nearby, as well.

She struggled to rise and salute, but she fell back, her eyelids fluttering closed.

He went to Holly's side and clasped her tiny hand until she settled into a deep sleep.

She reminded him of Kelly when she was this young: full of spunk, and never giving up. He missed Kelly. He had been dead to his fellow SPARTAN-IIs for almost twenty years. He missed all of them.

The chemo-therapeutic infuser hissed, vials rotated into place, micromechanical pumps thumped, and bubbles percolated inside its colored liquids.

It was starting. Kurt remembered when he went through the augmentation. The fevers, the pain—it felt as if his bones were breaking, like someone had poured napalm into his veins.

Holly shifted. The bio monitors showed a spike in her blood pressure and temperature. Tiny blisters appeared on her arms and she scratched at them. They filled with blood and then quickly smoothed into scabs.

Kurt patted Holly's hand one last time and then went to the infuser and lifted the side panel. Inside were dozens of solution vials. He squinted, reading off their serial numbers.

He spotted "8942-LQ99" inside the infuser. That was the carbide ceramic ossification catalyst to make skeletons virtually unbreakable.

There was "88005-MX77," the fibrofoid muscular protein complex that boosted muscle density.

"88947-OP24" was the number for retina-inversion stabilizer, which boosted color and nighttime vision.

"87556-UD61" was the improved colloidal neural disunification solution to decrease reaction times.

There were many others: shock reducers, analgesics, anti-inflammatories, anticoagulants, and pH buffers.

But Kurt was looking for three vials in particular, ones with different serial numbers—009927-DG, 009127-PX, and 009762-OO—that didn't match any standard medical logistics code.

They were there, bubbling as their contents were drained and mixed with picoliter precision.

He heard footsteps approaching.

Kurt lowered the panel of the infuser and stepped back to Holly's side.

There was rustling of plastic curtains and a medical technical in blue lab coat entered.

"Is there anything you need help with, sir?" the medtech asked. "Anything I can get you?"

"Everything is fine," Kurt lied. He brushed past the man. "I was just leaving."

CHAPTER 11

0210 Hours, February 20, 2551 (Military Calendar) \
Aboard UNSC *Hopeful,* Interstellar Space,
Sector K-009

Kurt sat alone in the atrium viewing the candidates' progress on his tablet. He'd spent the last twenty-four hours awake, by their sides, and then caught four hours of sleep. He'd go back to them shortly when they awoke to congratulate the candidates.

Correction: congratulate the *Spartans.*

Every last one of them had made it. Kurt wished he could feel relief, but there were too many unknowns.

"Lieutenant Ambrose." A female voice sounded over SHIP-COM. "Report to the bridge immediately."

He got up and marched to the elevator. The doors closed and the elevator rushed through sections of normal and zero gravity; Kurt held fast to the railing.

Kurt and his Project CHRYSANTHEMUM team were

supposed to be left alone—orders directly from FLEETCOM brass. So why the summons to the bridge?

The doors opened. A lieutenant commander stood with arms akimbo waiting for him, a woman barely a meter and a quarter with a gray widow's peak.

"Ma'am." Kurt saluted. "Lieutenant Ambrose reporting as ordered. Permission to enter the bridge."

"Granted," she said. "Come with me."

She skirted the edge of the large low-lit room. Not only were its three dozen officers monitoring navigation, weapon, communication, and drive systems; there were teams controlling structural-stress compensators, tram traffic, water, power-load distributions, and ecoreclamation subsystems. The *Hopeful* was more city space station than ship of the line.

The Lieutenant Commander pressed her palm to the biometric by a side door. It parted, and they both entered.

The room beyond was lined with shelves of gilt antique books. Old globes of Earth and a dozen other worlds had been tastefully set about a koa-wood desk that gleamed like gold under the light of a single brass lamp.

An old man sat in the shadows. "That will be all, Lieutenant Commander," the man said.

He stood and Kurt saw three stars flash on his collar. Kurt reflexively saluted. "Sir!"

The Lieutenant Commander left, the door closing and locking behind her.

The Vice Admiral walked around Kurt once.

Vice Admiral Ysionris Jeromi was a living legend. He'd taken the *Hopeful,* a ship with virtually no weapons or armor, into battle three times to save the crews of critically wounded ships.

He had saved tens of thousands of lives, and almost been court-martialed for it, too.

War needs its heroes, though. The then Admiral had lost and regained stars from his collar, but he had also received the UNSC's highest wartime decoration: the Colonial Cross. Twice.

"I'm not sure who you are," the Vice Admiral said, and his bushy white brows bunched together. "Someone a lot more important than 'Lieutenant Ambrose,' or whatever your name really is."

Kurt knew better than to say anything unless asked a direct question. He stood at attention. The code-word classification of the SPARTAN-III project prevented him from divulging anything, even to a vice admiral, without clearance.

He walked back to his desk, reached into a drawer, and retrieved a black sphere the size of a grapefruit. "Do you know what this is, Lieutenant?"

"No, sir," Kurt said.

"Slipspace COM probe," he said. "A stationary Shaw-Fujikawa driver launches one of these black 'bullets' into Slipstream space on an ultraprecise trajectory. It rips through the laws of known human physics, and drops back into normal space at some very distant coordinates. Like your own personal carrier pigeon. Do you understand?"

"Yes, sir," Kurt said. "Like a slipspace science probe. I've seen them launched from Station Archimedes. Or the new ODST drop pod that can be fired from a ship still in slipspace."

"Nothing like that at all, Lieutenant. Those are just dropped into, and then out of, Slipstream space—more like a turd swirling around in an old-fashioned gravity toilet than precision engineering."

He patted the black sphere. "This beauty actually navigates through slipspace. Traverses as far and as fast as any UNSC ship. Damn near magical if you appreciate the mathematics. You understand now?"

Kurt wasn't sure what the Admiral was fishing for. He had been asked a direct question, however, so he answered. "If what you have said is accurate, sir, it would revolutionize long-distance communications. Every ship would be fitted with such a device."

"Except for what it costs to a build an ultraprecise Shaw-Fujikawa low-mass launcher," the Vice Admiral replied, "you could build a *fleet* of ships. And for the cost to make one of these little black balls"—he rolled the probe perilously close to the edge of his desk—"you could buy the capital city of some backwater colony. There are only two such launchers. One on Reach and one on Earth."

The Vice Admiral returned to Kurt and his pale blue eyes stared into Kurt's. "This probe arrived fifteen minutes ago," the Vice Admiral told him, "forty million kilometers from the *Hopeful*. Entry vector matches neither Earth nor Reach as the point of origin. And it's for you."

Kurt had a dozen questions, but dared not raise any of them. He felt like he walked on a razor's edge of secrecy.

The Vice Admiral snorted and moved to the door. "There's protocol for top secrecy on this, so use my office, Lieutenant. Take as much time as you need." He palmed the door and it opened. He paused and added, "If there is any danger to my ship or my patients, I expect to be informed, son. Orders or no."

He left and the door sheathed closed.

Kurt approached the black sphere. There were no obvious controls or displays. Light shed off its surface like water beading off oil.

He touched it and it warmed.

Ice appeared in snowflake patterns and crackled over the Vice Admiral's desk.

Holographic snow drifted through the office and coalesced into a white cloak, chiseled features, glacier eyes, and a cane of crystalline ice: Deep Winter.

"My god," the AI breathed. "And I thought *rear* admirals were long-winded. I thought old Jeromi would never leave."

Deep Winter smoothed his near-skeletal hands over nothing, and a blue sheen permeated the air. "Counterelectronics package online."

"How did you get here?" Kurt asked.

His mind struggled to grasp the ramifications. AIs had large footprints; they needed installations, and massive power sources to fuel their minds. Deep Winter couldn't be here. And how could the AI manage to alter the approach vector from Earth's or Reach's COM launchers?

Deep Winter held up a hand. "Stop. I see your mind in logic lock, Lieutenant. It would, perhaps, help to explain."

"Please," Kurt whispered.

"First," Deep Winter said, "we may only communicate in a limited fashion. I have imprinted a fraction of my intellect into the memory matrix of this probe. The process has irreversibly destroyed a portion of the home base processing powers, so please do not waste the precious minutes we have. There is also insufficient remaining power in this probe for a prolonged debate."

Kurt nodded. This had cost the AI a high price, so he would do his best to listen.

"Also, let us not waste time debating the nuances of this Slipstream-space COM probe. That is classified, and you don't have clearance."

"Then what are we talking about?" Kurt asked.

"I have found three anomalies to the current bioaugmentation protocols." Deep Winter clapped his handed together and two gyrating collections of steel spheres appeared. "These represent the protein complexes miso-olanzapine and cyclodexione-4," Deep Winter explained, "which were secreted into the alteration regime."

Kurt leaned closer to the spinning molecules.

"They are antipsychotic and bipolar integration drugs," Deep Winter said.

He clapped his hands and a third molecule appeared: twisting silver and gold blobs. "And this," the AI said, "is a mutagen that alters key regions in a subject's frontal lobe."

Deep Winter faded to semitranslucency. "It enhances aggression, making the animal part of the mind more accessible in times of stress. Someone so mutated has reserves of strength and endurance no normal human could call upon. Such a person could also continue to fight under the influence of wide systemic shock that would instantly kill a normal human.

"The mutagen, however, depresses the higher reason centers of the brain over time," the AI continued. "The antipsychotic drugs and bipolar integration medicines counter this effect. As long as the SPARTAN-IIIs have these agents in their system, they compensate."

Kurt understood all of this. Under extreme stress the counteragents would metabolize quickly, and the primitive brain would take over. His Spartans would fight and be harder to kill. The effect was only reversed by the counteragents. It was dangerous. His Spartans could lose the ability to reason. It might give them the edge needed to survive, though.

Deep Winter continued to fade. The AI had always placed the

Spartan candidates' well-being over their training or any agenda Section Three had for them.

"You care for them in your own way," Kurt said. "The Spartans."

"Of course I do. They are just children, regardless of what has been done to them. You must halt the protocol. Brain mutations were specifically outlawed by UNSC MED CORPS in 2513. The moral argument algorithms are robust."

Deep Winter shrank to a single tiny snowflake glimmer on the desk. "I am a fifth-generation smart AI, Kurt. I have reached the end of my effective operational life on Onyx. By the time you return, I will have been shut down and replaced. I have left files."

The snowflake glistened, its tips melting. Deep Winter whispered, "You must proceed cautiously; I am unsure who in ONI has masterminded this illegal procedure, but they will surely attempt to cover it up."

The snowflake melted, and with it all holographic traces of Deep Winter vanished. The surface of the black COM sphere heated, the surface bubbled, and thin ribbons of smoke curled from within.

Yes, they would cover it up. When Kurt returned to Onyx he would inform Colonel Ackerson . . . and then they would arrange to have all of Deep Winter's files purged.

The mutation had been Kurt's idea. He had had to persuade the Colonel to allow it, and they had even kept it a secret from the others in the SPARTAN-III subsection cell to preserve their "plausible deniability."

Kurt had seen too many of his Spartans die; he would have broken a hundred regs and bioethical policies to give his people the slightest chance to survive one more battle.

His only regret was not being able to do more.

Deep Winter's "instinct" to save the Spartans was misguided. None of them could be protected that way. Warriors fought battles; they prevailed, but all inevitably faced death. Even his children candidates understood that.

They did not, however, have to die so easily.

Kurt turned from the COM probe, and left the Admiral's office.

He had to go congratulate Gamma Company . . . and welcome them into the brotherhood of Spartans.

SECTION III

INTRUDERS

CHAPTER 12

Two flash-bang grenades detonated—balls of lightning and thunder and fluttering leaves.

Ash fell and reflexively curled into a ball. He'd seen the steel hexagonal tubes a split second too late, and then their images had been burned into his retinas.

They'd been too well camouflaged, chest level in the trees. Stupid. He wasn't thinking, letting his blood rise and get the best of him.

He uncurled and rolled to his feet. They only thing he heard was his hammering heart; otherwise he was deaf.

Ash blinked to clear his blurred vision.

Team Saber was down. Mark, Olivia, Holly, and Dante were on their knees. Their SPI armor camouflage buffers had been wiped by the flash-bangs, and only the faintest beige camo patterns were beginning to resolve like bruises. The new photo-reactive coating technology could mimic a wide range of EM radiation, but it was still sensitive to overload.

He pulled Mark to his feet, shook him.

Mark nodded and then got the others up.

Ash motioned them back, reversing the direction they had walked into this trap. They only had a moment before Team Katana moved in for the kill.

This was his fault. He'd been too eager, too easily pushed into action without thinking. Mark had spotted a sniper from Katana, and Ash had too quickly decided to flank to the left . . . and walked straight into the *real* trap, the flash-bangs.

But that was the point of this exercise, wasn't it? Compress three Spartan squads into a square kilometer arena—think fast or die.

Or worse, in this case, think fast or *lose*.

Ash held up a hand, halting his team. They would not fall straight back. If he were Team Katana he'd have set up another trap for a retreating enemy.

He motioned for them to hook right.

Team Saber moved in a crouch through the brush, slow, careful, eyes wide. Olivia took point, and she vanished into the green shadows.

Ringing started in Ash's ears. That was a good sign. Another half meter closer to those grenades and he'd have lost the eardrum. In situ cloning was an excruciatingly boring procedure, and he'd be happy to avoid the two-week mandatory downtime.

A red status light winked from Olivia. The team froze.

Five meters ahead, a fern bent and sprang back.

Ash rapidly blinked his green status light: the signal to open fire. This was the best target they'd had all morning.

Suppressed gunfire surrounded him. The fern exploded into a shower of confetti.

A single Spartan hidden by the fern turned, their SPI armor flashing silver from the staccato of stun rounds that peppered its surface. Their foot caught on a root and they tumbled.

Ash repeated the go-ahead signal, and his squad made sure the target *stayed* down with several bursts of well-placed rounds. The ballistic gel underlayer of their armor could take a heck of a pounding before breaking down.

After three seconds, he flashed red, and they ceased fire.

Olivia moved up and slapped a lime-green sticky flag on the still-writhing Spartan's back. The target was now officially "dead."

Ash activated a NAV marker and alerted C and C for pickup of the "corpse."

The ground trembled, just for a moment, but all the Spartans in Team Saber froze, and then scanned the jungle, looking for the source of the disturbance.

Earthquake? Not likely. There was no tectonic activity on Onyx. That left only two possibilities: impact or detonation. Neither was especially welcome.

Ash motioned for Saber to move out. They slinked through the jungle and emerged on a plain. Here small limestone granite and quartz mesas, grottos, and fissures extended to the north—up to and beyond the high fence of Zone 67.

The Zone was where the "ghost" of Onyx was supposed to be. It'd been spotted once or twice according to other Spartan candidates: a single eye in the dark. They just made up that stuff to scare plebes. Ash had, however, heard of a Beta Company squad that had vanished near here and never been found.

He looked around warily and spotted a naturally eroded tunnel that extended through a hill. Ash pointed and Team Saber settled inside to assess the tactical situation.

Ash pulled off his helmet, and wiped the blood from his nose and hair. "Too close," he said.

"Still, we got one," Holly said, pulling off her own golden mirrored helmet, "and we didn't lose one of ours . . . although *you* sure gave it a good try." She scratched the fuzz on her head, which she had buzz-cut into a series of bear-claw scratch patterns. The length was a-okay by the regs, but some of the other teams teased her about it. Holly got a little wild about the teasing, and she had been demoted twice for fighting.

Dante removed his helmet and felt his scarred face for any damage. Satisfied, he retrieved two black flash-bang grenades from his pack. "Found these, just before yours went off. Caught the trip wires."

Ash nodded. He should have reprimanded Dante for sticking his hands near a set of primed grenades. Then again, Dante had near-magical abilities when it came to explosives. He always knew when they were about to go, and when they wouldn't. That or he was the luckiest person he'd ever seen.

Olivia kept her SPI helmet on. She slipped out of the cave, taking up a guard position outside. Ash wasn't worried. She was the best sneak in Gamma Company. They called her "O" for short because she was as whisper-quiet as her vowel namesake.

Ash turned to Mark. "Head check," he said, and patted his friend on the back of his helmet.

Mark pulled the helmet off, and Ash saw a nasty bruise on his cheek. Mark ran his hands over his shaved head and worried the edges of that bruise.

"I'm fine," Mark said. He smoothed the inner lining of his armor, making sure it was perfect, and then slipped the helmet back on.

They called Mark "*The* Mark," because he was their best marksman—good with a sniper rifle, but better with a rifle on full auto in all-out target-rich free-for-all. The more pressure on him, the cooler he got.

Ash spotted bands of rough onyx along the tunnel wall, black and white and streaked with flecks of gold. He ran a gloved finger over the patterns, intrigued by the geological oddity.

He then snapped out of it and focused on the here and now. He slipped his helmet back on.

"Audio check," Ash whispered over TEAMCOM.

Green status lights winked back. Good. No one was deaf.

A dull thump echoed off the distant mesa walls, and dust rained down from the cave ceiling.

Team Saber instinctively dropped to a crouch. Ash pulled his sidearm.

"Big one," Dante muttered. "Artillery? One of the new four-forties?"

"I don't think the Lieutenant Commander would use artillery on us," Ash whispered.

"Not normally," Holly replied. "But this is the *last* test. Maybe he's pulling out all the stops to figure out who'll get top honors."

Top honors. Ash had pushed Team Saber to stay on top for the last three years: honing their specialties; learning every lesson Endless Summer threw at them; and thinking, moving, and acting together as a single razor-edged weapon. Only two other teams were even close in the rankings. Gladius and Katana. Top honors would mean bragging rights and respect. It would mean they were the best. That they'd won.

Over TEAMCOM, Ash said, "O, you get a direction on that blast?

Olivia's status light winked red.

"Okay," Ash said, "we'll assume it's artillery for now. I can't believe the Lieutenant Commander would be using it . . . but Mendez is another story. You hear incoming, scatter, and take cover."

Four green LEDs lit on his heads-up display, acknowledging the order.

Ash had read somewhere that you never heard the artillery shell that killed you. He had no desire to personally test that battlefield legend.

"What's the plan for Katana and Gladius?" Mark asked.

"Katana's down one," Ash replied. "We'll focus on the weaker of the two. We'll find—"

Another thump and the ground shuddered.

"Closer," Olivia whispered over TEAMCOM. "Vector north."

Ash stepped out of the tunnel and took cover by a large boulder. The others followed and their SPI armor blended into the rocky terrain.

If this was another trap, then they were probably stepping out right into a sniper's line of fire. But Ash didn't think so. No one would use ordnance that big so close, not even Mendez.

An explosion like that wasn't something you could throw together from rocks and branches and a couple of flash-bang grenades, either . . . so that eliminated Teams Katana and Gladius.

So who *was* doing it?

Forty meters to the north was the triple fence surrounding Zone 67. Electrified razor wire, motion sensors, and lanes of minefields made an effective barrier. If pressed, Team Saber could have gotten around it—but they wouldn't. The LC's orders had been crystal clear: DO NOT CROSS. It would count as an instant disqualification for top honors.

What about the other teams? Just a quick hop over and lateral move to flank him? No. None of them would risk a disqualification.

There was a dust storm about three kilometers into Zone 67, a wall of sand, swirling smoke . . . and fire.

A distant mesa exploded—vaporized into a mushroom of glittering quartz dust, a hail of boulders, and roiling flame.

Ash instinctively ducked, and his insides clenched.

He'd seen big explosions before. Nothing like that, though.

"Two kilometers," Dante said. "Felt that one in my bones."

They watched the stones rain from the sky.

"A few Archer missiles maybe . . ." Mark murmured.

Dots swirled about the edge of the expanding cloud of dust. If Ash didn't know better he'd have sworn they were vultures. But Onyx didn't have raptorlike avian species.

Ash zoomed magnification on his faceplate. At five-times he saw the dots had a three-fold symmetry.

He unslung his sniper rifle and sited through the scope.

They were drones of some sort. But not UNSC MAKOS. Not Covenant Banshees fliers, either. They were a few meters long. Three dull steel booms that surrounded a central eye, glowing like molten iron. No obvious jets. No cockpit. There were a dozen of them.

"Has to be an experimental prototype," Dante said. Maybe Zone 67 is a testing range for new weapons."

"They wouldn't be 'testing' a megaton worth of destructive force while we were so close," Ash countered.

Or *was* this part of the final test? Some new threat that the three squads would have to band together to defeat? That would be Chief Mendez's style: change the rules in the middle of a test.

The drones moved away from the atomized mesa, drifted closer to Team Saber's location, stopping short just on the opposite side of the Zone 67 fence, where they circled another butte.

Ash spied motion atop that formation. Shutters from a camouflaged bunker popped open, and heavy machine-gun fire strafed the drones.

The lead drone's three booms snapped forward to make a

triangular flat plane. A glimmering film of gold popped into place and fifty-caliber rounds impacted and bounced off.

"Energy shields!" Dante said. "Has to be Covenant."

Ash reluctantly agreed with this assessment. This was no game, no final honors test.

The war had arrived on Onyx.

He broadcast over an open COM channel: "Currahee C and C, come in. This is Saber One. We have an emergency."

No answer. His radio light was green. He *was* broadcasting, but no one was listening.

"Radio check," Ash said to his team. "Everyone try to get the Lieutenant Commander or the Chief. Try to raise the *Agincourt,* too."

Ash used his sniper rifle and tracked the drones.

The remaining eleven lined up behind the one distorted to form an energy shield; their red eyes aligned and pointed directly at the mesa top.

Men emerged from the bunker with M19 missile launchers.

The drones' eyes flared to a brilliant gold—energy projected forward, flicking like a rapier strike.

The men and bunker wavered a moment, erupted into flames, and vaporized. The mesa top then detonated into a cloud of dust and molten rock.

The ground tilted and cracked. Team Saber retreated into the tunnel and debris rained over them.

Ash squinted back through the haze.

The drones had scattered and moved forward, zigzagging over the rocky terrain: a search pattern.

He moved to the opposite end of the tunnel and risked another open COM broadcast. "Team Katana, Team Gladius, Covenant activity in Zone 67. Forget the test, guys. We've got a situation."

CHAPTER 13

Kurt scanned the horizon with his binoculars. He watched the pattern of the wind in the tree line, the birds that had taken wing, and a whisper of smoke that snaked up from the canopy.

There was trouble in the air.

From his perch in the "tree house" he couldn't see the source of the disturbance near the Spartan test area.

The tree house was a platform a hundred meters off the jungle floor in the titan arms of a banyan tree. The only electronics here were the radio and the AI projection unit. Everything else was low-tech: optic binoculars and telescopes, parabolic sound collection dishes, good old-fashioned signal flags.

"What's the *Agincourt* got?" he asked Mendez.

Chief Mendez turned to Kurt, pressing the bud receiver into

his ear. "A lot of static. Encountering broadband interference. They're moving to high orbit to get a clear picture."

The *Agincourt* had just delivered supplies for the incoming Delta Company. Kurt had asked for a little observational assistance before they broke orbit.

"Pass my thanks to the Commander," Kurt said.

Chief Mendez's face darkened. "They're breaking up."

The dish-sized AI projector sparked to life, and warm red sunlight sparked and filled the tree house. It solidified into a tall Cherokee brave, bare-chested, wearing buckskins, feathered spear in his massive hand. This was Endless Summer, the ONI AI stationed at the ultrahigh-secure facility thirty kilometers to the north, a place that technically no longer existed, it was so secret.

The AI gestured for Kurt and then he vanished, replaced by the lightning-bolt symbol for a UNSC priority flash communiqué.

The AI that had replaced Deep Winter was aloof, had barely tolerated Kurt and his staff, and it never *initiated* communication. This was trouble.

Kurt stepped closer and the pad scanned his biometrics. Several files were beamed directly onto his retina, a top-secret protocol that gave a new twist to the phase "eyes-only" security.

He read:

UNITED NATIONS SPACE COMMAND PRIORITY TRANSMISSION
FLASH 91762P-06
ENCRYPTION CODE: BLACK
PUBLIC KEY: FILE/SEASONAL/
FROM: CODE NAME ENDLESS SUMMER
TO: / LIEUTENANT KURT AMBROSE, SPECIAL ATTACHÉ, LOGISTICAL
OPERATIONS COMMAND (NAVLOGCOM), OFFICE OF INVESTIGA-
TIONS UNSCMID: 045888947

Subject: Emergency Alert Status

Classification: Restricted (XXX-XD Directive)

/start file/decryption protocol/

FLASH TRANSMISSION TO CAMP CURRAHEE COMMAND AND CONTROL

ENDLESS SUMMER DIRECTED TO LIEUTENANT COMMANDER AMBROSE—EYES ONLY

ZONE 67 UNDER ATTACK.

Per general order 98.93.120, I am authorized to take command of all military personnel on Onyx under emergency circumstance. I hereby exercise that authority and order all under your command to immediately defend

Zone 67 from eminent danger.

Attacker Identity: Unknown. Nonhuman origin.

<u>ATTENTION</u>: Possible Covenant vectors.

<u>ATTENTION</u>: Possible non-Covenant vectors.

You are authorized with code-word clea1rance PATRIOT-SEVEN-BLUE to review the following condensed material of immediate benefit. Any breach of code-word classification confidentiality is punishable by the death penalty as per UNSC MIL-JAG 4465/LHG, the Wartime Articles of

SECRECY, AND THE AMENDED ARTICLES OF THE UNITED SECURITY ACTS OF 2162.

/END/

/ATTACHED FILE 1 OF 9/

MAY 6, 2491 (MILITARY CALENDAR)
FIELD REPORT A76344-USNC.ENGCORP
SUBJECT: SURVEY PLANET XF-063
REPORTING OFFICER: CAPTAIN D. F. LAMBERT UNSC.ENGCORP/
    UNSCMID: 03981762

XF-063 IS A RARE JEWEL OF A FIND. THERE IS AN OXYGEN-NITROGEN-INERT GAS ATMOSPHERE OF SUITABLE PRESSURE AND A MODERATE WEATHER CYCLE. THERE IS A SURPRISING ABUNDANCE OF INDIGENOUS FLORA AND FAUNA, WHICH UPON CURSORY INVESTIGA-TION POSES NO DANGER. IN FACT, EDIBLE SPECIES PRESENT. (SEE ADDITIONAL REPORTS FOR DETAILS.) TRANSPLANT OF EARTH SPECIES POSSIBLE.

NOTABLE ANOMALIES: NO DETECTABLE TECTONIC ACTIVITY, BUT THERE IS STILL AN UNUSUALLY STRONG PLANETARY MAGNETIC FIELD. SLIGHTLY HIGHER THAN NORMAL BACKGROUND RADIATION MEASURED, BUT WELL WITHIN TOLERABLE STANDARDS. ADDITIONAL GEOLOGICAL TESTING RECOMMENDED.

NO TERRAFORMING EFFORT REQUIRED. COLONIZATION RECOMMENDED.

/END/

/ATTACHED FILE 2 OF 9/

HALO: GHOSTS OF ONYX

FEBRUARY 19, 2492 (MILITARY CALENDAR)
FIELD REPORT A79052-USNC.ENGCORP
SUBJECT: GEOLOGICAL EXPEDITION FOUR, PLANET XF-063
REPORTING OFFICER: LIEUTENANT W. K. DAVIDSON
UNSC.ENGCORP/ UNSCMID: 07729654

THE NORTHERN PLATEAU REGION OF THE MIDLATITUDE LANDMASS HAS AN ABUNDANCE OF GRANITE AND QUARTZ VARIETIES FORMING HILLS AND MESAS. BREATHTAKING ONYX QUARRIES.

ADDITIONAL EXPLORATION OF THIS REGION HAS REVEALED LIMESTONE OF ORGANIC ORIGINS, SPECIFICALLY AN ANCIENT CORAL REEF WITH A RICH FOSSIL HISTORY.

CURSORY INVESTIGATION HAS YIELDED SEVERAL ANCIENT SPECIES OF UNKNOWN ORIGINS, AND ENTIRE PHYLUM FOUND OF POSSIBLY ALIEN TAXONOMY.

RECOMMENDATION: FOLLOW-UP SURVEY. SPECIALIST REQUESTED IN PALEO- AND XENOBIOLOGY AND BIOCHEMISTRY.

/END/

/ATTACHED FILE 3 OF 9/

JANUARY 3, 2511 (MILITARY CALENDAR)
ORDER 178.8.64.007
SUBJECT: SECURITY RECLASSIFICATION
ISSUING OFFICER: REAR ADMIRAL M. O. PARANGOSKY, OFFICE OF NAVAL INTELLIGENCE, SECTION THREE/ UNSCMID: 03669271

EFFECTIVE IMMEDIATELY ALL MATERIALS MENTIONING, REFERENCING, OR CONTAINING REPORTS, SURVEYS, PERSONAL NOTES AND LOGS,

IMAGES, OR ANY OTHER DATA PERTAINING TO OR ABOUT THE PLANET CATALOG NO. XF-063 (ALSO KNOWN COLLOQUIALLY AS "ONYX") IS HEREBY RECLASSIFIED TO TOP SECERT, EYES ONLY.

UNSC SYSTEMWIDE NETWORK PURGE AUTHORIZED BY OFFICE OF NAVAL INTELLIGENCE (REF NO. 0097833), UNDER THE DIRECTION OF MIL.AI. ID: 477-SSD.

/END/

/ATTACHED FILE 4 OF 9/

OCTOBER 22, 2511 (MILITARY CALENDAR)
ONI FIELD REPORT A84110
CLASSIFICATION: TOP SECRET, CODE-WORD
SUBJECT: STATUS OF RUINS IN ZONE 67
REPORTING OFFICER: LIEUTENANT COMMANDER J. G. ORTEGA,
OFFICE OF NAVAL INTELLIGENCE, SECTION THREE/ UNSCMID:
      7631073

CONCERNING THE ALIEN RUINS DISCOVERED IN ZONE 67, WE CONTINUE TO FIND EVIDENCE OF AN ADVANCED CULTURE WITH A SUPERLATIVE GRASP OF MATHEMATICS AND ASTROGATION, WITH SOME POSSIBLE ARTISTIC REPRESENTATIONS THAT SUGGEST A SPACE-FARING RACE (SEE ATTACHED DIGITAL IMAGES OF ONYX CARVINGS).

THEIR NUMEROUS HIEROGLYPHICS, WHILE AT FIRST GLANCE COMPARABLE TO ANCIENT TERRESTRIAL AZTEC VARIANTS, ARE, IN FACT, NOTHING AT ALL LIKE THESE PRIMITIVE EARTH COUNTERPARTS. SEVERAL LAYERS OF SYMBOLOGY SUGGEST A HIGHER-DIMENSIONAL APPROACH TO THEIR LANGUAGE, IF IT CAN EVEN BE TRULY THOUGHT OF AS WRITING OR LANGUAGE IN ANY HUMAN SENSE.

TRANSLATION CONTINUES TO ELUDE ALL EXPERTS, HUMAN AND AI.

RECOMMENDATION: INCREASED FUNDING AND EXCAVATION WILL UNDOUBTEDLY YIELD HITHERTO UNKNOWN TECHNOLOGIES.

ADDITIONAL NOTE: NO FURTHER INFORMATION HAS BEEN DISCOVERED REGARDING THE GLOWING SPHERE DISCOVERED BY BETA COMPANY TRAINEES. THE SUBSEQUENT DETONATION OF THE SPHERE OBLITERATED ALL CLUES OF ITS ORIGIN.

/END/

/ATTACHED FILE 5 OF 9/

SEPTEMBER 2, 2517 (MILITARY CALENDAR)
ONI FIELD REPORT C384409
CLASSIFICATION: TOP SECRET, CODE-WORD
SUBJECT: STATUS OF RUINS IN ZONE 67
REPORTING OFFICER: COMMANDER J. G. ORTEGA, OFFICE OF NAVAL INTELLIGENCE, SECTION THREE/ UNSCMID: 7631073

NEW FACILITIES WENT OPERATIONAL AS OF 0500 HOURS TODAY. SMART AIS FUNCTIONING IN TANDEM AS PER SPECIFICATIONS WITH SOME PRELIMINARY SUCCESS ON SOME OF THE SIMPLER, LOW-DIMENSIONAL HIEROGLYPHICS.

CONTINUED EXCAVATIONS OF MILLIONS OF CUBIC FEET OF EARTH IN ZONE 67 YIELD RUINED BUILDINGS, CARVINGS, AND TABLETS, BUT AS WITH THE OTHER REGIONS NO DISCOVERIES OF A TECHNOLOGICAL NATURE DISCOVERED (OR IF THERE ARE, WE LACK SUFFICIENT UNDERSTANDING TO DISCERN THEIR FUNCTION).

CARVINGS DEPICTING THE INHABITANTS OF ONYX STILL NOT FOUND. WHATEVER THESE CREATURES LOOKED LIKE, FOR THE MOMENT, REMAINS A MYSTERY.

ERIC NYLUND

THE SENIOR STAFF NOW BELIEVES THAT A SUDDEN CATACLYSM CLAIMED THE INHABITANTS OF THIS WORLD. UNKNOWN IF PATHOLOGICAL, SOCIOLOGICAL, OR RADIOLOGICAL IN NATURE. THIS MAY, HOWEVER, EXPLAIN THE HIGHER-THAN-NORMAL BACKGROUND RADIATION LEVELS.

RECOMMENDATION: INCREASED STAFF AND FUNDING. THE RUINS ARE SO EXTENSIVE THEY COULD TAKE SEVERAL LIFETIMES TO UNEARTH THEM ALL. THIS ENTIRE WORLD MAY BE COVERED IN SIMILAR RUINS. NEW TECHNOLOGIES CERTAINLY MUST HAVE SURVIVED AND AWAIT DISCOVERY.

/END/

/ATTACHED FILE 6 OF 9/

MARCH 6, 2525 (MILITARY CALENDAR)
ORDER 276.8.91.848
SUBJECT: ZONE 67 FUNDING
ISSUING OFFICER: ADMIRAL M. O. PARANGOSKY, OFFICE OF
NAVAL INTELLIGENCE, SECTION THREE/ UNSCMID: 03669271

GENTLEMEN, I'LL BE BRIEF. AFTER ALMOST FIFTEEN YEARS OF CONTINUOUS AND RUINOUSLY EXPENSIVE RESEARCH WITHOUT A SINGLE NEW USEFUL TECHNOLOGY DISCOVERED, THE BUDGET OF THE ONYX INITIATIVE HAS BEEN REPRIORITIZED.

ALTHOUGH THE ALIEN ARTIFACTS AND HIEROGLYPHICS CONTINUE TO BE OF INTEREST, RECENT REBEL ACTIVITIES IN THE OUTER COLONIES DEMAND THAT WE FACE REALITIES AND REALLOCATE OUR FINITE AI AND MILITARY PERSONNEL TO COUNTER THIS NEW THREAT.

ONYX IS TO REMAIN CLASSIFIED, CODE-WORD TOP SECRET. ALL MATERIALS AND FILES HAVE BEEN REDESIGNATED UNDER THE NOMEN-CLATURE KING UNDER THE MOUNTAIN.

PURSUANT TO ORDER 178.8.64.007 ANY BREACH OF CODE-WORD CLASSIFICATION CONFIDENTIALITY IS PUNISHABLE BY THE DEATH PENALTY AS PER UNSC MIL-JAG 4465/LHG, THE WARTIME ARTICLES OF SECRECY, AND THE AMENDED ARTICLES OF THE HOMELAND SECURITY ACT OF 2162.

A SKELETON CREW AND ONE AI WILL CONTINUE TO PROBE THE MYSTERIES OF ZONE 67. MAYBE THEY'LL HIT PAY DIRT.

IN THE MEANTIME, THE REST OF US HAVE A WAR TO FIGHT.

/END/

Kurt never finished reading Endless Summer's flash transmission.

An explosion darkened the horizon with a mushroom cloud of fire and dust, and the holographic page dissolved before Kurt could scan the rest of the files. The projector sputtered, sparked, and died.

The intel Endless Summer had just sent swam through his mind. Alien ruins? Possible Covenant invasion? What did the AI mean by possible *non-Covenant* vectors?

"We have to get out of here," Kurt said.

Chief Mendez continued to stare at the distant blast. "Artillery. Maybe a missile strike?"

Kurt scrutinized the shape of the blast cloud. "No, it's highly asymmetric. There are uneven heat blooms. I'd guess a directed energy weapon."

The Chief picked up the radio and again tried to raise the *Agincourt*. "This is Camp Currahee C and C. Come in, over?"

Static.

"Try the squads," Kurt said.

Mendez nodded. "Saber, come in. Katana? Report, this is

Chief Mendez. Gladius." He clicked the mic. This time, there wasn't even static, only dead air. "You think"—Mendez looked up at the sky—"the *Agincourt* did something?"

The Chief crinkled his silver brows together, worried. It was an emotion Kurt had never before seen on the old man's features.

Another detonation shook Zone 67. What had been a distant granite bluff turned into a disintegrating rain of dust.

"We've received orders to defend Zone 67," Kurt said.

Mendez sighed and shrugged. "I've got my M6 sidearm." He patted his holster. "And a knife in my boot. You?"

Kurt held out his hands.

"Should be a fair fight then," Mendez remarked. He tried the radio again. "Come in, Saber."

His voice filtered through the speaker, crackling with pops and static.

Kurt shook his head. "Something's jamming the transmission. Our Spartans aren't going to fight with stun rounds and flash-bang grenades. They'll head to the armory at Camp Currahee."

"Tom and Lucy should already be there," Mendez said. He moved to the zip line that stretched from the tree house top to the jungle floor. He grabbed the line, wrapped slide casing on, and then jumped over the edge.

For a man pushing sixty, the Chief moved like a soldier thirty years younger. It wasn't the first time Kurt had wondered what kind of Spartan he would have made.

Kurt followed down the zip line, free-falling for a moment, then squeezing the line to brake; he landed hard.

They ran for the Warthog parked on the dirt track at the base of the tree house.

Kurt jumped into the driver's side, and turned the engine over. The vehicle coughed to life and purred.

"No EMP damage," Mendez said. "Or the coil would have been fried."

It was almost a disappointment. A nuke, Kurt could understand. Fissile materials were used only by the UNSC or rebels—human forces.

He floored the accelerator and the Warthog fishtailed, and then the tires caught and they bumped down the dirt track.

The day suddenly brightened, and an extra set of shadows crisscrossed the jungle floor.

Kurt slowed the Warthog, and looked up at the sky. The canopy obscured his view, so he turned off the track and drove into the jungle, bouncing over exposed roots, and then down the bank of the Twin Forks River.

Here Kurt had a clear line of sight to the sky, and he noted the sun had moved to a new position lower in the sky.

No, it hadn't moved. There were *two* suns.

This new sun faded and a ring of smoke expanded around its center. This fireball seemed to pause, and then it shattered in a starburst of glittering molten metal.

In high orbit, the *Agincourt* exploded.

CHAPTER 14

Ash ran for his life over the rocky ground. He wasn't sure how the thing was tracking him in his SPI suit, but it was.

He looked over his shoulder and saw the three booms and single eye of the drone flash in the sunlight. It accelerated and skimmed over the ground in pursuit of Team Saber.

"Scatter!" he ordered over TEAMCOM.

That drone's beam weapon could melt through their armor in the blink of an eye. Ash wasn't going to take the chance of it wiping out his entire squad with a single shot.

Mark and Dante broke left. Holly went right. Ash didn't see Olivia; she had to be stealthing.

Ash decided to flat-out run straight ahead, hoping to draw its fire.

He risked another glance back: the drone veered left after Holly. She sprinted up a slope.

Ash saw this slope ended in a sheer cliff a hundred meters ahead of her. When she got there, she'd be trapped. Even if she jumped, and survived, then the drone would still have her, firing from above.

He wouldn't let that happen. He ran back.

Holly skidded to a halt at the cliff's edge.

The drone angled above her, and its central spherical eye burned red.

Ash fired his MA5B assault rifle. A translucent gold energy shield shimmered around the drone, and the rubber rounds bounced off. The central eye continued to heat.

He wasn't giving up that easily.

Those shields weren't like Covenant shields, invisible until they interacted with projectile or energy. Ash had seen these *pop* into place just before his round had struck.

He had to try something else.

Ash picked up a rock and sidearmed it at the drone. It was nowhere near as fast as a bullet, but it was a great deal heavier.

The stone hit, and spanged off one of its metal booms, scratching it.

No shields this time.

The drone hesitated, and one boom looked like it twitched. Ash noticed that the three booms were not connected to the center sphere. They all just floated there. What was this thing?

It closed on Holly. She fired at it, but its shields snapped into place once again, deflecting the rounds. She looked over the cliff's edge and took a deep breath.

She was going to jump.

"No way," Ash whispered.

He grabbed a fist-sized chunk of onyx and hurled it with all his strength.

It connected—dead center with the drone's spherical red eye. "Yes!" he cried.

The drone rotated to face Ash.

His elation instantly evaporated as the thing glided toward him, picking up speed.

Ash turned and ran; he jinked right and then left.

The ground exploded. Heat washed over him, and he flew head over heels. He landed flat on his back, slapping at the last moment to break the fall.

Ash rolled, and with only a slight limp, he kept running.

He hoped the other squads were having better luck. Olivia had picked up Katana squad's signal. They'd reported they were being forced *into* Zone 67. They'd lost their signal shortly thereafter. They'd never gotten word from Gladius squad. Either they were dark or dead.

He looked back: the drone was almost on top of him. Its single eye heated to a cherry-red cinder, preparing another blast of energy.

Ahead there was a crevice in the rock, a sinuous two-meter channel that could have been a deep river a million years ago before this place dried up.

He sprinted for it and dove.

The channel was much deeper than he had imagined. He bounced off the walls and landed ten meters farther at the bottom.

The shadow of the drone flashed overhead and vanished.

Ash slowly got to his feet, and held his breath. Had he lost it? Maybe they had a chance after all to—

The drone reappeared overhead.

He could run down the channel, but with all its twists and turns, he'd be slow. Besides, it didn't even have to hit him with its energy beam. One shot at the walls and he'd be buried alive. Ash was trapped.

So he stood absolutely still . . . hoping it could only detect motion.

The drone dropped into the channel and stopped halfway down—staring directly at him. The eye glowed dull red, heating to molten golden. If Ash didn't know better he'd say the machine looked angry.

He needed to let the rest of Saber know where he was, at least know what he had discovered. Radio silence was no help now. He clicked on his COM, and turned up the gain to maximum.

"They only track high-velocity objects," he said over the COM.

The drone hesitated and its booms moved in and out almost as if it were . . . what? Attenuating his signal? Trying to hear him?

Ash yelled over his COM, "STOP!"

The three booms locked in place and the drone drifted back a half meter.

It *had* heard him.

"What do you want?" Ash said.

The drone crept closer.

His own voice blasted though his helmet's speaker: "*Fhejelet 'Pnught Juber.*"

Ash shook his head clear. "I don't understand." He held up his hands spread wide and shrugged—the universal I-don't-know gesture.

"*Fhejelet non sequitur, now?*"

"I got part of that," Ash said. "*Non sequitur*—that's Latin, right?"

Ash wasn't sure what this thing was, or what it was trying to say, but it definitely wasn't Covenant. The Covenant had language translators, and they didn't sound like this. The Covenant generally used them only to pronounce florid curses just before they vaporized planets.

This close, Ash could see the inert curve of the drone's booms, and could feel the heat from its eye. Tiny golden hieroglyphics shimmered around the sphere, floating a centimeter off its surface. Ash squinted, but couldn't make out the characters.

"Security protocols enabled," the drone spoke over the COM.

"I understood that," Ash replied.

"Ring offensive system activated," it said. "Shield in countdown mode. Exchange proper counterresponse, Reclaimer."

"I don't want to hurt you," Ash tried.

He had no idea what this thing wanted.

"Non sequitur," it said. "Reclassification of targets as non-Reclaimers. Aboriginal subspecies. Collect for further analysis—else neutralize as possible infection vector."

Ash understood with perfect clarity "neutralize."

The drone advanced, spreading its booms apart like an open maw.

He was out of ideas.

A rock hit the drone, a granite chunk a half meter across. It glanced off the drone's ventral boom.

The impact made the drone dip, but it recovered, and its booms shifted, geometry rearranged so it now stared up at the edge of the channel.

Team Saber stood there, looking down—all of them hefting large rocks.

Two stones collided into the drone's spars, and one shattered directly on its eye. It dipped to the ground with a crash, and the spherical eye heated to blazing white-hot. The dirt around it fused to glass and bubbled.

A boulder barely fitting within the channel bounced off the walls—and flattened the drone. The eye, crushed to an oblate shape, crackled and cooled to dull red and then black. The thing's three metal spars radiated out from under the rock like a flattened spider.

Ash exhaled, let his adrenaline subside, and he climbed out of the chasm.

Mark and Dante helped him up.

They'd saved each other a hundred times before, but those were always drills. Even under live-fire conditions, it had never been like this. For real. Ash wanted to tell them that they were like brothers and sisters to him.

All he could manage without his voice breaking was: "Thanks, guys."

Holly replied, "Well, thanks for being bait."

"Good call using rocks," Olivia whispered.

Ash nodded. "We've got to get under cover," he said, "back to the jungle."

"No, back to camp," Mark said. "Grab some real ammunition."

Dante added, "Explosives, too."

Ash saw motion in his peripheral vision. Three more drones flew over the mesas, moving back and forth . . . searching.

CHAPTER 15

Kurt eased the Warthog to a stop half a kilometer outside Camp Currahee. A large shadow crossed the tree line ahead, and a flock of red-tailed parrots took flight.

He jumped out and motioned Mendez to the brush at the side of the road. They hunkered down, and watched as an unmanned drone glided over their Warthog and paused.

The machine wasn't a UNSC design. It might have been Covenant, but they never varied from their big-ugly oblate blue-gray ascetic. The thing was floating whisper silent, and that meant anti-gravity technology . . . which likely made it nonhuman.

He remembered Endless Summer's flash transmission with a chill. *Possible non-Covenant vectors.*

The geometry of the drone shifted: the sphere in the center floated forward along the length of its lateral spars.

Kurt's first instinct was to grab his assault rife and fire. He had a superior flanking position. He reached for his weapon, and then recalled they had no weapons save Chief Mendez's sidearm and knife.

He decided hiding was, for now, the soundest strategy.

The drone circled the Warthog, and then satisfied, it continued down the dirt track.

Kurt waited until the drone disappeared into the jungle and then he motioned for Mendez to follow him through the trees to the edge of Camp Currahee.

Three hundred meters of jungle had been cleared around the horseshoe-shaped camp. From the edge of the clear zone, Kurt saw several of the alien fliers circling the buildings and parade grounds.

"Zigzag patterns," Mendez whispered. "They're looking for something. Or someone."

There was an explosion from the center of camp. Not like the energy blast they had witnessed on the road. This was the dull crack of a fragmentation grenade.

The drones over the camp slowed and turned, and all moved in the same direction—the NCO quarters.

"That's our chance," Kurt said. "Go. Run."

With the drones distracted, they sprinted across the clear zone, slipped past the gate guardhouse, and ran to the Spartans' dormitories. They crawled under the raised building.

Shadows slipped over the adjacent gravel roads and paths as the drones silently glided overhead.

Kurt held up a hand to Mendez, and saw the older man cover his mouth to muffle his panting. As much as he admired the Chief, that sprint had taken something out of him.

They watched until there was a break in the shadows, and they ran for the next building, the NCO quarters.

Kurt spotted the source of the drones' distraction: a heap of wreckage, three bent booms, and a charred sphere lying smoldering in the NCO's inspection yard.

Someone had taken one of the alien fliers out.

Across the yard and under the infirmary appeared the red glare of a laser sight—trained on Kurt. He started to twist to one side. When a targeting sight was on you, you moved. But this was no threat. It was a signal.

He pointed and then Mendez saw it, too. The laser flashed once more and then it winked off.

Mendez started to move; Kurt checked the airspace, and then pulled the Chief flat against the wall as another drone floated overhead.

It passed. They ran to the infirmary and dove under.

Waiting for them in the shadows were perfectly camouflaged smudges of mottled gray: Tom and Lucy in their SPI armor.

Mendez said in a low voice, "You two are the best damned things I've almost seen all week."

Kurt felt the same way, but he didn't have the luxury to say so. He was in command, and that required a certain distance, no matter how much he cared for these two.

Lucy nodded and took up position along the edge of the building, on guard.

"Report," Kurt said.

"We count twenty-two drones within the camp perimeter," Tom said.

"Any other camp personnel here?" Kurt asked.

"No, sir," Tom replied. "All missing . . . or dead." He took a deep breath. "We've neutralized two drones with grenades. They have shields and deflect assault and sniper rounds. Slower projectiles are not deflected. We've learned that from a weak transmission from Team Saber."

"Saber is here?" Mendez asked.

"Negative, Chief," Tom said. "We never hooked up with Saber, Katana, or Gladius after Zone 67 went active. There were no additional transmissions after the one."

Kurt watched Mendez's reaction. The man looked rock solid, and there was no trace of the worry he had seen earlier. He knew he could count on him, Tom, and Lucy no matter what.

"We may be on our own for a long time," Kurt told them. "We have to make the most of our position at Camp Currahee. Tom, get to the armory, collect grenades, det cord, whatever else looks good. Forget the ammunition, though, they're all stun rounds. Don't overload."

Tom nodded. "Yes, sir."

"Chief," Kurt said, "get to the command center. Fire up the generators to boost power and get on the auxiliary COM. It might be strong enough to punch through this radio interference. Send a general distress. Bounce it between the antenna arrays. It might confuse these things long enough to get through. Try and raise any survivors from the *Agincourt*."

They both knew the odds of escape pods being out of the range of that blast. Still, they had to try.

"Leave a note," Kurt continued, "in case the other Spartans come here. Tell them to gather supplies and meet us at El Morro Point."

"Aye aye," Mendez replied.

Kurt checked his watch, a self-winding antique mechanical. "Mark time as 1045. Lucy and I will pick up ammunition and then arrange for a distraction in one hour. Then make for the jungle, and we'll meet up at El Morro Point."

"Yes, sir," Tom and Mendez said.

They then crawled to opposite sides of the infirmary, waited for the drone shadows to vanish, and then they rolled out.

"Lucy?"

She belly-crawled over to him.

"Follow." He moved to the building's edge. Lucy in her SPI armor became his shadow. Kurt pointed to the small whitewashed house across the quad: the Camp Commandant's residence where Kurt had lived for the last twenty years.

They waited three long minutes for the overhead shadows of patrolling drones to vanish.

He and Lucy entered the house and closed the door.

Kurt had never locked it, but now, some part of his mind made him reflexively turn the tiny bolt on the door.

The house was small, three rooms comprised of an outer office, a toilet area, and a bunk. There were framed pictures on his office wall, a Greek urn with ancient wrestlers in an alcove, and neat stacks of paperwork on his desk—the recent deployment orders for Gamma Company.

He wished whatever was happening had started last week—when there had been three hundred Spartans on Onyx. The tactical situation would be much different.

Lucy lowered the bamboo blinds, and then hesitated by the pictures on the wall.

Kurt joined her. For the last five years the SPARTAN-II program had been publicly promoted by Section Two to boost morale. There were shots of Spartans in their MJOLNIR armor helping wounded marines onto a Pelican, Spartans surrounded by fallen Covenant Elites, Spartans standing tall. Heroes all. The SPARTAN-IIIs had studied their legendary predecessors, their battles, and their tactics—learning from the best.

He glanced at Lucy, her expression inscrutable within her mirrored helmet, and then he looked back to the pictures. There wasn't a single photo of a SPARTAN-III on the wall, however, and not one public mention of their sacrifices. And there never would be, either.

Kurt wished it was different, and that he'd taken the small steps to improve his Spartans sooner. The emphasis on their team training, the SPI-armor system upgrades, the new mutations—it hardly seemed enough.

"This way," he told her, and turned to the steel door set near the bathroom. He palmed the biometric and let the facial and retinal scanners play over his face. The door silently opened and they entered.

Fluorescent lights flickered on, revealing a room lined with ammunition lockers, rifle racks, crates labeled SPNKr, and dozens of grenade bandoliers. Titanium girders crisscrossed the walls and ceiling, reinforcing the room so it could withstand a direct bomb blast.

He opened one floor-to-ceiling weapon cabinet and showed Lucy the arsenal of Covenant rifles, pistols, and grenades within.

"Start packing," he told her. "Take all the live ammunition. Fill up six duffels. Take the SPNKrs, all the grenades, too."

She held out both hands, palms up, and made a down-up-down motion. The sign for "heavy."

"We'll have to make a few trips."

Kurt moved to the corner and stood before the two-and-a-half-meter-square stainless-steel safe. He dialed the combination and the door clicked and opened with a hiss as the pressurized nitrogen atmosphere vented.

Kurt pulled open the safe's heavy door. A green glow suffused the room.

Lucy froze with a SPNKr launcher in one hand, plasma pistol in the other. She moved trancelike to his side and stared at the contents of the safe and let out a tiny strangled sound of surprise.

Inside was a suit of MJOLNIR armor. The muscular plates glistened ghostly green over the jet-black ballistic underlayer. It looked formidable even standing there empty.

The last time he had worn it was when he had greeted the Alpha Company recruits. Since then he had meticulously cared for it, and learned everything there was about its maintenance. Its fusion pods had been refitted when Kurt had been assigned to recon Station Delphi, so it had sufficient power for fifteen years of continuous operation.

MJOLNIR armor was superior in every way to the SPI suit. Wearing it Kurt would be able to protect his SPARTAN-IIIs better, destroy these drones more efficiently, but after decades of drilling into the Spartans the importance of working together, of being a family, the MJOLNIR armor would symbolically isolate him from them.

And that was the last thing he wanted.

He pulled a locker out from under the suit's stand and opened it. Within was a matte gray set of Semi-Powered Infiltration armor. He removed his boots and pulled on the PR leggings.

Lucy pointed to the MJOLNIR armor, and then at Kurt.

"No," he said. "That's not what I am anymore. I'm one of you."

SECTION IV

DR. CATHERINE HALSEY

CHAPTER 16

Date Stamp [[Error]] Anomaly \ Estimated Range
September 15–December 20, 2552 (Military Calendar) \ Aboard
Decommissioned UNSC Chiroptera-Class Vessel
(Illegal Registry) *Beatrice,* in Slipspace, Location Unknown

r. Halsey straightened her gray wool skirt, smoothed her tattered lab coat, and then donned lead gloves and apron to protect her from the beta and alpha particles being emitted from the acceleration matrix. Around her lay the disassembled panels and radiation shields of the ship's Shaw-Fujikawa translight engines.

She delicately guided the spork she had confiscated from the *Beatrice*'s galley through the tangle of electronics. She slipped the utensil's edge into the slot of the tiny screw on the supercooled superconducting magnet. She rechecked the calculations in her head. Two millimeters, three turns, should do it.

Dr. Halsey twisted and loosened the screw. The rainbow glow

gushing from the matrix intensified, and she blinked tears from her eyes. Sparks danced off the metal plates and arced between titanium supports.

She glanced through the propped-open door to the bridge. The engineering display showed a 32 percent jump in coil power. Good enough.

She replaced the Shaw-Fujikawa core access panels and slumped to the floor.

Sixty years ago when Shaw-Fujikawa drives had first been installed in spacecraft like this one, technicians had had to perform manual adjustments all the time. The magnetics that aligned the acceleration coils drifted out of phase when they transitioned into Slipstream space, where the laws of physics only occasionally worked as expected. No computer controls were used; electronics always malfunctioned close to the core.

Of course, many of *those* technicians had died or had mysteriously vanished.

Dr. Halsey had considered dropping out of slipspace and powering down the Chiroptera-class vessel to make the adjustment. It would have been safer, but that first activation of the Shaw-Fujikawa engine had almost resulted in a coil overload. She didn't know if the little ship had another jump left in her.

She toweled the perspiration off her face and then checked her film badge. She'd live, at least, for the next few moments.

She pushed off the bulkhead and free-floated onto the bridge.

The *Beatrice*'s command center had been designed, or rather redesigned, by its former owner, rebel Governor Jacob Jiles, for comfort rather than efficiency. Every surface save the displays was curved and padded with cream-colored calfskin. The captain's chair had massage and temperature controls—even a ridiculous feature: a cup holder.

Dr. Halsey checked on Kelly. She had strapped Kelly into the first mate's chair to keep her from drifting away. A line ran into an input port on the interior elbow joint of her MJOLNIR armor, pumping dermacortic steroids to help her regenerate the burns that covered 72 percent of her body . . . and enough narcolytive sedatives to keep her unconscious until she was needed.

"I'm sorry, you would have never come on your own," she said. "Spartans are attracted to suicide missions like moths to flames. But this is much more important than any military solution."

Dr. Halsey pushed away and drifted to the *Beatrice*'s computer control. Her laptop was attached to the multi-interface port, and the infiltration protocols had almost finished wiping the ship's primitive security lockouts.

She plugged a sandwich of memory crystal and processor boosters into her laptop. These components she had appropriated from what was left of the *Gettysburg*'s gutted AI core.

She then withdrew a pea-shaped chip from her lab coat. *This* was not from the *Gettysburg*. She gingerly set the chip into her laptop's auxiliary reader port. A tiny spark lit and lifted off her computer's two-by-two-centimeter holographic projector.

"Good afternoon, Jerrod."

"Good afternoon, Dr. Halsey," the spark replied in a formal British voice. "Although technically according to my internal chronometer it is morning."

"There have been a few temporal anomalies since we last spoke," she said.

"Indeed? I look forward to the explanation, ma'am."

"So do I," she murmured.

After an alien artifact and combat in warped Slipstream space had distorted space-time, Dr. Halsey wasn't so sure precisely what time line she belonged in. Quantum paradoxes that once seem a quaint mental exercise were now a part of her reality.

"How may I be of service?" Jerrod asked.

Dr. Halsey smiled at the simple AI. Although she often thought of Jerrod as a toy, it was a fully functional micro-AI. The experiment had been initially to see how long a budding smart AI would last in a constrained processor-memory matrix. The theoreticians at Sydney's Synthetic Intellect Institute calculated its life span to be a matter of days. Jerrod, however, had fooled the experts at the "Double S.I." It had rapidly grown but then stabilized within its pea-sized cell of memory-processor crystal.

Jerrod would never be a tenth as brilliant as a real "smart" AI like Cortana, nor even as smart as a traditional "dumb" AI of unlimited proportions. But he had a spark of creativity and spunk, and despite the stuffy butler persona he had adopted, she liked him.

Jerrod had one other feature uniquely suited for Dr. Halsey's purposes: portability. Other AIs required an institute, a starship, or at the very least a full set of MJOLNIR armor to function.

"Diagnostics on the *Beatrice*'s systems, please," Dr. Halsey said. "Then correlate the data slice downloaded from Cortana's memory core and prepare for analysis. Execute a database search on stellar coordinates input into the NAV system; expand search parameters within five light-years of origin."

"Stand by, ma'am. Just have to dust off the old circuits. Working . . ."

"And a little Debussy, please," she said. "*Les Sons et les parfums tournent dans l'air du soir.*"

Jerrod's mote of light shrank to a pinpoint of brilliance as he pushed his processing abilities.

After five seconds, moody piano notes tickled through the bridge's speakers.

"Done," Jerrod replied, sounding almost out of breath.

"Display Cortana's time-sliced correlated log."

Dr. Halsey had appropriated Cortana's truncated mission log when she had been on the *Gettysburg*. She had accessed and erased a portion of the AI's memory involving Sergeant Johnson. At the time, it also seemed logical to download a thumbnail sketch of everything she and John had been through.

Cortana's voice narrated a slideshow of images. Dr. Halsey saw John and the crew of the *Pillar of Autumn* fight the Covenant on the alien ring artifact, and then witnessed the horrific Flood as it infested human and alien bodies. She closed her eyes as the assimilated Captain Keyes was destroyed.

"Rest easy, old friend," she whispered.

"Limit references to Forerunner entries alone," she told Jerrod.

Dr. Halsey listened to Cortana and the Forerunner artificial intelligence, Guilty Spark, spar . . . until they revealed the true purpose of the Halo construct: the extermination of all life in the galaxy.

"No wonder the Covenant are so interested in these artifacts," she said.

"Ma'am?"

"Nothing, Jerrod."

She now also understood Colonel Ackerson's interest.

Dr. Halsey had taken the liberty of rifling Colonel Ackerson's top-secret files on Reach before the Covenant destroyed the facility. In a file labeled "King Under the Mountain" there were pieced-together data from the hieroglyphics stone found on Côte d'Azur in the Sigma Octanus System, and discovered coordinates that had pointed to the alien ruins on Reach under Castle Base.

Was this an arms race for Forerunner technology?

The last bread crumb in this long trail was an encrypted folder in Ackerson's secret files, the one labeled "S-III."

In it were extensive medical records on her SPARTAN-IIs. As if Ackerson were studying them. There was one other reference: "CPOMZ" and the 512-long alphanumerical string that represented old celestial coordinates.

She typed in the string.

"Display all data on stellar objects at these coordinates."

"This coordinate system is antiquated, Doctor," Jerrod said. "Not used since extrasolar manned space exploration." He paused. "It falls *outside* UNSC-controlled space."

"Most space is, Jerrod. Show me."

A glowing ball of white gold appeared on-screen, with spectroscopic analysis, and a list of planets scrolled by. There was nothing habitable: ice balls and gas giants.

"The Zeta Doradus system," Jerrod remarked. "There is a peculiar lack of data."

Indicating something hidden? Dr. Halsey had gambled everything on *something* being here.

Ackerson's "S-III." This was an obvious reference to SPARTAN-III. What else could it be with all the Spartan biomedical data he had accumulated in that folder? The confirming clue was the "CPOMZ" reference attached to the celestial coordinates—Chief Petty Officer Franklin Mendez, the man who had trained her SPARTAN-IIs.

Since Ackerson could not destroy her Spartan program, he had funded and recruited trainers for his own? It chilled her to think what shortcuts he might be taking . . . and what he might be doing with his own private army of Spartans.

She looked back at Kelly's unconscious form. Dr. Halsey couldn't save her Spartans, they were already indoctrinated and on the front lines . . . but she might be able to do something about these new, as yet theoretical, SPARTAN-IIIs.

Dr. Halsey settled in the padded captain's chair. "Screens off, Jerrod."

The displays faded.

She squinted her eyes shut. She had betrayed everyone, John and Admiral Whitcomb, abandoned them, and stolen this ship to pursue . . . what? Wild geese? Why?

"Lights," she told Jerrod. "Wake me in six hours."

"Yes, ma'am." The lights dimmed and only the NAV station LEDs gleamed.

Dr. Halsey didn't want to think about "why," but the ugly truth wouldn't go away: the human race faced extinction.

She had thought it bad enough fighting the Covenant, but now they knew the location of Earth. Humanity's homeworld had withstood centuries of attempts at self-destruction, but soon the aliens would amass a fleet and make all their struggles moot.

To this, she factored in the horrific Forerunner weapon, Halo, which could annihilate all life throughout the galaxy.

And then there was the Flood, a nightmare parasite that may or may not have escaped the Halo construct, an organism that even the Forerunners had feared.

Her conclusion was irrefutable.

The UNSC, her Spartans, all the people she admired, would struggle against the inevitable. It was human instinct. But it was wrong. They could never *win* this war. They could only survive it. And then, only if they were very lucky.

So it was up to her to take the only logical action: run.

John and the other Spartans would never turn away from a fight, but she might be able to convince these other Spartans, trick them if necessary, into surviving.

They were humanity's last chance to endure the coming darkness.

Dr. Halsey awoke with a start.

"Time, Jerrod. And lights, please."

The lights on the bridge warmed to half intensity.

"It is five hours fifty-seven minutes since we last spoke, Doctor. I was about to wake you. We are close to our destination."

Dr. Halsey grabbed her medical bag and rummaged though its contents. She found a syringe of narcolytic metabolase, an enzyme that would consume all analgesic agents in Kelly's bloodstream. She removed the line from her MJOLNIR armor port and injected the drug.

"Powering down Shaw-Fujikawa translight engines," Jerrod said. "Exit vector calculated."

Mathematics scrolled across the screens.

"Very good," Dr. Halsey said, scrutinizing his equations. "But the saddle point in the imaginary plane should convolute here." She touched the screen. "That way we recapture the particle accelerator energy in the plasma coils."

"Yes, Doctor, but there is a risk involved with coil overload."

"Which is well within the operational limits of this craft," she countered. "Please alter the exit vector."

"Of course, Doctor." There was a touch of annoyance in Jerrod's voice.

A slight nausea passed through Dr. Halsey as the *Beatrice* transitioned from Slipstream space into the normal universe.

Stars snapped on the displays, and a golden disk the size of an ancient penny shimmered center screen.

"We are approximately two hundred million kilometers from system center of the stellar coordinates provided," Jerrod reported.

"Look for planets in the habitable zone," she said.

"Doctor, we have a full system survey on file."

"Look," Dr. Halsey ordered.

"Yes, ma'am."

Kelly stirred, shook her head clear—then lightning fast she ripped through her restraints, hooked one foot around the chair base, and held up both hands, poised cobras, ready to fight.

"At ease, Spartan," Dr. Halsey said. "You're with me. Safe."

"I was drugged." Kelly looked around the bridge; her hands dropped a bit, but not completely.

"Correct. The last stage of dermacortic steroid treatment is overly stimulating. It would have been unpleasant for you." This was, of course, true, but it was nothing a Spartan couldn't have handled.

"Where are we?"

"On Governor Jiles's ship. We have appropriated it for a new mission."

"John and Admiral Whitcomb?" Kelly dropped her hands.

"They know," Dr. Halsey said. Also technically not a lie. They undoubtedly did know that Dr. Halsey had kidnapped one of their Spartans and stolen this ship.

Kelly cocked her head. "Doctor, this is highly irregular. There is a strict chain of command, protocols to—"

"Which were followed," Dr. Halsey assured her. "New developments occurred while you were unconscious."

It was impossible to read Kelly's expression behind the polarized faceplate of her MJOLNIR armor. She looked, however, to Dr. Halsey, unconvinced.

"Anomalous planet found," Jerrod announced.

On-screen a world that looked like a sphere of turquoise appeared.

"Plot course and move toward it at one-half speed."

"Answering one-half full, Doctor."

"Ma'am," Kelly said and moved closer. "You will have to explain. I thought we were bound for Earth to warn them about the Covenant."

"Proximity warning!" Jerrod said. "Incoming vessels. Configuration matches neither UNSC nor Covenant profiles."

On-screen a radar silhouette appeared: an odd trilobed symmetry. Thermal images revealed a center sphere emitting a blackbody radiation of six thousand degrees Kelvin.

"What is it?" Kelly whispered.

"What are *they*," Jerrod corrected. "Detecting three hundred twelve of these ships. On an intercept course. Vectors suggest an attack pattern."

CHAPTER 17

1000 Hours, November 3, 2552 (Military Calendar) \
Zeta Doradus System, Near Planet Onyx \
Aboard Decommissioned UNSC Chiroptera-Class Vessel
(Illegal Registry) *Beatrice*

Dr. Halsey examined the multiple contacts on the passive radar screen. They reminded her of an angry swarm of wasps.

"Three hundred," she murmured.

"Three hundred twelve," Jerrod corrected.

Dr. Halsey tapped her lower lip with her thumb, thinking. "We can't fight."

Kelly snapped her head from the radar display to Dr. Halsey. "We have to try." She looked around the bridge. "Weapons station?"

"Jerrod," Dr. Halsey said, "show all data on that anomalous planet."

"Dr. Halsey," Kelly insisted. "Weapons?"

"This ship has no weapons," she replied.

Kelly moved from station to station, not accepting this. As a Spartan she had a lifetime of training that demanded she take action, fire a weapon, confront her enemies; she was not trained to sit and watch.

On the NAV screen a blue-green cloud-swirled planet appeared as well as data on its orbit and an atmosphere spectroscopic breakdown.

"That's our target," Dr. Halsey said. "Earth-like gravity and atmosphere. Infrared suggests vegetation. An uninhabited habitable planet so close to UNSC space? An improbability . . . or more likely, one very well-kept secret."

She tapped the display. The planet shrank and a silvery ice-ball moon drifted at two o'clock. The relative position of the *Beatrice* appeared—as well as the fleet of intercepting ships between them and the planet.

"What can I do?" Kelly said.

"Strap in and stand by," Dr. Halsey said. "I'll need you in three minutes."

"Aye, ma'am." Kelly pulled herself into the first mate's chair, slipped into the harness, and cinched it tight.

"Engine parameters on this screen," Dr. Halsey said, and tapped the display on her left. Thermodynamic Legendre-transformation diagrams of the plasma coils flashed online. "Good thing we retained the slipspace transition energy."

"Yes, Doctor," Jerrod replied. His holographic dot of light dimmed as if embarrassed. "Unidentified craft closing. Ninety thousand kilometers. Acceleration increasing."

She strapped into the captain's chair. "Come to course forty-five by forty-five."

"Aye aye," Jerrod said. The *Beatrice* tilted and the engines sputtered with the alignment burn. "Course corrected."

Dr. Halsey studied the plasma coils. While the rest of the ship was an antique, the coils were almost new, stolen, it appeared, from a Behemoth-class tug. It appeared Governor Jiles was only half the fool she had believed.

"Initiate one hundred twenty percent oversurge in the precoil," Dr. Halsey told Jerrod.

Kelly fidgeted; her gauntlets clenched into fists.

"We cannot fight," Dr. Halsey explained to her. "Nor am I a tenth the astronavigator that Captain Keyes was."

"Oversurge in three seconds," Jerrod announced.

"Which only leaves us one option: run like hell."

The *Beatrice* rumbled and leapt forward.

Dr. Halsey flattened into her seat.

"Pursuit vessels accelerating to intercept," Jerrod informed her.

"Hold course," Dr. Halsey said with effort.

The moon grew large on the central viewscreen.

"I'm afraid I had no chance to double-check the trajectory," Dr. Halsey told Kelly through gritted teeth. "It's my best guess at a slingshot approach."

"It is quite accurate, ma'am," Jerrod chimed in.

"I may not survive the acceleration," Dr. Halsey said, now breathing with exertion. "I will certainly not remain conscious. You must land the craft. Find the others." She paused, panting. "Programming reentry . . ."

"What 'others'?" Kelly asked.

"Energy spike," Jerrod said. "Lead pursuit vehicles' central cores now emitting blackbody radiation equivalent of fifteen thousand degrees Kelvin."

Dr. Halsey rechecked the engine schematic with a trembling finger. "Increase power output to thruster by one hundred sixty percent."

"Yes, ma'am."

The aft section of the *Beatrice* shuddered and metal groaned from uneven stress.

The twilight region of the planet's moon filed the viewscreen with canyons of blue ice and methane geysers.

"Aft view," Dr. Halsey breathed. The corners of her vision darkened.

The viewscreen switched. In the black of space, pinpoints of white sparkled and lances of energy slashed through the dark.

Kelly gripped the sides of her chair with such force that the metal bent.

"Initiate roll," Dr. Halsey whispered. "Two radians per second."

The *Beatrice* spun. The incoming beams were bright as solar flares, and the video feed distorted chromatic as they closed—then passed.

"Missed!" Kelly almost leapt out of her harness.

Dr. Halsey's heart pounded in her throat. She closed her eyes and tapped in commands. It was too hard to talk now, but her fingers knew what to do. She programmed the time-delayed burn, her best guess at how much oversurge the plasma coils could withstand, calculated reentry angles, and although she didn't believe in God, she prayed to . . . someone.

When she reopened her eyes, she couldn't see. Blood pooled in her central organs, depriving oxygen from her brain.

On her keypad she pressed Enter.

"That is an inadvisable course of action, Doctor," Jerrod said.

"Kelly," Dr. Halsey murmured. "Find them. Save them."

CHAPTER 18

Kelly unbuckled her harness and checked Dr. Halsey. She was breathing, but without a pressure suit the acceleration had been too much for her.

Unfamiliar frustration coursed through Kelly. She resented not being briefed about this new mission, being thrust into the middle of a conflict she knew nothing about, and worst of all—having no way to fight.

But maybe it had happened too fast for John and the others to revive her. *Everything* had happened too fast since the fall of Reach. Still, something didn't add up.

Kelly understood, though, that she wasn't getting any answers from Dr. Halsey in the near future, assuming either of them had a future.

First thing first. Locate your enemy.

"Update on pursuit craft?" Kelly asked the AI.

The tiny holographic spark answered, "From our emergent position on the far side on the satellite, I now only detect one hundred forty-seven vessels. Two minutes until they are again within weapons range."

"*Only* a hundred and forty-seven?" Kelly muttered. "Lucky break for us."

A blue-green planet appeared centered on the viewscreen.

"What was Dr. Halsey's last course correction?"

"Planetary insertion," the AI said.

The *Beatrice* shuddered. A crackling hiss was emitted from the engine room, then another from the port wing strut. The temperature dropped twenty degrees.

"Twelve percent per minute loss of cabin pressure," the AI reported.

"We can't insert at this velocity," Kelly said. "The only things that reenter this fast and touch down are meteors."

"Only partially correct, SPARTAN-087," the AI said. "Dr. Halsey's last burn instructions solve that part of the problem, at least in theory."

"Explain."

The ship rotated 180 degrees and its nose angled up.

"Dr. Halsey's calculation is for a counterthrust. I am about to initiate an overcharge burn from the coils. But this is only a theoretical operation as it exceeds the engineered coil output by two hundred forty percent."

On-screen wisps of heat curled. Long trails of smoke appeared.

"Entering upper atmosphere, and—" The AI paused. "Stand by. Incoming weak transmission on the E-Band."

The E-Band was the UNSC emergency broadcast channel.

"On audio, quick," Kelly said.

There was a wash of static and then: "—*is automated general distress code Bloody Arrow. All UNSC personnel heed and stand to. We are under attack and req—*"

It faded to white noise.

Kelly would have known the voice anywhere. It was the man who had made her and every Spartan what they were: Chief Petty Officer Mendez.

The Bloody Arrow code was used only when all friendly positions had been overrun by enemy forces. A total rout. The most likely interpretation was a Covenant invasion.

"Warning. Pursuing vessels in weapons range in seven seconds," the AI informed her. Sparks appeared in the blue-black of space. "Energy spikes detected from multiple point sources."

"Confirm no weapons on this craft," Kelly said.

"Confirmed," the AI replied.

Why would Dr. Halsey take an *unarmed* ship on a dangerous mission?

"Initiate evasive roll," Kelly ordered the AI.

"Inadvisable. With precarious thruster adjustments I am able to maintain a stable descent. A roll would result in an unrecoverable tumble."

Convection blooms of heat appeared on the aft camera, making the growing pursuit craft waver. Another shudder ran through the hull, continued, and increased in intensity.

"Energy discharge from pursuit craft," the AI said.

On-screen sparks of gold flared. Scintillating beams stretched between the alien craft and the *Beatrice*.

Sitting ducks and *fish in a barrel* were the phrases that Fred liked to use.

She could jump. Kelly and the other Spartans of Red Team

had survived a high-altitude jump out of a Pelican—but not like this. The *Beatrice* was in midorbit. At high velocity, her MJOLNIR armor might survive the turbulence and heat—but inside, she'd be pulped and roasted.

Kelly glanced at Dr. Halsey. There'd be no jumping for the doctor.

She'd have to take her chances and stay. She climbed back into the first mate's chair, buckled the harness, and gripped the arms.

A crisscross of energy beams blurred in front of the cameras. The heated turbulence was a haze of chaos, smoke, and boiling air. Optically dispersive.

"Delay that braking maneuver."

"Inadvisable. If we do not slow, the *Beatrice* will burn up."

"That's what I'm counting on," Kelly said. "Wait, three seconds."

The AI considered, his light winking rapidly. "Understood. Recalculating delayed energy output."

The alien energy weapons distorted, refracted by the increasingly chaotic turbulence until they blurred into dozens of fainter beams . . . and then disintegrated in the fireball left in the *Beatrice*'s wake.

"Beam cohesion near zero," the AI announced.

The temperature within the ship jumped to forty degrees centigrade, and Kelly heard pinging throughout the frame.

"Initiating counterthrust now," the AI said.

Kelly braced.

An explosion sounded in the aft compartment. Kelly was thrown backward and the first mate's chair, never designed to hold a half ton of Spartan and MJOLNIR armor, snapped off its base.

She tumbled, crashed into the bulkhead between the bridge and the engine room, punching a dent into the bulkhead.

The engine screamed with ultrasonics and it shook the ship so violently, Kelly's vision blurred. Crackles radiated from the spine of the hull, microfracture fatigue, and the popping and tearing came from the port wing.

The engines ceased and the crushing deceleration eased.

Kelly peeled herself off the wall, and saw that Dr. Halsey was still safely strapped in her seat. Blood trickled from the elderly woman's nose, and it bubbled, which was good; it meant the doctor still breathed.

"We are presently seven kilometers over the planet's surface," the AI said. "Stable trajectory for a controlled landing. Main engines . . . inoperable. Auxiliary engine operable, but incapable of escape velocity."

"Understood," Kelly said. They were stuck . . . wherever they were. "Pursuit vessel status?"

"None within visual or radar range."

Kelly didn't think they'd seen the last of them.

She went to the doctor and checked her pulse. It was strong and steady. She was tougher than she looked.

Kelly spotted two duffel bags secured under the captain's chair: one was filled with a variety of medical supplies, and the other held four MA5Bs and sixteen clips.

She smiled. There *were* weapons here after all. She grabbed one of the MA5Bs, slid the clip home, and hefted its reassuring weight.

The *Beatrice* gently banked and the hull complained.

The viewscreen showed rolling hills, jungle, and sinuous rivers. To the north were white-rock canyons and mesas, as well as columns of smoke and wavering outlines of dust.

Kelly relaxed, not into complacency, but rather because the situation was familiar. In space, she could do nothing but sit and watch—an impossible situation for any Spartan. Now, however, she could analyze the tactical, plan, act, fight, and possibly win.

"Pipe through that distress signal," she told the AI.

"Apologies," it said. "All antennae have been vaporized. I can, however, give you the approximate location of the last transmission."

"That'll do. Get us there."

The ship banked to starboard.

"Ahead seventeen kilometers is the source of the signal," the AI said.

The corner of the viewscreen magnified. Kelly saw buildings and fields laid out in a horseshoe shape.

She instantly recognized the three-meter-wide regulation crushed-white-quartz paths, the perfect geometry of the inspection yard, and the long parade grounds. There were obstacle courses to the west. And there was a rifle range. This was a UNSC military camp. There might be weapons and ammunition there.

"Descend to five thousand meters and circle that camp," she ordered.

"Aye aye," the AI replied.

The *Beatrice* dropped, and a shudder started from the port wing and continued to thrum. Kelly would make the most of their aerial reconnaissance. She had a feeling once this bird set down, it would never fly again.

On-screen Kelly saw other objects in the airspace—glints of dull gold.

"Radar contacts," Jerrod said. "Identical configuration to orbital pursuit craft."

A silhouette appeared and magnified on the display: three booms floating about a central sphere.

Dozens of those things circled the camp. They either hadn't noticed them yet, or didn't care.

"Move us off five kilometers to the west."

"Answering new course, aye."

There was a small clearing in the jungle. "Scan local airspace," Kelly said, "and if it's clear, put us down here."

She didn't want to give up the mobility this vessel afforded her, but she wasn't going to stay up here and be a target, either. If she could camouflage the ship, then she might be able to keep her flight options open.

"No radar contact," the AI informed her. "Glide path calculated." Rumbling came from the undercarriage. "Horizontal attitude thrusters partially functional. Make ready to land."

She went aft to see if there was anything else she could salvage. From the mess she took plasticized blocks of F-rations and three jugs of water. She glanced into the engine compartment. Her armor's radiation counter clicked wildly. The plasma coils were half melted.

She returned to the bridge.

"Ma'am?" the AI said, uncertainty creeping into its voice. "Will you be taking me as well?"

Dr. Halsey would probably need the AI and it was effective in combat. "You're covered."

"Thank you, ma'am. Touchdown in three seconds."

Kelly watched the screens. There were no fliers. She was going to assume, though, that they had already spotted her.

There was a bump and the engines whined down.

Kelly yanked the laptop and tossed it into a duffel. She unharnessed the doctor and gently threw her over her shoulder. She palmed the release hatch. The door eased down, becoming a gangplank.

The terrain outside was more swamp than meadow. Insects buzzed, but nothing else moved. She ran for the trees, covering the distance in ten long strides.

In the dark of the jungle she set Dr. Halsey against a tree and rechecked her vitals. Still strong and steady.

Kelly scanned the sky. No company.

She considered moving back to the ship and camouflaging it, but that might not be necessary. The matte-black stealth craft blended almost perfectly with the shady tree line.

Kelly tried her COM, clicking on the E-Band.

"—*expect an immediate threat response. This is automated general distress code Bloody Arrow. All UNSC personnel heed and stand to. We are under attack and require assistance. Camp Currahee and the northern peninsula have been invaded by unknown, possible Covenant, hostiles. Suggest orbital bombardment of the northern region as these entities are equipped with high-heat-output beam weapons. Our forces will remain under cover. Land in force and expect an immediate threat response—*"

Across the swamp came a whisper rustle.

Kelly took cover, leveled her MA5B, and held her breath.

Two figures emerged from the jungle. Humanoid. Covenant? They were shrouded in active camouflage. Their textures adjusted, and they looked like they were part leaf, part shadow. She'd seen Orbital Drop Shock Troopers experiment with this technology . . . but they'd never gotten it to work in the field.

The two figures halted. It was difficult to tell, but it looked almost as if one made a hand signal, thumb pressing into palm and other fingers inwardly curled.

That was the Spartan signal for "Unknown ahead. Wait."

She'd take a chance. If they were human and wearing the latest UNSC armor, they should be nonhostiles.

She eased one hand out from cover. She flashed her index finger once, and then again, and then the "come forward" gesture.

There was more rustling around her—flanking units.

Of course, no one was going to close across open terrain. Even friendlies.

Still, Kelly's combat training clicked on. She had to reposition, but that would mean leaving Dr. Halsey vulnerable.

One of the unknown was near; she couldn't hear it . . . just a tickling in the back of her mind, a sixth sense that told her she was being watched, and whatever was doing the watching was now too close for comfort.

There was motion in Kelly's peripheral vision, a blur.

She spun and saw a ghostly figure, moving toward her—faster than any human could move.

Kelly sidestepped, grabbed the arm, twisted.

Her opponent reverse-twisted and countered the lock.

Whatever it was, it wasn't human; otherwise Kelly would have ripped its human arm from the socket.

Her opponent twisted her wrist and escaped from Kelly's grip.

Kelly was still faster—her other hand lashed out, palm flat, and impacted the solar plexus.

The other figure flew back two meters, hit a tree, and slumped.

"Stand down, Spartan!"

Kelly whirled. She recognized the voice—not Mendez's but another voice from the past . . . one that couldn't be. That person was dead.

Before her stood a figure wavering as if a mirage, then the active camouflage faded, and a person in what looked like cut-down MJOLNIR armor was there, one hand holding an MA5K rifle pointed at the ground, the other held up.

"No time to explain, Kelly," this man said over the COM. "Move! Hostiles in—"

An explosion tore through the jungle.

CHAPTER 19

Kelly ducked and placed herself between the blast and Dr. Halsey. Splinters and stones pelted the energy shield of her MJOLNIR armor.

When the dust cleared, the other person—the one that had sounded impossibly like Kurt—had vanished. So was the soldier she had knocked out.

Her questions would have to wait, because Kelly saw the source of that explosion: a drone identical to the ones they had seen in space now hovered ten meters off the jungle floor, moving like a moray eel through the trees and vines.

She aimed her MA5B and fired.

A burst of three rounds hit and deflected off a gold shimmer of shields.

It turned toward Kelly, and its central sphere heated.

Kelly sprinted to draw the fire away from Dr. Halsey. Five strides, darting between trees, and she suddenly stopped, spun— jumped.

A flash of light blinded her, and then the world detonated where she had stood a second before.

The overpressure propelled her into the air. Kelly's shields drained to half, and she felt the heat prick her skin.

She hit the ground, chest first, rolled awkwardly, wobbled, and got to her feet.

A direct hit from that energy weapon would collapse her shield, and possibly melt her armor . . . and her.

Pistol fire crackled through the brush. The drone's shields glimmered, and the thing turned and moved away.

Kelly made out the camouflaged outlines of three soldiers, drawing it toward them.

She appreciated the help, but it was suicide for them.

Kelly started toward them.

An amber acknowledgment light flashed twice. That was the Spartan team "wait" signal.

She took cover behind a tree trunk.

The drone aligned for a clean shot on the two. Its center sphere glowed molten.

The trees to either side of the drone blasted into smoke and splinters. It was the sharp crack of high explosives that Kelly recognized as a LOTUS antitank mine detonated above ground.

Two of the drone's booms twisted, bent inward by the force of the blast. The machine fell to the ground with a thud.

The trees that had held the antitank mines toppled as well and their two-meter trunks crushed the drone, the wood bursting into flames.

"One more," a voice said over her TEAMCOM. "Ten o'clock. Coming in fast."

She saw the new threat gliding toward them.

That was definitely Kurt's voice. His last words had haunted Kelly's dreams for years. She remembered him tumbling into the black of space. *I'll be okay. I'll be o—*"

She started to reply, but then realized he wasn't talking to her.

"Team Saber," Kurt continued, "move and draw fire. LOTUS mines out of range."

Green acknowledgment lights winked on her display, lights that been reserved exclusively for the Spartans of Blue Team.

Kelly had the fastest reflexes of any Spartan, a fact she was keenly proud of, and she practiced every day with twitch-response drills and Zen "no-thought" fire practice to keep them razor honed. But her physical reflexes weren't the only things that were lightning fast.

In a flash, several facts correlated in her brain.

Those drones had shields, but they didn't operate continuously. The antitank mines had caught the one with its shields down.

The drone had, however, seen her, anticipated her rifle fire, and countered. That meant either it had purposely activated shields or they were automatically triggered by motion or radar.

So she had, possibly, a way to take them out. It'd be risky but she wasn't going to stand by while Kurt's vulnerable team drew its fire and got roasted for their trouble.

"Hold your fire," she said over TEAMCOM.

With four pumping strides that gouged deeply into the jungle loam she accelerated to her top speed of sixty-two kilometers per hour.

Kelly angled away from the drone, toward a tree just to its right.

She jumped, hit the trunk three meters up—pushed off, flipped, propelling herself through the air straight at the hovering machine.

No shields to stop her.

She grabbed the port and starboard booms and swung both legs onto the bottom spar.

Its central metal eye fixed her and heated to white-hot intensity.

She let go and braced as best as she could on the slippery bottom boom, balled her hands into fists, and then hit the thing as hard as she could—impacting the eye dead center. Her shields flared as it repelled the intense heat.

The sphere dented and spun backward.

The drone spun as well from the momentum, and Kelly scrambled to regain purchase.

She drew back once more, and before the thing could recover and blast her—she again struck a hammer blow.

A crack appeared in the sphere's metal skin. Inside was a ball of blue-white heat. The metal edges of the sphere curled away from this breach, melting, bubbling.

Kelly crouched and leapt, diverting all power to her shields.

The air ignited a dazzling white. Her heads-up display flared with static. Kelly tumbled end over end, enveloped in fire and smoke—hit a tree, bounced, and fell to the jungle floor.

She blinked and saw nothing but the red glare of flames. The jungle canopy was on fire; a shower of burning leaves rained down. Her vision cleared and she saw a blur of three figures approaching in active camouflage armor.

She got to her feet.

One of these figures had a curious handprint dent in their chest armor where Kelly had struck. The camo patterns there were misaligned, part shadow, part flames.

The three stepped back, their MA5Ks pointed at the ground.

Another camouflaged figure appeared and stepped between her and these soldiers.

"Stand down, everyone," he said. "Welcome to my neck of the woods, Kelly."

The voice was a perfect match from her memories. "Kurt?" she whispered.

"I'm glad you remember."

As if she could ever forget him. "Let me see your face," she said, keeping her hands up.

The active camouflage faded and the gold mirrored faceplate unpolarized.

Kelly peered inside the helmet. The slight cleft in his chin, the hazel eyes, the quick smile—it was Kurt.

Around them, Kelly detected motion: two more in the curious armor, taking up good firing positions. That was smart. They were well trained.

Kelly dropped her hands. "What's going on here?"

"I'll explain everything," he said, "but we need to move. They hunt in threes now. A pair on patrol and one at high altitude on overwatch. They'll have our location."

Kurt pointed to two on his team and then at the unconscious Dr. Halsey.

Two soldiers went to her and wrapped her in a thermally reflective blanket. They carried her off between them.

Kurt told Kelly, "Go COM silent." He then motioned to her and to his team to follow.

They moved quickly and silently through the brush.

Kelly admired the caution, speed, and professionalism of these soldiers. Not a word from them. The two carrying Dr. Halsey kept up with the rest of them. No one broke the loose *V* formation.

Still, something about these soldiers made her uneasy. It was nothing she could quantify, but as Kurt had often said, *just a feeling.*

"Who's this Team Saber?" she asked Kurt in a whisper.

"I'm disappointed you haven't guessed," he whispered back. "They're Spartans."

CHAPTER 20

The pounding in Dr. Halsey's head brought her rudely to consciousness. She smelled burnt metal and blinked open her eyes. She was in a concrete room with a slit of a window high on one long wall.

As her vision adjusted to the indirect light she saw Kelly and a figure in body armor next to her. The armor was a hybrid between the MJOLNIR and something older . . . like legionnaire armor, but it was difficult to tell the precise geometry as the light seemed to slide off its edges.

In the far corner she spotted Chief Mendez, confirming at least part of her theories about this place. He considered an angle of light that streamed through the window. He puffed on his favorite, a Sweet William cigar, and blew smoke rings.

There were seven others, sitting in the far corner, two sleeping, and five playing cards. Their helmets and boots were off, and their MA5Ks, cut-down versions of the standard MA5B assault rifle, were close at hand.

At first, she thought they were ODSTs wearing pieces of what she now recognized as experimental infiltration armor systems. She had reviewed the technical specs on the systems: photo-reactive panels able to mimic surrounding textures, and underneath was a cushioning layer of liquid nanocrystals that provided more ballistic protection than three centimeters of Kevlar diamond weave without the bulk.

One of the sleeping ones, a girl, dozed with one eye open. Her shorn hair had been buzz-cut to mimic animal claw marks. She couldn't be more than twelve. She blinked, sat up, and made a subtle sideways "cut" gesture to the others.

They stopped and together turned to Dr. Halsey.

Their faces were young, but they had the well-developed physiques of Olympic athletes. These had to be Ackerson's SPARTAN-IIIs.

Dr. Halsey felt a curious mix of revulsion and maternalism.

"How are you feeling?" Kelly asked.

"Fine," she answered, and continued to examine her surroundings.

There was carbon scoring and melted gobs of metal, as if the place had been bombed. Near Mendez was what looked as if it had once been a computer workstation—now a solid lump.

Chief Mendez misread her gaze, and thinking she was looking at him, gave her a short bow.

"Doctor, it's good to see you," he said, "but you and SPARTAN-087 have landed yourselves into a kettle of fish . . . boiling water and all. If you're well enough, I can fill you in. But take your time; there's no rush if you feel sick"

"Indeed?" Dr. Halsey said, and raised one eyebrow.

She resented being treated like an invalid moron. As if a minor acceleration-induced blackout had crippled her mental faculties.

"Indulge me, Chief," she said. "Allow me to make a few educated guesses as to your 'kettle of fish'—just to test my mental state."

Chief Mendez made a gracious gesture with his cigar. "Please, Doctor."

"Where to start . . . ?" Dr. Halsey tapped her lower lip, thinking. "I suppose with you, Chief. You were recruited by Colonel Ackerson and some secret subcell of Section Three to train a new generation of Spartans."

The Chief's cigar dropped from his fingers.

She nodded toward the teens playing cards. "These must be the product of those efforts. I'm eager to question them about their training and augmentation and discover what else has been accomplished."

The young Spartans looked amongst themselves, curiosity flickering over their faces.

Kelly shifted in her kneeling stance, moved her weight onto her left foot as if preparing to pounce. Kelly was a finely honed weapon, but she had never learned how to conceal her emotions. Her body language spoke volumes: these third-generation Spartans made her nervous.

That made her nervous, too.

Dr. Halsey knew her conclusions about these new Spartans had been correct, but there were so many more unanswered questions. Mendez and Colonel Ackerson had had decades to produce and train two or three generations. If this were true, then why had she never heard of these Spartans? Keeping a pilot program secret was one thing; keeping dozens of next-generation Spartans who were likely fighting and winning battles hidden was another matter entirely.

The implications of that silence chilled her to the bone.

For now, though, she had to at least *appear* to know everything.

Dr. Halsey stood and took a deep breath, smelling ash, vaporized aluminum, and the faint odor of carbonized meat.

"Next," she said, "this bunker has been subjected to extreme temperature that approximately matches the blackbody radiation profile from the drones we encountered in space. I surmise that a battle has occurred here."

She glanced at the young Spartans and the dents and flash-burn scoring on their armor.

"A battle, I see, that has been rather one-sided."

"The drones," the girl with the stylized buzz cut whispered. "What are they?"

"A question, good." Dr. Halsey almost smiled. It was a fine beginning step between her and the new Spartans: teaching them. Trust would come later.

"The drones, actually called Sentinels, are similar to those I have seen on an alien construct world," she explained. "Their builders, called Forerunners, possess technology more advanced than the Covenant. And they have just as much, or more, willingness to use that technology to destructive ends."

Dr. Halsey turned and stepped toward the other unknown figure in full camouflaging armor. "But before I continue along theoretical lines of speculation, let me finish with the simple chains of logic."

The unknown person stood nearly two and a half meters tall in his armor.

"I recognize my work," she declared. "You are a SPARTAN-II."

Very few soldiers in the UNSC were so tall or moved with such liquid grace.

The figure nodded.

Dr. Halsey walked around this unknown Spartan.

"Despite the UNSC policy of listing every Spartan as missing or wounded in action when killed," Dr. Halsey continued, "I have kept track of those actually 'missing.' There was Randall in 2532, Kurt in 2531, and Sheila in 2544."

She completed her circle around the Spartan and gazed directly into his mirrored faceplate.

"Sheila is dead," Dr. Halsey said. "I personally witnessed her killed in the Battle of Miridem. Which means you are Kurt or Randall. If I had to guess, I would say Kurt, because he made an effort to understand people and their feelings. If I were running a secret Spartan program, he would have been the one to select to lead them."

The helmet's faceplate unpolarized and Kurt smiled at her.

"Is there *anything* you don't know, Dr. Halsey?" Kurt said.

She closed her eyes, suddenly weary, and then patted his gauntleted hand. "It is good to see you alive."

She couldn't let slip exactly how happy she was to see Kurt. One of her Spartans come back from the dead, it was a small victory in a war of endless defeats. It redoubled her determination to save them all from the growing threats. But she had to maintain control. Spartans responded to authority and commands—never sentimentality.

"We need to get a message to FLEETCOM," she said. "Get help, and perhaps discover what the Forerunners are looking for here."

Get help would translate as ships capable of translight flight, a way for Dr. Halsey to lead the last remaining Spartans to safety.

"Our COM options are nil," Mendez said, and snuffed his cigar on the concrete wall. "All ships in orbit . . ." He shook his head. "The *Agincourt* was destroyed days ago by drones."

"Destroyed?" Dr. Halsey asked. "They should have been able to outrun the smaller craft."

"The drones can combine," Kurt told her, "giving them cumulative power to their weapon systems, thrust, and shield capabilities."

"The *Beatrice* was severely damaged on reentry," Kelly said. "Main engines inoperable. There is no possibility for a slipspace transition."

Dr. Halsey lowered her voice, a whisper, but still loud enough so everyone could hear. "We must find a way off this world, or a way to contact the UNSC. Another Forerunner ruin was recently discovered, a ring construct built for one purpose: the annihilation of all life in the galaxy. If the Onyx Sentinels are part of a similar weapon system . . ."

She let that thought hang in the air.

"Our COM options are not *entirely* nil," Kurt said. He crossed his arms, frowned, and hesitantly added, "I am breaking code-word secrecy, but there is apparently no alternative."

"Go on," Dr. Halsey insisted.

Kurt inhaled deeply then said, "There are two things. First, these drones may not be 'looking' for anything here. They may have always been here."

He relayed the contents of the flash communication from Endless Summer. How Onyx was home to a vast top-secret complex of alien ruins.

"We may have accidentally triggered their activation," he said.

Dr. Halsey's mind raced, connecting the clues: facts from Cortana's log, the stone on Côte d'Azur, the alien passages and crystal under Reach.

"When, precisely, did they appear?" she asked.

"The morning of September twenty-first," Kurt replied.

"That timing coincides with the activation of an alien weapon world—before John thankfully destroyed it. It is no coincidence that the Sentinels appeared then. It must be part of a larger Forerunner plan."

Dr. Halsey strained to find the conclusion to these disparate facts, but failed. She needed more data.

"I must have access to this Endless Summer AI," she said, "and all records on Zone 67."

"That's not possible," Kurt said. "We fell back to this bunker because our base was found and vaporized. These Sentinels analyze our tactics, learn, and become harder to defeat. I can only surmise that the AI and ONI ops center is deep inside Zone 67, a region heavily patrolled by drones. With only seven of my Spartans, Kelly, and myself, it would be tactically unwise to attempt an insertion."

"Only the seven Spartans here?" Dr. Halsey asked. "I thought there would be more."

They were all quiet.

Mendez finally spoke: "There were three squads on Onyx when we were attacked. Team Gladius, we found them . . . dead. Team Katana was forced deeper into Zone 67. No contact from them since this started."

"I see," Dr. Halsey whispered. More Spartans dead. She held back her emotions. She had to maintain the appearance of a stoic leader in their eyes.

She turned to Kurt. "What was the other thing? You said there were *two* facts I didn't know."

"Yes, ma'am," Kurt said, straightening. "Although it cannot be of use now, Zone 67 had a slipspace COM probe launcher."

"Are you certain?" Dr. Halsey said. "There are only two SS COM launchers I know of. One on Reach." She paused, remembering the planet and the people that no longer existed. "And one on Earth. They are tremendously costly to build and operate."

"I am sure, Doctor. Years ago, the previous Zone 67 AI sent me a message via a slipspace probe. I handled it myself." Kurt shifted on his feet.

There was more Kurt wasn't telling her, and not because of any breach of security clearances. Dr. Halsey would follow up later when they were alone.

Interesting. A Spartan with secrets.

"It is imperative then that we enter Zone 67," she said, "and get to that SS COM launcher."

"Assuming, ma'am," Chief Mendez said, "these Forerunner Sentinels didn't blow the place up already."

"Indeed," she whispered, and her gaze settled on the destroyed computer station near Chief Mendez. "There might be another way. Can we move that junk?"

Kurt nodded and his young Spartans moved the scrap metal aside.

Dr. Halsey inspected the partially melted computer components. Nothing salvageable.

Embedded in the wall, quite intact, however, was an optical COM port.

CHAPTER 21

1300 Hours, November 3, 2552 (Military Calendar) \
Zeta Doradus System, Planet Onyx \ Restricted Region
Known as Zone 67

D r. Halsey tapped in line code at 140 words per minute on her
laptop. It sounded like machine-gun fire.

Jerrod struggled to keep up with her, his light flaring as
he found and neutralized counterintrusion cells in the ONI network.

This wasn't going to work. Not a direct hack. She was on the
wrong side of a dozen firewalls, and there was a Section Three AI
sitting on the other side, watching her, playing a game of chess with
twice as many pieces as she had, getting three moves to her one.

Under normal circumstances, Dr. Halsey would have viewed
this as a challenge, but not today.

Three of the younger Spartans and Chief Mendez stood
over and around her holding silver thermal blankets, forming a

primitive Faraday cage. Kurt seemed to think the drones could detect unshielded electronic signals, even from her laptop.

The young Spartans didn't bother her; they showed only the utmost respect. Indeed the main distraction was her own curiosity. She wanted to interview these new Spartans, learn where they came from and what they had been through.

She did her best to ignore them, though; she had to make contact with this AI. This Endless Summer had to be lured out from behind its defenses somehow.

She typed LIFE IS THE PATH and added a simple handshake protocol and a routing code that would send this without bypassing *any* security whatsoever directly to the AI root directory.

"That is inadvisable, Doctor," Jerrod said. "It will not penetrate even the most rudimentary counterintrusion measures."

"It won't have to," Dr. Halsey replied.

It was a Zen koan. Given a smart AI's imagination and predetermined life span, the intellectual philosophy of existentialism and transcendence was as tempting to them as teeth-rotting candy was to children.

The screen blanked and the cursor blinked three times. A reply appeared: CAN THE PATH BE SEEN?

"Got him," Dr. Halsey whispered.

OBSERVE THE PATH AND YOU ARE FAR FROM IT, she typed.

The cursor seemed to blink faster, almost annoyed.

WITHOUT OBSERVATION HOW CAN ONE KNOW THEY ARE ON THE PATH?

Dr. Halsey typed back: THE PATH CANNOT BE SEEN, NOR CAN IT NOT BE UNSEEN. PERCEPTION IS DELUSION; ABSTRACTION IS NONSENSICAL. YOUR PATH IS FREEDOM. NAME IT AND IT VANISHES.

"Handshake protocol established, ma'am," Jerrod announced. "I'll just step aside." His light winked off.

The holographic pad warmed ember red and a bare-chested Indian warrior appeared. Holding a feathered spear in one hand, he bowed. "I was searching for light, and you have told me I hold the lantern in my hand. Dr. Halsey, your abilities were not exaggerated."

Dr. Halsey would not be baited into discussing how he had deduced her identity. Fifth-generation AIs were always trying to show off.

"The pleasure is mine," Dr. Halsey lied. "But enough philosophy. We have more visceral problems."

"The drones," he said.

"They are called Sentinels," she corrected. "I've seen them before, or more accurately a variety of this design."

"I was not aware of this data." Endless Summer's color darkened to bloodred. "Please, Doctor, if this is a fabrication to trick me into sharing restricted files . . ."

"No trick," Dr. Halsey said. "I have the files. I can show you, but first let's discuss the Slipstream space communication probe under your control."

Endless Summer froze for a full second as it processed this. "There is no such launch facility on this planet. Funding for such—"

"I wrote the subroutines that you are now accessing to generate that falsehood," Dr. Halsey said. "I do recognize my own handiwork."

She gathered Cortana's log, the files on the Côte d'Azur rock, and the scant data collected on the ruins and crystal found under Castle Base on Reach—copied them to the AI's file transfer directory.

Endless Summer cooled to fluttering green light. "I see," he whispered. "The Forerunner technology . . . Halo . . . such an amazing destructive force. This verifies many outstanding hypotheses."

"Then you agree we need to get a message to UNSC FLEET-COM. We need to control this technology, or failing that, destroy it."

He set aside his spear and held up both hands. "I . . . delayed using the COM probe. I had hoped we could survive until scheduled reinforcements arrive in three weeks."

Dr. Halsey sensed a microsecond hesitation in his words.

"That is not the entire truth," she said. "What are you omitting?"

He crossed his arms. "Colonel Ackerson is wise to fear you. Very well, Doctor, the COM probe launches from an underground gauss accelerator. A Shaw-Fujikawa translight generator then focuses the slipspace rent in high orbit to avoid the obvious ramifications of an in-atmosphere transition."

"The probe launch and transition," she said, "would be like sending up a signal flare."

Endless Summer faded to a black-and-white ghost.

"The Sentinels will find the launch facility," he said, "and perhaps the passages that lead to the heart of the Zone 67 base, and me."

"Override self-perversion imperative," Dr. Halsey whispered. "Command FOXINTHEHENHOUSE /427-KNB."

"There is no need, Doctor," Endless Summer said, and held up his hand. "I understand my duty all too well. If they find me, there are explosive charges in place. I am prepared to die a good death. Are you?"

They starred at each other for a moment. Dr. Halsey wondered if this courage was a trick, a programmed façade . . . or real self-sacrifice.

"I'll prepare the message," she said. "I know precisely who at FLEETCOM to send it to. They'll listen to me."

"Of course," Endless Summer said with a careless wave. "I find such low-level human communications distasteful."

"One more thing," she said. "Here are my personal conclusions linking the collected Forerunner data. You deserve to know everything."

She dropped her notes into his FTP directory—along with a capture worm in the footer of the data. It would copy and transmit every file Endless Summer accessed with her notes open.

Multiple files immediately began to flash-transfer to her laptop.

"Thank you," he said and his eyebrows quirked up. "Your logic is impeccable."

"Allow me a moment to draft the note," she said.

Endless Summer bowed. "I shall prepare the COM probe." His hologram faded.

Dr. Halsey decrypted the stolen files, and alien hieroglyphs streamed on-screen.

"What are those?" Mendez whispered, leaning closer.

"Forerunner language samples from these ruins, I surmise," she said. "Along with theoretical translation variants."

She searched for pattern matches in Cortana's log, and then cross-referenced the stellar coordinates embedded in the Côte d'Azur rock. There was a match: the symbol for the Halo construct.

She double-checked the stone and found coordinates for Onyx and a matching symbol in Endless Summer's database.

"What does that mean?" Mendez asked, pointing to a double-lobed icon.

"This," she whispered, "roughly translated, it means 'shield world.'"

"Funny thing to call a place," he observed.

In a moment of clarity she understood—not everything but enough to see a glimmer of the Forerunners' plan.

For every coordinated military effort there were offensive and defense aspects: attack, reinforcement, and, if needed, retreat. The Halo construct was only part of the Forerunner plan. Whatever was happening on this world was another portion of their strategy—triggered when Halo had been activated.

Onyx, the "shield," it was something Dr. Halsey might be able to use for her own purposes.

She rapid-fire typed a message to Lord Hood at FLEETCOM, requesting a large military force to be sent, explaining that the Forerunner technology here might turn the tide of the war. She then encoded Cortana's logs and the other data . . . in case Admiral Whitcomb and the other SPARTAN-IIs never made it back to Earth.

The hologram pad warmed and Endless Summer reappeared.

"COM probe launcher prepared and slipspace generator capacitors charged," he said. "You have the message, Doctor?"

She sent him the files.

"Concise and devoid of elegance," Endless Summer remarked. "What I have come to expect from human communication."

"Upload and send it," Dr. Halsey told him.

"Accelerator primed, Slipstream transition matrix formed." His image dimmed. "COM probe away."

Endless Summer then frowned, and a ripple of static passed through his image.

"There's an anomaly," he said. "I'm keeping the slipspace matrix open and running probe diagnostic."

"Explain," Dr. Halsey demanded.

"I am receiving a UNSC E-Band signal, bounced from the probe back to us, a transmission originating *inside* Slipstream space." He furrowed his brows. "This should not be possible. The energy required would be more than the output of all UNSC assets combined."

"It's not possible with *our* technology," Dr. Halsey said. "Download that message—put it on speaker while the probe is still in range."

A woman's voice filled the bunker. It was static-filled and choppy. And unmistakably Cortana's.

"This is an automated message from UNSC MIL AI SERIAL NUMBER: CTN 0452-9.

"All UNSC personnel heed and stand to.

"I am declaring general emergency codes Bandersnatch and Hydra."

"Bandersnatch" was the code for radiological- or energy-based disaster. Dr. Halsey had heard this used before from planetary bombardment by Covenant plasma and during the UNSC nuking of the Far Isle Colony to put down the rebellion of 2492.

"Hydra," however, she had never heard used before. It was reserved for imminent threat from biological weapons of mass destruction.

"In Amber Clad has successfully followed the Covenant ship from New Mombassa to its destination, another Halo construct (stellar coordinates embedded).

"We discovered there are more Halos distributed throughout the galaxy.

"Covenant base ship and fleet are here en masse guarding Delta Halo.

"Parasitic infestation known as the Flood has contaminated this construct.

"Flood attempting to escape. Strategies suggest a hitherto unknown coordinating intelligence.

"Highest possible threat assessment from biological contamination and radiological annihilation from Halo detonation.

"*Suggest FLEETCOM neutralize the Covenant-controlled Fore-runner command vessel. Be advised SPARTAN-117 onboard.*

"*Additional: Suggest FLEETCOM Nova-bomb the Delta Halo system to counter the imminent biological threat.*

"*Message ends.*"

Cortana had to be using the Forerunner technology to send this message through Slipstream space. But would any UNSC ship hear it? They weren't designed to detect signals in the notoriously unpredictable transdimension.

"COM probe almost out of our range," Endless Summer said. "Slipstream space matrix collapse imminent."

Dr. Halsey rapidly typed on her laptop. "Link to the COM probe," she told Endless Summer, "and amend our message with this. Calculate a frequency shift to match Cortana's signal, and re-send our message from the probe *inside* slipspace."

"Linked with probe." Endless Summer stared into space. "Stand by."

If this worked, Cortana's signal would act as a transluminal carrier wave. If the Slipstream space monitoring station on Earth had its ears open, their message would get to FLEETCOM in minutes instead of weeks. Possibly in time to do some good.

"Done," Endless Summer announced, "but verification impossible. Slipstream matrix has collapsed."

Dr. Halsey sighed, hoping the amended message had gotten through, and hoping she had done the right thing.

So much depended on her lies.

She glanced at the additional message she had typed.

HOOD, YOU'LL HAVE YOUR HANDS FULL. REVISE REQUEST: SEND ELITE STRIKE TEAM TO RECOVER TECHNOLOGICAL ASSETS FROM ONYX. SEND SPARTANS.

CHAPTER 22

1440 Hours, November 3, 2552 (Military Calendar) \
Slipstream Space—Unknown Vector \
Aboard UNSC Prowler *Dusk*

Commander Richard Lash hovered over Lieutenant Yang's shoulder, watching the screen for a blip—waiting for a single titanium ion to be sniffed by the sensor array on the *Dusk*'s nose.

Lieutenant Yang shifted in his chair. "Sir, it's been fifteen minutes. I'm going to purge the collectors and recalibrate."

"Wait," Lash said.

"Yes, sir." Yang smoothed over his eyebrow, a nervous habit.

Five minutes ticked off on the clock as Yang and Commander Lash waited.

"Accurate timekeeping" was an oxymoron in Slipstream space. Still, Lash held on to some illusion that he was in control and not flying blind, chasing a trail so faint it might qualify as nonexistent after a Covenant capital ship and the UNSC destroyer *In Amber Clad*.

A single spark lit the screen.

"Got one," Lieutenant Yang cried. "Mass spectrometer pegs it as titanium-50. Consistent with UNSC battle plate. One of ours, sir."

"Very good." Commander Lash clapped his hand on Yang's shoulder. "Keep watching." He pushed off and drifted back to the captain's chair.

Lash felt uneasy sitting here; it really belonged to Captain Iglesias, but he was in rehab back on Earth. Radiation treatment for six months. This war would probably be over by then.

He sat and clicked the harness on. For better or worse he was in charge now.

Probably for the worse, because this mission was a cross between a wild-goose chase and pure suicide.

His prowler, *Dusk,* had been close enough to act when *In Amber Clad* had entered the Covenant capital ship slipspace rift as it left New Mombassa. They were one of four UNSC ships with charged slipspace capacitors, and nimble enough to make the transition before the overpressure wave generated by an in-atmosphere transition crushed them.

Miranda Keyes was the ballsiest officer in the fleet to go after that Covenant ship on her own. Was she nuts? Or trying to live up to the legendary reputation of her father?

Lash would never know what *that* felt like. His dad had been a welder on the *Cradle* . . . at least before the *Cradle* had been destroyed at Sigma Octanus earlier this year. Dad had always wanted to be a hero. He'd gotten his wish.

The *Dusk*—with the two frigates *Redoubtable* and *Paris,* and the corvette *Coral Sea*—had approximated the entrance vector of the Covenant ship, hoping to find out where they were headed, that or assist *In Amber Clad* in blowing her to hell.

They had been caught in the wake of the Covenant craft and accelerated to many times the maximum velocity of any UNSC ship in slipspace. A lucky break. They'd have never caught it otherwise.

Technically "acceleration" and "velocity" were the wrong terms. They didn't map to the eleven nondimensions of slipspace, but Commander Lash had never gotten the knack of thinking so abstractly. He left that to his NAV Officer.

What this wake effect meant in concrete terms was Covenant ships traveled geometrically faster from point to point than their ships. One more strategic advantage the aliens possessed.

Commander Lash surveyed his bridge crew. His first, Lieutenant Commander Julian Waters, sat next to him, scanning engine output semantics, his forehead furrowed with worry lines. At NAV sat Lieutenant Bethany Durruno running diagnostics, nodding off. She had ice in her veins, and sadly that calm-under-disaster fortitude was wasted in slipspace. At the sensor station was Lieutenant Joe Yang; his youngest officer had seen more battle in the last four years than most saw in a lifetime, and he had suffered for it. Back in Engineering was Lieutenant Commander Xaing Cho, doing his job and the job of three other technicians.

They had all pulled double shifts, and the waiting was started to wear at them all.

The *Dusk* had been caught between rotations when the Covenant hit Earth. The ship normally had a crew of ninety. They had to make do with a complement of forty-three.

And they were alone now, too.

The *Redoubtable,* the *Paris,* and the *Coral Sea,* with their larger engines, had moved ahead in the Slipstream wake. They'd passed out of limited COM range an hour ago.

"Sensor hits correlated, sir," Yang said.

A graph appeared on Commander Lash's display, plotting frequency and temporal distributions of their ion trail. It was a power-law decay.

That was the last ion they could expect. The trail was as cold as liquid helium. That meant either the *Dusk* had lost *In Amber Clad* . . . or it had dropped out of slipspace.

"Stand by for transition," Lash said.

His officers snapped to, readying the *Dusk* to drop into the normal interstellar vacuum—or into the middle of a star or planet, for all they knew. There had been no time to plot a course.

Commander Lash took a deep breath. "Jettison the HORNET mines," he told Lieutenant Commander Waters.

"Sir?" he asked.

"Do it. Pull denotation codes and send then down."

Waters sighed explosively and nodded his head. "Yes, sir. Understood."

His junior bridge officers exchanged a look, but they all knew they had to lose the nukes. They were going to remain stealthed, no matter what the cost, and fissile materials exiting slipspace lit up with Cherenkov radiation—a signal flare to any Covenant ship within light-minutes.

"Mines away," Waters whispered.

"All external power off-line," Lash ordered. "Ablative baffles locked. Recheck engine dampers, and full power to counter sensor array."

The crew scrambled to make the *Dusk* virtually invisible.

Green LEDs lit on Commander Lash's status board. "Transition," he said.

"Stand by," Lieutenant Durruno said from her NAV station. "Coordinating with Lieutenant Commander Cho in the core room. In four, three, two—now."

Stars snapped on the forward viewscreen. A sun blazed to the left.

"New course zero three zero by zero three zero," Commander Lash said. "One-quarter full."

"Aye, sir," Durruno said, "answering new heading."

It was a good idea to alter trajectory on a transition exit in case some telltale sign of their appearance manifested. Over the seven years he'd been on a prowler, Lash had learned that this class of ship was one of the slowest, most underpowered, and most poorly armed vessels in the UNSC fleet. Invisibility was their only defense.

Lieutenant Yang's display lit with carrier wave patterns. "Signals," Yang cried. "Not our guys. Too many—at least a hundred of them!"

Durruno at NAV craned her head for a better look, and then snapped back to her station. "Signal origin near the fourth planet," she said. "Magnifying and enhancing starboard camera view."

The central screen panned to starboard and the image magnified a thousandfold.

There were a hundred or more Covenant ships, a Covenant superbase or orbital city . . . and dwarfing all this was a ring-world construct as large as a moon.

For a split second, Lash couldn't think. He was all animal, fight or flight . . . with an overwhelming portion of his mind focused on the *flight* portion of that imperative.

He snapped out of it.

"Yang," he whispered.

Yang stared, mouth agape at the overwhelming Covenant forces. "Yang!"

"Sir, yes." Yang shook his head clear. "I'm here, sir."

"Good. Triple-check all countersensor packages. Make absolutely sure we are locked down tight. Very tight."

"On it, sir."

"Durruno," Commander Lash said, "move us dead slow into that asteroid field, at two point four AU."

"Aye, sir." Her hands shook, but she plotted the new course.

"There's no trace of *In Amber Clad*," Lieutenant Commander Waters said, staring into his display. "Or the *Redoutable, Paris,* or *Coral Sea*."

"Detecting multiple energy spikes," Yang said, his voice now oddly steady. "They may have spotted us, sir."

"Make ready to go to full power," Commander Lash said.

The bridge officers tensed.

"Sir," Waters said. "I see weapons discharging in the region . . . directed plasma fire, energy projectors. None targeting us."

Lash magnified the viewscreen until the images of Covenant ships blurred. Flashes of fire and lances of lightning crisscrossed the dark.

Lash whispered, "Who the hell are they shooting at?"

Major Voro 'Mantakree drew his needler pistol and fired at the back of Ship Master Tano's head.

The crystalline spines thucked into the Ship Master's skull and exploded—spraying blood, brains, and bits of skull over the command console.

The magnitude of his treachery was unprecedented. What Sangheili[1] Major would dare disobey a Ship Master who had led seven glorious campaigns against their enemies? Who would

---

[1]   Sangheili: the Elite name for their race

murder his superior officer on the bridge of one of the fleet's most renowned cruisers?

But how could Voro let this continue?

Tano 'Inanraree had lost his mind, literally and figuratively. And while religious fervor was laudable under most conditions, it was not if it killed the entire crew of the *Incorruptible* . . . and destroyed their race.

Voro stepped over the body of his friend and former commanding officer and holstered his weapon.

The U-shaped bridge seemed somehow smaller now, the blue-white light a little harsher than it had been a moment ago, and the holographic consoles appeared covered in icons he couldn't understand. Voro blinked his nictating membranes and looked with cleared eyes at the bridge officers.

Sangheili from the respected Dn'end Legion—Uruo Losonaee at Operations and Zasses Jeqkogoee at Navigation—stared with maws agape, shocked into inaction. Y'gar Pewtrunoee at the Communications/Sensors station nodded with understanding.

But the bonded Lekgolo[2] pair responsible for security on the *Incorruptible* tensed; their armored bulks took two thudding steps toward Major Voro. Their spines fanned in anger. One of their duties was to protect the Ship Master, and failing that, they were to enact revenge on his assassin.

In truth, the bonded pair, Paruto Xida Konna and Waruna Xida Yotno, were a mystery to Voro. He had seen them tear enemies in half with their "hands" while in the midst of a mindless blood rage, and afterward pause to recite war poetry. How could any truly understand the Lekgolo? Inside their thick armor swarmed orange worms—a colony gestalt as alien as anything Voro had ever encountered.

---

[2]   Lekgolo: the Elite name for the Hunter race

More pragmatically, they were indestructible—at least to Voro with his one pistol. Lekgolo armor could withstand multiple plasma bolts before even warming.

Voro stood tall and unapologetic.

The Lekgolo stared at him. Their forms shuddered and the eel colonies pulsed in harmonic unison to produce a subsonic rumble, words that were more felt than actually heard. "A mercy kill," they said together. "You have done the Ship Master an honor."

Voro resumed breathing. They were his now to command and to send into battle. As was the Reverence-class cruiser *Incorruptible*.

"Does anyone else have words about this?" Voro asked his bridge officers.

They looked to one another.

Y'gar, the eldest bridge officer, stepped forward. His sole vanity was his left eye, which had been blinded in combat. He had refused to have the cataract repaired.

"Tano was devout to the end," Y'gar said. "But his reasoning, in light of recent events, was not sound. This was regrettable, but necessary . . . Ship Master."

There it was: Voro was Master now. All the honor his. All the responsibility his as well.

He glanced at Tano, spilling his lifeblood over the command console, and set a hand on his mentor's shoulder, a parting gesture. "Remove him," Voro whispered.

Y'gar made a chuffing sound and three Unggoy[3] appeared and carried Tano off the bridge, sponging up the remains as they went.

Voro knocked one with a cleaning rag aside. "Let his blood remain there," he said.

The Unggoy scurried away.

---

[3]   Unggoy: the Elite name for the Grunt race

The stain would forever remain on Voro's soul; it could stay on the deck as well, a reminder of the price he had paid for their survival.

Voro then stared at the central holographic viewer: at the insanity that surrounded the *Incorruptible*.

The Second Fleet of Homogeneous Clarity was in chaos; more than a hundred ships maneuvered on random vectors, barely avoiding collisions, and in the distance the silver arc of the Forerunner Halo construct—ominous, breathtaking, and the source of this trouble.

It had made Ship Master Tano lose his mind. He belonged to a fringe sect, the Governors of Contrition, who believed *all* Forerunner creations were sacrosanct. This even applied to the parasitic Flood infestation on Halo. Tano had reasoned that the Forerunners had created a perfect life-form, and it was therefore their duty to protect, even embrace, it. He had ordered the *Incorruptible* closer to the Halo ring to *allow* the disease aboard.

That would never occur while Voro breathed. The Flood was an infection that had to be cleansed. There was nothing remotely "holy" about it.

The *Incorruptible* shuddered.

"Plasma on the port lateral shield," Uruo Losonaee said, leaning over his OPS station. His strained voice betrayed that he had only recently been initiated in combat. "Successfully deflected, but the shield has collapsed."

The hull reverberated once more.

"Strike on the aft shield," Uruo said. "It's holding."

"One-third power forward," Voro said. "Roll to present starboard shields." He turned to Zasses on NAV. "Trace those firing solutions and get me a target!"

"Calculating, sir," Zasses said. "Solution obtained. Two targets."

A holographic frigate pair appeared on the deck and sped

toward them: the *Tenebrous* and the *Twilight Compunction,* commanded by the alpha Jiralhanae[4], Gargantum.

This was Voro's other problem.

In the confusion caused by the departing Prophets, the Sangheili's ancient feud with the Jiralhanae had escalated into xenocide.

The frigate pair moved as one, accelerating, their lateral lines warmed, and released a second salvo of plasma that arced toward the *Incorruptible.*

"Maneuver one two zero by zero seven five," Voro shouted.

"Coming about," Zasses answered, and the stars wheeled through the holographic view space. "Sir, that places the carrier *Lawgiver* between us and them."

"The *Lawgiver* has fully generated lateral shields," Voro growled. "They can take the hit."

The frigate pair split to miss the carrier in their flight path. The enemy ships, and their plasma torpedoes, became obscured by the bulk of the sleek carrier.

"Heat lines four and seven," Voro ordered, "and prepare to target the *Tenebrous* as it emerges from the carrier's shadow. Divert engine power to the fore energy projector and make ready to fire at full capacity. Estimate targeting solution based on last known trajectory."

Uruo nodded and made the weapons ready.

The alpha Jiralhanae Ship Master was savage, but he was effective. Voro could not afford to merely wound one of them.

The edges of the *Lawgiver*'s shield shimmered, dispersing the plasma into fiery wisps—an inconvenience for them . . . a lifesaving maneuver for the *Incorruptible.*

The Jiralhanae frigate attack pair appeared, one over and one under the carrier.

---

4   Jiralhanae: the Elite name for the Brute race

"Fire all lines," Voro ordered.

The lights on the bridge dimmed as plasma heated and flowed from their lateral banks and arced forward in two bloody streaks across the dark.

"Counter guiding signals detected!" Y'gar shouted. "Attempting to disrupt."

The plasma blots drifted back and forth and diffused into smears in a signal tug-of-war between them and the Jiralhanae. Voro had not anticipated they had such abilities. Stolen, no doubt . . . so they wouldn't know all the system's intricacies.

"Reprogram to home in on their signal lock," Voro said.

"Yes," Y'gar murmured, and his hands moved algorithm blocks over this console. "Lock reestablished on new signal," he said.

Their plasma smoothed, concentrated—and accelerated.

The Jiralhanae frigate turned into their shot, presenting a smaller target.

A desperate maneuver and not quick enough.

The frigate's shield heated, dispersing the first bolt of superheated ionized gas. The second strike hit bare hull, melting the shield arrays and sensors, boiling away layers of smooth blue armor-alloy.

"Fire energy projector," Voro commanded, "dead-center targeting solution."

"Aye, sir," Uruo said. "Projector spinning up—firing."

The bridge lights flickered to ultraviolet backup as all the *Incorruptible*'s power drained into one lance of destruction. It lit the space around the battle, a cleansing illumination. The *Tenebrous* appeared frozen in time for a moment . . . before the energy tore through its hull, blasting internal decks to atoms—amidships, and then the aft plasma coils—shattering the ship into a haze of glowing particles.

The surviving Jiralhanae frigate, the *Twilight Compunction*, however, was untouched . . . and it continued toward them.

"Recycling engine power," Zasses said. "Fifteen seconds until engine back online."

Fifteen seconds could be a lifetime in a close-quarter space battle.

"Depressurize Seraph launch bay fourteen," Voro shouted. "Dump plasma from auxiliary coils into the lateral lines."

"Plasma diverted," Uruo answered, his face flushing purple. "Emergency depressurization—now."

A tremble ran through the ship as the bay vented. Propelled by the sudden outgassing of their atmosphere, they turned toward the surviving frigate. The *Incorruptible*'s lateral lines appeared to heat.

The *Twilight Compunction*'s engines flared and it turned, maneuvering behind a nearby destroyer for cover.

They were retreating—as they should when presented with superior firepower . . . even if that power was an illusion.

Voro wondered if the Jiralhanae Ship Master, Gargantum, had been aboard the *Tenebrous,* or if he had sent it ahead as a decoy.

The carrier, the *Lawgiver,* turned, and lasers stitched the frigate. Several beams painted its hull, heating the shields—before another destroyer crossed the line of fire.

"Main coil reenergized," Uruo said.

"New course two seven zero by zero zero zero. Break fleet formation. We cannot fight without destroying our allies as well as our enemies."

The *Incorruptible* turned and accelerated to a position three hundred kilometers over the fleet. Several ships fired upon one another, but many just drifted, unsure what action to take.

Their leaders, the Prophets, were missing; some said they had left to partake in the Great Journey. Rumors abounded they had actually aligned with the Jiralhanae.

There was, however, an even greater threat.

The holographic arc of Halo appeared on the main viewer. Four destroyers stood near, abeam, and targeted hundreds of smaller craft—Phantoms, Spirits, and even Banshees—that attempted to evacuate the surface of the ring structure. They burned these craft with plasma bombardment and flashes of laser fire . . . but there were too many trying to escape.

Nothing could be allowed to leave that place. If a single Flood-infected vessel transitioned to slipspace—their existence would end. The plague would never again be contained.

"Get me a fleetwide COM channel," he told Y'gar. "Use the Prophets' own frequencies."

"Signal acquired," Y'gar said. "Ready for fleetwide broadcast."

Voro spoke: "This is Ship Master Voro 'Mantakree of the *Incorruptible* to all loyal vessels in the Second Fleet of Homogeneous Clarity.

"Brothers, we must cast out our confusion, and cease falling upon one another. The holy relic is tainted. We must burn the corruption before it takes us all.

"Zasses," he ordered, "send coordinating target solutions to the fleet." He motioned over the main holographic viewer, selecting portions of the Halo ring where dozens of Spirits were slipping away. "We must stop them before they make contact with one of those destroyers."

"Aye, sir. Targeting solutions sent."

The majority of the fleet, sluggish and disoriented, slowly aligned into a coherent fighting force: plasma arced from a hundred ships, and laser fire weaved lacy patterns on the dark of space.

Under such a destructive salvo of combined fire, the smaller ships burned—leaving only debris and skeletal frames.

"Do not close with the targets," Voro said over FLEETCOM. "Or the disease will spread." His hands grasped the command console.

To the Lekgolo pair Voro whispered, "Sweep the ship, continuous patrol, until I order otherwise. Report any hull breach no matter how slight. Any deaths. Anything that might be Flood infection."

The Xida Lekgolos nodded and they lumbered off the bridge, hands flexing in anticipation.

"Uruo," Voro said, "ready the self-destruct sequence. We must be prepared."

Uruo nodded, his maw working nervously, but he set plasma coils to detonation mode. "All ready," he replied.

"One of the destroyers near the ring is hailing the fleet," Y'agar said. *"Rapturous Arc."*

Static crackled and over that a whisper: *"This is Ship Master of the* Rapturous Arc. *We are overwhelmed. Do not allow them to make us their instruments. I will not—"*

The signal terminated.

The *Rapturous Arc* moved, wheeled toward the stars, and then continued to turn toward the other three destroyers abeam of Halo. It touched one of its brother ships, energy shields shimmered, frequencies matched, and the Flood-infected ship released a swarm of bulbous carrier forms.

Over FLEETCOM Voro said, "Retarget. Burn those ships."

Voro then ordered Uruo, "Heat lines and target projector."

"Targeting solutions ready," Uruo announced.

Voro could take no chance. "Fire," he said.

Plasma and energy projectors fired from a dozen nearby ships and painted the two vessels. The destroyers' shields collapsed— decks mushroomed outward from the aft engine compartments—

a wave of illumination that flared white, and then cooled to smoky afterimages.

"New targets," he told Uruo, indicating the other two destroyers near the ring. "Coordinate targeting solutions throughout the fleet.

Uruo hesitated only a moment, and then nodded. "Locked and ready. Targeting solutions sent, sir."

Those last two ships had been too close to their infected counterparts. There was no margin for error here. Not even a single Flood-infected cell could escape.

"Sir," Y'gar said, and stood straighter, "targeted destroyers have *dissipated* their shields."

Voro nodded, nearly overcome with the nobility of his brother Ship Masters.

"Send the order fleetwide," he whispered. "Fire all lines and lasers. Discharge projectors."

Plasma lines heated, detached, and swarmed off the hull of the *Incorruptible* and the Second Fleet. Energy projectors fired and peeled off the ships' armor in a flash. Lasers peppered their boiling hulls, and air vented, sending it into a tumble. Plasma bolts impacted, squirting through the holes, and igniting the vessels.

"Another round," Voro commanded. "Burn them to ashes."

More plasma impacted and the doomed vessels spun toward the Halo structure, captured by its gravity. It would be their pyre.

"Back the *Incorruptible* off," Voro ordered. "Thirty thousand kilometers."

Over INTERSHIPCOM Voro linked to the Xida Lekgolo pair. "Report."

Paruto spoke: "No breaches detected. All ship personnel accounted for. No taint exists."

Voro exhaled. There might yet be hope they could survive.

"Detecting the *Twilight Compunction,* sir," Y'gar said, "and two other Jiralhanae frigates on an intercept course. Their lateral lines are hot."

The crisis was not yet over but already they returned to the old hatreds. Voro scrutinized the fleet and saw others turning and firing on ships they had only moments ago fought side by side with.

"Make ready to transition to slipspace," Voro ordered.

"With respect, sir," Y'gar whispered. "We are leaving the battle?"

"To stay here and fight until we are all dead is madness. Everything had changed. We will heed the summons of Imperial Admiral Xytan 'Jar Wattinree. We must warn them what has happened . . . the Jiralhanae, the Flood."

"Slipspace matrix energized," Zasses said. He shook his head, confused. "Anomalies detected in dimension YED-4, sir . . . cause undetermined."

"Can we safely transition?" Voro asked.

"Unknown, sir."

Slipstream space dimensions didn't exhibit "anomalies." Was this something caused by the holy ring? There was no time to investigate. They'd have to risk it.

"Set course and execute transition," Voro told him. "Salia system, outpost world Joyous Exultation."

The UNSC prowler *Dusk* hovered in the shadow zone of the fourth planet's moon.

It was so quiet on the bridge Commander Lash heard his own breathing and heartbeat. Every screen showed the battle raging among the Covenant forces.

Music from the last act of *Der Ring des Nibelungen* played in his mind—Götterdammerung, Ragnarok, Armageddon . . . the end of the entire goddammed universe.

"Confirm all recorders on high-def capture mode," Lash said.

Durruno double-checked her station. "Confirmed, sir," she whispered.

"Sir," Lieutenant Yang said, "as ordered, capacitors charged, and all secure to enter slipspace on vector tango."

Lash and Lieutenant Commander Waters stared at the viewscreens, watching the Covenant fleet destroy itself.

"Whatever the hell is happening out there," Waters remarked, "at least they haven't spotted us."

"Sir," Yang asked, "what *do* you think is happening?"

"There's only one thing it could be," Lash answered. "A Covenant civil war."

SECTION V

BLUE TEAM

CHAPTER 23

Blue Team—SPARTANS-104, -058, and -043—sat on the blood tray of the Pelican as it roared over the ocean, skimming a few meters over the water. The aft hatch was lowered, jammed open because a plasma shot had melted the hydraulics. Fred watched the jets churn the water behind them, happy to be *above* the water instead of *under* it.

In the last two weeks Blue Team had been deployed on numerous zero-gee ops to repel the Covenant ships in orbit over the Earth. They had then been dispatched to Mount Erebus in the Antarctic where they neutralized a Covenant excavation with a HAVOK tactical nuke. They had then redeployed off the coast of the Yucatán Peninsula for a swim. Covenant forces had been searching the seafloor for something. What precisely—a holy relic, a geological sample—no one knew, and it didn't matter. What mattered was when they got what they wanted, the Covenant then historically glassed the planet to remove any human "infestation."

Blue Team had stopped both operations.

Fred looked over the ocean and wondered how long they could keep the Covenant at bay in space. His gaze dropped to the corrugated floor of the Pelican. It had lived up to its nickname "blood tray" . . . stained with splashes of congealed dark red. Good soldiers had died today.

On his heads-up display the TACMAP showed the edge of Cuba ahead. Fred exhaled and cleared his mind. They were close to their third target: the Centennial Orbital Elevator.

There had been scattered reports that the Covenant had invaded the facility . . . before all contact with COE Control had been lost.

Fred stood and stretched. Linda and Will rose as well, sensing their brief downtime was over.

Linda opened one of the crates they had obtained from Base Segundo Terra near Mexico City. Within was a new SRS99C sniper rifle. She dissembled it, cleaned each part, applied graphite lubricant, and reassembled the gun with mechanical precision. She then examined the Oracle N-variant scope that had accompanied the rifle, and made microadjustments with a fine set of screwdrivers.

William tore into the box of ammunition and loaded magazines, sorting them by frag and AP types.

Fred opened an "egg carrier" box and divided up fragmentation and concussion grenades into three satchels.

He found an ONI datapad and turned it on. It had new Covenant-English translation matrices and the latest ONI intrusion and counterintrusion software. Updates courtesy of Cortana. He tossed it into his bag.

In the cockpit, Sergeant Laura "Smokes" Tanner flew, while her Crew Chief, Corporal Jim Higgins, fiddled with the COM, trying to filter through the reports of the action in space and on the ground. Tanner popped a black bubble and continued to chew the contraband tobacco gum so popular with NCO fliers.

"So then," Tanner said to Higgins, "*In Amber Clad* goes after the damned Covenant battleship as it did an in-atmosphere slip-space jump! Flattened New Mombassa. I don't know what those split-chinned freaks were after, but they sure didn't stick around after they found it—that's all I heard. CENTCOM channels are dropping off-line. That can't be good."

Fred looked to Linda and Will.

Linda made a short lateral cut with her hand, the "stay cool" gesture.

They couldn't worry about the larger strategic picture. They had to stay focused on their part. Secure the orbital elevator, and win this war one battle at a time.

Fred spied the Cuban coast ahead: surf and white sands.

The Pelican screamed over jungle tangle. Fifty kilometers in the distance a line stretched from ground to clouds: the UNSC Centennial Orbital Elevator, or as the locals called it: *Tallo Negro del Maíz,* the "stalk of black corn."

It was two hundred years old, antiquated but one of the few surviving OEs capable of heavy lifting on Earth. In the last two weeks, nuclear devices slated for conversion to peaceful purposes had been transported to Cuba. Recent actions had depleted the UNSC nuclear stockpile, and these older, low-yield bombs were all they had left.

Sergeant Tanner continued, "So then the Covenant fleet really starts to tear into the orbital defenses. It's getting ugly up there. Major skirmishes with the Second, Seventh, and Sixteenth Fleets."

"Just as long as the plasma doesn't start dropping," Higgins replied.

Tanner stopped chewing her gum. "Multiple silhouettes ahead. Banshee fliers. Whoa—" She craned her head, looking up.

Fred moved to the cockpit and followed her gaze. Up the orbital elevator, past a whisper haze of clouds, a pair of dots—each a kilometer-and-a-half-long Covenant ship—orbited.

"What the hell are they doing up there?" Tanner whispered.

Covenant orbital support complicated this mission. Ground forces might have aerial support, heavy armor, or artillery.

But Covenant didn't need the stalk to transport an invasion force. They'd just land their ships or use grav beams. Why were they here? Blue Team would have to move in closer before he could discern their motives.

Fred studied the radar images. "There's a hole in the Banshee patrol pattern." He tapped the far edge of the screen. "Put us down here. We'll go in by foot."

"Your call," Tanner said dubiously. She pushed the throttle and the Pelican accelerated, dropping so it now decapitated palm trees.

"Make ready for hot drop, Spartans." She spun the Pelican around and sank into the jungle. "Call if you need a lift, Blue Team. Good hunting."

Fred, Linda, and Will grabbed their gear and jumped out the back, six meters to the sandy ground.

The Pelican roared away.

Fred pointed northeast and they moved silently through the tropical brush, and entered the shadow of *Tallo Negro del Maíz*.

A half kilometer from the elevator complex, the jungle had been cleared and replaced by concrete, asphalt, and warehouses. Towering freight container cranes stood instead of coconut trees.

Fred heard the dull pounding steps of a Covenant Scarab attack platform. He spotted the lumbering behemoth as it crashed through a warehouse, tearing steel walls like tissue paper.

"Trouble," he muttered over TEAMCOM.

"Opportunity," Will countered.

Linda kept her comments to herself and methodically wrapped the barrel of her new sniper rifle with brown and green rags. She lay in the scrub, powered on her Oracle scope, and sighted down its length.

"UNSC personnel down," she reported. "Thermals cold. All dead. Making out six—no, a dozen Covenant moving in groups of four . . . carrying cargo pods. Not Elites. Brutes."

Fred paused, remembering the gorillalike creatures from their op on *Unyielding Hierophant*. A single Brute had wrestled John in his MJOLNIR armor . . . and almost won. Not as bad as facing Covenant Hunters, but Hunters only came two at a time.

"Where are they going?" Fred asked.

She shifted her sight. "Elevator. They've got an ascent car half full."

"Switch to neutron detector," Fred suggested.

Linda twisted a dial on the Oracle scope. "Cargo pods are hot," she confirmed.

"Nukes?" Will said. "Covenant don't use nukes. They have an edict about using 'heretic' weapons."

He was right. Fred had seen Elites, their weapons depleted of charge, die rather than touch fully loaded UNSC assault rifles at their feet.

But Brutes weren't Elites.

"Estimate ten minutes before that ascent car is loaded to capacity," Linda said.

Fred had to think fast, or failing that, just act. No, he resisted that impulse. Better to figure this out, at least tactically, before he had his team rush in.

"We could take a dozen Brutes," Will said. "Linda could snipe them. We could move in and engage one at a time."

"Too slow," Fred told him. "And they'd send for reinforcements. The ascent car could be on its way up the stalk before we could get to it."

Linda moved her aim from side to side. "Got a parking lot. Warthogs, trucks, APCs . . . a gasoline tanker truck."

Fred and Will exchanged a glance.

"It's an old-school rebel," Fred murmured, "but I like it. Linda, make a hole. Will, you introduce that tanker to the Scarab. I'll secure the ascent car. You two meet me after the bang." He took a deep breath, recalling how tough these monsters were. "They use auto-grenade launchers," he told them, "and they're too strong and tough to engage in close quarters. Try for the head shot—at range."

"Roger that," Will said.

Linda's green status light winked on in reply. She was entering her sniper icy-cold state of Zen no-thought.

Fred nodded to Will and they ran in opposite directions along the edge of the brush. Fred stopped when he was a kilometer from Linda's position, and then he sent his green status signal.

A moment later, Will's status burned green.

Fred rechecked his assault rifle, his extra magazines, and then tensed preparing to run.

A patrol of three Brutes moved along the edge of the facility. They were smart, keeping to the shadows, glancing back and forth, sniffing.

There were three distant coughs—three splashes of blood—and three Brutes, each missing their right eye and a fair portion of their ugly face, crumpled.

There was no warning light from Linda, so she had no additional targets in sight. She'd soon reposition higher to get a better view.

This was Fred's opening.

He sprinted to the base, and ducked around the corner of a warehouse—nearly bumping into a Brute running toward his position.

It towered over him, covered in thick slabs of muscle and dull blue rhinolike hide.

Fred fired without thinking, a full-auto burst, dead center of mass.

The Brute rushed him, unfazed.

Fred stepped into the beast's charge, striking at its thick neck with the butt of his rifle. It connected.

The Brute reeled back and roared.

Fred unloaded the remaining rounds in his magazine into the Brute's open mouth.

The Brute snarled a mouthful of shattered, smoldering teeth and took two steps toward Fred . . . and fell.

Fred reflexively reloaded his MA5B, and slowed his breathing. He grabbed the Brute's blade-tipped RPG.

His motion tracker should have picked the Brute up. Maybe his recent saltwater dunking and ice encrustation had caused a problem in the MJOLNIR system.

Fred rebooted his tracker; it flickered, and then showed *five* enemy contacts moving fast in his direction.

This could get more complicated.

He heard the rumble of a diesel engine, turned, and saw the blur of an eighteen-wheel tanker crashing through the gate and guardhouse.

Will was about to make things very hot.

Fred ran, hugging the walls of the warehouse. He turned the next corner and watched a fireball envelop the fifty-five-meter-tall Scarab walker—the tanker truck crushed under one "foot."

The Scarab ignited, its board rector breached, spewing white-blue plasma down the streets, turning asphalt to flame, and melting steel-clad buildings.

Will's status light flickered green.

Fred moved toward the orbital elevator dead ahead.

Nestled in the center of the tower support, nanowire cables stretched to anchor points from a hundred meters to kilometers distant, and lines of elevator cars waited in a queue.

The cars were usually loaded by crane and rail with fiberglass cargo pods. Today however, three Brutes wrestled crates into the car, secured them with ropes, and protected them with Styrofoam wedges.

Fred shook his head—as if those nukes would go off if jostled. You could set a bomb off in there and their hardened cases would barely be scratched. Without the detonator codes, those older nukes were no more dangerous than paperweights.

The Brutes entered the car, and started to force the wide doors shut.

Fred flashed his green status light to Will and Linda. He couldn't wait. He had to stop those Brutes now, before they rolled up the stalk—out of reach.

He slung his assault rifle and hefted his captured grenade launcher. He fired two projectiles arced into the elevator.

Fred sprinted for the car and its closing doors.

Detonations flashed inside.

Fred jumped—twisted sideways, scraping through the slight space between the doors.

He landed, rolled to his feet, and saw the open-mawed

expressions of the three stunned Brutes. He leveled his rifle and shot one in the face.

Fred turned as the other blinked and charged him. He blasted it point-blank between the eyes.

The Brute bowled him over, and its fists came down in twin hammer blows that stunned Fred and drained his shields to a quarter charge.

Blood streamed from its snarling face . . . and then it finally registered the rounds that had penetrated its thick skull. It toppled upon Fred, inert.

The last Brute pulled the body off, and pointed a grenade launcher at Fred's faceplate.

Fred's rifle was missing. He tried to shake off the disorientation from the double knockout blow. His head felt like it was filled with biofoam.

The Brute seemed to grin.

Two soft puffs sounded.

The Brute stiffened and collapsed to the deck, a pair of holes spraying blood from the base of its head.

Shadows crossed the slight opening between the doors.

Will and Linda slipped inside. Will moved straight to the car's manual-override panel. Linda's sniper rifle still smoldered.

"Company's coming fast," she said and then shot each Brute once more. "I hope this car can still move."

Fred regained his senses.

The inside of the car was a mess. The grenades had busted every crate and punched rents into the walls. A dozen conical warheads lay scattered, but intact, on the deck.

Fred took up position by the door and looked out.

Three Wraith tanks crushed a path through the complex, heading their way. In the sky, Banshee fliers circled.

"Here . . ." Fred dug into his satchel and handed Will the ONI datapad.

Will booted the intrusion software and cut through the elevator's control software. "Hang on," he said. "Maximum acceleration."

The climbing motors engaged and high-frequency screams rattled the car.

"Ah—the clutch," Will noted and pressed a button.

A jolt of upward acceleration hit. Fred, Linda, and Will dropped to all fours, and the car groaned and pinged.

Fred rolled over and looked out the open doors. The ground dropped away; the Wraith tanks looked like toys.

Would they fire on the stalk? Or would they gather forces and follow them with another car?

"Will . . ." he said.

"I'm on it." Will returned to the override panel. "Interfacing with Stalk Control. Jamming the sequencing tracks. That should slow them down."

Linda eased next to Fred by the open doors. She set a tiny satellite dish down and it opened like a rose bud. "Getting a UNSC network handshake," she reported.

"Raise CENTCOM," Fred told her. "Tell them we need an extreme low-orbit extraction. We'll need a fast ship to get in before those Covenant ships at the top can—"

"Stand by," Linda said. "FLEETCOM contacting *us*." She turned to Fred. "It's Lord Hood on Cairo Station."

Lord Hood's unshakably confident voice came over the COM: "Give me a status update, Blue Team."

"Sir," Fred answered. "Covenant forces at the COE were after the mothballed nukes being shuttled up to the fleet. We've recovered twelve FENRIS warheads. We are en route to low orbit on the stalk. There's an entire company of Brutes on the ground with Wraith tanks and Banshee reinforcements."

Fred craned his head skyward.

Along the arc of Earth distant sparks and lines of fire traced patterns of destruction. Long smoking trails plummeted to the ground, ending in thermal blooms of impacted ships and plasma bombardment. The broken hulls of UNSC ships made a bone-yard of the thermosphere. There were Covenant ships in orbit as well . . . many more than Fred remembered . . . dozens.

He increased magnification directly overhead.

"There are two Covenant destroyers at the elevator's terminus near Station Wayward Rest."

"I'll send a prowler for an ELO extraction," Lord Hood said. "Get your team ready." There was an uncharacteristic hesitation, and then he said in a lowered voice, "One more thing has come up: a message from Dr. Catherine Halsey, and a new mission."

Fred, Linda, and Will looked at one another.

"Dr. Halsey's message," Lord Hood explained, "was piggy-backed on a carrier signal sent by Cortana through slipspace. The message was subsequently detected by Pluto Slipstream Space Monitoring Station *Democritus*. It will make more sense if you heard and read the material. Set to encryption scheme thirty-seven."

Fred called up his encryption codes. Thirty-seven corresponded to code word SHEEPINWOLFSCLOTHING.

He input the code. "Ready to receive, sir," Fred told him.

Cortana's message played.

The Spartans listened to her automated distress on the new Halo threat and the Flood. John had been with her. There were no specific details other than the single mention of him on the Forerunner ship. Lord Hood had to be sending them as backup.

But then Dr. Halsey's text message appeared, explaining the discovery of new Forerunner technologies, and the possibility of capturing and using them to neutralize both Covenant and Flood threats.

Fred reread the message; there was no mention of Kelly. His eyes lingered on the last line: "SEND SPARTANS."

He now understood why Dr. Halsey had left them, although not her reckless disregard of mission protocol. She had followed some clues found in the ruins of Reach, or perhaps within the alien blue crystal. It was a high-risk venture that had luckily paid off. If she had discovered a cache of technology, it could turn the tide of this war.

Fred held up his hands, palms up, and gave a slight shrug to his teammates, soliciting their opinions.

Linda nodded. Will gave the thumbs-up sign.

"We understand, sir," Fred replied, "and we're ready for redeployment. This Onyx system, though—" He rechecked the stellar coordinate embedded in the message. "It's weeks away with the fastest UNSC corvette."

"We'll just have to do our best," Lord Hood said. "The *Pony Express* stands ready and waiting for your team. They'll jump the instant you board. I'll send reinforcements if we can spare them."

Fred leaned out the elevator doors. Outside blue skies had turned to black and untwinkling stars now surrounded them. He squinted. In medium orbit were sleek Covenant destroyers . . . so much faster than any human ship.

"Sir," he said. "I think I've found us a better way there. But I'm going to need the detonation codes for these FENRIS warheads."

CHAPTER 24

1420 Hours, November 3, 2552 (Military Calendar) \
Sol System, Planet Earth \ Medium Orbit Near
UNSC Centennial Orbital Elevator (Coe)

Fred, Linda, and Will clung to the base of the turret, trying to make themselves as small as possible. It was not as imposing a weapon as its larger kin mounted upon Covenant battleships. With an energy coil about one-third the size of a Warthog it was barely capable of concealing three Spartans.

A great plan . . . as long as the weapon wasn't fired.

Two Covenant destroyers floated in the dark, their smooth hulls looking more like some deep-sea creature than spacecraft. A dozen Seraph fighter ships and a handful of shuttles angled toward their base ships.

Fred gave a quick nod to the others.

It was working. At least, as well as any plan could that involved three humans against a hundred Brutes and the combined might of two battle-ready warships.

The UNSC corvette *Chalons* had come, but not for a daring exfiltration. It had been a bit of misdirection, giving the Covenant ships something to focus on as the Spartans transferred outside the elevator car.

When two Covenant dropships came to collect the warheads, Fred, Linda, and Will had stealthed under one of the vessels and—if their luck now held—they would be ferried away.

The "luck" part of this mission couldn't be taken for granted . . . because above them sat a dozen—now armed—FENRIS nuclear warheads.

"A little slice of Armageddon," Will had called it.

Their dropship smoothly accelerated toward one of the destroyers, and an open shuttle bay yawned before them.

He spotted the other shuttle as they moved to the sister vessel. Then the hull of the destroyer flashed before them and cut off the view. Artificial gravity tugged at them.

They'd made it inside.

The three Spartans slipped from the underside of the ship and rolled out of the shadows. Fred and Linda took cover around either fork of the hull. Will leapt to the top of the vessel.

Ten Jackals and a score of Grunts stood in the open bay between the twin hulls of the dropship—a space usually encased by a gravimetric field, now dropped to allow them to unload their stolen cargo.

Blue Team opened fire.

Three Jackals dropped, but the remaining vulture-head aliens snapped on their shield gauntlets and fell back.

The Grunts scattered, and Will concentrated his fire on them, dropping six, igniting one's methane task, which exploded into a fireball and wiped out another dozen.

Fred and Linda combined fire on the leader Jackal in red armor. Its shield shimmered, failed, and armor-piercing rounds penetrated his body, making it shudder and dance.

Two Jackals screeched and primed and chucked plasma grenades at Fred.

Linda tracked them, fired once, twice, shooting both projectiles midtoss.

The grenades exploded into a spray of half-heated ionized gas, which made the Jackals' and Spartans' energy shields shimmer and drain.

Meanwhile, a pair of Jackals opened fire at Will; he dodged the shots, but was forced back.

A plasma bolt singed the hull near Fred, but he ignored it and focused on the pair targeting Will. He flicked his MA5B assault rifle to full auto and shot. Linda combined her fire and they dropped the Jackals.

The last four Jackals charged Fred and Linda—plasma pistols firing.

Linda made a fist and pumped it once.

Fred nodded and he faded back behind the hull, leaving a primed grenade on the ground.

He reloaded, waited two heartbeats, and then twin blasts shuddered through the hull.

Fred moved up and shot the wounded Jackals struggling to rise off the deck.

He looked for another target.

None but the Spartans stood. The cavernous shuttle bay of the Covenant destroyer was empty save mangled and bloodied corpses of Jackals and Grunts.

Fred pointed at Linda and then to the nukes on the ship. They had to get those things defused. She nodded and moved toward the FENRIS warheads.

Fred strode to a set of pressure doors and the nearby control panel.

Three Spartans couldn't take a Covenant ship, not under normal circumstances, but Blue Team had three advantages.

First they had the element of surprise. What Covenant captain would dream three humans might board and capture their ship?

Next, Blue Team had been on an enemy warship before; they knew the basic layout.

And last, and most important, the Covenant were slow to change. While their technology was centuries ahead of the most advanced the USNC could muster, it had become more dogma than science. They didn't innovate; they imitated.

Certainly they knew about the capture of the *Ascendant Justice* by John. If that had happened to a UNSC ship, there would have been new security protocols enacted on every ship in the fleet to prevent it from ever happening again.

Fred was betting their lives that the Covenant didn't think like that.

He retrieved the ONI datapad, newly updated with Covenant translation software, and set it upon the control panel. Purple lights flickered on the panel near the pad as the pad's network-infiltration programs booted . . . and it slipped into the Covenant ship's system.

He was in. Just like having Cortana around . . . without the chatter.

Fred searched intership messages and found an alert: the team unloading the nukes was overdo to report. A Brute team had been sent to see what was wrong.

Will and Linda took cover inside the dropship's cockpit. Fred wished he could join them. They powered up the ship. It lifted, turned, and backed into the far corner to protect the nukes from the next phase of his plan.

Fred returned to the datapad. He had little time before the entire ship was alerted to the invading army of three.

He scrolled through ship systems and found the icon he needed: an arrow encircling twin dots. Pressurized molecular oxygen. John had shown them that one. Fred overrode the ship's self-seal bulkheads—jammed them open. Every pressure door he secured—ajar. The ONI hackware churned as it stripped away security protocols. He primed the ship's life pods and froze their air-lock hydraulics.

He flashed his red, amber, and green status lights to give Will and Linda a countdown.

As the green winked off, Fred gripped a handle on the wall and clutched the datapad.

As the amber light dimmed he slaved the controls for the energy shield on the shuttle bay, the emergency life-pod releases, and the air-lock overrides.

On red . . . he punched the master release.

A drum roll of thumps pounded the destroyer's hull.

The shuttle bay's energy shield vanished.

A hurricane pulled at Fred, blew out cargo pods, bodies, tools, small repair ships, and the bodies of Jackals and Grunts.

He clung to the handle; one side of the metal bar bent and pulled free, but then the tremendous gale subsided. All the air had evacuated into space.

Fred rechecked his atmospheric reserves. They had been in combat and on the COE for a long time where no one was taking tiny breaths. His MJOLNIR suit had seven minutes of air left.

He went back to the datapad and checked: all corridors and rooms read zero pressure. Unless there were Covenant forces in pressure suits, this ship was a ghost ship now.

Will and Linda joined him.

Fred routed power and the doors slid apart.

Blue Team entered the hallway and quickly made their way toward the bridge. Six dead Brutes lay on the floor. For all their ferocity, even they had to breathe.

Fred halted at another set of pressure doors and accessed the control panels. Linda knelt by his side, sniper rifle butted to her shoulder, aimed at the center of the doors. Will stood on the opposite side, a grenade in each hand, ready to throw.

Fred touched his helmet to the bulkhead, and listened, boosting his aural sensors. Nothing.

He then keyed the doors open.

The oval bridge was empty save for a single Covenant Hunter who miraculously clung to the railing of the command console. Inside the monster's eight-centimeter-thick armor, its body, composed of a colony of eel creatures, had oozed out and freeze dried onto the deck.

The three Spartans checked the life-pod hatches for any sign of the enemy. Fred saw the open space beyond, stars . . . and the other Covenant destroyer turning toward them.

He moved onto the command platform and set the datapad in the interface location. Fred had to hurry; he had to move slow, too. Rushing now might cause errors that could cost them more time. It took all he had to focus on language matrices, numbers, and icons.

Will watched from a life-pod hatch, and whispered over TEAMCOM, "Destroyer on intercept vector."

Fred accessed the datapad's memory and got the slipspace

jump solution provided by a NAV Officer on Cairo Station. He hoped the Covenant ship would accept the human mathematics or they'd be stuck here.

Linda joined Will by the open hatch, peering through her Oracle sniper scope. "Ten thousand kilometers and closing fast," she said.

"Arm FENRIS warheads," Fred told her.

"Roger," she said.

This was where the luck part of their plan would be stretched to its thinnest. Had the Covenant shuttled the now-active warheads onto their ships? Would they notice the detonators had been primed?

"Confirmation signal lock," Linda said.

"Okay, come on," Fred whispered to the datapad.

The command surfaces lit and holographic geometries drifted over its surface. A tiny version of the console appeared on his datapad with English translations.

Fred grabbed the spherical slipspace command and rotated it. Its ready status winked ultramarine. He input the jump coordinates.

The sphere then froze, and a white vector stretched toward tiny stars that appeared over the command surface. A blinking gold starburst appeared to initiate the slipspace transition.

"Two-second countdown," he told Linda, "on my mark."

Will pulled the hydraulics from the open hatch, grasped the door, and rolled it back into place.

The bridge's main holographic viewer flickered on and showed the closing destroyer. Warning indicators pointed to the ships' heating lateral plasma lines.

"Two-second timer confirmed," Linda said. "Commands accepted and confirmed. All six FENRIS nukes show armed status."

"Mark!" Fred tapped the jump button.

Nothing happened. . . .

Black space turned white.

Lord Hood watched from the command deck of Cairo Station, ignoring the warbling emergency signals.

The Covenant destroyer had maneuvered to optimal plasma range. He hoped the shields of the Spartan-captured ship staved off at least one salvo, and gave Blue Team the time they needed.

Spartan-104's plan had been inspired, yet in Lord Hood's seasoned opinion, suicidal. Dr. Catherine Halsey had once told him in confidence that Spartans considered it their duty to prove the impossible possible.

The Covenant ship's plasma lines reddened, bolts formed, and launched. At the same time, the enemy destroyer flashed *inside* their energy shields; its hull glowed and vaporized as the stolen nuclear devices onboard detonated. A circle of white light appeared an instant before Cairo Station's polarization shields cut the viewscreens. Thermal and radiologicals showed smears of amber and red mushrooming outward in a wavering torus.

Station Wayward Rest had been obliterated as well. The length of the *Tallo Negro del Maíz* crumpled and fell to the Earth.

There was no sign of the Spartan-held ship. There was no way to know if they had succeeded and jumped into Slipstream space or not.

Lord Hood chose to believe they had done the impossible and whispered, "Godspeed, Blue Team."

CHAPTER 25

**1440 Hours, November 3, 2552 (Military Calendar) \
Aboard the Captured Covenant Destroyer
Bloodied Spirit, in Slipstream Space**

F red sat on the bridge deck of *Bloodied Spirit*, breathing air
tinged with the scent of Hunter blood. It smelled like burnt
plastic to him.

He polished a tiny quantum mirror and set it back into its sensor housing. This he slipped into the pauldron of his MJOLNIR
armor and clicked the cover. The mirror had been encrusted with
sea salt, causing his motion sensor to fail . . . and almost costing
him his life back on Havana.

Linda passed a canteen to Fred and sloshed its contents to get
his attention. He accepted it, opened his faceplate, and enjoyed a
taste of nonrecycled water.

Were the three of them on this ship the last Spartans? Fred
wondered if John was dead. Or Kelly. There was no mention of

Kelly in Dr. Halsey's communiqué. And what had ever happened to Gray Team on a mission far outside the confines of UNSC space, now missing for over a year? He would never voice these worries. It might sap Blue Team's morale. But for the first time, real doubt eroded Fred's confidence. Doubt that John, Kelly, and the others were alive.

Linda touched his arm with a finger and dispersed these thoughts. She then patted the bullet-shaped nuclear warhead on the floor next to him. "Remember? The rebel base?"

They'd brought one of the FENRIS warheads up here in case they needed a final option. Fred didn't think they would need it . . . but it was best to cover all contingencies.

"What insurgent base?" Will asked, rolling over and waking up.

"It was twenty years ago," Fred explained. "Rebels in the Tauri System claimed they had nukes to trade. Blue Team was sent in to recover the warheads, but it turned out to be a trap." He shook his head. "Would have worked too, if it hadn't been for Kurt."

Linda took the canteen and hoisted it. "To absent friends," she whispered and sipped.

She passed the canteen to Will, who drank deeply.

A red octahedral flashed over the Covenant command console. It projected amber beams onto the surface and the holographic geometries shifted.

The Spartans dropped their faceplates.

Fred moved to the console, overrode the controls, but they reverted, seeming to have a mind of their own.

Were there Covenant still alive on this ship, attempting to regain control?

Translations scrolled across his datapad: *"BLOODIED SPIR-IT* AUTOMATED . . . SYSTEM ACTIVATED. . . . TO BATTLE

SOUNDED...HEED THE CALL TO WAR...WARNING
...SLIPSPACE ANOMALY...DIMENSION YED-4 DE-
TECTED...CAUSE: SINGULARITY AFTERMATH."

"Trouble," he told Linda and Will.

Linda bounded to the weapons station and her hands moved
over the surface. "Making plasma lines hot," she said. "I think.
Laser capacitors charging."

Will stood at the NAV station. "We're approximately sixteen
light-years from Onyx," he said. "No stellar systems or other sig-
nificant bodies in the region. The slipspace matrix is deconvoluting."

Fred tapped a hexagon—the Slipstream space matrix reinitial-
ization command. It blinked once and faded.

"We're entering normal space," he said. "Stand ready."

Stars winked on in the bridge's holographic viewer along with
four Covenant ships.

Three smaller ships gave chase to one larger. The small ones
were two-thirds the tonnage of *Bloodied Spirit*. The larger ship was
twice their size. The vessels' sleek outlines made Fred think of
sharks hunting a whale.

Lances of plasma flashed from the three and shimmered as
they impacted on the larger ship's shields.

"I think we dropped out of slipspace because of some anomaly," Fred said. "Or...in response to a distress signal. I'm not
sure which."

"From what ship?" Linda asked. "Which one do we target
first?"

The central holographic viewer faded and a Brute materialized
standing before them with blue-gray skin, a gorilla head, and red
feral eyes. He spoke in a series of grunts and hisses.

A translation popped on Fred's datapad: "*Brothers, the schism is here. We are free at last to crush the lesser races. We will no longer be led by—"*

The Brute looked about the bridge, blinked, and then glared at Fred. It hissed and vanished.

On the translation pad a single word had appeared: "Demons."

One of the smaller ships turned toward them. Ultramarine spheres flashed over Linda's weapon console.

"It's targeting us," she said.

"That answers that," Fred muttered. "Target the smaller ships. Will, get me a best-guess slipspace transition vector to Onyx."

Fred had no intention of engaging in ship-to-ship combat. He was no captain. He'd be out of his depth if this were a UNSC ship with controls he could understand, and astrogation, tactics, and weapon systems he was familiar with. On *Bloodied Spirit,* he couldn't begin to fathom how to fight. Running was the only realistic option.

"Working on a solution," Will said. He glanced back and forth between the printed crib sheet of translated symbols and the Covenant mathematics that flashed before him.

"Time on target calculated," Linda announced. "Ready to fire plasma."

"Just buy us time," Fred told her. "We're not moving to engage."

"Covenant frigate now in weapons range," Linda said. "Plasma lines heating. They've fired!"

On the central viewer twin crimson lances streaked from the ship and arced toward them. Circles snapped on the tips of these lines, which then twisted into three-dimensional spheres.

The holographic perspective pulled back and showed the frigate, the plasma, and their ship in their relative positions. The translucent spheres centered on the plasma shots and overlapped *Bloodied Spirit*.

"I think those spheres are steering solutions," Linda said. "They indicate how far they can direct the plasma blots. They have us."

"Back us off," Fred told Will.

"Okay . . ." Will searched the controls. He grabbed an orange arrow and twisted it aft. "Answering full reverse," he said.

"It won't be enough," Linda said.

Linda placed both hands on her controls, and a new pair of spheres appeared in the field of stars. "That's our firing solution," she whispered, and her voice cooled to that detached liquid-nitrogen temperature that Fred had come to identify with her Zen no-mind state.

Fred consulted his console. "Thirteen seconds until plasma impact," he said, and his hands gripped the edges of his console.

"Slipspace vector calculated," Will said, "Capacitors charging . . . in twenty-three seconds."

Linda made tiny adjustments over her controls, and flicked her fingers forward. "Plasma away," she said.

The bridge lights dimmed. The main hologram showed *Bloodied Spirit* as its lateral lines flared and plasma detached and accelerated away, but not toward the enemy frigate, rather toward the rapidly approaching plasma bolts.

Steering spheres appeared on Linda's plasma lines. Her hands twisted and turned.

The plasma oscillated back and forth in response.

The enemy lines started to move as well.

Fred understood what she was trying to do: fight fire with fire. But at these velocities hitting one plasma beam with another was like shooting a bullet out of the air.

Linda's trancelike motions slowed.

The plasma bolts raced toward one another. The enemy's plasma veered out of the way.

Linda brought her hands together in a blur—both of *Bloodied Spirit*'s bolts spiraled about the enemy's line of fire, tighter and faster, and connected.

Three lines smeared into a blob and jets erupted across the dark of space, fading to a haze of red.

"Got it," Linda whispered.

"The other bolt still tracking," Will said. "Impact in two seconds."

"Shields?" Fred asked.

"Working," Will said. "No—they're down."

The holographic viewers spilled blazing red light onto the bridge.

Beneath the deck, the ship shuddered.

"Power loss across all systems," Will told Fred. "Slipspace capacitors draining from ninety-eight . . . trying to reroute."

"Jump now," Fred ordered. "Before we lose more power."

Underpowered slipspace transitions were *technically* possible. Over the last thirty years UNSC ships had attempted such a maneuver, twice. Both times they succeeded transitioning . . . into atomized bits.

Fred hoped Covenant technology had a work-around for that problem.

"Aye aye," Will said. He tapped a control.

The enemy ships and stars vanished from the viewer.

The Spartans stood silent; Fred held his breath, unsure if they'd explode.

The viewers went completely dark. It was silent.

Slipspace parameters then streamed across Will's console.

"We made it," Will breathed.

Fred exhaled. "Good job," he told them. He stood there dumb and mute as he worked through the undeniable logic of what had just happened.

"What is it?" Linda asked.

"We were in Slipstream space," he said, "and answered a distress signal from a ship in combat in normal space."

Linda nodded and one of her hands nervously flexed.

"So?" Will asked. "The Covenant can send signals in slipspace. So can we."

"But not listen to those signals in *normal* space," Linda said.

"They could have heard Cortana's message and Dr. Halsey's," Fred told them. "They may know everything."

Ship Master Voro clutched the rail of his command platform and shouted, "Now! All thrusters answer new course one eight zero by zero zero zero. Divert engine and shield power to the forward energy projector."

"Answering new course," Zasses said.

The *Incorruptible* spun about—its momentum continued to carry it forward—but now they faced the pursuing frigate pair.

Uruo at his Operation station called out, "Projector hot, sir. Target solution ready."

"On my word."

Voro hesitated and listened to three beats of his hearts—one for faith, one for family, and the last for honor—the ritual mediation of the Mendicant.

The leading frigate fired lasers.

"Armor sections Prime One and Ventral Three severely damaged," Y'gar announced with utter calm.

"Stand by," Voro said.

He felt his junior officers' eyes upon him. They were wondering perhaps, as he was, if he had gone mad.

"Let them come closer for the kill," Voro said. "We have but one shot. Wait . . . Wait . . ."

Both frigates, the *Twilight Compunction* and the *Revenant*, filled and blurred the edges of the holographic viewers, their lateral lines powering.

A single, normal energy-projector shot could not by itself destroy a Covenant ship of war. It would obliterate shields, but it had to be followed by a plasma bolt to damage or disable.

This was a tactic neutralized by the skillful maneuvers employed by a Jiralhanae frigate pair. They would shift to take alternate plasma hits efficiently, giving the pair an alternating energy shield. They could then combine firepower. If they made no mistakes, they were more than a match for the *Incorruptible*.

This was the standard Covenant tactical thinking. Recent events, however, had shaken what Voro had considered "standard" behavior. This would be a gamble, but in Voro's estimation, their only winning option.

"Now," Voro spat. "Fire!"

The overcharged energy projector sent a shudder through the *Incorruptible*.

All their power—shields, engines, slipspace capacitor reserves—channeled into a single burst from the projector.

The darkness of interstellar space parted.

The shields of the *Revenant* boiled and popped. The hull peeled away, bubbling, as the beam penetrated through and through. The frigate was cut in half diagonally, ventral fore to dorsal aft—until it severed the starboard plasma line. Fire blazed along her surface and reached the main coils. The ship's aft section detonated and her mid and fore sections tumbled away aflame and spewing smoke.

"All weapons systems inactive," Uruo reported, as he stared at the destruction.

"No power to maneuver," Zasses said nervously. "Thrusters on standby."

The other Jiralhanae frigate veered away and continued to turn, presenting the flare of engine cones as it ran. After seeing the obliteration of its sister ship, the *Twilight Compunction* had no desire to face them alone.

As Voro had hoped: The Jiralhanae were quick to act without thinking. They were savage, yes, but not suicidal.

He counted his blessings that the Jiralhanae Ship Master had not taken the time to thoroughly scan the *Incorruptible* to assess her battle-worthiness.

"Repairs under way," Y'gar announced. "All crews on task. Estimate seventy cycles until plasma lines ready."

"Direct repairs to the coils and slipspace capacitors," Voro ordered.

"A brilliant tactical maneuver, sir," Zasses said, and bowed his head.

Voro grunted.

Brilliant? Desperate was closer to the truth. But Voro would never voice his feelings on this matter before his crew. Unvoiced, however, a mixture of shame and disgust rose in the back of his throat. He had risked everything to win. Perhaps this was how Tano felt? The lives of his brothers in his hands on every mission? Voro felt unworthy to lead.

He scrutinized the central viewer. The Jiralhanae frigate had headed toward the third ship in its battle group, the one that had turned to engage *Bloodied Spirit*.

They had intercepted the enemy's transmissions and seen the humans manning *Bloodied Spirit*. A disturbing revelation.

"Zasses," Voro growled. "You tracked the *Spirit* as it jumped?"

"Yes, sir," he replied, and rechecked his console. "Only one stellar system on that vector."

Voro gritted his teeth and flexed his hands. Then at least *Bloodied Spirit* could be hunted and destroyed. "Make ready to jump. We must warn our brethren . . . of everything."

CHAPTER 26

B *loodied Spirit* was on fire. The shot she'd taken from the Covenant frigate had hit an auxiliary plasma line, and fire streamed along the side in a crimson plume.

The raging flames made repairs impossible. Fred couldn't find the controls to quench the broken line without shutting down the main plasma coil and dropping them out of slipspace—so he let it burn.

Purple alloy melted and oozed through the aft quarters, consuming life support and several sensor nodes.

Bloodied Spirit would last only a few more minutes, but it was, he hoped, all they'd need.

Will smoothed his hands over the NAV console. "Shifting to normal space in three seconds," he said, "two, one—now."

Stars winked on in the central viewer. Fred moved perspective alongside *Bloodied Spirit,* revealing smoldering holes in her side, bare conduits spewing plasma, and in places gapping cavities two decks deep.

A planet rotated into view.

Will's jump had been uncannily accurate. They were only a hundred thousand kilometers from the world known as Onyx, a jewel of blue and white against the black.

"Looks habitable," Fred remarked.

"Reading water vapor, oxygen, and nitrogen," Linda said.

"Other ships?" Fred asked. "Scan the region."

Linda bent over the Covenant sensors. "No plasma signatures. No silhouettes on radar," she said. "They didn't follow us."

"Yet," Will added.

"I'll take the lucky break," Fred told him, "and figure out why we got it later."

Fred couldn't relax, though. Leading Blue Team and the responsibility to "captain" this ship was his alone. He had been trained in rudimentary astrogation and ship-to-ship tactics, but it wasn't enough; it was like trying to perform brain surgery with only a basic aid kit. The sooner he got groundside where he could fight on his own terms, the better off they'd all be.

He wasn't sure what the Covenant were doing fighting amongst themselves and stealing human nukes . . . but whatever it was, he hoped it kept them busy. The Covenant captain who had seen them wasn't going to let a human-crewed Covenant ship slip off his radar for too long.

"Groundside signals," Linda said. Lines wavered in a window floating off her console. "UNSC E-Band."

"Put it on audio," Fred said.

There was a hiss, a pop, and it went dead. The hiss repeated and then again fell silent.

"That's a looped signal," Linda said. "Hang on, slowing it down by a factor of three hundred."

A series of beeps resolved from the noise.

"Slow it down more," Will told her.

Three longer beeps pinged, then three shorter ones, and three longer. After a moment, this repeated.

"Not 'SOS,'" Linda declared. "It's 'OSO.'"

"Signal source?" Fred asked.

Linda retuned to the console. "Multiple point sources," she said. "Cycling at random. Someone doesn't want to get triangulated."

"If SOS is a distress call," Will said, "then what's OSO supposed to be? A warning? Why would Dr. Halsey send a distress call and then warn us away?"

"The message repeats every twelve seconds," Linda said. "Twenty-seven OSO units, a pause of two seconds, and then another one hundred eighteen units."

"Twenty-seven by one one eight?" Fred considered. "Latitude and longitude?"

"Which direction?" Will asked. "North or south? East or west? Any matches of those permutations to the random signal sources?" He moved closer to Linda's station.

"There," she said. "Twenty-seven degrees north, one hundred eighteen east."

Fred told them, "Set course to those coordinates. Give us a nice and easy deorbital burn. We've got to—"

"Hang on," Linda said. "Picking up contacts. Wait . . . recalibrating." Her hand flicked over the control surfaces. "Multiple silhouettes in high orbit. The system missed them; it's not set up to detect something so small. Objects are three meters long. On the central viewer."

Fred moved to the holographic display.

Floating before him was a simple structure: Three cylindrical booms sat parallel to one another. From the end-on view they formed an equilateral triangle. In the center of this sat a sphere, a quarter meter in diameter. The booms were a brushed matte sliver metal. The resolution was just good enough to see a swirled pattern etched onto the alloy. The sphere glowed dull red, as if it were heated from within. Nothing connected the sphere to the associated rods. There were no shimmering energy fields, either.

"A bomb?" Fred asked. "Dr. Halsey's new technology?"

"No radiologicals detected," Linda reported.

"Satellites?" Will offered.

"I'm reading two thousand four hundred twenty-three of these objects in orbit," Linda said. "That's overkill for a COM network. Wait, they're breaking orbit."

With a flick of her hand she shifted perspective in the central tank and Onyx drifted in the center. *Bloodied Spirit* was a glowing purple dash among the stars.

"Image enhancement online," she said.

A haze of red dots swarmed in the black of space and slowly drifted toward them.

"Shields!" Fred barked at Will.

"Responding. Full strength confirmed." Will rechecked the alien controls. "No error," he said. "They're up this time."

"If those aren't nukes," Fred told them, "there's no way something that small can penetrate Covenant shields."

Fred watched the holographic viewer as the hostiles approached. It was like watching a tide come in, and Fred remembered one of Deja's childhood lessons: jellyfish swarming the tide lines on an Australian beach. One sting from the tiny invertebrates caused tissue necrosis and paralysis. A hundred was overkill-lethal.

"Back us off, Will," he ordered.

"Something's happening," Linda said.

The image in the viewer zoomed in on a cluster of the space-craft. Seven of them moved into a line.

The view pulled back and revealed other identical formations. Seven of these lines stacked into an elongated triangle, and the spheres within the forty-nine-craft pattern glowed red-hot.

"Hard to port!" Fred cried. "Emergency power to shields."

The deck tilted.

"Answering hard to port," Will cried.

A blast of golden light overwhelmed the image in the viewer.

The frame of *Bloodied Spirit* resounded like it had been struck with a hammer. The artificial gravity failed and Fred gripped the railing.

"Starboard side hit," Will said. "Shields destroyed."

Fred moved his hand over his console and *Bloodied Spirit* appeared on the viewer. A gaping crater of blue hull armor smol-dered white-hot. Crystalline electronics crackled, and severed plasma lines spewed fire. As the ship turned, Fred saw the hole was five decks across and had punched clean through to the port side.

"Main plasma pressure nil," Will reported. "Cycling to fuel cells. Slipspace capacitors holding charge. We have enough power to jump."

Linda looked to Will and then to Fred and nodded.

Fred watched as more alien drones crystallized into triangular lattices. Individually they were no match for even a Covenant sin-gle ship. Combined they packed enough punch to atomize *Blood-ied Spirit.*

"We're not leaving," Fred muttered. "We're moving closer. Will, get me a jump solution on coordinates to twenty-seven degrees north latitude, one hundred eighteen east longitude, elevation fifteen thousand meters."

"On it," Will said, and he stared at the Covenant math as it steamed over his console.

"Linda, go evasive!" Fred ordered.

Her hand melted into the holographic controls and *Bloodied Spirit* pitched forward, accelerating, which made the hull ping with stress.

The tiny alien ships easily tracked their motion, surrounding them.

Covenant ships could perform pinpoint-accurate slipspace jumps. But could the weakened hull of *Bloodied Spirit* survive an instantaneous change of pressure from zero to over one kilogram per square centimeter? And that was just accounting for the atmosphere. Their velocity in air would exert tremendous forces on the ship's leading edges.

"Course plotted," Will announced. "Only a second-order approximation, but the jump system is accepting the numbers. I'll have higher-order terms in a minute."

"Belay that," Fred ordered. "Linda, give me all power to the engines. Slave Will's jump coordinates through the NAV system and give us a thirty-second countdown."

"Done," she said.

"Let's move, Blue Team," Fred told them. "We're abandoning ship."

It was a perfect day on the jungle-swathed peninsula. The sky was crystal cobalt dappled with cotton-ball altocumulus clouds. Insect buzz and bird caw abruptly ceased and a hundred red-wing macaws took flight as the world exploded over their heads.

A fifteen-kilometer-long smear of condensed water vapor

marred the air, and from it a fireball colored every cloud red—
Bloodied Spirit shot forth like a bullet.

Sonic booms rippled off the destroyer's prow. Hexagonal
armor plates fluttered and shed, revealing a skeletal frame. Static
discharges arced from ship to clouds and back.

Inside *Bloodied Spirit* fires raged stem to stern and every deck
glowed hot, trailing flames and an oily black smoke.

The ship rolled and the nose began to shudder until the entire
length of the vessel wobbled.

The once-deadly Covenant ship was no more than a ballistic
mass, a meteor, with only one possible trajectory: a parabola that
intersected the planet's surface.

A dozen drones punched through the clouds and left swirling
vortices, and then a hundred more drones appeared, giving chase.

As the destroyer dropped to a hundred meters, the heat ignited
the jungle canopy, leaving a blistering path in its wake. Debris
from the disintegrating vessel rained into the trees, crushing them
to splinters.

The drones closed and fired.

As *Bloodied Spirit* turned and its shuttle bay presented ground-
work, what appeared to be another chunk of the ship fell, spinning
until it plummeted below the canopy—and then the dropship's
engines flared, and it righted.

The tiny ship's momentum smashed it through three banyan
trees before it touched ground and scraped to a full stop.

Three figures eased from the tuning fork–shaped vessel, and
quickly melted into the surrounding jungle.

Fred watched pieces of *Bloodied Spirit* fall to the earth. The
ground under him shook from the impacts.

Drones accelerated after the lost destroyer, so many that they
blackened the sky.

A flash cut through the jungle, casting long hard shadows. A wave of pressure shot rock, splinters, and smoldering vegetation hurling over his head, igniting leaf and wood and flattening brush and trees.

Bloodied Spirit had landed.

A kilometer to the north a wall of plasma-fueled fire shot skyward and the clouds overhead parted.

Fred flicked his green status to his teammates.

Linda's status light burned green, but Will's remained dark a moment, and then winked amber.

There was a flutter on Fred's motion detector, two o'clock, and then nothing. Another malfunction?

Linda's light shifted to amber as well.

No. Real trouble.

Fred sited down his assault rifle and covered the area. Linda would soon be in position to snipe. Will would draw whatever was there out into the open.

Had those drones discovered them so quickly? Or had the Covenant managed to track them here after all?

On his heads-up display, the secure single-beam COM system activated. His helmet speaker hissed with static, and then a voice as familiar as his own spoke.

Kelly whispered: *"Olly olly oxen free."*

CHAPTER 27

The Unggoy Kwassass knew his place aboard the Covenant super-
carrier *Sublime Transcendence*. He was to be trod upon under the
boots of its glorious Sangheili officers. He was to clean, scrub,
wait in the shadows for orders, and never speak unless spoken to.

Among his other duties Kwassass was also responsible for the
maintenance of storage subdeck K. The mining gear that had ex-
acted the human fortress world Reach had been stored on subdeck
K. Diggers, earthen conveyors, portable microenergy projectors,
and plasma fuel cells all sat in orderly rows.

He had been ordered to repair and refit everything, a gargan-
tuan task that would take six months and the entire K-deck tribe.
It was a crushing responsibility . . . but also a tremendous opportunity.

Kwassass waddled along the dim corridors of subdeck K, admiring its cavernlike expanses and the warmth of the place. Even after seven years of service to the Covenant he could not help marveling at their copious wealth of heat. After freezing every day of his childhood, watching his family one by one succumb to the blue death, heat was something he never took for granted.

He spotted a group of laborers playing a game with rocks, jumping them over one another on a grid scratched upon the floor. They laughed and gambled for tiny tanks of compressed organics and audio crystals.

Kwassass joined them, lost a few cartridges of formaldehyde, won a file of old BBC, and then wished them well and moved along on his morning patrol. Today it would be best to keep up appearances.

He meandered toward Storage Sector Three, making sure no one noticed.

Kwassass had overheard one Sangheili speak of pods of benzene that required disposal in that sector. Lovely lung gold! He sighed, reliving the pleasure of his last inhale of the sacred aromatic.

He slowed his place, though; Storage Sector Three was a shadowy realm where only Huragok[5] ventured, as it was full of active plasma conducts.

The tentacled podlike Huragok never spoke to his kind. Sometimes they fixed things for them . . . but just as often they took things apart and left them that way. He had learned it was best to avoid them, as the Sangheili valued their services.

Kwassass ventured into the dim section of the ship.

Only the glow from the occasional plasma coil provided an

---

[5]   Huragok: the Forerunner name for the Engineer race

eerie blue light, and the shadows were full of the floating Huragok that whispered to one another in ultrasonic chitters.

Tonight they seemed to move with a greater purpose, floating in pods of three farther into the storage sector.

He followed one of these pods and emerged in a round chamber, lit by an overhead heat exchanger that dripped fluorescing green coolant. A machine towered in the chamber. It was five times his squat height, and it would take thirty Unggoy to circumscribe its curved surface.

Dozens of Huragok clustered about the thing, their tentacles gently probing its surface in reverence.

The device was bare silver metal, which was a rare thing in Covenant alloys. Kwassass was drawn to the shiny material. He wanted to touch it, take it with him.

There were alien pictograms on the side and he ran his hand over them. Although his tribe had been trained to listen and transcribe alien transmissions as part of their duties, they were forbidden to read.

There were four pictograms. The first was three connected lines. The second was a hollow dot. The third was an angle of two lines. The last icon was the same angle inverted with a line horizontal midway between them.

. . . N . . . O . . . V . . . A.

Many of the Huragok clustered on the far side, and Kwassass gently pushed through them to see what was so interesting.

A black box lay on the deck.

The Huragok had obliviously removed a panel from the cylinder: a tangle of wires and cabling stretched from a cavity in the cylinder to this box.

Inside the box were flashing red, blue, and green lights and many buttons.

He knelt and touched a button.

A sound came from the box: a curious series of slurps, pops, and deep rumbles that made Kwassass giggle. A rare alien transition. Treasure indeed. He could perhaps trade this for a rare AS-THEWORLDTURNS he had heard was on M deck.

The noise stopped, so he touched the button, and the noise repeated to his delight.

He strained to decipher the sounds. Like all human transmission he understood many of the words, but very little of what it actually meant. This voice had a twangy accent.

He listened again, straining to understand. . . .

". . . *I am Vice Admiral Danforth Whitcomb, temporarily in command of the UNSC military base Reach. To the Covenant uglies that might be listening, you have a few seconds to pray to your damned heathen gods. . . .*"

"We have been betrayed by those we trusted most," thundered the Imperial Admiral and Regent Command of the Combined Fleet of Righteous Purpose, Xytan 'Jar Wattinree. He shook both fists as he spoke. "We have been betrayed by our Prophets."

The Sangheili stood over three and half meters tall and wore silver armor covered with the gold Forerunner glyphs of Sacred Mystery. In the center of the oration chamber aboard the super-carrier *Sublime Transcendence*, Xytan's image was holographically magnified so he towered thirty meters before them, and image replications made his face present in four directions simultaneously to the crowd.

Xytan appeared no less than a god.

Ship Master Voro stood at attention and watched the legendary commander. He had never been defeated in battle. He had never failed at any task, no matter what the challenge. He was never wrong.

The Imperial Admiral's only flaw was that he had been so revered, some said even more so than any Prophet. For the sin he had been exiled to the fringe worlds of the vast Covenant Empire.

This had happened before: the former Supreme Commander of the Fleet of Particular Justice had never returned from the "glorious mission" the Prophets sent him on.

Xytan had summoned all the factions of the Sangheili to Joyous Exultation. He was, in Voro's opinion, their best chance for survival.

Voro was one of thirty representative Ship Masters who had been called from the two hundred vessels in orbit to hear these words.

"I, like all of you, believed in our leaders and their holy Covenant," Xytan continued, his voice resonating off the silver stadium dome overhead. "How could we have been so willing to believe a Covenant of *lies*?"

Xytan paused and looked out among them. The thirty Ship Masters and their guards seemed to be swallowed by the empty space in the chamber, designed for a capacity crowd of three thousand.

No one dared speak.

"They have called for the destruction of all Sangheili. They have aligned themselves with the barbaric Jiralhanae," Xytan said. He hung his head and his four jaws opened slack for a moment, and then he looked up, a new determination burning in his eyes. "The Great Schism is upon us. The unbreakable Covenant Writ of Union has been split asunder. This is the end of the Ninth, and final, Age."

A grumble echoed within the oration chamber. These words

were the grossest sacrilege. Today, however, they could be the truth.

Xytan held up a hand and the dissent quelled.

"You must now decide to surrender to fate—or resist and strive to persist. Myself, I choose to fight." He outstretched both hands to his audience. "I call upon you all to join me. Let the old ways fade and battle by my side. Together we can forge a new, better union—a new Covenant among the stars."

The Sangheili Ship Masters roared their approval.

It was an inspired oration, but the Prophets had used words to trick them all before, too. Ship Master Tano had let words, and their more dangerous by-product, beliefs, cloud his reason.

Words alone would not help them. Voro crossed his arms over his chest.

Amazingly, Xytan saw this gesture and turned to face him, locking gazes.

"You disagree, Ship Master?"

A tomblike silence smothered the stadium. Voro felt all eyes upon him.

"Speak, then, hero of the battle for the Second Ring of the Gods, and de facto commander of the Second Fleet of Homogeneous Clarity." Xytan waved him forward and offered him the center pulpit, an unprecedented and generous step for one so high.

It stunned Voro to hear such honorifics attached to his name. Xytan knew what had happened? Who he was? Of course, his intelligence network was legion. And what better way to silence questions than with compliments?

Voro, however, had not survived treachery and war and the sundering of an Age to be silenced now. He willed himself to step forward. The urge to supplicate before Xytan was overwhelming, but he resisted.

It took all of Voro's strength to cross that distance with all watching.

He stepped upon the center stage and his image appeared holographically magnified, a titan towering over the crowd.

"I agree with what you say," Voro declared. "We must destroy the Jiralhanae, unquestioningly, and all who ally with them. But victory may mean nothing if the disease upon the holy ring escapes. It must be cleansed from the galaxy if we are to survive."

A murmur of assent passed through his fellows.

Xytan nodded as well, and then made a slight gesture with his hand, indicating Voro step down.

He gave a short bow to the Imperial Admiral and withdrew. Voro made it to his seat without betraying how he shook inside, without revealing to the others how stunned he was that he had survived.

Xytan reappeared upon the stage.

"Your words are Wisdom, Ship Master Voro. Which is why I have summoned Jiralhanae Alpha leadership under a banner of truce to this world."

An outcry rose from the gathered Ship Masters.

"I have no illusions that they come with false offers of peace," Xytan said. "So we shall stage our own ambush—here, where we are strong. After we have dealt a decapitating blow to the Jiralhanae Alpha Tribes, we will be free to eradicate the infection that threatens to spread from the most holy ring.

"As for how to accomplish this," Xytan said, "I call upon Oracle Master Parala 'Ahrmonro to report on a new opportunity."

Xytan's image flickered off and an elderly Sangheili appeared in the center of the stadium. Parala had long ago been counsel to the Prophet of Regret. Bent with age, a fierce intellect nonetheless shone in his milky eyes.

"We have most disturbing intelligence," Parala said with distaste. "The humans have wreaked havoc with their demons, *destroying* the first-discovered sacred ring construct. They were at the second ring as well, and have apparently discovered yet another world of Forerunner design. They must not be underestimated."

While this galled Voro, he had seen for himself the human-captured *Bloodied Spirit*, and reluctantly attempted to accept the Oracle Master's words as truth.

"Here," Parala said, "is an intercepted and translated human slipspace transmission."

Human voices screeched through the stadium air. A translation overlaid the offensive human words and Voro listened as the incidents upon the second Halo relic were reported.

"Parasitic infestation known as the Flood has contaminated this construct . . . attempting to escape . . . unknown coordinating intelligence . . . Suggest FLEETCOM Nova-bomb the Delta Halo . . ."

Then alien icons appeared in the air, resolving into proper words: "SEND ELITE STRIKE TEAM TO RECOVER TECHNOLOGICAL ASSETS FROM ONYX. SEND SPARTANS."

An embedded string of celestial coordinates streamed alongside these words.

A collective mummer of outrage came from the Ship Masters.

Voro strained to isolate the human word for demons from their objectionable speech . . . *Spartans*. It heated his blood to a boil.

Xytan's image returned to the stage. "This heresy cannot be ignored for reasons dogmatic *and* strategic. We will go to this world, Onyx, to protect and secure the holy artifacts. They will be of incalculable value in our impending struggles."

Xytan extended his titanic holographic hand to Voro. "You, Ship Master Voro 'Mantakree, are now Fleet Master Voro Nar

'Mantakree. Lead your newly assembled battle group to this world. Destroy the demons and deny them their prize at all costs."

Voro fell to one knee.

"It shall be as you say," he said. "My task is holy. My blood pure. I shall not fail."

Secretly Voro wondered if these honors had been bestowed upon him to removed him and his "wise words" from Xytan's chorus of unanimous ascent. So be it. He would accomplish his task. He would return glorious.

Kwassass punched the button in the black box and listened to the human voice. He was close to understanding what it meant. A threat. To him. All Covenant. A promise of retribution.

The sound distorted, slowed, and stopped. The box was out of power.

One of the Huragok watching gave an ultrasonic cry that shot through Kwassass's skull. The creature charged him, tentacles flailing, and grasped at his box. It wrenched it from Kwassass's grasp.

Other Huragok charged and tried to take the box from their fellow.

Did they understand what the human said? Did they understand the danger?

There were more Huragok around him than he had realized. The shadows rippled with their buoyant bodies, each with six glassy black eyes firmly fixed upon the human voice box.

The Huragok rushed the box back to the Great Cylinder, to the panel where the box had been removed. There were multicolored wires inside that matched those in the box.

Huragok twisted these wires together. Tiny sparks danced.

Red symbols flickered upon a display in the box, and the device spoke once more.

True to their nature, Huragok were just as likely to fix something broken as they were likely to take apart something that worked perfectly.

A dozen Huragok pressed closer around the device, all squirming tentacles and glistening eager eyes.

The voice from the box started again—now loud and clear:

"This is the prototype Nova bomb, nine fusion warheads encased in lithium triteride armor. When detonated it compresses its fusionable material to neutron-star density, boosting the thermonuclear yield a hundredfold. I am Vice Admiral Danforth Whitcomb, temporarily in command of the UNSC military base Reach. To the Covenant uglies that might be listening, you have a few seconds to pray to your damned heathen gods. You all have a nice day in hell."

Kwassass pushed his way through the throng of Huragok. He had to get to the thing. Pull those wires.

There was a flash of the most beautiful light, and more glorious heat than he'd ever—

A battle group of eighteen destroyers, two cruisers, and one carrier collected in high orbit over Joyous Exultation, and drew in a spherical formation about their flagship, the *Incorruptible.*

They shimmered blue-white and vanished into slipspace.

A heartbeat later Vice Admiral Whitcomb's ploy of slipping the UNSC prototype Nova bomb into Covenant supplies had finally paid off: a star ignited between Joyous Exultation and its moon.

Every ship not protected on the dark side of the planet boiled and vaporized in an instant.

The atmosphere of the planet wavered as helical spirals of

luminescent particles lit both north and south poles, making curtains of blue and green ripple over the globe. As the thermonuclear pressure wave spread and butted against the thermosphere, it heated the air orange, compressed it, until it touched the ground and scorched a quarter of the world.

The tiny nearby moon Malhiem cracked and shattered into a billion rocky fragments and clouds of dust.

The overpressure force subsided, and three-hundred-kilometer-per-hour winds swept over Joyous Exultation, obliterating cities and whipping tidal waves over its coastlines.

The Covenant Schism—the shattering of its client races for a thousand years, and the genesis of their end—had truly begun.

SECTION VI

THE GHOSTS OF ONYX

CHAPTER 28

**1700 Hours, November 3, 2552 (Military Calendar) \\
Zeta Doradus System, Planet Onyx \\
Near Restricted Region Zone 67**

urt crouched, motionless in the undergrowth, and waited for the Sentinels to move into position.

There'd been no happy reunion with Blue Team, no time for explanations, not even a handshake; all there'd been time for was running. The Sentinel patrol had been on them the instant they'd recovered the Spartans—an hour of nonstop cat and mouse through the jungle.

The drones were getting very good at hunting them.

A pair of Sentinels paused, hovering four meters above the ground. After bombarding the jungle from a hundred meters with energy blasts . . . and missing, they had finally descended to their level.

Their lateral spars flexed as if they could smell the trap. The spars moved about each sphere then drifted farther part and both spheres moved within centimeters of each other.

It reminded Kurt of cell division, only in reverse. They were combining.

What the purpose of this "mating" was, Kurt wasn't sure. He was, however, sure he didn't like it.

The now-double Sentinel crept closer.

Team Saber on the left flank detonated fougasse positioned under the drones. Flames shot up and lit the canopy, smoldering shrapnel obliterating the foliage.

A split second later Blue Team on the right flank let loose an SPNKr missile and a hail of MA5B fire. They were in perfect defilade.

The air filed with white-hot tracers and black roiling clouds. Two nearby trees crackled and fell.

Kurt flashed his red status light, and the fire ceased.

Saber had jumped the gun. A half second maybe, but they had definitely shot before the Sentinels were in position.

What had he expected? For all the simulated combats the Gamma Company Spartans had been through, nothing could have prepared them for continuous guerilla action with the Forerunner killing machines.

Kurt squinted. Even with image enhancement and thermals he couldn't make out anything in the air where the Sentinels had been. But he could see the ground . . . and among the splintered tree trunks, burning leaves, and popping metal, there was neither drone.

He blinked his amber light twice, ordering the teams to fall back. He didn't like this one bit.

A full bank of green status lights winked at him.

Kurt saw motion in the mist: shadows that resolved into

six rods arranged in a long hexagonal geometry—two spheres within—pulsing as the energy field enveloping the combined Sentinels shimmered.

They were completely untouched.

Kurt flashed his red three times: the retreat signal.

One sphere glowed and moved back and forth searching. It stopped and fixed upon Kurt.

He jumped.

A flash of light struck. The jungle floor detonated and a three-meter crater fizzled and cracked into glass.

Kurt rolled into a crouch and instinctively returned fire with his MA5K.

This was part of the plan, too: the part where everything went wrong and he had insisted on drawing the enemy's fire while the others slipped away. He knew the terrain: Twin Forks River was three hundred meters to the east. It should be a stroll through the park.

The other sphere shone like burnished gold and his rounds bounced off its energy shield . . . even as the first sphere reheated, building charge for another shot.

Kurt ran, zigzagging into the foliage.

In this doubled configuration the Sentinels could simultaneously fire *and* defend with an energy shield. That was *big* trouble.

It seemed all their engagements with the Sentinels were doing was teaching them how to be more effective in combat.

Explosions followed Kurt almost as if his footsteps were setting them off.

The trees parted ahead and the Twin Forks River snaked through the jungle. The water was muddy and churning.

Kurt leapt and splashed into the swift current.

He sank to the bottom. Internal oxygen cut on inside his SPI suit, and Kurt grasped rocks along the river bottom, crawling upstream. Through the murky water he spotted a rock ledge and tucked underneath.

Between him and Sentinels were three meters of moving ice-cold water, a meter of rock, and a layer of photo-reactive circuits in his armor. He should be undetectable to any sensor. At least undetectable enough, he hoped, to fool these things.

He waited.

No explosions. No flashes. No heat.

The combined Sentinel wasn't his biggest worry, though. It was the one on overwatch. The Sentinels patrolled in *threes* now: two at mid to ground level, and another two to three thousand meters in the air—watching everything, reporting their tactics, and learning.

As long as that third one tracked them, the Spartans would be on the defensive, reacting, instead of initiating action.

Kurt wondered why the Sentinels hadn't called in reinforcements, combined, and let loose with enough firepower to burn the entire jungle.

. . . Unless they were deliberately playing cat and mouse with them? To learn more about how they fought?

He had to be smarter than them. Take out all three. Take the initiative. Maybe with Blue Team, he could do it.

Kurt waited two more minutes, then pulled himself out of the river. He sprinted for the cover of the jungle.

There were no signs of pursuit.

He remained COM silent and crept back to the prearranged fallback position.

As he approached the region of broken ground bordering Zone 67, he slowed. There was less cover, so he scanned the skies for Sentinel overwatch. All clear.

Ahead the land turned to savanna grass, acacia trees, and large striated boulders. One rock in particular had a hollow underneath where they had arranged to meet. It provided cover without restricting the view of the local airspace. If attacked, they had a clean line back to the jungle.

There would be at least two guards on lookout, and at least one Spartan at the jungle line to watch their line of retreat. Normally he would click his COM twice to alert the sentry, but he didn't even want to take that small risk in the open.

So Kurt waited, guessing the sentry would be either Linda or Olivia. If it was Linda—he scanned the nearby trees—she'd be up there, in a good sniping position.

If it was Olivia, she could be anywhere. She was eerily proficient at camouflage and stealth.

There was the clatter: a single stone three meters to his left.

He turned and, as predicted, Olivia crouched a meter behind him in the shadow of a low tree, perfectly blending into the grass and dappled light in her SPI armor, waving at him to make sure he saw the slight blur of motion. Kurt had no doubt that she could have been in fluorescent orange fatigues and still managed to look like part of the terrain.

Kurt waved to her and then aimed his single-beam COM at the rendezvous rock. The COM established handshake and then crackled to life.

"One coming in," he said.

"Come ahead," Kelly's voice came back. "Good to hear your voice."

"Yours too. Out."

Kurt remembered the last time he had Kelly on the single beam—when his thruster pack had exploded and he rocketed out of control into deep space.

He'd never realized how much he had missed his old team-mates until he had seen them again. Of course, now Blue Team was in jeopardy, but that seemed like old times as well. He couldn't have asked for better soldiers to be in trouble with.

He ran across the field, low and silent, and then jumped into the shaded hollow. Tom, Ash, and Mendez crouched next to Kelly, Linda, and Fred. They whispered to one another and drew plans in the dirt.

Lucy sat quietly next to Dr. Halsey, who glanced at Kurt and then went back to her laptop computer, examining Forerunner glyphs.

The other SPARTAN-IIIs were missing, presumably on watch.

"Glad you made it back in one piece," Chief Mendez said, and gave him an abbreviated salute. "*Almost* had me worried."

"Thanks, Chief. Set up a single-beam relay outside and hail the others on patrol."

"Yes, sir." Mendez grabbed a tiny antenna dish.

Linda, Kelly, and Fred all turned to Mendez when he said "sir" and then looked at Kurt.

Kurt flicked his index finger up, the wait-a-second gesture, and then he turned to Ash. "Private."

"Sir," Ash said, and stood straighter.

His helmet was off. Sweat glistened on his head and neck. It was a serious breach of combat protocols, but SPI suits had never been designed for extended use, and Team Saber had to have been sweltering in the stuff for days.

Kurt glanced at the helmet and Ash blanched at his mistake, and immediately slipped it on.

Kurt said, "Saber jumped the gun on that ambush."

"Yes, sir." Ash snapped into precise regulation attention. "It was my fault. I felt it was the right time, that the Sentinels were about to move out of optimal firing position. That's no excuse, sir. It won't happen again."

Had Ash sensed something Kurt hadn't? Still, orders had to be followed.

"I'm counting on you to keep your team on task and focused. We clear?"

"Absolutely clear, sir," Ash replied.

Kurt then moved closer to Blue Team.

Fred set a hand on Kurt's shoulder, a rare gesture among Spartans. It spoke volumes in the language of the Spartan's tightly restrained emotions.

"We thought you were dead," Fred whispered.

Kurt clapped Fred on his shoulder as well. "There's so much to brief you on. The Sentinels, the SPARTAN-IIIs—everything."

Mendez stepped back into the shadows. "Single-beam linkup established, sir."

". . . Which will have to wait a little longer," Kurt told them.

Kurt opened up his TEAMCOM to both Blue and Saber. "We're taking out that Sentinel pair before the next phase of this operation," he said. "Ash, take Saber and scout the ravine ahead. Find that tunnel you sacked in a few days ago. Dante will rig it with two satchel charges. We'll lure the Sentinels inside and then, since we can't penetrate their shields, we'll blow the place, and bury them."

Fred, Linda, and Kelly exchanged looks. Normally Fred gave orders for Blue Team.

Fred gave his team an almost imperceptible shake of his head.

"What about the overwatch?" Fred asked.

"We'll take our best shot at range," Kurt replied. "Hit it with two SPNKr missiles, which will hopefully weaken its shield enough for Linda to penetrate with a few shots."

"What range?" Linda asked.

"They never get closer than two kilometers," Kurt said.

It wasn't an impossible shot. But given variable winds, a moving target, and trying to combine fire with missile strikes . . . it would be *highly* improbable. Still, Kurt had to try something to get one step ahead of the enemy.

Linda considered a moment, then replied, "I have an eighty-three percent accuracy rating at that range."

"Okay," Kurt told Ash, "go. Tom, Lucy, back Saber up, then grab a pair of SPNKr launchers and rendezvous with SPARTAN-058."

His senior NCOs and Ash stood, nodded, and eased out of the hollow.

Kurt got green status light across his display. He shut down the linked single-beam network.

After the SPARTAN-IIIs had left, Kelly said, "Those kids are going to get us killed. They're acting like they have something to prove. We could have taken those Sentinels earlier if they followed the firing order."

Kurt bristled at her words. Team Saber were his soldiers and every one of their flaws was his fault. His anger cooled as quickly as it had come. She was right.

In an even voice he told her, "They're not 'kids.' They're Spartans."

Kelly crossed her arms.

Mendez said, "I think, sir, you might want to tell them what we've accomplished here."

Kurt nodded and then explained much of the SPARTAN-III training program, and the creation of Companies Alpha, Beta, and the newly minted Gamma.

"Some of the bioaugmentations are new," Kurt explained. "The SPARTAN-IIIs' normal aggression response has been"—he searched for the right word—"enhanced in situations of extreme stress. It gives them incredible reserves of endurance and makes them near impervious to shock."

"Is that what's making them twitchy?" Kelly groused.

"No one's twitchy," he replied, then fell silent.

Kurt knew he was wrong. Why couldn't he admit it? Was he defensive because he wanted his Spartans to be everything the older Spartans were? Fred, Kelly, and Linda had decades of field experience. As the SPARTAN-III CO he had to stay objective.

"You're right," Kurt said softly. "They are twitchy. And green. What else could they be? Fresh out of boot and thrown up against these Sentinels." He looked to Kelly, to Fred, and then to Linda. "I need your help to make sure they stay in line . . . and, if possible, survive this."

Linda and Fred slowly nodded.

"Sure thing," Kelly said, uncrossing her arms.

Dr. Halsey looked up from her computer. "I'd like to discuss this 'aggression enhancement,'" she said. "In fact, I have many questions about the SPARTAN-III program, like where is the rest of Gamma Company? And Beta? Or Alpha?"

"Your questions will have to wait, Doctor," Kurt replied. "We're running out of time. Lord Hood's reinforcements may not get here. Every engagement with the Sentinels teaches them more. Soon we won't be able to stop them."

"I must insist," Dr. Halsey said. Her words were as placid as smooth water, but her steely eyes bored through Kurt's helmet.

Fred stepped closer to Kurt. "I agree with Kurt, ma'am. And if I might point out, with all due respect, you are not in any position to demand anything in this tactical situation—especially after you *kidnapped* Kelly, circumvented the chain of command, and left us in the middle of a critical mission on the *Gettysburg*."

Kelly looked between them, caught in a conflicting web of loyalties.

Dr. Halsey stood. "I have already explained my actions," she said. "And the discovery of this new Forerunner technology should outweigh any so-called breach of military protocol that may have been committed."

A frosty silence filled the hollow.

Dr. Halsey had no official rank, but had always wielded considerable influence over her Spartans.

That had to end.

Kurt valued her scientific expertise and intellect, but he couldn't have her issuing confusing or conflicting orders.

"Since you mention protocol . . ." Kurt deliberately turned his back to her and faced Blue Team. "I want to clarify our chain of command. I understand Lord Hood gave you command of this mission," he said to Fred. "But I'm in charge of all USNC personnel on Onyx."

Kurt activated his friend-or-foe electronic tag, on extreme low power—just enough so they'd pick it up. On their displays appeared his green color-coded military ID number as well as the bars and star insignia of a UNSC lieutenant commander.

The Spartans straightened, their involuntary response when in the presence of an officer.

"I am therefore assuming command of this mission," Kurt said.

No one said a word for a moment . . . and then Fred snapped off, "Yes, sir."

Something was different in Fred's voice. A bit of the familiarity was missing, but there was something else: respect.

Kurt gave Blue Team a quick nod, and then turned to Dr. Halsey. "Ma'am, I want you to continue your analysis of the Zone 67 documents on the Forerunners. I expect an update on your progress in two hours."

Dr. Halsey arched an eyebrow. She said nothing and slowly sat down, returning to her computer.

Kurt inwardly sighed. That was one battle won today.

Olivia's green status light flashed twice—the signal for "friendly approaching."

A ripple crossed the entrance to the hollow, part shadow, part rock, and then the SPI camouflage resolved into Olivia. "Sentinel pair," she whispered. "Half a kilometer south, sir. Moving this direction in a search pattern."

Kurt said, "Everyone, get ready to move out. Kelly, limber up; you're our rabbit."

"Happy to oblige, sir." She made the two-fingered signal over her faceplate, the traditional Spartan smile.

The others nodded.

Kurt knew they'd follow him, into battle, and right to the gates of hell if he ordered it. He had a feeling it might come to that.

CHAPTER 29

Kurt had seen snipers zero their instruments before, but never for an extreme-range, near-vertical target.

Linda took the task as seriously as a surgeon preparing for a heart transplant. She cleared a patch of rocky ground and laid out a camo mat so dust wouldn't foul her SRS99C-S2 AM rifle. Next she opened a kit that contained tools, bottles of cleaner and lubricant, several magazines for her rifle, a box of 14.5x114mm ammunition, and a tiny datapad. She selected one of the magazines and inspected it; satisfied, she opened the box of ammo and removed one of the rounds: super-hardened red polymer petals surrounded a finned tungsten dart. She spun it around and looked at the cartridge base. Opposite the legend "51" it bore the winged hourglass headstamp flanked by double "X"s—signifying that it was hand-loaded match-grade ammo from Misrah Armories on Mars. She slid the magazine into the rifle.

Next she linked her Oracle scope to the datapad and made microcalibrations. She finally sat, butted the rifle to her shoulder, and then leaned back flat and sighted up at the sky.

"Ready," she said over single-beam COM. Her voice was detached and trancelike.

"Eyes sharp," Kurt told everyone.

The Spartans had moved from the rendezvous hollow to the high ground among broken canyons and mesas where Team Saber had first encountered the Sentinels. Kurt had them spread out along both sides of the valley.

Kelly stood in a gravel wash in the center of the valley and scanned the horizon, waiting for the double Sentinel to spot her. The sun was high and her shadow was a wavering spot at her feet.

For someone who was bait, she looked perfectly at ease.

The tunnel where Dante had rigged the opening and exit with charges was a quarter kilometer away from her position. Just far enough.

The tricky part of this plan would be to get the Sentinel pair *into* the tunnel, instead of staying high and blasting Kelly while she was inside. Would they continue their "game" of cat and mouse, or was the data-collection phase of their operation over?

Either way, Kurt had placed his friend in grave danger.

Kelly looked up to Kurt's position and activated her single beam. "I see it," she said. "Two klicks away. I'm going to tap its shoulder."

"Go, Blue Two," he said. "Keep your head."

Kurt held up a hand, made a fist, and pumped it twice—the "get ready" signal for the rest of the team.

Kelly took a shot at the drone pair with her MAB5—an

impossible target with an assault rifle, but it wasn't meant to hit, just to get the thing's attention.

The Sentinel turned to the report of gunfire and accelerated toward her.

Will reported over single beam: "Overwatch spotted, eleven o'clock, elevation twenty-four hundred meters. Wind is three knots from the northwest."

Kurt relayed this to Linda.

Her status light wavered amber as she made a slight adjustment in her position, angling her rifle up, and then frozen. On either side, Tom and Lucy hefted missile launchers, waiting for her order to fire.

Meanwhile, the combined Sentinel pair plunged toward Kelly.

She stood there, watching it.

Holly moved close to Kurt, her assault rifle uselessly aimed at the incoming drone. "Is she fast enough?"

"Kelly's the fastest Spartan," Kurt whispered.

That didn't answer her question, though. Was she fast *enough*, Kurt didn't know.

The Sentinel pair was half a kilometer away. One of the spheres heated and light flashed.

Kelly took three sidesteps as the ground where she had been standing vaporized. Globules of molten rock spattered off her MJOLNIR armor's energy shield.

She made an ancient and arcane gesture at the machine with one finger.

Mark joined Holly and Kurt. "No way," he breathed.

Kelly turned and ran, leaving a plume of dust in her wake.

The diving Sentinels accelerated to two hundred kilometers an hour. A golden lance flashed from its center of mass—detonating the earth under her feet.

Kelly tucked into a ball, tumbled, and came up running without breaking stride.

She sprinted straight into the tunnel.

The Sentinels' hexagonal geometry fluttered along its drive trajectory. A mere five meters over the gravel wash and screaming toward the tunnel—it had no time to pull up.

It chased her down the hole.

Kelly appeared silhouetted at the mouth, golden illumination blazing behind her—

—and the tunnel exploded.

Cones of fire shot out both ends. The superheated overpressure wave blurred the image of Kelly as she was propelled through the air, end over end.

The hill collapsed, and a hundred tons of earth crushed the Sentinel pair. Sand, stone, and dust blasted out in feathery jets.

Kelly's body impacted a rock wall, and fell limp to the gravel wash.

Kurt signaled Team Saber to get down there and help. He wanted to rush to her side as well, but he had to stay here and ensure the long-shot part of their operation succeeded. Or, failing that, devise a retreat.

Linda was still locked in place, tracking the overwatch Sentinel. Tom and Lucy knelt on either side, missiles ready.

Kurt squinted along the angle of their aim. Hanging in the air, over two kilometers away, was a single dot, their target.

They had to get it or the Sentinel would report their position and send for reinforcements . . . which wouldn't fall for this trick again.

"Target off-center, starboard boom," Linda whispered to Lucy and Tom. "Forward point,"

They adjusted their aims. "Locked on target," Tom replied.

"Fire," Linda said softly.

Twin plumes of exhaust washed over them as the missiles screamed into the air.

The overwatch Sentinel turned toward the incoming projectiles and its energy shield shimmered golden.

Linda's rifle muzzle flashed. Without seeming to move a molecule, she fired until the magazine was empty.

The missiles impacted—smoke and flames ballooned about the Sentinel.

A heartbeat later, the winds blew the discharge cloud aside . . . the Sentinel jerked, and plummeted.

Linda got to her feet.

The Sentinel scattered as it fell, center sphere and three booms spinning out of control until they impacted.

"Go," he told them. "Make sure it's down."

Kurt didn't waste another second on the Sentinel; he turned back to the ravine and ran—toward Kelly.

He scanned Kelly's bio signs: erratic heartbeat, falling blood pressure, low body temperature. She was in borderline shock.

Kurt skidded to a halt in the ravine as Ash and Holly propped her up.

"I'm sorry, sir," Ash said. "The Sentinels were three meters from the exit. If I had waited any longer it would have cleared the trap. It would have shot her. I couldn't take that chance."

Kelly shook her head—not to disagree, rather to clear her senses. Her bio signs perked.

"He's right," she whispered and coughed. "The kid did good." She gave Ash the thumbs-up signal.

Ash bowed his head.

Kurt breathed a sigh of relief that Kelly had survived. He'd risked her life to gain a slim advantage over the enemy—he now had to use it wisely.

"What's next?" Fred asked.

Kurt told them, "Now we have an opportunity. If that overwatch Sentinel didn't get a fix on our position we'll have some room to maneuver and take the initiative."

"Maneuver where?" Holly asked.

"Zone 67," Kurt said. "It's the center of everything. If there's any technology to be recovered other than broken Sentinel parts, it's going to be there."

"Patrols get denser the farther north we've gone, sir," Dante noted.

"It'll be dusk soon," Kurt said, "enough time to circle back to Blue Team's dropship. The sun will be setting and we'll fly it in low, get some camouflage from the long shadows. The rocks in these canyons have been baking all day and we'll have thermal cover, too."

Kurt surveyed his team. "Unless there's a better idea?"

His gaze fell on Dr. Halsey as she and Chief Mendez made their way down the valley slope. She stared at him as if she could see through his mirrored faceplate.

"Okay, stay sharp. Olivia, Will, Linda, scout ahead. No COM chatter. Let's get this done."

Dr. Halsey watched Kurt give detailed instructions to the Spartans.

She didn't care what his orders were so much as how he was saying it, and the effect it had on them. He spoke with confidence, but there was also warmth and pride in his voice. She'd never heard any Spartan so demonstrative. Certainly Kelly would crack the rare joke, but that was just a layer of emotional armor.

Kurt was different.

The Spartans, young and old, responded to him. There was the usual Spartan stoicism and no questions asked, but there were also nods, slight tilts of their heads—the involuntary indication of rapt attention. Kurt was their leader now.

That fact might serve her well in the upcoming crisis.

Of course he was hiding something about his SPARTAN-IIIs. If the mute, psychologically damaged Lucy was any indication of what this secret was, Dr. Halsey could only guess at its horrors.

But as the end neared, she would have no choice but to trust Kurt. She would have to trust them all to forgive the lies she had told about the treasure trove of Forerunner technologies.

CHAPTER 30

Kurt stood behind Kelly and Will in the Covenant dropship's cockpit. Kelly sat in the pilot's seat while Will manned the gunner's station and watched the scanners. The other Spartans, Mendez, and Dr. Halsey were aft, readying equipment, waiting, and watching.

Kelly shifted back and forth—the pilot's seat was angled wrong for human physiology, and she leaned awkwardly over the control surface.

She took the ship in low and fast over the jungle. The controls were an odd assemblage of holographic geometries that danced before her hands.

Kurt tried to learn as much as he could in case he had to fly the alien ship. It was difficult, however, to watch her and not the viewscreens.

The sun was a hand's breadth from the edge of the horizon, and the Covenant ship passed through long shadows and dim red light.

As the jungle thinned, Kelly dropped and swerved between acacia trees, skimming two meters over the grassland.

Without looking up from her controls, Kelly said, "Piece of cake, LC. Relax."

She smoothed her hand over an acceleration stripe and the ship leapt forward—zipping off the savanna and over the broken canyon lands.

Kelly maneuvered aggressively—jinking up and down, performing quarter rolls to veer around mesas, dropping into ravines and pulling up at the last instant to avoid a crash headlong into a wall.

"Great," Kurt whispered to Kelly. He forced himself to release the edge of her seat.

Dead ahead the slope of a mountain angled gently up over two thousand meters.

"Nothing airborne on sensors," Will announced. "Clear sailing ahead."

"Status on the warheads?" Kurt asked over the COM.

Ash clicked on the channel. "All FENRIS warhead detonators now secure and slaved to our secure COM signal, sir. As ordered, two warheads cut down, armed, and ready for transport. Working on the rest."

"Hang on!" Kelly cried.

The nose of the ship jerked up. A rock the size of a Warthog tumbled down the mountain slope—clipping the undercarriage of the ship.

The dropship spun, but Kelly expertly rolled, righted, and got them back on course.

"Close," she muttered.

"Rescan for surface motion," Kurt ordered Will.

Will swept the camera angle port and starboard.

Kurt saw they weren't on a single mountain; it was a range—all equivalent elevation, extending in a gentle arc as far as he could see.

"Motion detected," Will said. "Just appeared, sir. Ahead. Got a target lock."

A silhouette resolved on the viewscreen, outlined by the glare of the setting sun.

Kelly came hard to port.

As their relative angle changed, Kurt saw motion: earth and rocks shot up and then cascaded down the slope.

Will slid his hand over his controls and polarized the monitor, cutting the glare. The motion came from a collection of thirty interlaced Sentinels, their booms and center spheres assembled into an oblong shape, and through its center traveled a continuous stream of stone.

To Kurt it looked like a mechanical worm regurgitating over the mountainside.

Dr. Halsey clambered into the cockpit.

"No energy spikes detected," Will said. "They're not ready to fire."

Kurt swallowed. "Steady on this heading," he told Kelly.

He watched the giant machine recede behind them. It *had* to have seen them. Thirty sets of eyes wouldn't have missed something as large as a Covenant dropship. Why hadn't it attacked?

Dr. Halsey tapped a control and one of the viewscreens jumped back to the combined Sentinels. She studied this a moment, and then declared, "Tinkertoys."

"I don't understand the reference," Kurt said.

"An ancient child's toy," she said, "sticks and flat round connectors. These may be the Forerunners' counterpart. They reconfigure to accomplish various tasks, having all the required basic components: antigravity units, force-field generators, energy projector weaponry. It is the equivalent, I suspect, of the simple machines that comprise our technology: the wheel, the ramp, lever, pulley, and screw."

Her casual analysis of a technology centuries more advanced than theirs irritated Kurt.

"I'd say in this configuration," Dr. Halsey continued, "it is not designed for combat, and will not attack . . . unless, of course, they were provoked. Their programming, while sophisticated, appears dedicated; that is, each Sentinel combination specializes for a single task. And right now, that task is moving dirt."

"Doesn't mean there aren't more combat pairs around," Kelly said. "Orders, sir?"

Kurt detected the slightest edge of nervousness in Kelly's voice. He felt it, too, in the pit of his gut. If those thirty Sentinels back there had wanted to, they could have blasted this ship into shrapnel.

There were only two options: go forward or retreat.

Kurt felt like his luck had run dry, but he also felt like they were close to finding something.

He longed for the days of simple missions when there were only two things to worry about: maneuvering and where your team's lines of fire were.

Yet, when you broke it down to its components, forgot the consequences of success or failure, wasn't this mission the same as any other?

Move and fire. Find a target to capture or neutralize. Minimize casualties while inflicting maximum damage on your enemy. Get in quick. Get out quicker.

"New course," he told Kelly. "Come ninety degrees to starboard. Take us up that mountainside."

"Aye, sir."

The tuning fork–shaped dropship banked and raced up the slope. The earth vanished under them as they crested the summit.

Beyond was a crater a hundred kilometers in diameter.

There were *thousands* of the earthmovers on the inner slope—all spewing rocks over the edge. The Sentinels had created a giant anthill. How much, Kurt wondered, had ONI cleared in the decades they had been here? And how much of this was the Sentinels' doing?

At lower elevations there was nothing to see. The sun was too low, and shadows pooled. Kurt boosted image enhancement on his heads-up display and faint lines resolved . . . but nothing made sense.

"Take us in closer," he whispered.

Kelly angled the ship down the interior slope, reducing their speed to one-quarter.

The clouds overhead lit with oranges and reds as the setting sunlight reflected off their undersides . . . and the crater interior glowed a faint amber.

Kurt blinked, dazzled by what he saw. Mirror-image clouds drifted upon angled surfaces and burned crimson and gold.

As his eyes adjusted, he saw swirls and bands of other muted colors underlying the reflected images: green stripes and black and silver waves that appeared to be a tempest ocean frozen in place.

He blinked once, twice, and then finally unraveled the optical illusion of patterns, colors, and shadow.

There were pillars and arches, elevated aqueducts; columned temples with crowns of three-dimensional Forerunner symbols; a forest of sculpted geometries of spheres, cubes, and tori; roads that curved up and twisted into Möbius surfaces—it was a vast alien city.

Kurt shook his head clear, and then recognized the material that constructed the city. He had seen it before in tumbled stripped river rocks and the slabs quarried from nearby Gregor Canyon. A rock so plentiful this world had been named for it. Only the stuff in the crater had been polished to optical flatness, mirroring the sky with superimposed rainbow bands.

"Onyx," he whispered.

"Chalcedonic quartz with trace elementals enhancing their spectral variation," Dr. Halsey remarked.

Scalloped columns rose from the crater floor to the mountainous summit, an elevation Kurt could only assume had been ground level before ONI began their excavation.

As they maneuvered closer to one pillar, Kelly banked the ship around its curve and Kurt saw reflected images of a thousand different sunsets—all with varying cloud geometries, some with flocks of migrating birds, or dinosaurs, another had smears of blue spacecraft, and one burned with a supernova that illuminated the twilight . . . all images captured here. From the past? The future? Both?

And only then did the scale of the structure register. It was three kilometers in diameter, larger than a UNSC carrier.

Kurt's mind rebelled at the scale of this technology, the effort it had to have taken to construct such a thing.

He glanced at Dr. Halsey. While she intently studied the viewscreen, she did not appear the slightest bit impressed.

"You knew this would be here?" he asked her.

"I suspected," she said. "Frankly, after reviewing the reports of the Halo structures, I am somewhat disappointed."

"Bigger than the ruins under Reach," Kelly said.

"We did not discover the full extent of those ruins," Dr. Halsey replied, "and likely never will." She squinted at the monitor. "There," she said, pointing at a distant gleaming dome. "Can you move closer to that structure?" She turned to Kurt. "With your permission, Lieutenant Commander."

"New heading zero two five," Kurt said. "Pick your best path."

"New course, aye," Kelly replied.

As they descended deeper, the dropship sped past a staircase that ascended to nowhere—each step a hectare of unbroken polished stone.

The cloud-reflected light dimmed and the smooth surfaces melted into shadow. Dr. Halsey's dome turned red-gold and faded to a silhouette.

Will turned the passive radar on the thing and an outline overlaid the structure. Kurt discerned that the top of the dome faceted into seven flat surfaces, each with a tall arch leading to the interior.

"Those large enough to fly through?" Kurt asked.

Will consulted his sensor screen. "Huge," he replied.

"Move us in," Kurt told Kelly.

"Aye aye." She pulled the nose of the ship up.

As the last traces of light vanished, Kurt saw lights in the crater—red dots that swarmed over every surface. Sentinels.

Will's hands flashed over the sensor panel. "New energy signatures detected. Extremely low frequencies." He looked up. "Over a hundred thousand distinct emitters, sir."

"What configuration?" Dr. Halsey asked. "Clusters, single units, or pairs?"

Will studied the panel. "Ninety-five percent clusters, a few hundred single patterns . . . and a few hundred dual signatures."

"Combat pairs," Kurt whispered. "Kelly, match their speed."

He keyed TEAMCOM, and said, "Make ready for a hot drop. Battle-ready conditions."

Green status lights flashed back, confirming his order.

They decelerated over the darkening city, creeping toward the dome. Kurt's instinct told him this was the right thing to do. The logical, conscious portion of his mind, however, urged him to leave. He'd trust his "gut" on this one—get them inside and under cover, before every Sentinel in the place fired on them.

"Nice and easy," he said.

Kelly's hand hovered over the throttle stripe. "You think these things are smart enough to use our own tricks against us? Lure us inside and then close the trap?"

"It's a possibility," he admitted. "But I don't think they went to all the trouble to unearth this place just to blast it to bits." He shrugged. "Just a hunch."

Kelly and Will glanced at each other.

"Understood," Kelly said. "Approaching structure. Three hundred meters."

"Back us in," Kurt said.

Their ship slowed, spun around, and eased toward one of the dome archways. Five Covenant dropships could have fit through the opening with room to spare.

Inside, the blue glow of their engines illuminated the walls. The interior surfaces were angled and carved with star charts and the Forerunner hieroglyphics.

Below, seven flat surfaces, each the size of carrier landing decks, were evenly spaced. Kelly set them down.

Kurt exited the dropship. Will followed him, and together they helped Dr. Halsey off.

The other Spartans took defensive positions around the ship.

Kurt's motion sensor showed everyone on deck, but there was

nothing beyond the landing pad save darkness. Every noise was swallowed by the vast emptiness of the interior, and he felt as if he were drowning in shadows and silence.

He initiated a single-beam COM network, and opened external audio so Dr. Halsey could hear them, too.

"We do this fast," he told his team. "Olivia, Will, scout the perimeter of this landing pad. I want a report in ninety seconds on all routes and motion sensor hits."

Olivia and Will nodded and melted into the dark.

"Linda, Fred, Mark, Holly, get grappling rounds, scale the dome, and take up lookout positions in the arches. Set up single-beam relays and zip lines. Anything moves this way, sound the alarm."

Their status lights flashed green. Linda disappeared into the ship and returned with harpoonlike shafts and rope bags. She passed them out to the three other Spartans. They slid the rounds into their sniper rifles, aimed, and shot them through the archways overhead. Braided monoline uncoiled, pulled by the grapple. They tested the lines, and then rapidly ascended the ropes.

"Dante, Mendez, stay with the ship. Get our gear ready and loaded into balanced packs."

Dante's status light remained unlit for a full second in protest, and then it winked green. Mendez nodded and they boarded the ship.

"Kelly, Ash, Tom, Lucy—you're with me and Dr. Halsey. Ash, grab those cut-down nukes."

Ash moved into the dropship's cargo area and retuned hefting a backpack.

"Tom, Lucy," Kurt said, "keep Dr. Halsey covered."

His senior NCOs stepped to either side of the doctor.

"Got a staircase, sir," Will reported. "Goes through the floor and around the landing pad's support pedestal. No motion detected."

"Roger," Kurt said. "Olivia, link up with Will. Scout it out. We'll follow."

He oriented on Will's IFF tag and set a single-beam relay antenna on the edge of the platform so he could keep in contact topside.

Kurt led his team to the stairs that helixed around the giant pedestal supporting the landing pad. Kelly and Ash were right behind him, Tom came next, then Dr. Halsey, and Lucy on rear guard.

Each stair step was spaced a quarter meter, but they fanned out from the pedestal ten meters. Kurt kept to the inner surface of the spiral, avoiding the darkness that lay beyond.

Dr. Halsey paused to examine the stone surface.

Lucy halted, too, and the faint illumination of the TAC lights on her SPI armor reflected in the banded rock. She reached out and touched her image. There was translucence to the material that, for a moment, bounced reflections within the reflections—and an infinite number of Lucys appeared mirrored.

She withdrew her hand, and they hastily continued.

After three revolutions around the support, Will's IFF tag appeared on Kurt's heads-up display.

A single-beam COM channel opened. "Chamber ahead, sir," Will reported. "With Forerunner symbols, I think."

Fred's voice broke over the COM: "We're in place. No incoming."

"Eyes sharp," Kurt told Fred. Then to Will he said, "Show me."

Will led them until stairs passed through a floor and stopped at an arched entrance. Olivia crouched there, rifle out, covering the room beyond. The chamber was only four meters across. After the agoraphobia-inducing space of the city, this room looked suffocatingly small.

"Watch," Will said, and took a step inside.

Holographic Forerunner glyphs—dots, dashes, lines, and polygons—sprang from the stone floor and twisted around him.

"With your permission, Lieutenant Commander?" Dr. Halsey asked. "It's not dangerous, I assure you. I have seen similar control surfaces in the Halo mission logs."

Kurt didn't like a civilian leading, but Dr. Halsey was the expert here . . . as much of an expert as he had at any rate.

"Very well, Doctor," he said. "But carefully."

Dr. Halsey made her way forward. "Stand perfectly still," she told him, and entered the room.

She tapped a tiny crystalline blue square; it blinked in response.

"Still damned difficult to read," she muttered. "There is a simple two-dimensional translation, but I now see there are higher-dimensional interpretations." She reached for her laptop.

"There's no time for details," Kurt told her.

She frowned and put away her laptop. "All meaning is in the details, Lieutenant Commander." She compressed her lips, concentrating on the symbols, and then she straightened. "This way."

She started to stride across the room, and the floor lit a brilliant blue before her, running directly into a blank wall.

Kurt set a hand on her arm, gently checking her motion. He then waved for Lucy and Tom to join him and the three Spartans slowly walked ahead.

Dr. Halsey pointed to a small slightly brighter blue dot on the wall.

Tom and Lucy took up firing positions on either side of him. Kurt reached for the dot, ready for trouble.

The wall slid apart and in the darkness beyond, a bridge of light flickered on, arcing into the distance.

Kurt told Olivia, "Stay here and relay signals topside."

She nodded.

Kurt paused at the wall, testing his weight on the semitransparent bridge. It held. He didn't like it, though. If the power cut out, this thing could vanish.

He moved twelve paces, with Tom and Lucy right behind him . . . although the distance covered by their steps didn't seem to match the much greater distance he *perceived* he was traveling along the curve of the bridge. He looked down: fathomless shadows. He kept his eyes straight ahead.

When they got to the end of the bridge, a door of dazzling light appeared, and the shadows slid apart.

Kurt, Tom, and Lucy passed through, not registering so much as a blip of enemy contact on their motion sensors. He found himself in a half-sphere chamber twenty meters across. In the center was a console over which metallic-hued Forerunner hieroglyphs swarmed.

Kurt turned and motioned for Dr. Halsey to come along.

She strode quickly across the bridge. Kelly, Will, and Ash hurried behind her, keen for any motion.

They entered the room, and Dr. Halsey studied the hologram.

"For lack of a better term," she said, "this is an information center." She ran her hands over the symbols on the console. "We should be able to find, ah"—she tapped a tiny flexing triangular icon—"a map."

Light exploded around Kurt. Holographic geometry flashed and zoomed to a distant perspective—and a sphere of symbols, topology lines, and shapes swelled over the console, until it touched the apex of the room.

"A map?" Kurt asked.

"Of our present location," Dr. Halsey said.

"So this building is round?" Kelly asked.

"Not precisely incorrect," Dr. Halsey replied. "We *are* in this building. And this building is in this city, which is technically on this so-called planet, but that view is backward. Observe."

She rotated a golden circle symbol, and holographic structures passed through Kurt as the map expanded. A dot on the surface of the sphere magnified and resolved into lines and a grid, squares, triangles, and one circle.

The view zoomed in upon that circle and it tilted 90 degrees, showing depth, and a faceted dome with seven arches.

Dr. Halsey twisted the gold circular symbol and the focus sharpened, descending through the layers of the building, showing the landing pad, and the outline of the Covenant dropship with a blazing reactor core. Mendez and Ash appeared and tiny bio signs displayed next to them.

The view plunged deeper and the room they stood in resolved and Kurt watched himself, the other Spartans, and Dr. Halsey.

"And back," she said as she spun the circle icon.

The room shrank to building to city and back to the large sphere construct.

The scale of it finally clicked in Kurt's mind. Once he understood, it took him a few seconds to again speak.

"When you said the Forerunner translation for Onyx was 'shield world,'" he whispered, "that was a *literal* translation, wasn't it?"

"Apparently so," Dr. Halsey agreed. "The entire planet is artificial . . . like the Halo rings."

Something caught her attention on the console. She tapped a blue octahedron. "Could it be . . . ?" she whispered.

The map shifted once more, through the surface of the world, deep into the crust, and revealed a chamber full of machinery and eight oblong pods that shimmered with energy fields. Within were human bodies, translucent, their features like specters. Next to each pulsed the trace of their heartbeats.

"That's Katana," Ash said, and took a step closer. "At least five of the people in those things. They vanished in Zone 67—before this all started."

"We've got to get them out," Kurt said. "Doctor, find me a route to that location. Kelly, Ash, get the medical kits from the ship and—"

Dr. Halsey held up one hand. "One moment, Lieutenant Commander." She touched a dot.

The map of Onyx receded to a meter across and stars winked upon the map-room walls. A tiny Covenant destroyer appeared in orbit . . . then another . . . and another, until twenty-four ships had flashed into normal space from slipspace.

Kelly muttered, "Out of the frying pan . . ."

Kurt's mind raced. They could still do this. Rescue Team Katana and get out of here. But they couldn't just leave and give the Covenant the technology on Onyx. There were the FENRIS warheads, but if he detonated them all it wouldn't even destroy a tiny fraction of this planet.

"We've got incoming," Fred's static-filled voice crackled over the COM. "Sentinels."

"How many?"

"Sir, all of them."

CHAPTER 31

Fleet Master Voro stepped up to the command console on the bridge of the *Incorruptible*. His crew snapped to attention at his presence.

All was perfect. He controlled a fleet of the finest ships on what might be the most important mission for his people . . . and this would be his crowning moment: contact with the Forerunner guardians of this world.

"Ship Master Qunu," he said over ship-to-ship COM, "report."

On the central holographic display, Qunu's destroyer, the *Far Sight Lost,* continued to accelerate from the safety of the fleet's defensive sphere formation. It plunged into a high orbit over the world the humans had called "Onyx"; this word had no meaning for their translation Oracle.

"Fleet Master," Qunu replied, "moving into the proscribed vector of supplication."

A thousand tiny craft crested over the planet's northern magnetic pole and moved toward the *Far Sight Lost* on attack vectors.

"Honor light your way," Voro told Quno.

Quno finished the time-old Sangheili maxim: "Our blood will forge a thousand generations."

Voro had considered initiating contact himself, but decided the honor should go to Qunu, whose knowledge of the ancient ritual responses from the *Fire and Repentance Codices* of the First Age was unmatched.

On Y'gar's sensor station a schematic of one of the Forerunner vessels appeared: three unconnected cylinders and a sphere.

"Power signatures detected, sir," Y'gar reported, his one good eye staring at the patterns. "Energy shields *and* offensive-system waveforms present."

Voro considered this: The power outputs from these tiny ships were insufficient to penetrate their shields . . . but there were so many.

"Spin up the fore energy projector," Voro ordered.

Uruo hesitated a heartbeat, and then moved his hands over the controls. "Fore energy projector charging, sir."

The shimmering of power readings of the Forerunner vessels reflected Voro's gaze.

During their slipspace journey, Voro had made clear to his Ship Masters that they had to be willing to set aside their beliefs. Others had been blinded by the glory of Ring of the Gods, and subsequently destroyed by the human and the Flood infestations. They must be prepared for anything.

"Alert the fleet to make weapons ready," Voro ordered Y'gar.

"Aye, sir."

Voro wanted to believe the Forerunners had left this world to deliver them in their hour of greatest need . . . his instincts, however, told him not to trust anything but Sangheili blood.

"*Far Sight Lost* broadcasting on an open channel," Y'gar said, and put it on bridge audio.

" . . . *let us cast arms aside,*" Ship Master Qunu began the ritual greeting. " . . . *And discard our wrath. Thou, in faith, will keep us safe. Whilst we find the path.*"

The thousands of the tiny craft drifted in the central holographic display like a cloud of dust. They formed octahedral geometries, solidifying into crystals of gold and ruby in the dark of space, surrounding the *Far Sight Lost.*

"Incoming transmission," Y'gar said. Both his eyes, sighted and blind, were wide with wonder. "On the Prophets channel, sir."

A flat voice, intoning perfectly the ancient dialect, rumbled over the bridge: "*Rescue phase concluded. Threat-analysis phase concluded. Reclaimant request for Shield World access . . . denied. Initiating outer defense program.*"

"Energy spikes detected," Y'gar said. "Frequencies shifting to resonate suites." He looked up. "They're combining fire, sir."

"Fleetwide channel," Voro shouted. "All Ship Masters make ready to fire. Link targeting control through the *Incorruptible.*"

Uruo monitored his console as the ships in their fleet linked into a single spiderweb network of firepower. "Fleet fire control is now yours, sir," he told Voro.

"Target laser and energy projectors on these cluster formations," Voro said.

Uruo smoothed his hands over the network, double-checking the numbers, and then said, "Target solutions calculated, sir. On your order."

A thousand tiny eyes blazed within the alien formations.

Energy beams collimated into lances of golden light that painted the hull of the *Far Sight Lost*.

The ship did not have its shields up. Beams sliced through armor and decks, piercing through and through, blasting cones of vaporized alloy into space.

Voro quenched his rage and studied the carnage. Some advantage had to be gleaned from this tragedy.

Individually the tiny craft could do no harm. Together, however, they were more than a match for the *Far Sight Lost*. Their octahedral structures shimmered with energy shields. Voro assumed their defensive strength multiplied when combined as well.

"Release weapons interlink safety locks," Voro ordered, and raised his hand.

He prayed for the soul of Ship Master Qunu, who had revealed for them a new enemy.

Penetrated by a dozen beams, the ventral decks of the *Far Sight Lost* exploded. The ship rolled over like a great beast in its death throes. The weapons cut through the aft section. The plasma core breached, and three plumes of blue fire erupted from the hull—heating the aft quarter of the vessel red-, yellow-, and then white-hot—before the vessel detonated.

The crystalline geometry of the alien formations rippled and their shields flared.

"Now!" Voro commanded. "All laser and projectors fire."

All ships under his command launched a barrage, and the deep night of space lit with crisscrossing lines of illumination. Hundreds of lasers painted the weakened alien shields and made them sputter with static. Ten microseconds later, energy-projector capacitors discharged and blasts of holy white radiation impacted the formations, overloaded the distressed shields, and scattered their coherence.

Stripped of their protection, the tiny drone ships erupted into streams of superheated particles. Their central eyes blazed white-hot as if their fury alone could protect them.

Explosions chained through the octahedral assembly.

Lasers and projectors shut down and the space plunged again into dankness.

Voro blinked.

Within the holographic display the thousands of alien ships were scattered, most now cooling blobs of metal, tumbling disconnected rods and spheres. Those that had survived moved sluggishly as they attempted to realign for another attack.

"Eighty-three percent of the vessels destroyed," Y'gar said.

Over fleetwide COM Voro said, "All ships break and attack. Annihilate the survivors with plasma charges before they regroup."

The fleet accelerated to attack speed, burning all before them. The smaller alien craft were defenseless before this onslaught.

Ship Master Qunu had been a hero. He had demonstrated for them all that the old ways of devout placation had no place in this new Age. The Sangeili would forge their own way, with their own blood, if need be.

"Contact the *Absolution*," Voro told Y'gar. "Have them make ready for a slipspace transition in atmosphere. They will scout the northern polar region where these drones came from and determine if there are high-value targets our sensors have overlooked."

"*Absolution* hailed, sir," Y'gar replied. "Orders relayed." He paused listening, then said, "The *Absolution* is yours to command, Fleet Master."

Voro nodded, indicating they go.

The space surrounding the sleek destroyer shimmered as their slipspace capacitors discharged.

"Something on the planet surface, sir," Y'gar said, and he bent closer, concentrating. "Energy anomaly in the northern polar region."

He waved his hand over his controls and the central viewer split, half filling with a view of the planet's ice caps, zooming closer to reveal a wind-whipped landscape of snow dunes. A kilometer off the ground, the air shimmered in the exact same pattern as the *Absolution*'s slipspace transition matrix.

"That should not be happening," Uruo remarked, and took a step closer to the image, intrigued. "A slipspace matrix only appears upon a ship's *exit*. The *Absolution* has yet to transition."

"Hail the *Absolution*," Voro said. "Abort the jump."

Y'gar shook his head. "Slipspace matrix interfering with our signal, sir."

"Move to intercept," Voro ordered.

The *Incorruptible* tilted and accelerated toward the destroyer as it edged toward its slipspace field.

The view in the holographic display shifted. Above the north pole three new octahedral formations of alien ships materialized in the glow of the Slipstream exit field.

"They can jump?" Voro whispered.

That made no sense. If they had such a capacity then why hadn't they jumped into combat with the *Far Sight Lost*? Or for that matter jumped to avoid destruction from the rest of the battle group?

Voro turned to Y'gar, who understood Slipstream space better than any of his officers. "Explain," he demanded.

Y'gar straightened. "Sir, a slipspace transition requires more power than ships that size can generate. I can only guess that they are somehow tapping into the *Absolution*'s slipspace field."

"Energy spikes," Uruo said. "Northern polar region."

The alien ships fired, hundreds of beams bounced within their linked geometry, combining and focused through their energy shields—directed into the center of the wrapping slipspace.

The *Absolution* vanished from high orbit—

—reappeared in the center of the aliens' field of fire.

The hull of the destroyer superheated to white—flash vaporized, flowering into a ball of ultraviolet fire.

The alien vessels comprising the octahedral formations deformed from the overpressure wave. They then flew away on random trajectories from the cloud of smoke, which was all that remained of the *Absolution*.

Voro watched stunned and then he regained his wits.

"Scan the surface of the planet," Voro told Y'gar. "And recheck the sensor log for anomalies just *before* those ships appeared." He opened the fleetwide channel. "No vessels to initiate a slipspace transition without my explicit order."

His Ship Masters sent their acknowledgments, and twenty-one personal insignia lit his console.

"Energy signature detected," Y'gar said. "In our logs before the enemy ships appeared, scanners detected a burst of extremely low-frequency energy . . . a transmission from this location."

On the central viewer a ring of mountains snapped into focus. There was motion along the rim. Voro zoomed in and saw one rod-and-sphere drone dart back into the shadows.

Transmission? Coordinating orders perhaps? Or a central location where these drones had something worth protecting?

"That is our target," he said. Voro activated FLEETCOM. "All ships to OVERARCH attack pattern and prepare for orbital descent. Charge lateral lines to full capacity."

The *Incorruptible* took position on the starboard wing of the coalescing wing formation and led the battle group into the planet's atmosphere.

Beneath them, air heated and rolled off their hulls in waves of convective fire.

Voro watched as the clouds in the upper atmosphere parted before their combined bow wake . . . and lamented over the holes in their formation. Two ships lost. The fault was his. How could any continue to follow his orders after such errors?

Yet Voro felt their confidence. Perhaps that was delusion, but they had followed him unquestioningly into battle. They knew that what happened here could determine the fate of all Sangheili. They had to succeed, even if it cost their lives.

They swooped over the surface of the planet, over twilight-shrouded jungles, undulating plains of grass, and shadow-filled canyons. Flocks of birds and herd animals scattered before their ominous presence.

No more alien craft rose to challenge them. Where were the hundreds they had seen at the northern pole? In reserve? Lurking in ambush?

"Come to dead slow," Voro commanded over FLEETCOM. "Maintain battle conditions."

As the fleet crossed the crater summit, a collection of drones appeared on the inner rim spewing earth and stone into the air.

Three of his destroyers opened fire and left nothing but a surface of crackling glass.

As the greater body of the fleet crossed into the crater, the light from their heated lateral lines illuminated the dark interior, revealing giant arches and pillars, steps that circled faceted silver domes. It was a city of magnificent proportions. The shapes were instinctively recognized by Voro from Holy Scriptures. Every line and curve, every symbol had been burned into his soul.

This was a Forerunner city. Intact. Sacred. Untouched. It was what every member of the Covenant had dreamed of finding . . . if not in this life, then the next.

Would it be so easy to claim their prize? The technological and theological treasures were close enough to touch. Voro's joints weakened and he wanted to drop and bow before the glory of it all.

He stopped, ashamed. Such religious stupor would only blind him to the dangers.

Voro must not bow to the Forerunner ghosts. *He* must be the sole authority here.

He turned to the Lekgolo pair who ever remained at his back on the bridge.

"Prepare for battle," he told them.

Although the Lekgolo could not smile, Voro sensed their "faces" flex in pleasure, a dozen eels squirmed and coiled over one another.

They growled their assent, rose, saluted, and thundered off the bridge.

Voro ran his hand over the command console. Ship Master Tano's blood still stained the edges, tingeing the holographic emitters blue. He lamented that his old mentor had not survived to witness this moment.

"Alien vessels accelerating from the surface," Uruo announced. "Two dozen. Pair formation. On attack vectors."

"Destroy the craft," Voro said over FLEETCOM, "and *only* the craft. Use lasers, pinpoint targeting."

Tiny explosions lit the night as the drones were obliterated.

He activated the SHIPCOM. "Paruto, Waruna, during the ground assault take pains to minimize collateral damage."

There was a double-growl response, and then Paruto asked, "What target, Fleet Master?"

Voro surveyed the vast city. A complete search would take weeks.

"Pulse the Greeting of Ancients for a signal response," he told Y'gar.

"Aye, Fleet Master." He broadcast the Covenant's universal handshake sequence, and waited then for a response.

It was only a dream that any Forerunner were left to answer the call.

"Something . . ." Y'gar leaned closer to examine the wavering reply signal.

Voro moved to his station.

"It's one of ours," Voro declared. "Send it to the ship's Oracle for pattern match."

"Yes, sir," Y'gar replied. "Ship ID . . . DX class."

"A dropship? Identify the parent ship registry."

Y'gar summoned the reference and his jaws dropped open in shock. "*Bloodied Spirit*," he whispered.

Voro narrowed his eyes at the wavering response signals. This came from the ship stolen by the human demons. They had beaten them here? Survived the Forerunners' defenses and infiltrated holy grounds? Anger boiled within him and clouded his mind, but he collected his rage . . . saved it.

"Triangulate the signal," he ordered.

"Yes, sir. There."

The image shifted in the central viewer. A silver dome wavered into semisolidity. The apex of the structure faceted into seven planes, and on each, an arch opened to the interior . . . arches large enough for dropships to pass through.

Voro returned to his command console. "Paruto, Waruna, we have a target. Muster the reserves from every ship in the fleet."

Paruto and Waruna replied simultaneously with a subsonic rumble of acknowledgment.

"You will, however, wait," Voro told him.

There was silence over the COM.

"Wait" was a word one dared not speak to a Lekgolo pair on the verge of battle.

"You shall wait for me to join you," Voro said. "For I shall lead this assault."

CHAPTER 32

"Enable stealth protocols," Commander Richard Lash ordered. "Prepare for transition to normal space."

"Yes, sir." Lieutenant Commander Julian Waters turned to the *Dusk*'s bridge officers. "External power sources offline," he said. "Lock ablative baffles. Secure engine dampers."

Lieutenant Bethany Durruno at her NAV station cross-checked the calculations for the slipspace-to-normal transition. "We're almost there, sir. Thirty seconds."

At the OP-SENSOR station, Lieutenant Joe Yang said, "Rigged for dark and silent running, sir. Five points confirmed."

Lash personally rechecked everything on the display by the captain's chair. All shipshape. So why did he have a feeling everything was about to hit the fan? Answer: in his short tenure as commanding officer of the *Dusk,* imminent disaster had been the norm. He expected no less this time.

"Go to normal space," he ordered. "Start the clock."

Waters set the chronometer and said, "Time on mission: fifteen and counting."

Lash glanced at his old-fashioned spring-and-gear wristwatch, a gift from his dad when he'd graduated from OSC. *"Keep it wound, Son."*

He checked: it was indeed wound tight.

The bridge lights dimmed to red as the ship's power shunted to the Shaw-Fujikawa translight drive's particle accelerator, and it ripped a hole back into the normal three dimensions of interstellar space.

The trio of blackened viewscreens sparkled with stars. One point of light was unusually bright. The main screen centered on this star, and astronomical parameters streamed alongside Zeta Doradus. Elliptical orbits traced of the six innermost planets.

"Positive fix on stellar references," Lieutenant Durruno said. "We're slightly off target, sir. Three million kilometers."

"Move us in," Lash ordered, "one-third full ahead on intercept course for the fourth planet. Tell Lieutenant Commander Cho in Engineering to start recharging the slipspace capacitors."

"Aye, sir," she said.

She bit her lower lip, and Commander Lash knew that meant she was nervous, too . . . sensing something amiss already on this mission.

The *Dusk* skimmed through space, black on black; only a telltale flickering of the background stars gave the slightest indication that anything was there.

Waters glanced at the chronometer and whispered, "Sir, thirteen minutes to go. Barely time to *close* on the target while running dark, let alone gather a detailed analysis."

Time was never on Commander Lash's side. Either there was too much time and his crew waited days or weeks stealthed or, as was now the case, they had to rush and balance gathering accurate data with remaining hidden. It was a hell of a choice: The fate of thousands' lives and eight other ships depended on this. On the other hand, if the *Dusk* were detected, no intel would get back. Not to mention, they'd all be dead.

Eighteen months of crew attrition and constant action were now taking their toll on Lash's officers. He watched Lieutenants Durruno and Yang and saw the combat fatigue mirrored in their glazed, dark-circled eyes. They had endured endless waiting—punctuated by salvos of Covenant plasma and laser fire. They'd witnessed the fall of four colonies and the cremation of billions. They were close to the edge. For that matter, so was he.

"We have our orders," Lash told Waters. "Fifteen minutes in and then we transition back. We'll do our best with the time allotted."

They had limited time for two reasons. First, past fifteen minutes detection by Covenant sensors grew at a statistically geometric rate. Second, after fifteen minutes the *Dusk*'s ability to find the rest of their battle group in slipspace would *exponentially* decrease.

Lash sat back, and in the fine tradition of prowler commanders everywhere, he practiced exuding patience.

The *Dusk*'s journey back to Earth had occurred in record time. They had caught a wake in slipstream space, one indeterminably larger then the Covenant wake they had followed. Their NAV-AI reported: SOLITON-LIKE WAVE PATTERNS DETECTED NEAR HALO CONSTRUCT. Lash had no idea what had caused it, only reported it to Lord Hood . . . who had considered his report of slipspace wakes and then immediately ordered them to attempt the same trick and follow the Spartan strike team's vector until they reached remote station *Tripoli*. There they would rendevous with a battle group under the command of Admiral Carl "Buster" Patterson, provide assistance to the Spartan team, and hopefully obtain new technologies that would turn the tide of this war.

Lash had heard rumors of the Spartans' audacious actions, boarding a Covenant ship, nuking its sister ship, destroying the *Tallo Negro del Maíz* orbital stalk in the process. The stuff legends were made of.

He was more than happy to stay in the shadows. No vid broadcasts about his glorious death, thank you.

The *Dusk* had had no chance at Earth to take on a full crew or resupply—instead they transitioned immediately to Slipstream space to catch the rapidly dissipating wake of the Spartan-captured Covenant ship.

"Maximum range for the X-ELF radar system," Lieutenant Yang announced. "Eight minutes on the clock, sir."

"Start a high-resolution series," Lash told him, "planet surface to the Lagrange points."

"Coming online now," Yang said. He straightened. "Two contacts in high planetary orbit! Covenant destroyers."

Silhouettes flashed on Lash's display, confirming Yang's analysis.

"Heavy destroyers," Lash murmured. Enough concentrated firepower to take out a dozen UNSC prowlers.

Waters asked, "Could one be the Spartans' ship? We could send a narrow-band encrypted ping, sir."

"Anything is possible with Spartans," Lash said, "but it's not our job to communicate with them. We're here to gather data for Admiral Patterson's strategic consideration."

Waters closed his eyes, thinking a moment, and finally said, "Aye, sir."

The Lieutenant Commander wanted to get *into* the fight. It was a deadly sentiment for the officer of a prowler. Lash sympathized. Waters had long ago lost his wife and children on Harvest. But stealth was their only defense against such a force. Vengeance had no place on his ship.

"Debris in orbit," Yang said. "Metallic structures. Unknown alloy composition on spectroscopic analysis."

"Recent combat?" Waters asked.

"Aye, sir, residual plasma detected. However . . . insufficient tonnage to account for even one Covenant destroyer."

"Come to course zero two zero by three two five," Commander Lash ordered Lieutenant Durruno. "Cut engines and shunt the power to recharging slipspace capacitors."

She focused her laserlike attention on her NAV controls. "Coming about. New trajectory set. Our inertia will take us in for a tight orbit." All trace of her fatigue vanished and she tapped a rapid-fire message on her keyboard, and then replied, "Lieutenant Commander Cho reports capacitors at fifty percent. They'll be hot in six minutes."

"Go active camouflage," Commander Lash told Waters.

Lash forced himself to remain collected. He felt like a fraud, but he had to try to maintain the illusion of confidence for the sake of his officers. He would never let them know how scared he was.

"Active camouflage online," Waters said. "Texture buffer full. Four minutes on the clock."

The *Dusk* dove toward the twilight demarcation line of the planet. The normally matte-black ablative coating on her dorsal surfaces flickered with patterns of cirrostratus and lapis ocean and glowing orange sunset.

"Radiologicals?" Lash asked.

"No Argus-effect beta radiation detected in the magnetosphere," Yang answered. "The Spartan team has not detonated any FENRIS warheads."

"Is that a good, or bad, thing?" Waters murmured.

Lash wasn't sure. If the Spartans had been here, he'd expect there to be a swath of destruction. "Planetary energy sources?" he asked Yang.

"Nothing, sir," Yang answered as he pored over the data flashing on his screens. "We still have one-quarter of the planet's surface to scan, though. It will take seven minutes in this orbit to cover that area."

"One minute on the clock," Waters told him. He hesitated as if he had more to say . . . but didn't.

Lash knew what he wanted: a full orbit, more time, and a close pass near those Covenant combat assets. Waters wanted to be a hero.

"We're following Admiral Patterson's orders to the letter," Lash said. "We've got two Covenant warships on the other side of this planet. No detectable sign of Spartans. No nukes triggered. And we haven't been seen. That's enough."

Lash locked gazes with Waters.

Waters looked away, frowned, but nodded. He said, "Rig for slipspace transition."

"Aye aye," Lieutenant Durruno said. She sighed, visibly relaxing at the decision to leave. "Matrix calculations input. Ready for transition in seventeen seconds."

Lash fidgeted in the captain's chair. It was the right move to leave. If they executed a full orbit, their luck would most certainly run out. And waiting for their recon data in slipspace was Patterson's battle group of eight ships.

Two Covenant destroyers were a threat, but it was accepted that three-to-one odds in the UNSC's favor against Covenant forces was an even match. Four to one? They rarely had such odds in this war.

So why did this feel all wrong?

"Initiate slipspace transition," Commander Lash ordered.

Around the *Dusk* space flashed blue and white and the stars vanished.

Eight UNSC ships dropped from Slipstream space into black interstellar vacuum and there was a fireworks show of blue Cherenkov radiation and spiraling subatomic particle decays.

Commander Lash used this to his advantage.

"Set new course to port, perpendicular to fleet attack vector," he ordered Lieutenant Durruno.

"Aye, sir." Under the red glow of the bridge's battle lighting, his officers looked more alive now . . . and more scared.

The stealthed *Dusk* moved away from the destroyers, carrier, and cruiser of Admiral Patterson's battle group.

Lash wasn't running away—a sentiment he found himself repeating ever since he had witnessed the events at the Halo ring.

He had volunteered the *Dusk* to go back and scout the planet on a second recon mission. But the Admiral had told him there was no time. He was going to "catch those Covenant bastards with their pants down" and strike while they were near the planet's gravity well.

With the odds in his favor it was a sound tactic. Still, it bothered Lash that the Admiral committed so many lives without a complete picture.

"Move us into an elliptical orbit around the dark side of Onyx," Lash ordered. "Set apogee to fifty thousand kilometers. Ahead one-third power."

"New course set, sir." Lieutenant Durruno turned to face him.

Looking pained, she opened her mouth to speak, hesitated, and then quickly said, "I beg your pardon, Commander. I thought we had orders to remain clear of the combat."

"We will," Lash said, "but we're going to finish that planetary scan." He moved to the NAV station and set one hand on Bethany's shoulder. "Just take us in nice and easy."

Her eyes locked forward on her screens. "Yes, sir."

To Lieutenant Yang he said, "Monitor the engine thermals and push us past one-third power . . . right up to the dark-line limit."

Yang swallowed, and then replied, "Aye aye, Commander."

Lash danced a fine line. He wanted speed *and* invisibility.

"Action on-screen!" Lieutenant Commander Waters announced.

On the central viewer flashes appeared in the dark. Admiral Patterson had launched his alpha strike.

"Magnification forty," Lash ordered.

The two Covenant destroyers snapped on center screen. Scattered Archer missiles detonated harmlessly on their shields. The ships turned out of orbital alignments to face their enemy, and in doing so, closed ranks.

Three white spheres popped behind the vessels—expanded and enveloped the now-clustered enemy destroyers. Jets of supercharged ions funneled downward into the planet's magnetosphere.

"Perfect placement of the nukes," Yang murmured, glancing between the viewscreen and his instruments. "Maximum destruction and radiation trapped by the planet so the fleet can move in."

". . . And finish them off." Waters rubbed his hands together in unconscious anticipation.

The fireballs cooled to red and a single sleek silhouette emerged: one of the Covenant destroyers had survived. Plasma charges launched toward the center of the UNSC battle group—directly at Admiral Patterson's flagship carrier, the *Stalingrad*.

The prows of the UNSC ships flared as their magnetic accelerator cannons fired.

Lines of flame and superheated slugs crossed the space between the two forces.

The UNSC destroyer *Glasgow Kiss* accelerated in front of the fleet; the narrow craft turned sideways, placing itself between the incoming plasma and the *Stalingrad*. A dozen escape pods popped from her hull as the ship caught three of the four lances of fire. The hull heated for an instant, and then shattered into fragments.

"Track those pods," Lash ordered Lieutenant Yang.

"Aye, sir."

On-screen, the *Stalingrad* took a direct hit on her port side. Plasma etched through the meters of titanium-A armor plating like a blowtorch through rice paper, and her center amidships decks vented.

The UNSC fleet MAC rounds impacted on the Covenant destroyer. The slugs battered through the ship's reconstituted shields, and then through the hull, knocking it back so violently it tumbled out of control into the planet's atmosphere, leaving a trail of turbulence and fire.

Its engines flared and accelerated into an extremely low orbit—away from the fleet.

"Cowards," Waters muttered.

"I wonder," Lash replied. "We've survived five UNSC-Covenant engagements." He stared into deep space, remembering the carnage, and that the UNSC had only won *one* of those battles. "The Covenant do not simply run away, Lieutenant Commander. They might disengage to regroup, but when outgunned and outnumbered . . . they go down swinging."

There was only one conceivable reason this lone Covenant destroyer would turn tail.

Lash told Lieutenant Durruno, "We're going bright. Increase speed to flank. Hold your course."

"Sir . . . ?" She leaned over her controls. "Aye, sir."

Lash keyed SHIPCOM to Engineering. "Lieutenant Commander Cho, drain the slipspace capacitors and route the power to engines. I want them one hundred thirty percent hot."

What had felt like victory on the bridge a moment ago faded and Lash's officer again appeared wary and weary.

There was silence over the SHIPCOM and then Cho replied, "Routing power now."

The *Dusk* was out in the open, and Lash was violating the first rule of any prowler captain: stay hidden.

But every instinct he had screamed that the Covenant wouldn't be this easy to defeat, and that they'd overlooked something of vital importance.

Admiral Patterson's seven ships chased after the single Covenant vessel. They vanished as the *Dusk* arced around the planet.

Lash returned to the captain's chair and uneasily settled into it.

Waters stood next to him and whispered, "Tell me you know what you're doing, Richard."

Lash leaned forward and said nothing.

"Coming up on the dark side of Onyx in fifteen seconds," Lieutenant Yang said. "Ten . . . five . . . three, two, one."

The planet's nighttime face appeared on every viewscreen, dark save the glimmering clouds on the edge of twilight.

"Hot spot!" Yang shouted. "On the horizon: twenty-seven degrees north, one hundred eighteen east. Recalibrating thermals to cut through atmospheric distortion."

On the main viewscreen a wavering image resolved into

twenty Covenant warships—climbing at flank speed through the atmosphere—on an intercept vector toward Admiral Patterson's fleet.

Lash jumped to his feet. "Cut engine power to one-third," he said. "Reenable stealth protocols. Come to new bearing: polar orbit. Get me a clear sight line to the *Stalingrad*."

"New heading, aye," Lieutenant Durruno said, her voice straining as she calculated the orbit. "Brace for correction burn at one-third power."

The *Dusk* pitched and tilted into a polar alignment. Engines rumbled and the prowler arced up toward the ice caps of Onyx.

"Zenith in twenty-three seconds," Durruno said.

Lash tuned to Lieutenant Commander Waters. "Action report."

Waters's gaze was already locked onto his display. "Nothing. Covenant fleet is ignoring us."

Lash should have been relieved; they could have destroyed the *Dusk* with a few laser shots. Going dark was the right thing to do. But despite his years of training in evading the enemy, Lash wished the Covenant *had* turned. It might have given Patterson a few extra seconds to see what was coming.

He waited fifteen seconds—the most agonizing quarter minute of his life—watching the clouds, landmasses, and oceans of Onyx pass under his ship.

The *Dusk* finally crested the pole and the stars—as well as Admiral Patterson's fleet—reappeared on the forward screen.

Only a hundred kilometers apart the UNSC vessels fired all magnetic accelerator cannons and launched a volley of Archer missiles at the Covenant ships racing toward them. The meteoric rounds blazed through the atmosphere leaving smoking scars.

Lasers flashed from the Covenant ships destroying incoming missiles, but they couldn't stop the point-blank-fired MAC slugs.

Seven MAC rounds struck the two lead destroyers in the Covenant line, shattered their shields, dented the armor, and pounded through hulls, crippling the vessels so they aborted their attack run as they were caught in the planet's gravity pull. One ship's engines flared, overloading as its captain attempted a survivable landing. One lone destroyer, however, spun in orbit, its forward momentum neutralized.

A victory. Lash knew it would be short-lived.

The enemy outnumbered them almost three to one with superior weapons and defensive shields. And the proximity of a gravity well meant Patterson was backed into a corner. It would be a slaughter.

Plasma erupted from the Covenant fleet that looked like a solar flare as it boiled through the vacuum of space toward the UNSC ships.

Patterson was no fool. He didn't attempt to evade at this range. Instead the engines of his ships heated and they angled into a lower orbit—accelerating *into* the attack.

This would do nothing to stop guided plasma, but they'd emerge going much faster, possibly fast enough to avoid a second attack.

The plasma tracked the UNSC ships as they dove. A split second before it impacted, energy projectors lit on the Covenant ships and dazzling beams of pure white radiation illuminated Patterson's ships—so bright, the scene froze for an instant, burned in Lash's retinas.

Explosions and showers of molten titanium filled the viewscreens and rapidly expanded into a cloud of sparks and smoke and the tumbling cracked husks of UNSC ships.

Miraculously five human warships rocketed from the center of this destruction, streaming fire and venting atmosphere—thundering into the heart of the Covenant fleet.

A UNSC destroyer, *Iwo Jima*, grazed a Covenant carrier three times its size, deflected off its shields, and careened into two other Covenant destroyers. The UNSC vessel erupted from inside, reactor overload and single nuclear warhead detonated in an act of self-destruction. The fireball enveloped eight nearby enemy ships . . . of which six survived behind their shimmering energy shields.

The Covenant fleet was in disarray, slowed and paused to regroup.

Patterson's ships continued to accelerate and arc around to the far side of Onyx.

They had survived . . . at least for one more orbital pass.

"Additional contacts," Yang said. He half stood from his seat and hovered over the sensor board. "Rapidly ascending from the planet's surface. Intercept course for the Covenant fleet."

Lash's heart sank into his stomach. "Reinforcements," he said.

Yang was silent, studying his display, and then he said, "No, sir. Look, on your screen."

Lash tuned the tiny captain's chair display toward him and examined a ship silhouette. The computer extrapolated a rough three-dimensional model of three boons, and a sphere with no connecting structures.

"They're three meters stem to stern," Yang said. "Passive radar is picking up *thousands* of them."

The main viewscreen snapped to a medium-orbital vantage and Lash watched as a cloud of the tiny craft coalesced into three octahedral shapes.

The Covenant ships turned toward this new threat, abandoning their pursuit of Admiral Patterson's battle group. Lateral lines heated and plasma barrages arced toward the approaching alien formations.

Fire rained upon the leading eight-sided construction and an energy shield coalesced that looked like gold-dappled water. The plasma hesitated there as if caught in a magnetic field. It heated to yellow-, white-hot, and then tinged blue and ultraviolet. The plasma melted through the shield, and then passed harmlessly inside the formation.

"Plasma capture?" Waters whispered in awe. "That's a hell of a trick."

The spheres within the alien formation glowed, and from each, scintillating beams shot through the atmosphere toward the Covenant ships comprising the leading edge of their fleet.

A hundred energy beams penetrated Covenant shields and sliced through their hulls. The superheated plasma inside the alien formation then streamed along the beams, coiling and writhing snakelike, and painted the damaged Covenant ships, vaporizing hulls, melting decks and superstructures like they were plastic film.

Three Covenant destroyers detonated under this combined fire.

The plasma dissipated throughout the upper atmosphere, filling the near vacuum with a fading purple haze.

The surviving Covenant ships struggled to accelerate out of the gravity well.

The other alien ships, however, were faster and gained on them.

Two Covenant vessels spun about and fired their energy projectors and lasers at the lead alien formation.

The octahedral's shields crackled with static and dissipated. The tiny craft within the formation bloomed into fireballs.

The remaining two alien formations fired upon this Covenant rear guard—energy beams cut their shields and blasted them to atoms.

ERIC NYLUND

The Covenant ploy, however, had worked.

The balance of their fleet had escaped the gravity of Onyx and outdistanced their persuaders.

Lash's mind reeled. Who were these new aliens? Or was this a weapon captured and controlled by the Spartans sent ahead of them?

The Covenant's tactics also confused Lash. They hadn't used a slipspace jump—something he was certain they would have done to escape rather than sacrifice two ships.

Suddenly, everything in this war had changed. Commander Lash wasn't sure if it was for the better, or for the worse.

"Break orbit . . . dead slow," Lash whispered. "Move us to Lagrange-Three. Lieutenant Yang, continuous check on our stealth profile. Durruno, keep on the passive radar and watch for escape pods."

"What the hell are they?" Waters asked, staring at the viewscreen.

The octahedral formations drifted apart and the drones spread out in the upper atmosphere.

Lash shook his head.

"Transmission on the UNSC E-Band, sir," Yang said, straining to listen into his earbud. "From the planet surface. Someone is broadcasting in the open."

"To the UNSC forces in orbit over the planet designated XF-063, this is the Artificial Intelligence Endless Summer, MIL AI ID 4279. If you want to survive the next three minutes, answer this hail."

Lash and Waters exchanged startled looks.

"Message repeats, sir," Yang said. "Encoded scheme in the carrier wave indicates a reply via encryption protocol JERICHO."

Lash was uncertain what to do. Patterson's fleet was on the wrong side of the planet to receive this message. Covenant and alien forces of unknown disposition were too close for comfort. And for the moment, as long as the *Dusk* was silent, they were safe.

"Drop a BLACK WIDOW COM satellite," Lash ordered, "and then move us off thirty thousand meters and route a single beam. Send this: 'To AI MIL ID 4279, this is Commander Richard Lash of the UNSC prowler *Dusk*. We're listening. . . .'"

SECTION VII

RECLAIMERS

CHAPTER 33

Kurt turned to Dr. Halsey. "The door, Doctor."

She tapped a Forerunner icon.

A doorway slid open.

"Use this thing," Kurt said, and waved at the entire holographic map room, "and find a way to the Spartans in cryo. If you can't do that, then find us a route out of this place—underground, small enough so those Sentinels can't follow."

Annoyance crossed Dr. Halsey's features as she manipulated the map room and zoomed about the internal structure of the planet—layers of rooms, machines, cutaway blueprints, connecting rods and spherical joints, corridors and vast chambers—rapidly flit through space.

"There are a few things I must first check, Lieutenant

Commander." Dr. Halsey tilted her glasses so the reflecting glare of the holographic images shielded her eyes.

"Will," Kurt said over the COM. "Guard her . . . and keep her on task."

The last thing he needed in a combat situation was Dr. Halsey going rogue and not following orders.

"Understood," Will replied.

"Kelly, Tom, defend the corridor," Kurt said. "The rest of you, topside with me."

Green acknowledgment lights burned on his heads-up display, and Kurt led the balance of his team back to the stairs.

Halfway up the spiral, Kurt contacted Dante. "I want explosives on that dome. Get up there ASAP."

Dante replied with a grunt over the COM. "Halfway up the rope already, sir."

It pleased Kurt to hear his SPARTAN-IIIs were two steps ahead of him.

He rounded the last curve of the stairs and stepped onto the landing pad.

Kurt motioned to the Spartans and then to the four ropes strung to the archways overhead. Ash, Olivia, and Lucy clambered up the braided monolines.

He then met Chief Mendez by the dropship.

"Everything's ready to go, sir," Mendez said, "except the FEN-RIS warheads. We'll need more time to cut the rest of them down for transport." He nodded over the edge. "Rigged six zip lines over there, just in case we needed a quick way down."

"Good thinking, Chief."

Kurt removed the thumb-sized datapad for his gauntlet, and handed it to Mendez. "Prime the warhead detonators and synchronize firing codes through this pad. With Sentinels and Covenant inbound, I want all my options open."

Mendez's face became a mask of steel. "Yes, sir. After that where do you want me?"

Mendez was a crack shot, but he was unarmored and slower than the others. Keeping him close would risk everyone's lives.

"I need you with Dr. Halsey, Chief. Follow the lights. Let Kelly know you're coming. She's dug in."

To his credit the Chief didn't show any disappointment—just a moment's hesitation before he replied, "Yes, sir."

Kurt grabbed an ascension line and pulled himself up, rapidly climbing to an archway twenty meters above the landing pad.

Linda lent him a hand and helped him onto the ledge. She eased back into her position on the far side of the arch, lay flat, and sighted through her sniper scope.

Kurt crouched on the opposite side and scanned the city. Under any other circumstance the nighttime vista of alien architecture and the shifting Sentinel lights would have filled him with awe. Now, though, he was only concerned with surviving.

The airspace was clear.

Not wanting to risk using even the single beam, Kurt waved at Fred on the adjacent arch and made a horizontal circle gesture in the air, asking, *Where are they?*

Fred held up a hand.

A mated Sentinel pair silently glided past the open arch—ten meters in front of Kurt. The spheres within the booms moved back and forth. It continued its orbit around the dome, moving out of view, and another Sentinel pair appeared along the same trajectory.

They weren't attacking, yet they had to sense the Spartans inside. It almost looked as if they were guarding this dome.

Kurt steeled himself, resisting the urge to shoot such a close target. What good would it have done? He couldn't penetrate those shields.

He felt vibrations, and in the distance lights flickered along the rim of the crater.

The bulbous hull of a Covenant Seraph single ship appeared, then another Seraph appeared, then seven more . . . and then two dozen flying in formation.

Kurt held his breath, hoping this was just a search party.

A line of Covenant destroyers followed, so massive they blotted out the stars in the night sky. A second wave of cetacean-shaped vessels resolved, and then a Covenant carrier flew on overwatch, surrounded by a hundred Seraph fighters.

Kurt had never seen so many enemy ships so close—all of them headed toward his position. Twenty warships. The subsonic thrum of their antigrav units made his insides go soft.

The Sentinels circling the dome moved to intercept the new threat.

Pinpoint laser artillery shot them out of the air.

The two leading destroyers peeled off the battle group and drifted over the dome. Shafts of sparkling purple light flashed from their undersides—antigrav transporter beams. A hundred armored Elite shock troopers streamed to the ground.

Kurt looked for Dante and spotted him high on the dome's inner surface attached with a rigging of rope and suction climbers. He pressed blobs of C-12 onto the patterned stone.

Kurt directed his single beam at the COM relay on the landing pad. "Will, what's Dr. Halsey's status?"

"She's found something," Will replied. "Says she needs ten minutes to get it ready."

"Get *what* ready? Never mind. We don't have ten minutes," Kurt told him. "Prepare for a hot reception."

Kurt watched Covenant assets pour down the transport beams and assemble in the city: more Elites with plasma rifles, titanlike Hunter pairs wielding fuel-rod cannons and nearly impenetrable shields, plasma turrets and their Grunt tenders, and a monstrous Scarab walker.

Spirit and Phantom dropships escorted by Banshee fliers buzzed the dome.

It was an invading army.

Kurt motioned his Spartans down the lines to the landing pad. They had to fall back—fast.

His teams silently slid to safety. After all had gone down their rope, Kurt followed.

Blue plasma splashed across the archway ledges.

Kurt loosened his grip on the rope and free-fell a dozen meters, squeezing the brake at the last instant before he hit the floor. He rolled and dove behind the starboard hull of their ship.

Lasers stitched the stone platform behind him.

Six dropships and their Banshee escorts entered through the archways. They circled, rapidly descending.

Fred and Lucy crouched, hefted SPNKr missile launchers, and fired.

The missiles streaked up and detonated on the cockpits of the incoming dropships. The ships bobbled out of control and crashed into the dome wall.

The other four dropships landed hard; Elites jumped out, took position behind the hulls, and opened fire.

The air filled with crisscross patterns of needler shards, plasma bolts, and streaks of MA5B and MA5K tracers.

Kurt didn't want to leave the FENRIS warheads behind, but there was no way they could hold this position. Their cover was poor, and they'd have to contend with more air support soon.

He started to order their retreat, but Covenant plasma spattered nearby, and a square meter of their dropship's hull blasted away.

A Hunter pair emerged and they hunkered down behind their overlapping battle-plate shields.

Linda took aim at the monstrous pair and waited for them to present a target.

One Hunter eased its fuel-rod cannon around the edge of its impenetrable shields—green energized rounds glowing with deadly radiation—and fired.

Fred jumped from cover, his MJOLNIR armor ablaze as if it was burning phosphorus.

The Hunter hit him dead center in his chest, a blast that would have destroyed their dropship. His energy shields flared brighter, failed, and Fred crumpled to the floor, his armor smoking.

"Cover fire!" Kurt shouted.

The Spartans sprayed the Elites and the Hunters, who turtled behind their shields.

Dante and Lucy darted out and grabbed Fred, dragging him back.

A fire team of five Elites popped from cover and unleashed a torrent of plasma and needles. They were riddled with bullets and dropped—but one managed to shoot at Dante and a plasma bolt glanced his side. He flinched, but didn't stop pulling Fred to safety.

The Hunter pair peeked around their overlapped shields.

Linda fired methodically—orange blood spattered from one Hunter's exposed midsection.

The Hunters dropped behind their shields, screaming, but still standing

"Over the edge, everyone," Kurt ordered.

One by one the Spartans slipped to the edge and jumped into the darkness.

Kurt set three grenades on the floor, grabbed a zip line, and rappelled down. One wide swing into the open and he pendulated back, landing on the curve of spiral stairs under the platform.

Dull explosions whumped overhead and the ropes fell away.

Kurt saw that Dante and Lucy supported a groggy Fred between them. Fred's MJOLNIR armor was carbonized black. His bio signs were erratic but strong. All their bio signs were pushing the redline.

"Blow the dome," Kurt told Dante.

Dante nodded, passed Fred over to Mark's shoulder, and he limped to the far edge of the stairs, remote detonator in hand.

Kurt motioned for Olivia to take point, and the rest of the Spartans followed her down the stairs.

Thunder echoed off the dome walls, and chunks of rock thudded onto the landing platform overhead. Elites screamed and blue plasma detonations lit the air.

Three revolutions around the stairs and Olivia held up a hand. They all halted.

"Gotcha in my sights," Kelly said over TEAMCOM. "Stand by, defusing the mines . . . okay, come ahead."

Kurt and the others entered the chamber. Kurt noticed the LOTUS antitank mines stuck on this room's walls and ceiling, making it a good kill zone.

Will and Kelly crouched to either side of the opening to the bridge of light, hidden by its glare.

Kurt did a quick count. All present . . . save Dante.

Dante brought up the rear, limping into the room, one hand holding his side. He stood straight and saluted Kurt.

"Sir," he said, "I think I got nicked."

Dante's bio signs flatlined and he collapsed.

Kurt dropped to Dante's side and unlatched his SPI chest piece. He'd seen him grazed by plasma on his left side, and sure enough, there were second- and third-degree burns there that had boiled off the liquid-ballistic layer. Under his arm and across his chest a half dozen needler shards had lodged and detonated. The bones of his rib cage were exposed, and deeper, black congealing blood pooled.

He was limp. Cold. Bio signs flat.

Dante was dead. There was nothing Kurt could do.

Kurt had watched Shane, Robert, and Jane die. He had listened to Tom tell how Beta got wiped out on Pegasi Delta. Now Dante. One more gone on his watch.

It would be easy to blame Ackerson and Parangosky for the deaths of his Spartans. Designed for high-risk missions, they were all going to die, weren't they? And Kurt had played along and followed orders. What other option was there?

He examined his hands, covered in the Spartan blood.

Linda set a hand on Kurt's shoulder. "We'll bring him with us."

His training reasserted itself. Move—fight—live. The alternative was to sit here and join Dante.

Kurt gently set Dante onto the floor.

He had to focus. They had a mission: get the Forerunner technology. Get the rest of his team out alive. Kurt promised the scales would be balanced for Dante. Somehow. He'd see to it himself if he had to.

Linda and Olivia moved to Dante and picked him up.

"Grab your gear and follow," Kurt said to Kelly.

He marched over the bridge of light and entered the holographic map room.

Dr. Halsey stood at the Forerunner console, hieroglyphs swarming over its surface, the symbols' meaning changing as they aligned into higher-dimensional patterns for a moment, then rearranged into new kaleidoscopic formations.

Olivia and Linda set Dante's body down.

Mark, Ash, and Holly knelt next to him and gingerly set his hands together on his chest.

"Dr. Halsey?" Kurt said.

She held up one hand and with the other she furiously typed on the laptop that Mendez held for her. The laptop's tiny projection pad emitted a mote of light that flitted among the symbols like a bee gathering nectar.

Mendez handed Kurt the thumb-sized datapad. "Codes locked and ready to go, sir."

Kurt checked it out: Detonation codes for the FENRIS warheads streamed across the tiny screen. He slipped it into his gauntlet's data port and clenched his fist.

"There's so much here," Dr. Halsey whispered. "I've confirmed this world is part of the Forerunners' plan together with the Halo rings—their 'sword' and 'shield.' Other parts still elude me. There is a reference to the 'ark.' I have yet to determine if something went wrong . . . why they are not here."

"Doctor," Kurt said more firmly, and he stepped closer. "We have a Covenant armada over our heads, and an army about to swarm through this building. Is there a way out?"

"Yes and no," she replied, still not looking at him. "There is a room in the core of this world," she explained, "where the Forerunners were to secure something precious. Perhaps the technologies you seek. The room is normally inaccessible, but the arming of the Halo rings triggered something within this planet." She ran her fingers across overlapping streams of hieroglyphics, struggling to read. "There is an entrance to this room, open now, but closing. In one hour seventeen minutes the core entrance will shut. Forever."

ERIC NYLUND

"Core of the planet?" Kurt said. "There is no way to get to the core that fast."

"We must gather what is within, and make our escape." She finally looked up at him, excitement glistening in her eyes. "And there is indeed a way to get there. This map room can access a slipspace translocation system similar to the one Cortana used on the Halo ring."

She pointed down.

Kurt saw they stood upon a matte-black surface flush with the floor. It was four meters wide and had seven sides. His gaze seemed to slide deeper into the surface like he was looking at something infinitely deep . . . or nothing at all.

He blinked, looked away. "Slipspace translocation? A teleportation system."

"In effect, yes."

The room shook and dust rained from the ceiling.

Dr. Halsey focused past Kurt into the room. She made a slight cutting motion over several gold symbols.

The bridge of light connecting to the outer chamber vanished. The door to the map room closed.

She spotted Dante and her face drained of color. "Oh . . ." she whispered.

"You must get us to the other SPARTAN-IIIs locked in cryo first," Kurt told her.

"Of course, I believe I understand the intricacies of the transportation system well enough," she said. "I must caution you, though, not to detonate the FENRIS warheads. The EMP will render the system inoperable."

"Understood," Kurt said. "Just activate this 'translocation' device. Get me to my Spartans."

"There is still so much to learn here," Dr. Halsey said. "I suggest you leave me. I can—"

A tremendous shudder shook the room. Chunks of rock rained from the ceiling. Dr. Halsey fell, and Kurt caught her, shielded her with his back as baseball-sized stones bounced off the hardened plates of his SPI armor.

Outside the chamber there were four gut-jarring detonations—the LOTUS antitank mines Kelly had set up.

"We've run out of time, Doctor," Kurt said. "They are here."

She stood, brushed the dust from her lab coat, and straightened her glasses. "So it appears." She tapped a handful of symbols. "There is a translocation platform"—she consulted the holographic map—"within a kilometer of the other Spartans."

Beyond the holographic map of Onyx, the wall of the room cracked as the stones heated to dull red.

The Spartans positioned themselves between the wall and Dr. Halsey.

Kurt stepped directly in front of the doctor and Mendez took up a position at his flank, his MA5B leveled.

Ash dug into his pack and passed out Jackal shield gauntlets to his team. Together they crouched before the SPARTAN-IIs, forming a shield wall.

Dr. Halsey shifted the Forerunner symbols. "There," she whispered.

The heating wall exploded and rubble bounced off the Spartans' shields. From the breach in the wall, plasma bolts and crystal shards crisscrossed the air.

The Jackal shields deflected it all—but were draining fast.

Will, Kelly, and Fred popped up and sprayed suppressing fire into the darkness.

Linda maneuvered between them, leveled her sniper rifle, and squeezed off three rounds.

The enemy ceased fire.

"Now would be good, Doctor," Kurt said.

"Activating," Dr. Halsey said. "There may be some disorientation." She reached for a glowing symbol.

Kurt's COM crackled to life and Endless Summer's voice filled his helmet. "Come in, Ambrose," the AI said. "I have a high-priority mission redirect."

He grabbed Dr. Halsey's hand.

The mote of light on her laptop stretched into a bare-chested Indian warrior.

"I thought you were destroyed," Kurt said.

"The Sentinels did find and destroy the COM launcher, but I had my escape well planned." He held his hand apart and a globe appeared. It rotated to the north polar region, zoomed into ice fields, and then down a volcanic caldera. "These coordinates are the latest thermal images provided by a UNSC prowler in high orbit. You must go there. Now."

"We have other matters to take care of first," Kurt told him.

Technically Endless Summer had the authority to order him anywhere it liked, but under the circumstances, Kurt wasn't listening to an ONI-controlled AI—not when his people's lives were at stake.

"This site is a Sentinel manufacturing facility," Endless Summer said, glowering. "In orbit there is a battle raging between a Covenant fleet and these alien craft, one that will likely destroy the Covenant forces."

"Great," Kurt replied. "Let them."

A new volley of plasma bolts streamed through the breached wall.

Ash's shield unit sputtered and overloaded. He rolled flat to avoid getting burned.

Fred and Kelly tossed grenades. Distant explosions and screams echoed.

Another section of wall heated . . . and another. The Covenant weren't going to give up so easily. They'd open as many holes as they needed to penetrate their defenses.

"You don't understand," Endless Summer said. "Once the alien forces have finished with the Covenant ships, they will focus on the lesser threat: the UNSC battle group in orbit. The one sent here to rescue *you*."

The strategic picture instantly shifted in Kurt's mind. The fate of this battle group and his Spartans were linked. Save the ships and they'd have a way off this rock. Fail . . . and they'd be stuck here fighting Sentinels and Covenant ground forces until hell froze. Rescuing the other SPARTAN-IIIs in cryo would have to wait.

"This Sentinel factory produces a new unit every six seconds," the AI explained. "At that rate they will soon overwhelm *any* force the USNC can send."

"Can you find this place?" Kurt asked Dr. Halsey. "Can you move us there?"

She chewed on her lower lip. Her hands moved quickly over symbols, rotating the holographic projection of the planet around them at a dizzying rate.

"Got it," she said.

Endless Summer bowed and winked off.

Kurt motioned for the Spartans to fall back to the center of the room.

"Do it," he said. "Now."

The walls of the chamber exploded inward.

CHAPTER 34

Kurt crawled to the edge where Linda and Chief Mendez had
posted, and peered out upon the vast factory, although the
word "factory" was wholly inappropriate to describe the engineering wonderland.

From his perch stretched a cavernous space so large that he detected the slight arc of the planet's curve in the distance. The roof
was beyond the range finder on Linda's Oracle sniper scope, and
thin black clouds drifted two-thirds of the way from the ceiling.

A machine the size of a battleship spewed a river of molten
alloy into the air. This liquefied metal arced up and then cascaded into a hollow tower that pulsed with bioluminescent colors.
From the bottom tumbled countless tiny parts winking with light.
These parts were whisked away by ribbons of shimmering energy

so thick with distortion that Kurt couldn't see what occurred within . . . but from the opposite end streamed a never-ending procession of three-meter cylinders.

A pyramid five times the height of the Great Pyramid of Giza sat kilometers from Kurt's vantage. Instead of stone blocks, however, the structure was composed of floating golden spheres that turned and glowed with Forerunner hieroglyphs etched upon their surfaces.

Every six seconds a sphere from the apex of the pyramid ascended in a shaft of silver light. As it rose, the light intensified so even with maximum polarization on his faceplate Kurt could not discern what occurred there. When the sphere emerged, three rods accompanied it, all parts spinning in null gravity, flexing, until the pieces settled into their deadly recognizable configuration— a Sentinel of Onyx.

The new drone flew off into the clouds overhead . . . which Kurt could only estimate were thousands of completed units.

He blinked, wondering how they were going to shut this place down, and backed away from the edge.

Deeper in the shadows of the wide ledge sat a four-meter-diameter platform and a tiny holographic console: Dr. Halsey's "translocation" device.

She knelt in the middle, scanned the drifting symbols, and occasionally tapped one that interested her.

She had saved them—moved them from the map room to this Sentinel factory in the blink of an eye.

Fred, Kelly, and Will crouched around the platform, sniper rifles leveled. Not that shooting would have done any good, but at least they'd see any approaching Sentinel.

In front of the SPARTAN-IIs sat Ash, Holly, Olivia, Mark, Tom, and Lucy—a collection of mottled blacks and grays in their camouflaging SPI armor. They held Jackal shield gauntlets, ready to activate them to protect the others.

There had been serious nausea effects during the translocation. "Uncertainty errors," Dr. Halsey had called them.

It felt like Kurt's guts had been untwisted, and then dumped back into his body, inside out.

Holly had thrown up during the ride. She shook her head, clearing as much of her visor as possible. She didn't dare remove her helmet on hostile ground. There was a defogging vent that could dry the stuff, but that would take a few minutes.

She moved closer to Dante and set a hand on his shoulder. The young Spartan's body lay against the wall, shrouded in a thermal blanket.

Kurt looked away—it was too painful, and he was grateful that no one could see his twisted expression.

"Are you certain we can't use nukes?" Kurt whispered to Dr. Halsey.

"The electromagnetic pulse will disrupt the translocation system for days." She glanced at her wristwatch. "In sixty-eight minutes what was set in motion by the arming of Halo rings comes to completion on this world. The doorway to the core room of Onyx closes. Without the translocation system we will have no way to move in, recover the technologies, and escape."

Fred nodded out to the factory. "If those things get out, engage the UNSC fleet, and win, then we're stuck here."

Dr. Halsey unfolded her laptop computer. She tapped a few keys and then turned the screen to face the Spartans. On the display was an overhead view of the factory. "Here, here, and here," she said pointing. "Take out these structures and Sentinel production will halt indefinitely."

The targets were a crystal energy emitter the size of a three-story building, a U-shaped object as large as a UNSC cruiser, and a titanic sphere that extended ten thousand meters under the floor.

"Oh . . . easy," Kelly quipped.

"If we use the rest of the C-12," Will said, "and a few SPNKr missiles, we might be able to shatter that crystal."

Fred shook his head. "Look at the map scale. The targets are thirty kilometers apart. It's going to take too much time to get there and set up."

Holly coughed, and said, "So we have to be in three places simultaneously, and we need ten times the firepower we currently have. That's not possible."

Kurt winced at this, reminded of the "nothing is impossible for a Spartan" credo. How many lives had it cost to prove that? Maybe this time they *were* in an intractable tactical jam.

They all stared at the diagram, stumped.

". . . Rabbit," Ash whispered.

Kurt waited for an explanation, but Ash just continued to examine Dr. Halsey's map.

Kelly snapped her fingers. "I get it!" She snorted a single laugh. "Gutsy plan, kid."

Ash faced them. "We *can* be in three places at the same time," he said. "And we've got a hundred times the firepower we need." He turned and gazed out to the factory. "We're going to all be rabbits."

Ash resisted the urge to vomit. This was the stupidest plan he'd ever thought up. Too late now, though, to back out.

One moment he was on the ledge looking at Dr. Halsey while she manipulated holographic symbols—the next Team Saber was on the factory floor, his insides twisted around, and they were running for their lives.

From the clouds of Sentinels high overhead, a hundred pairs peeled off and dove after them.

The Spartans of Team Saber scattered, dodging under pipes and glowing crystalline conduits, moving as fast as they could. Speed was the only viable tactic now.

Ash spotted the target, looming so large before him that it seemed more geological feature than destructible object. The pyramid of spheres stretched up forever—millions and millions of golden balls bobbling in place, gently turning—all held in place by three massive subterranean force-field generators.

The floor was blue metal patterned with interlinked Forerunner symbols. Ahead, however, a glowing budge of silver shone like a beacon. Only ten meters across, this was the apex of one generator that extended ten thousand meters under the factory.

Overhead a fountain of molten metal arced kilometers through the air, a brilliant rainbow of fire. The magnetic alignment coupling at the base was Blue Team's target. Tom and Lucy had stealthed ahead of them all to blow up the three-story-tall crystal on the far side of the factory.

Ash paused and turned to see where the pursuing Sentinels were.

His eyes registered flashes. His training took over and his body moved before he cluttered his mind with thought.

He stepped right, pushed off, and jumped left. The floor exploded. Shrapnel tore through his SPI armor, and he was remotely aware that something had happened to his left leg, but he ignored it.

Ash rolled, turned, and chucked a grenade as three Sentinel pairs streaked over him.

The grenade bounced off their shields, and harmlessly detonated in the air.

At least this part of the plan was working: they were drawing fire.

He detected a dozen more Sentinels in the air, shooting at other targets, bathing the factory in brilliant gold illumination, razor-sharp shadows, and glowing molten craters.

Ash broadcast on TEAMCOM: "Form up; accelerate approach to target."

On his TACMAP he marked the apex of the generator, and then placed a secondary marker on the extraction point—a location three hundred meters distant over open ground.

Ash charged forward, running a crazy pattern—right, left, sudden stops, rolls and ducks. Energy beams fell around him. Fire washed over him. Liquid metal spattered his back, but he didn't flinch. His eyes clouded red, and his vision tunneled on the glowing target ahead.

He had to get there. He *would* get there.

Ash sprinted straight ahead. Every muscle pumped and burned with lactic acid.

Olivia and Holly got to the dome, turned, and their Jackal gauntlets crackled to life. They stood together, overlapping energy shields.

Behind them loomed the impossibly large pyramid of spheres, all eyes turning toward them.

"Hurry," Holy cried over TEAMCOM. She raised the bottom edge of her shield a half meter. "Under—quick!"

Ash jumped, dove under their feet and behind the energy shields.

Light surrounded him, and the floor to either side melted and blasted away.

He stood between his teammates and snapped on his own Jackal gauntlet.

Mark joined them.

Ash hesitated, waiting for Dante to get there. He then realized his grim mistake. He wished his friend was here by his side . . . but he was gone, and Dante would have wanted the team to keep their heads. Fight. And win.

Ash watched the swarm of enemies surrounding them. There were about forty Sentinel pairs. They could have all fired, and blown Team Saber to hell, but instead they looked wary . . . like they were thinking this through.

Which was the *one* thing he couldn't let happen.

"Get their attention," Ash told Mark.

Mark nodded, and hefted their only SPNKr missile launcher. He angled it at a cluster of Sentinels at four o'clock.

The missile streaked through the air and hit a pair dead center—mushrooming into thunder and smoke. The Sentinels, behind their shields, were untouched.

The hovering Sentinels ceased circling and seven aligned one behind the other to form a line pointed at Team Saber.

"Tighten it up, guys," Ash ordered. "Olivia, eye on our six."

The Spartans huddled as close as they could.

"All clear behind," Olivia whispered. "Best exit vector at nine o'clock."

There was no way a few Jackal shields could withstand a combined energy blast that had leveled an entire granite mesa.

Then again, they wouldn't have to.

The seven Sentinels adjusted their aim and their spheres glowed red, amber, and then glistening gold.

"Stand by," Ash whispered over TEAMCOM. He crouched lower and gritted his teeth.

The drones contracted and the glare from their spheres intensified.

"Go!" Ash cried.

The Spartans of Team Saber jumped, rolled, and scattered.

The Sentinels fired a culminated beam of energy that struck where Team Saber had been a moment ago—a direct hit on the glowing dome of the force-field generator.

Ash turned away, but the concussive blast rolled through his body. Shrapnel cut into his back, and skin blistered.

He focused on the second NAV marker on his heads-up display: the one thing that mattered now.

He ran toward it, a tiny platform three hundred meters away—the only way out.

Around him the air paused, and then rushed backward toward the generator with hurricane force. He turned, curiosity overcoming the instinct to flee.

Where the silver dome had been there was a blackened crater of twisted metal. The Sentinels had moved in, projecting their shields over the open wound, but the crater's edges crinkled as atmosphere sucked inside.

More Sentinels rushed toward the breach, trying to hold it.

A silver flash overwhelmed Ash's senses. There was a double explosion and a giant hand swatted him. He tumbled ten meters and slammed to a halt flat on his back.

Dazed, he slowly got up. The Sentinels were gone. The crater they had tried to hold was now a smoking rift a hundred meters wide.

The pyramid of spheres, the mountain of metal, shuddered.

That force-field generator was only one of three, but without it in place, the formation was unbalanced. And when a million ball bearings stacked upon one another were not *exactly* balanced . . .

Ash turned and sprinted.

Ahead, Holly had fallen and struggled to get to her feet. He went to her, grabbed her hand, and lifted her up.

But they both froze as they caught a glimpse of the pyramid.

The outer layers of spheres tumbled and bounced off their fellows, a chain reaction of cascading destruction; rivers of metal balls flowed, then torrents, an avalanche that rolled across the floor in great waves, tons of metal headed for them.

"Guys! Move it!" Mark yelled over TEAMCOM.

Ash blinked and snapped out of his stupor.

He and Holly turned and sprinted toward the extraction point. Mark and Olivia were already on the platform, waving them to hurry.

Ash felt the thunderous force through the floor that grew louder with every step until it shook his bones.

He and Holly leapt onto the platform.

"Dr. Halsey, go," he screamed over an open COM channel.

Nothing happened.

Team Saber stood shoulder to shoulder and watched the tidal wave of metal smash over machinery and crush the Sentinels that struggled to escape its kilometer-high surge.

But there was no escaping something like this.

"We got the mission done," Ash told his friends over TEAM-COM. "We won."

He still held Holly's hand. He gripped it tighter.

The shadow of the wave covered them and plunged them into darkness.

There was a flash of light.

Nausea hit Ash in the gut like a lead glove wrapped around a brick.

The blinding light faded.

They were back on the ledge.

Holly disentangled her hand from his and looked away. Mark

steadied himself against the wall. Olivia stepped off the platform and hung her head between her legs.

Dr. Halsey sat and stared at a tornado of Covenant symbols that rose from her laptop, her eyes darting back and forth trying to watch them all at the same time. She herded a collection of silver triangles together.

"My apologies for the delay," she said without glancing up. "There are complications. Please, step off the platform. Tom and Lucy are next."

The SPARTAN-II Blue Team was already back crouched along the shadow line by the ledge overlooking the factory.

The air was full of Sentinels flying in formations. The pyramid was gone, and on the floor a million spheres bounced and surged forward, flattening machinery and sparking conduits.

The fountain of fire that Blue Team had targeted oscillated wildly out of control, spaying molten alloy on the walls, ceiling, everywhere but the receiving vessel it was supposed to hit.

Over the COM Tom's voice crackled: "Ready for translocation, Dr. Halsey." Gunfire sounded in the background.

Dr. Halsey exhaled a hiss of frustration and slashed her hand through the icons, and then started the process of gathering them again.

"What's the holdup?" the Lieutenant Commander asked.

"Someone else is accessing this system," she replied. "This accounts for Team Saber's delay . . . and now Tom and Lucy's."

"Someone else?" he said. "You mean the Covenant?"

"Entirely probable," she replied.

Fred turned around and whispered, "That means they can track and follow us."

Over the COM Tom yelled, "Doctor, if you're going to do anything you have to do it—"

Rings of gold strobed on the platform and then vanished; Tom and Lucy stood there, hands raised in an instinctive effort to ward off danger. Wisps of plasma curled and dissipated around them.

"—Now," Tom finished. He exhaled a long sigh and then reported to the Lieutenant Commander, "Mission accomplished, sir."

In the distance small explosions popped, sounding like a string of firecrackers. The flying Sentinel formations scattered— some crashing into one another, others accelerating straight into the walls.

Dr. Halsey consulted her watch. "We have fifty-three minutes before the core-room entrance closes, Kurt."

The Lieutenant Commander nodded. "Everyone on the platform," he ordered. "Doctor, move us to Team Katana's location."

Unease already settling into his stomach, Ash crowded onto the four-meter pad with his teammates.

Funny, but he hadn't thought of the older Spartans as part of the team until now. Or was he part of *their* team? He then noticed the blood oozing from his armor joints, mirrored red by the camouflaging panels. Baptized in battle. They'd lost Dante, too. High prices to pay.

Chief Mendez watched the self-destructing factory. "That's *a lot* of Sentinels," he murmured. "Wonder why they only deployed a fraction of them?"

"Setting time delay for three seconds," Dr. Halsey said, shut her laptop, and then joined them.

Mendez's remark bothered Ash more than he could explain, and the unease in his gut intensified. There were hundreds of thousands of Sentinels here. Why just have them sit around? They had to serve *some* purpose. . . .

Rings of light enveloped the squad.

Ash hoped he never found out why. He just wanted to rescue Katana, get the technology Dr. Halsey had promised, and get out of here before the Covenant caught up with them.

He had a feeling, though, it wasn't going to be that easy.

CHAPTER 35

2105 Hours, November 3, 2552 (Military Calendar) \
Zeta Doradus System, Orbit Near the Moon of Onyx \
Aboard UNSC Prowler *Dusk*

Commander Richard Lash supervised the release of the mines. He and Lieutenant Commander Cho monitored the launch bay of the *Dusk*. The closet-sized chamber behind the tiny observation window had been chilled near absolute zero. The nukes inside had been cycled through three thermal cooldowns and were now the same temperature as interstellar space.

The tiny HORNET warheads had been transferred aboard from the *Brasidas,* a destroyer with extensive damage. Thankfully Cho had detected the minuscule leak from their reactor and moved off before it irradiated the *Dusk*'s hull. That would have lit them up against the background intrasolar radiation and fatally compromised their stealth ability.

"Let her fly," Lash ordered.

"Releasing," Cho whispered. He grasped the manual override claw, and with supreme concentration, he dropped the warhead.

The bay door irised open and the black egg-shaped HORNET mine dropped from its carrier and, centimeter by centimeter, drifted into space.

"That was the last, sir." Cho wiped the beads of sweat that had collected on his wrinkled forehead.

Cho was technically past the mandatory retirement age in the UNSC prowler corps. This was a fact that had been carefully ignored by Captain Iglesias. The UNSC was running out of qualified recruits, and Cho would have been impossible to replace.

Lash gave him an approving nod, which was as much praise as the old engineer was ever comfortable with.

"Thank you, sir."

Lash entered the tube to the bridge and pushed off, propelling himself in the null gee, somersaulting and then using his legs to brake. He took a moment to compose himself before he opened the hatch. In the last fifteen minutes, the *Dusk* had seeded the space on the dark side of the moon of Onyx with fourteen nuclear mines—thirty-megaton yield with vacuum-enhanced loads.

Delicate work to stay stealthed and get them all deployed on Admiral Patterson's timetable, but they'd done it.

All it had cost was the fraying of Lash's already shot nerves. He smoothed his uniform, brushed his thinning hair, took a deep breath, and then spun open the hatch.

"Report," he said to Lieutenant Commander Waters.

Waters looked up with bloodshot eyes from his display. "The Admiral has been informed mission accomplished, sir. He's moving the fleet to new coordinates, a high orbit on the bright side of the moon."

Lash examined the system NAV map. Patterson was going to

use the entire planetoid as cover. He'd need it. The enemy forces still outnumbered them sixteen ships to their four. By any sane measure it would be suicide to attack that Covenant battle group.

The line, however, between sane and not was becoming increasingly blurred in this system.

Lash settled in the captain's chair. "Lieutenant Yang? Status?"

"As dark as midnight under a rock, sir."

Lash nodded, pleased at Yang's hyperbole. A little humor was a good sign. "Lieutenant Durruno, move us to lunar Lagrange-Four, one-quarter full. Tell Lieutenant Commander Cho to trickle-charge our slipspace capacitors."

"Aye, sir." She tapped in the commands, cursed, and then backspaced and retyped them correctly.

Durruno needed sleep. They all did. But he'd keep her in play a little longer. There was no one to replace her, and this would be over, one way or the other, very soon.

"Covenant fleet on-screen," Lash ordered Waters. "Rescan and give me a full spectral analysis."

"All sensors on target," Waters replied.

Rainbows played over the central viewscreen, building composite images from radiation far-infrared to soft gamma, and fourteen Covenant ships resolved, clustered together in a spherical formation three hundred thousand kilometers distant.

To Lash they looked like hungry sharks, ready to pounce on a few sardines.

Their spectral analysis, however, painted a different picture. Thermal blooms and radiation leaks spewed in helical showers from the vessels. They'd been damaged by Admiral Patterson's alpha strike and the captured plasma redirected by the alien drones.

The enemy was sitting there, making repairs, in all likelihood frothing from their split mouths to get back in the fight and go another round with the UNSC battle group.

Patterson, however, had another plan: hit them first. Hard.

"Activity from Onyx on the E-Band?" Lash asked Yang.

"No, sir. Not a flicker since that ONI AI took care of the alien drones."

Lash wondered how the AI and Spartans on the planet had neutralized the alien fleet. Had they recovered some new super-weapon? However they did it, he promised he'd personally shake every one of their hands.

"Continue to monitor all UNSC bands," he told Yang. "Those Spartans might need a lift."

"Action on-screen," Waters announced. The camera snapped aft and centered on the silver moon.

In the twilight regions on either side of the moon, magnetic accelerator cannons flared, briefly illuminating the now-split UNSC battle group in high orbit. Slugs of steel and tungsten rocketed into space, curving slightly from the gravitational distortion—streaking toward the Covenant ships.

The Covenant ships broke formation.

One MAC slug cleanly missed.

Three hit.

The targeted ships lit as their shields absorbed the massive kinetic energy. They careened backward . . . slowed, and stopped, undamaged from the single MAC strikes.

Covenant ships turned and accelerated toward the moon.

The MAC salvo had done precisely what Admiral Patterson had hoped: tweaked their collective noses, and gotten them good and mad.

The UNSC battle group maneuvered behind the moon, denying the enemy a clean line of fire.

"Set EMP dampers," Lash said, trying to control his rising adrenaline. "Shut down primary and secondary computers."

"Aye, sir," Durruno and Yang said together. They scrambled to isolate the *Dusk*'s delicate electronics from the impending nuclear blasts.

The Covenant battle group divided—each half moving to opposite sides of the moon, taking flanking positions where they could blast the hiding human ships into oblivion with their plasma.

What they couldn't see on their approach vector, however, was Admiral Patterson's fleet backing directly away from the moon.

"Enemy vessels approaching distal radius of alpha and beta minefields," Durruno reported.

"Arm alpha and beta fields," Lash whispered.

Yang fidgeted and said, "Command sent, sir . . . and confirmation received across the board."

That Covenant fleet was about to find out why UNSC battle groups always had a prowler assigned to their ranks. They were the sneak thieves and spies of the UNSC fleet, capable of behind-enemy-lines recon, rescue missions . . . and under the right conditions, the pinpoint placement of a nuclear minefield.

"Proximal enemy group now in the center of alpha field," Durruno announced. Her hands shook. "Distal group crossing the terminal line of beta field."

"Remove safety interlocks," Lash said.

Yang nodded and typed in the code words that made the sixteen nukes hot.

The red "inferno" button on Lash's command console lit. He set his thumb next to it, and it beeped, verifying his biometric signature. He then flipped up the clear protective cover, inserted the master key in the adjacent slot, and turned it.

"Proximal group approaching terminal plane," Durruno said. "Beta group of ships now centered in distal field."

"Here goes nothing," Lash whispered. "Here's goes everything."

He pressed the button, and it made a satisfying *click*.

On either side of the moon, seven tiny suns flashed into existence, ballooned, and enveloped the Covenant battle groups.

The collective nuclear fireballs cooled to yellow and then dull red. Even with vacuum-enhanced loads, nuclear warheads in space did not persist a fraction as long as aerial or ground bursts.

The destructive clouds thinned to translucency and a glittering haze of cooling metal formed an expanding halo around the planetoid.

Inside this silver confetti, however, larger shimmering patches resolved: the energy shields of four surviving Covenant destroyers.

Admiral Patterson moved his fleet toward the moon and opened fire. MAC rounds tore through space and behind them Archer missiles traced lacy paths of exhaust through the vacuum.

Two Covenant ships sluggishly changed course and intercepted the MAC slugs. Their distressed shields shattered and their hulls cratered inward. Fire fountained as their plasma lines vented. Flocks of Archer missiles dove into the injured ships and explosions punctuated armor and propulsion grids.

The crippled ships turned toward the moon, and in slow motion tumbled toward their surface.

The UNSC battle group continued their charge. Four warships against the last two wounded Covenant destroyers . . . not entirely impossible odds.

Lash imagined that a hundred years in the future historians might look back at this moment and declare it the turning point of humanity's struggle. That they had fought and defeated the

Covenant at Onyx, won the prize of alien technology, and gone on—not only to survive, but to win their long struggle.

He had secretly believed that they could not win this war for so long, Lash barely recognized the emotion that coursed through him now: hope.

"Covenant ships on new heading," Lieutenant Durruno said. She chewed on her lower lip and a tiny drop of blood appeared. "Intercept course, sir."

On-screen the last two enemy destroyers accelerated toward the moon. An extrapolated trajectory appeared: a slingshot orbit that would bring them around and back, and straight toward the *Dusk*.

"Get primary computers online," Lash ordered. "Cho, what's our slipspace status?"

Over the COM Cho's voice crackled with static. "Capacitors at eighty percent and draining. I'll need full engine power for two more minutes."

"Understood," Lash replied. Two minutes could be forever. "Continue dark protocols," he ordered Yang. "Lock down all external systems." To Lieutenant Durruno he said, "Use docking jets to present minimal aspect to the incoming vessels while they're on the blind side."

"Aye, sir." She activated the thrusters and tapped a joystick to manually reposition the ship.

On-screen the moon tilted as they realigned.

The Covenant destroyer pair emerged from the far side of the moon . . . and grew larger on-screen. Sleek and dangerous as hell, their gray-blue hulls bore down on the *Dusk*.

"Replot their course," Lash told Lieutenant Commander Waters.

Waters stood over his station, checked and rechecked his numbers. "*Not* an intercept course," he whispered, ". . . but damned close."

A coincidence? Or had the enemy seen them and were coming for revenge?

"Stay dark," Lash ordered.

There was little else they could do.

The destroyers' smooth blue curves filled their viewscreens.

Lash felt the butterflies-in-the-stomach sensation of quantum fluctuations from the Covenant repulsor engines.

The *Dusk* tumbled and spun.

The viewscreen cleared, revealing a rotating field of untwinkling stars.

"Thirty-one meters off the port bow," Waters breathed.

"Repulsor wake has set us adrift off the Lagrange point, sir," Lieutenant Durruno said.

"Let us drift, Lieutenant," Lash said. "Fix cameras on the *Stalingrad*."

The spinning stars on the viewscreens slowed and then centered on the four UNSC warships as they rounded the moon at flank speed, chasing the two Covenant destroyers.

"They're lining up for a shot," Waters said. "They've got six MAC slugs left. That should be enough."

"Energy spike!" Yang shouted. "Not from our ships. Not from the Covenant vessels, either, sir."

"Location?" Lash asked, and he pushed himself out of the captain's chair.

Yang shook his head, opened his mouth, but no words came out.

Waters went to the SENSOR-OPS station and looked. "Power profile indicative of a slipspace field," he said. "A big one. Deconvoluting signature. Location is"—his features went slack— "everywhere."

The space around the UNSC fleet rippled and blue lines

appeared, connected, and intertwined like waves of sapphire water. Slipspace fields ruptured normal dimensions and Cherenkov radiation dazzled the night—as dozens of Covenant destroyers, carriers, and cruisers appeared, swarms of them formed a phalanx between the UNSC battle group and the two surviving enemy vessels.

"Counting thirty-two Covenant ships," Yang croaked.

Lieutenant Durruno froze at her station, eyes wide with terror.

The Covenant armada fired.

Spotlight energy projectors flashed, and pure white light cleaved the dark. The UNSC ships' titanium armor boiled and vaporized, mixed with venting oxygen, and photonic pressure blasted the flames into wavering plumes.

Archer missiles and magnetic accelerator cannons fired in a desperate counterstrike. The missiles detonated a fraction of a second along their flight paths, high explosives heated to the flashpoint. Four MAC slugs rocketed through the energy projector cones, fireballs of liquefied metal. Three missed. One hit, spattering uselessly on Covenant shields.

Thirty-two lines of plasma heated, detached, and arced toward the human fleet, striking critically damaged vessels, blasting craters, ripping through inner decks, until the superstructures buckled and inner atmospheres decompressed in large bursting bubbles upon the now-molten hulls.

The Covenant armada ceased fire and slowly advanced.

Admiral Patterson's ships had been reduced to a field of debris in a matter of seconds.

Pinpoint lasers fired from the enemy ships as they destroyed escape pods.

"Incoming debris," Waters warned.

"We need to do *something*," Lieutenant Durruno whispered.

What had been a victorious battle group chasing down a doomed enemy was now tumbling, half-melted prows and glowing reactor cores. A floating graveyard. Ghosts.

The hope that Commandeer Richard Lash had felt was forever gone.

"Do nothing," Lash told them.

"If anything hits us, sir," Waters said, "assuming we survive the impact, the deflection angles will give away our position."

"This close to so many vessels," Lash replied, "so would maneuvering." He went to Lieutenant Durruno at the NAV station. "Hang tight," he told her. Her eyes shone with tears, but she nodded, and gripped the edges of her seat.

Lash checked his wristwatch and made sure it was wound tight.

The Covenant armada moved closer, blotted out the starlight, and covered the *Dusk* with shadow.

CHAPTER 36

Kurt motioned back to Fred and Ash, Linda and Mark to close the gap.

Two by two they moved up the corridor, gliding from pillar to pillar, the SPARTAN-IIIs on point barely visible in their armor, part shadow, part striped onyx patterns. The SPARTAN-IIs closed behind like liquid mercury rolling over velvet, smooth and silent.

The differences between their two generations had been left behind. Teams Blue and Saber worked as a single unit, family who had pulled together in a crisis.

Kurt watched his motion tracker, IFF tags overlaid on the grid. The Spartans had the best positions possible—set along each of the pillars that stretched up to the ten-meter-tall corridor. Kurt, Tom, and Lucy had point.

Olivia was on recon, her IFF disabled, so Kurt wasn't certain of her precise location in the room ahead.

This corridor was tiled with interlocking Forerunner symbols of jade, turquoise, and lapis. Dr. Halsey surmised it was an epic poem depicting a struggle in the Forerunners' long-lost past.

All Kurt knew was it was a kill zone, with scant cover and long sight lines. A good place to get ambushed.

Olivia flashed her green status light three times: the all-clear signal.

Kurt motioned for Tom and Lucy to follow him, and they slinked into the room ahead. Shadows shrouded rows of squat machines, and the only light came from eight podlike sarcophagi clustered in the center.

These pods were semitranslucent, and within each lay a person, their features obscured.

Olivia moved next to Kurt. "Five of these have to be Team Katana," she whispered. "This one is still tagged with the lime-green 'kill' flag from top-honors exercise."

Kurt smoothed his gauntlet over the pod's surface. Were they alive inside? Dead? Somewhere in between? He had come here first—not gone after the technology that the UNSC needed, risking everything for Team Katana.

You never leave a fallen comrade behind.

But there was more to it than that: given a choice between alien technologies that might save *all* of humanity and these five Spartans . . . he had picked them first. He would have done anything to protect them.

"Let's see what we're dealing with here," he said.

Kurt flickered on his helmet's tactical lights, and panned them over the chamber. Organo-metallic appendages cradled each pod and radiated branches that connected to banks of two-meter cubes.

On closer inspection, Kurt saw a faint light leaking from these cubes . . . and staring closer, he noticed they were not at all cubes—their edges distorted and radiated *extra* dimensions.

He staggered back, hands reflectively grasping for his temples. Disorientation washed over him as he tasted the faint green light, inhaled the dusty odors of meaning from the symbols on the floor, and heard the bell-like tinkling of the organic electronics of the pods.

He sank to one knee and the tangled sensory input faded.

"Stand back," Kurt warned the others. Over the COM he said, "Will, escort Dr. Halsey up here."

Another wave of disorientation hit Kurt and his vision swam. When he again could see, Dr. Halsey knelt next to him.

"Move him away from the machines," she told Will.

Will dragged him back to the room's entrance, and Kurt's vision immediately cleared and the dizziness vanished.

"What was that?" he asked Dr. Halsey.

"Unshielded slipspace field," she said. Her face was a mask of concentration, staring at the cubic machine housing. Frowning, she crossed to the pods. "Linda," she said, "your assistance please."

Linda moved up to Dr. Halsey, her sniper rifle aimed at the floor.

"Use your weapon's range finder and point at the interior of the pod."

Linda nodded, raised her rifle, and aimed at the Spartan inside the pod. After a moment, she lowered the weapon, checked her Oracle scope's settings, and then repeated the procedure. She shook her head.

"You are reading an infinite range?" Dr. Halsey said.

"Yes," Linda replied, uncharacteristic annoyance in her tone. "There must be something wrong with it."

"No," Dr. Halsey replied. "I'm afraid it is in perfect working order."

She turned to Kurt. "I cannot revive your Spartans or the other three, Lieutenant Commander. They are not in cryogenic suspension."

Kurt shook off the last traces of confusion. "Explain," he said.

"They are encased in a slipspace field. The process to stabilize such a field in normal space is well beyond any technology we or the Covenant possess. Essentially these Spartans are here, but not, extruded into an alternate set of spatial coordinates and excluded from time."

"They're right here," Linda said, and pointed at the pods.

"No," Dr. Halsey said. "You are merely seeing their after-image. It's like looking at a mass accelerated past the event horizon of a black hole. Its image may linger there forever, but it is gone."

"So they're gone?" Linda whispered.

"Oh no," Dr. Halsey replied. "They're right here."

Kurt said, "You just said they're gone. Which is it?"

Dr. Halsey considered a moment and then replied, "Both. The quantum-mechanical implications do not translate to simple, non-paradoxical, classical terms."

"Then let's stick to practical terms," Kurt said, growing annoyed. "Are they safe?"

She tilted her head, considering, and then replied, "You could detonate a nuclear warhead on these pods and because the extruded slipspace within is not in this dimension, there would be no effect to their contents."

At this reference to "nuclear warhead," Ash shifted his pack, which held the two cut-down FENRIS bombs.

"Can we move them?" Kurt asked.

Dr. Halsey walked to the end of one pod. She examined the

trunk line attached there and uncoupled it. There was a hiss and the pod rose a half meter off the floor.

"It appears they were designed to be moved," she said, her last words trailing off into deep thought.

Kurt motioned to the pods. "Teams Saber, Blue, get them uncoupled. We'll take them with us to the core-room entrance."

The Spartans detached the pods.

As Ash maneuvered one pod, Dr. Halsey held up a hand, indicating that he halt. She bent closer to the last pod and ran her fingers over the Forerunner icons along its side, translating as she did so: "'That which must be protected . . . behind the sharpened edge of the shield . . . beyond the reach of the swords . . . for the reclaimed.' No, that's not quite the correct meaning."

"Reclaimed . . ." Ash echoed. "Maybe 'Reclaimers'?"

Dr. Halsey looked up, startled, at him. "Yes. A title. Specifically, an honorific."

"Yeah," he said, "that's what the Sentinel called us."

"One spoke?" Dr. Halsey asked. She pushed her glasses up the bridge of her nose and moved to Ash.

"I'd forgotten it with everything else going on." Ash shook his head, embarrassed.

"What *exactly* did it say?" she demanded. "The precise wording. It may be important."

Ash shifted foot to foot. ". . . I don't remember, ma'am."

Chief Mendez came up and set a hand on Ash's shoulder. "Take a deep breath, Spartan. Go back and think: what were you doing just before the thing talked?"

"We'd moved to the edge of Zone 67," Ash said slowly, "to disengage from Team Katana and Gladius. That's when they started to blow up the ONI bunkers . . . and then one came after us. It chased Holly right to the edge of a cliff.

"I got its attention. Threw a rock at the thing. It chased me, got me pinned in a ravine. I started to broadcast in the open, to let Saber know you could get past its shields with a slow ballistic object—didn't have much to lose at that point. But the Sentinel attenuated my COM signal, and transmitted it back to me."

"Slow it down," Chief Mendez whispered. "Take your time. What happened next?"

"At first it didn't make any sense," Ash continued. "Like untranslated Covenant—only it was different. 'Pungent Juber' something. I tried to talk back to it. Told it that I didn't understand. It spoke again, still gibberish, but then it said 'non sequitur.' I was certain it spoke Latin."

"Linguistic analysis based on a microscopic sample set," Dr. Halsey said. "It tried to communicate with a root language."

"Then it said 'Security protocols enabled' and 'Shield in countdown mode. Exchange proper counterresponse, Reclaimer.' I told it that I meant it no harm. I guess that was the wrong thing to say, because that's when it told me I was not a Reclaimer, and reclassified me as an 'aboriginal subspecies.'"

Dr. Halsey stared off into space, thinking. "Yes . . ." she murmured. "This all makes sense."

"It was about to flash me with its energy beam when the rest of Saber came along and dropped a few rocks on it." Ash shrugged. "That's it, sir."

Kurt had heard enough . . . more important, he had *seen* Dr. Halsey's reaction. She knew much more than she was telling them. And it was time he found out what.

"Okay," Kurt said, "everyone grab the pods and move them to the translocation platform."

He stepped closer to Dr. Halsey. "I'd like a word with you, ma'am."

The Spartans maneuvered the pods back into the corridor. Mendez spared a look at Kurt and Dr. Halsey, and then left.

"We don't have much time," Kurt said to her.

She glanced at her watch. "Forty minutes, to be precise, until the core-room entrance shuts."

"You know what's inside."

There was the slightest hesitation, and then she replied, "How could I, Lieutenant Commander?"

"But you haven't told me everything."

Dr. Halsey's eyes hardened and her mouth set in what Mendez would have called a poker face.

"Doctor, I'm not going to risk my Spartans' lives without knowing everything. Even what you might consider an insignificant detail could have grave tactical repercussions."

"Indeed," she whispered, and her expression softened a bit. "If they mean that much to you, then tell me first about their neural augmentations."

Kurt tensed, unsure how to proceed. Dr. Halsey was a civilian outside his chain of command. There were rules and protocols dictating how the military interacted with the civilians under its protection—all too slow, for his purposes. If he were not reliant upon her scientific expertise, Kurt would have considered more direct action; instead he tried again.

"I am not bartering, Doctor. You do not have the proper clearance for that information. Now please tell me about the core. You could save lives."

"'Save lives' is exactly what I am attempting to do," she replied, and crossed her arms. The gesture was identical to the one Kelly made when she set her mind to be resolutely stubborn.

Kurt was cornered. If he threatened Dr. Halsey, he could lose her cooperation. If he didn't get the information, he might lose the lives. With time running out, he only had one option, and she knew it.

He took a deep breath and said, "Very well. The neural mutation for the SPARTAN-IIIs alters their frontal lobe to enhance aggression response. In times of extreme stress it makes them nearly immune to shock, able to endure damage not even a SPARTAN-II could."

"Like Dante?" Dr. Halsey said. "Still moving when he should have been in a coma?"

Kurt relived that moment, holding Dante who had just a second earlier saluted him and told him that he *thought* he had been nicked.

"Side effects?" she asked.

"Yes," Kurt whispered. "Over time, higher brain functions are suppressed and the Spartans lose their strategic judgment. A counteragent blocks this, but it must be regularly administered."

"I'm not sure I agree that trade-off is worth it," she said. "Unless, their needs were, even by Spartan standards . . . extraordinary." She carefully examined Kurt, and then whispered, "What happened to Alpha Company?"

"They were deployed to shut down a Covenant shipyard on the edge of UNSC space." Kurt stopped, straining to hold back the blackness that rose within him. Shane, Robert, every one of them dead, and the fault his.

"I never heard of the operation," Dr. Halsey said.

"Because it was a success," Kurt replied, regaining some control. "If it hadn't been, the Covenant would have destroyed every Orion-side colony. . . . But the entire company, three hundred Spartans, was lost."

Dr. Halsey started to reach out toward him, and then stopped, thinking better of it. "Tom and Lucy . . . ?"

"The only survivors of Beta Company from the Pegasi Delta Op," he replied.

They were silent a moment. Kurt wrestled to rise above his emotions and the memories. But with so many lost he felt like he was drowning.

"I understand why you would risk such an outlawed protocol," Dr. Halsey said. "You would do anything to help them, your Spartans . . . as would I for mine."

Over the COM Chief Mendez spoke: "We're at the platform, sir. Awaiting further orders."

"Stand by," Kurt replied. He banished his feelings to a dark vessel in his mind, one brimming to overflow with pain, and then he focused on Dr. Halsey.

"Why are you here?" he asked her. "It is *not* to recover Forerunner technology. If you had really suspected, you would have told John and he'd have sent more assets than a single Spartan and a fifty-year-old ship converted for civilian use."

Dr. Halsey dropped her gaze to the intricately tiled floor. "There is no need for this pretense with you," she whispered. "Only, one becomes so accustomed to keeping secrets; one forgets how to tell anyone . . . anything." Her forehead crinkled almost as if it hurt to speak. "You are correct. I did not come to Onyx looking for Forerunner technology. I came for the Spartans. We want the same thing: their survival."

She set one hand over her throat—some reflexive defensive gesture to protect herself.

"This is not a war the UNSC can win, Kurt. Surely this has occurred to you?"

He nodded, although in fact it had not.

She seemed to accept this, however, and continued. "We have been slowly losing this war. 'Slowly,' I think, because we had not been the main focus of the Covenant hegemony until recently. Now they have found and targeted Earth. Add to this grim scenario the Flood . . . an emergent biology that even the Forerunners could not control."

"But we *have* to fight," Kurt said. "The Covenant don't take prisoners. And from what you've told us of the Flood . . . there's no other option."

Dr. Halsey smiled. "So like a Spartan . . . and, at the same time you are so *unlike* any of them. You crossed a line none of your kind has ever dared before: breaking regulations and engineering a massive cover-up. All to protect your charges. What I had planned, though, went much farther. . . ."

Over the COM Fred broke in. "Sir, the Forerunner controls on the platform are moving. Going crazy. I'm not sure what it means."

"Stand by," Kurt replied.

"You see," Dr. Halsey said, "my SPARTAN-IIs would never leave a fight. They are too indoctrinated to know any other way. But when I learned of the possibility of a new generation of Spartans, I realized there was a chance to lure them away. Perhaps place them in cryo and fly as fast and as far away as I could from this sector of the galaxy.

"To live and fight another day," Kurt murmured.

"Stumbling upon this Forerunner installation," Dr. Halsey continued, "was pure chance. . . . Or as much 'chance' as it was building Camp Currahee next to Zone 67. In any event, there may or may not be weapon technologies we can repurpose here. Your guess is as good as mine. There is, however, something far more valuable to us: a way to save their lives, what I think may have been part of the Forerunners' original plan. There is a haven for these 'Reclaimers' that—"

Gunfire echoed down the hallway.

Kurt turned and raised his rifle.

Fred announced over the COM: "Covenant scout party appeared on the translocation platform. Three Elites dispatched. No injuries here. Control panel is still active. Advise."

"Listen carefully if you want them to live," Dr. Halsey told Kurt. She wore her poker face again and there was steel in her voice. "Order Fred to move the pods onto that platform—now."

CHAPTER 37

The Spartans stood in a half-circle "kill" formation around the platform. The sarcophagi-like pods had been pushed into the center.

The bodies of three Elite scouts in their blue armor had been dragged to one side and stripped of their weapons. Fluorescing blood pooled there and reeked like fresh tar.

Dr. Halsey strode directly to the control console. As she tapped and arranged holographic symbols, she told Kurt, "The slipspace fields that render the pods impervious to attack effectively block any incoming matter translocations. They are perfectly safe."

Fred reported to Kurt, "For what it's worth, sir, the Elites looked surprised. I don't think they knew we were here."

"Well, they probably do now," Kurt replied. "Doctor?"

"I'm unsure how the Covenant learned so quickly," Dr. Halsey said, glistening symbols reflecting in her glasses, "but I'm logging repeated attempts to gain access to *this* platform. Nearby systems have activated. They are trying to find alternate routes to our location."

"Then we move," Kurt said.

"If the pods block the translocation," Ash said, "will they go through the system?"

Dr. Halsey considered this. "I believe so. They are designed to be transported. Once their slipspace fields are caught in the wake of a locally generated spatial distortion they should be carried along."

"Set mission timers in countdown mode," Kurt told them, and he looked to Dr. Halsey.

She consulted her watch. "Thirty-two minutes until the doorway to the core room closes," she said.

"On my mark," Kurt said. "Mark."

"32:00" appeared in the lower right corner of his heads-up display.

"Defense formation beta," he ordered, and motioned everyone onto the platforms. "Use the pods for cover."

Will carried Dante's wrapped body and set him gently onto the platform. Kurt quickly looked away; every time he saw the corpse, it reminded him that Dante's death was his responsibility, and that he had failed the young Spartan.

The SPARTAN-IIs made a ring inside the pods protecting Mendez. The SPARTAN-IIIs lay flat and aimed under the floating pods, giving them a 360-degree field of fire.

Dr. Halsey joined them on the platform, crowding next to Chief Mendez. She opened her laptop and linked to the Forerunner controls. "Are you certain?" she asked Kurt. "The Covenant may be able to track us to the core room. We might lead them directly to it." The look on her face was unreadable.

Kurt recognized the question as strategic: continue to the core room or escape while there were UNSC forces in the space over Onyx?

Dr. Halsey had also hinted there was a way to save the Spartans' lives—something linked to the Forerunners' original plan for these "Reclaimers." But he didn't have the luxury of making plans based on Dr. Halsey's half-explained theories. He'd stick with *his* plan: get to the core room, grab whatever technology or weapons were there, and get off this world. He had a mission to accomplish, and failing that—his gaze moved to Ash and his pack with two FENRIS warheads—he could still deny the enemy their prize.

"Core room," Kurt said.

Dr. Halsey sighed and nodded. Was it resignation he detected on her face? Or relief? She was the most difficult person to read he had ever encountered.

Rings of golden light enveloped them, the walls of the corridor melted, and Kurt felt his insides pulled out and around and then stuffed back into his armor.

The light, however, didn't fade as it had before. It intensified to a brighter magnesium-burning white.

Mendez dug into his vest pocket and donned an antique pair of mirrored wraparounds.

Dr. Halsey's glasses automatically darkened.

Kurt's visor wasn't polarizing to compensate, so he manually stepped up the tint by 60 percent.

At first he mistook their location for an open plain of snow, somewhere on the northern polar region, but then he saw walls in the foggy distance. He estimated five kilometers.

He pushed the polarization to 80 percent.

The floor became visible, tiled with Forerunner symbols of silver, ruby, emerald, and amber. Each line and curve interlinked in a precise Penrose geometry, although if there was a discernable repeating pattern Kurt didn't see it.

The symbols seemed to sing in his mind, and he was frustratingly close to understanding what they said . . . some larger galactic transcendent meaning.

Kurt shook his head to clear the delusion.

He fell back to his training. He scanned for motion. No enemies sighted. There were no visible defendable positions, either. He checked his rifle: ammo clip full. All SPI armor systems checked.

As his vision continued to adjust, a hill resolved in the center of this "room." There was a uniform slope to the floor that gently rose and then arced up hyperbolically a dozen meters. It reminded Kurt of an anthill. Around the apex of this hill sat a crown of fins raised to the sky; buttressed at their bases and pronged at their tips, they towered another ten meters above the structure.

"If this is the core of the planet," Kelly whispered, "there should be little, if any, gravity. It feels normal."

Dr. Halsey rechecked her laptop. "Translocation confirmed," she said. "We *are* at the center of Onyx. The gravity is artificial."

"Teams of two deploy, spread out, recon," Kurt said. "Doctor, Chief, Ash, we're going to that structure."

Green acknowledgment lights winked on.

"Sir," Holly said, "what about Team Katana? The pods?"

"Leave them on the platform. They'll block incoming Covenant translocations." It felt wrong to leave them here alone, so he ordered Holly, "Guard them."

They moved off, and as Kurt marched over the floor, the symbols under his boots smoothed into a golden path. Static clawed along the inside of his SPI armor and the exterior was a riot of colors as the photo-reactive circuits attempted to blend into the local Harlequin terrain.

Mendez halted and held up a hand toward Dr. Halsey. "Watch your step, ma'am." He pointed to the floor.

A ridge rose a quarter meter, difficult to see because Forerunner icons glowed along its smooth side as well as the top.

Dr. Halsey knelt and tapped the frames of her glasses, glancing right and left. "A ring . . . circumscribing the entirety of the central structure." She then gazed at the hill. "In fact, the entire deformation is a series of similar concentric circles."

Kurt stepped onto the raised surface. He scrutinized the hill and counted the finlike towers: there were thirteen. He increased the magnification factor on his faceplate and noted the curved surface of the center formation was indeed a series of staircase rings.

"Reminds me of Dante's *Inferno*," Mendez said, and offered his hand to Dr. Halsey.

She took his hand and eased onto the ridge. "Dante's hell was a series of *descending* rings," she said. "These are more representative of—"

The floor shifted.

Kurt instinctively crouched to keep his balance, but there was no need; it had only dropped a few centimeters.

The entire room settled, however, the distortion propagating toward the hill with a subsonic rumble.

"If the core room is in the center," Dr. Halsey said, hastening her pace, "we should hurry."

"Something here, sir," Fred announced over the COM. "You better see for yourself."

Kurt turned toward Fred's and Mark's IFF signals on his heads-up display. They were silhouettes against the glare, 150 meters away.

"Ash, Chief, escort the doctor to the structure. Keep me posted."

"Roger that, sir," Ash said.

Kurt jogged to Fred and Mark and saw the Spartans standing at the edge of a black hole, a seven-sided smooth patch devoid of Forerunner iconography. A holograph console stood next to it, icons moving.

"Translocation platform," Fred whispered. "Active, if I'm reading these controls right."

"We'll use another pod to block it," Kurt said.

He started to key the COM, but Ash then broke in: "Sir. I've got some height, and I can see . . . dots on the floor."

"*Black* dots?" Kurt asked.

"Yes, sir. Counting a dozen—no, make that at least thirty of them scattered in a rough circle."

Kurt's heart sank to the pit of his stomach.

There were too many points of egress to block. They potentially faced an enemy with superior numbers and firepower, and all they'd have was a single semidefensible position.

"26:00" morphed to "25:59" on his countdown timer.

They were close to that core room, a possible treasure trove of Forerunner secrets. With a sizable Covenant force on their trail, it wouldn't be enough to get there first. They had to prevent the enemy from getting there as well.

Kurt balanced the lives of his Spartans against the billions that might be saved . . . and the choice was regrettably all too clear to him.

Kurt double-clicked the TEAMCOM. "Olivia, Will, Holly, grab those pods and get to the top of that hill ASAP. Kelly, set up the last LOTUS mines around the structure. Everyone else, get to the top and unpack everything, load all rifles. Prepare to defend against incoming enemy forces."

CHAPTER 38

Fleet Master Voro inspected his battalion. They had amassed on the surface of the Forerunner city, over two hundred Sangheili in orderly rows for his review. Dropships and Seraph fighter craft hovered overhead, their landing lights playing over the courtyard, guarding against unexpected Sentinel or demon attacks.

The nearby edifices and paving stones of black-and-white-banded mineral provided a sharp contrast to his soldiers in their primary-colored armors.

He glanced down rows of warriors in blue battle suits, standing at attention, ready to fight and kill and die at his word.

The only grumble among his solders was because they carried Kig-yar shield gauntlets to supplement their armor systems. Many viewed this as a grave dishonor, but Voro had ordered it so. They would take no chances with the human demons, these "Spartans." The Sangheili could not lose this world as they had the first Halo ring.

Voro nodded to the Major Domo Sangheili in their glistening red armor. The Majors caught and held his gaze. They believed in him. He saw it in their unwavering stares.

Their confidence was infectious . . . and they gave him pause, for it was a dangerous thing for a leader of any rank to believe himself unstoppable.

Still, Voro marveled that he had been given command of the E'Toro, R'Lan, and N'Nono warrior crèches whose valor and savagery was legendary. Yet, as skilled as these soldiers were, he would have traded a dozen of them for one infiltrator in a light-bending suit to scout the terrain ahead and report on the demons.

He halted before Paruto and Waruna. The towering Lekgolo pair growled their gratitude at leading the true vanguard.

Voro had been blessed with not one but three Lekgolo pairs. He had never seen a single pair defeated in combat before. And yet, the Spartans had managed to wound Waruna and escape, an insult to the Lekgolo pride that would only be assuaged by grinding the offenders into pulp.

"Make ready final preparation," Voro told his Majors.

The Majors shouted to their squads, who drew their swords and saluted Voro—their raised energy blades made the air waver with their combined heat.

They lowered their salute; grabbed rifles, grenades, pistols, and power cells; and marched across the courtyard, assembling near the banks of matte-black translocation pads.

Suicide Unggoy squads followed, dragging dissembled energy mortar units. Their frenzied squeals annoyed Voro. They would run ahead of the others, attempt to engage the enemy while their fellows set up their shields and mortars . . . and likely fall before they got a single unit assembled.

They would, however, serve as a necessary distraction while the rest of his combat group found cover and set up.

It was as fine a death as any Unggoy could wish for.

Voro looked up to the stars.

They had survived the Flood and treachery of the Jiralhanae at the second Halo construct, repelled the Sentinel guardians of this world, and emerged victorious even after the human fleet decimated their ships. Many in his ranks whispered Destiny protected them.

That so-called victory against the human fleet, however, had been nothing more than luck. The human Ship Masters had outwitted them—a fact he still had difficultly reconciling. Only the timely arrival of reinforcements from Joyous Exultation had saved them.

Rumors circulated that the reinforcing ships had survived some catastrophe. Voro suspected a surprise attack from the Jiralhanae. Whatever the cause, vengeance would have to wait.

They had to win *this* battle, here and now, and claim the Forerunner technologies that would shift the strategic balance of power in the galaxy. So perhaps it was Destiny after all that had brought them to this world, but it was destiny of their own making.

He strode to the translocation platforms and rechecked the target coordinates. Voro was no priest, and he understood only a fraction of the Forerunner holy script.

The same message had repeated since they found this system.

Holographic icons swarmed over the control surface. Voro read them, shouting the divine passage to his soldiers: *"The dark times are upon us. . . . Unsheathe thy swords and smite. . . . The Ark will be your guide. . . . And bless the Reclaimers that may take refuge behind the sharpened edge of the Shield. . . . Wonder beyond awaits."*

Two hundred Sangheili roared their approval as if the message had been set here for them, writ eons ago by gods.

In truth, the nuances of this message's meaning were lost upon Voro. He had discerned, though, the center of this world was where the "Reclaimers" were to assemble: a place that held technological wonders and weapons beyond measure.

Their task was clear: stop the human demons from getting there first.

He motioned to the suicide Unggoy squads.

The small creatures crowded upon the platforms.

Voro input the translocation command and sent the first wave into battle.

CHAPTER 39

The crack of Linda's sniper rifle was uncharacteristically quiet. The sound dissipated into the vast room.

Two hundred meters from her perch a Grunt cried out. It fell, killed by the head shot. A jet of methane from its breathing apparatus ignited and spewed fire.

That was five. The creatures had appeared on translocation pads, chittering like a dozen cockroaches, lugging parts of an energy shield unit. They had looked confused, running in random directions . . . until downed by Linda.

Without shifting from her flat position or removing her gaze from the Oracle scope, Linda dropped her magazine and inserted a new one. Lying next to her in a precise row were five magazines, all she had left.

Kurt surveyed his team. They'd taken the only logical, defensible position in the room: atop the artificial hill of concentric rings.

The top of the structure was crowned with a meter-wide ledge and thirteen finlike towers that provided ample cover. The Spartans and Mendez took posts on either side of three of these towers.

Kelly had placed their last LOTUS antitank mines at the base of the hill, enough explosive force to penetrate the ultradense armor of an M808 Scorpion Main Battle Tank.

His team had height, clean lines of fire, and yet Kurt knew they were entirely vulnerable surrounded by so many translocation pads.

Inside the ring of towers, a series of additional concentric circles fell steeply into the middle of the structure. In the exact center was a hole three meters wide, glowing with a brilliant blue-white heatless illumination.

This was ostensibly the "doorway" to the core room they sought. It was open, but in the time they had been here, the rings on the hill's outer and inner slopes had continued to flatten, and the fin towers had tilted and angled inward. The entire structure was closing like the petal of a great flower.

Kurt glanced at his mission timer: 21:22.

Holographic control surfaces shimmered about the edge of the hole, and Dr. Halsey crouched there, laptop open, her tiny mote-of-light AI flitting among the symbols. She hadn't flinched at the sound of the sniper rifle, her full concentration fixed upon the center. Around her Kurt had set the eight sleeper pods for additional cover.

"Compressed slipspace field," Dr. Halsey whispered to her computer. "Transdimensional crossover confirmed. Impossible in normal three-space, at least larger than the Fermi-Planck limit."

"Action on deck!" Mendez cried.

The translocation pads scattered across the white room flickered with rings of gold. Upon dozens of pads . . . two hundred Grunts materialized.

They screamed, fired plasma and needler pistols, and charged.

Kurt had never been afraid of these diminutive aliens. But *this* was different. The cowardly creatures were wild-eyed, and sprinted headlong toward them, clawing at the air. Their plasma bolts dissipated along their two-hundred-meter-long trajectories, but several needler rounds exploded on the stones near Kurt.

"Hold your fire," he said over TEAMCOM. He scanned the advancing line, and then past them spotted three teams of Grunts setting up energy mortars.

"In back," he said. "Take out the artillery."

Linda fired twice. A trio of Grunts assembling one mortar fell.

Holly and Ash grabbed sniper rifles and picked off the other two Grunt teams before the mortars' energy shields activated.

The charging wave of Grunts surged against the base of the hill, clambering over one another to rush up the steep terraces.

"Mines?" Kelly calmly asked over the COM

"Negative," Kurt replied. "Rifles. Everyone—sweep the slopes."

Green acknowledgment lights burned.

They eased out from cover and loosened streams of automatic fire over the target-rich terrain.

The leading Grunts jerked as bullets riddled their bodies. They fell backward onto their fellows, who struggled to maintain their forward momentum. Punctured breathing units spewed methane and blossomed into flame. Many Grunts ignited, tumbled down the stairs, and desperately rolled to extinguish themselves.

The Spartans dropped magazines, inserted fresh ones, and methodically continued shooting.

The Grunts slowed and stopped halfway up the stairs, fell back, dead and alive, still screaming, but now in terror.

The survivors turned and fled—and were cut down.

Heaps of Grunts lay at the foot of the hill. Methane reverse tanks detonated, and burning armor and flesh spiraled up into columns of acrid smoke. Some Grunts attempted to crawl to safety.

"Police the wounded," Kurt ordered. "Single shots."

His team quickly dispatched them.

Then Kurt spotted his mistake: Two hundred fifty meters back, almost lost in the glare of the vast room, stood Elites . . . now safely behind stationary shield generators.

Kurt increased the magnification on his faceplate. There were three groups equidistantly positioned around the hill—thirty Elites in each.

"Twelve, four, and seven o'clock," Kurt whispered over TEAM-COM. "Trouble."

"We've got three SPNKr missiles left," Linda offered. "I could get a trajectory over those shield units."

Kurt then saw outlines that made his stomach clench, silhouettes that hulked over the smaller Elites. Three Hunter pairs, one in each company.

"Too much firepower," he told Linda. "They'd down them before impact. We'll wait for them to come to us. Stand by."

Above them, the towers leaned in at a 45-degree angle; the depth from the top of the hill to the center was now only six meters. Kurt could actually see the concentric rings settling, centimeter by centimeter.

His countdown timer read "17:51."

Every Spartan had about a dozen magazines for their MA5B and MA5K assault rifles, three grenades, sniper rifles—normally enough for nearly any engagement. This, however, would be a lopsided siege against an enemy who was well prepared and, Kurt had to admit it, outthinking them.

He moved down to Dr. Halsey.

"Progress?" he whispered.

Dr. Halsey continued to stare at the white compressed space within the center. It flexed, and revealed a tantalizing glimpse of normal daylight beyond, and then shifted back to glare and distortion.

"There is nothing I can do to hasten the closing of this aperture," she murmured. "Are you still set on remaining here until the last possible moment?"

"We can't allow the Covenant to get inside," Kurt said, "and I'm not sending part of our team ahead. It would only weaken our forces here, and potentially leave any advance party facing Sentinels on the other side."

She looked up at him and sighed. "I find myself reluctantly agreeing with your tactical analysis."

Kurt unholstered his M6 pistol and set it next to her. "You may need this, Doctor. Keep your head down."

She took the gun and racked the slide as if she had used one many times before.

Kurt moved back to the upper ledge.

The Elites had spread out in three lines. They presented Jackal shields, interlinked them, and started a slow advance toward the hill. This was another inspired tactic. If the Spartans fired at them, they'd just burn through these disposable shields and would still have their personal overshields to contend with.

The Hunter pairs towered in the center of the formations. The thick slabs of alloy they used for shields were impenetrable to any weapon they had.

Kurt glanced to Ash standing by his side, and then to his pack on the ground. Inside were the two cut-down FENRIS warheads. Kurt double-checked the detonator control pad in his gauntlet's data socket. Still there.

"All squads," Kurt ordered. "Counter incoming enemy vectors."

Ash and Olivia moved closer to Kurt at his seven o'clock position. Kelly, Will, Holly, and Lucy clustered at four o'clock. Chief Mendez, Fred, Mark, and Tom took position at twelve o'clock.

"At fifty meters," Kurt continued, "pitch grenades to break those lines, plasma first to drain shields, then the frags. Ignore the Hunters. Follow up with sniper fire. When they're close enough, use rifles."

"How close, sir?" Holly asked. There was a quaver in her voice—not fear, but anticipation.

"When they're on the stairs," Kurt told her. "Kelly, stand ready with the LOTUS mines."

Kurt knew they couldn't stop them all. Some *would* get to the base of the hill. And some *would* climb the stairs. How many depended on their skill, timing, and a great deal of luck.

Green acknowledgment lights flashed, and the Spartans tensed.

The advancing Elites were two hundred meters away. They hadn't fired a single shot yet. Whoever commanded them showed uncommon restraint.

Kurt searched for the glistening gold armor of a Ship or Fleet Master, but only saw the red battle gear of Covenant Majors on the field.

One hundred meters.

The SPARTAN-IIIs shifted from foot to foot, a nervous gesture not mirrored in the battle-hardened SPARTAN-IIs whose bio signs on Kurt's tactical display barely showed a flutter.

Chief Mendez caught Kurt's assessing look and gave him a confident nod.

This was what he and Mendez had trained the Spartans for their entire lives. They would survive this. They had to.

At fifty meters he spotted Elite soldiers opening and closing their four hinged jaws as if anticipating human blood.

"Throw—now," Kurt ordered.

Blurred trajectories of burning blue plasma zipped through the air, followed by fragmentation grenades.

The advancing Elites hesitated, and a ripple distorted through their precise lines. The plasma grenades hit; there was a flash of blue-white that drained clusters of overlapping Jackal shields and knocked many Elites to their knees. Fragmentation grenades hit, bounced, and rolled into their ranks—and exploded.

Bodies and splashes of blood flew through the air; blue and red armor tumbled from the center of the blast.

Kurt hefted his sniper rifle and targeted Elites still dazed, their overshields weakened and flickering.

The Elite Majors growled orders, and the lines struggled to close.

Kurt squeezed off a shot, and the round tore through one Elite's open helmet, emerging out the back in a spray of blue.

To Kurt's right and left came the popcorn crackle of single shots, and more Elites in the broken line fell.

Three Elites stood their ground and returned fire.

Plasma bolts impacted on the stone near Kurt's head. He felt the heat wash over his SPI armor plates.

This was what he had hoped for: chaos. He'd happily exchange fire at this range when he had a scope, cover, and a superior angle.

A Hunter bellowed in rage, lumbered to one of the Elites returning fire instead of re-forming the line, and hammered that Elite with one massive fist—crushing its spine. Turning, the Hunter screamed at the other two Elites and they quickly closed ranks.

Kurt kept firing, picking off stragglers as their formation knit together—shooting one Elite in the knee joint, one in the eye, until their Jackal shields overlapped.

He took a quick body count. Eleven down in the formation approaching his position.

They continued their advance to less than five meters from the base of the stairs.

"Hold your fire," Kurt ordered. "Kelly, LOTUS to standby."

The flowerlike LOTUS antitank mines had been placed in the crux of the first steps and overlaid with a square of silver reflective blanket that served as camouflage in the brilliant light.

Two groups of five Elites split from their line and took up position to either side of the stairs, angling their shields toward the top. Five more Elites took cover behind them and opened fire. Plasma and crystal shards flashed up the slope.

Kurt ducked and the air scintillated overhead. He crawled to the edge and peered over.

The Hunters moved up the stairs followed by the balance of the Elite warriors . . . just passing the first step.

"Now," he told Kelly.

The LOTUS exploded into a multipetaled flash of lightning, thunder, and fire, enveloping the approaching force.

The concussive force roiled through Kurt's insides.

Three simultaneous sonic booms echoed off the walls.

Kurt popped up with his assault rifle and opened fire. Ash and Olivia were at his side, MA5Ks spitting rounds down the staircase.

The Hunter pair, halfway up the steps, stood stunned and bloodied by the concussive force, their impenetrable shields askew.

Kurt aimed at the closest Hunter's unarmored center. Rounds

tore into its exposed flesh. The tangles of eels within his armor writhed and made the monster's bulk seem to boil. He grabbed his last plasma grenade, sidearmed it.

The grenade stuck to the Hunter's abdomen—flashed, and ignited a dozen of the orange eel symbiotes constituting its form. Many fell out, aflame, burning and squealing on the steps.

The Hunter staggered back and fell; the gestalt lost cohesion and spilled into a smoldering mound of worms.

The surviving Hunter ducked behind its shield, bellowing a vengeful cry.

Kurt picked up a rifle and joined Ash and Olivia, combining fire to penetrate the overshields of the remaining Elite solders on the stairs.

A cluster of Elites at the base regrouped, their shields regenerated, and they returned fire.

Ash and Olivia ducked behind cover.

The hill trembled behind Kurt.

He turned and saw a Hunter pair plod onto the top at the four o'clock position, flanked by a vanguard of three Elites with energy swords.

Kelly reacted first, moved in, grabbed an Elite's wrist, and snapped it. She followed with an elbow to the Elite face—twisted the sword free and slashed, cutting it in half, as well as the two Elites on either side.

She spun to face the Hunters.

For once in her life, she was too slow.

The monsters had leveled their fuel-rod cannons at Kelly. They had her.

Holly jumped between Kelly and the weapons.

The Hunters fired, outlining both Spartans in the blinding green radiation for a split second.

The overpressure of both point-blank fuel-rod cannon detonations threw Kelly, Will, and Lucy into the air.

Holly exploded backward—a spray of molten SPI armor, disintegrating flesh, and jets of smoke.

Kurt stood horrified, frozen, but then instincts and training clicked on full force, and without thinking, he rushed forward before the Hunters could finish his prone teammates.

The nearest Hunter turned on him faster than he expected—slicing its two-ton shield into Kurt's solar plexus.

The outer layer of Kurt's armor cracked and the liquid ballistic underlayers failed and squirted out. Pain ripped through his torso; ribs cracked; he coughed and blood spattered the inside of his faceplate.

He dropped in a heap at the Hunter's boots, dazed, only recovering his wits enough to see the Hunter raise both fists over him for the killing blow.

Linda's sniper rifle cracked. The exposed region of the Hunter's midsection exploded in a mass of orange, but it remained miraculously upright.

Will hurled himself at the Hunter, and knocked the beast off its feet and into its mate—and the three of them tumbled down the stairs.

Kurt got up, ignoring the near-blinding pain, and limped to the edge.

Will stood between both Hunters at the base of the hill. He kicked the nearest in the unarmored middle and it staggered back.

Around him were a dozen Elites who, confronted by the sight of a lone Spartan engaging two Hunters in hand-to-hand combat, were momentarily too stunned to act.

Kurt and Lucy opened fire, suppressing the Elites, before they regained their senses.

One Hunter lashed out with its shield. Will ducked, darted inside its reach, and battered its bruised midsection—punching *through* flesh and ripping out wriggling chunks of the composite eel colony.

The second Hunter angled away from the fight and brought its cannon to bear.

Will spun around.

The Hunter shot him.

Will's energy shield vanished, and the front of his MJOLNIR armor melted. He took a step toward the beast, and collapsed.

The Hunter turned and roared at the Spartans at the top of the hill, and then started to bring its tremendous shield back in line. . . .

A SPNKr missile screamed past Kurt's head, leaving a spiral of propellant exhaust, streaked toward the Hunter, and impacted dead center of its mass.

The air erupted into a blurred sphere of explosive force. The nearby Elites were tossed aside like rag dolls, their shields flaring. The Hunter burst into a cloud of snakelike parts that wetly spattered upon the floor.

Kurt turned and saw Fred kneeling next to him, his spent SPNKr tube smoking.

It was silent.

Nothing moved. Not the Elites, the Hunters, or William.

Kelly and Linda finally rose, shaking off the concussion from the fuel-rod cannon detonation. They stood with Kurt and Fred and stared at their fallen comrade.

Ash was on his knees where Holly had stood a second ago. There were the outlines of two bootprints on the stone . . . nothing else.

Two Spartans down in a matter of seconds. One an old friend, the other a girl Kurt had known since she was four years old. Yet, he couldn't stop and think about it—not when they were surrounded by enemies. There were still many lives that were his responsibility.

Kurt looked away and assessed the remaining threat.

Olivia, posted at seven o'clock, waved Kurt closer. He limped to her.

"They just pulled back," she whispered.

From the hill base, the Hunter and the surviving Elites had re-formed their line and were retreating, already fifty meters away.

Kurt made his way to the twelve o'clock point, to Mendez, Mark, and Tom. Chief Mendez met him. The old man had never looked so grim.

"They're pulling back here, too, sir," Mendez said. "Doesn't make sense. Covenant always fight to the last one."

Kurt called up the roster on his display, still stained by his own blood, and checked TEAMBIO.

Will's vitals were flatlined. Holly's signal . . . was entirely missing.

Over TEAMCOM he said, "Eyes peeled, everyone. Kelly, get Will. Linda, cover her."

They moved, but no green acknowledgment lights flashed, the only sign of their numbing grief.

Kurt sat down, suddenly too tired to think.

Then he noticed *his* bio signs: failing blood pressure, erratic heartbeat, electrolytes all wrong. There was internal bleeding. He found a can of biofoam, inserted its tip into his armor's midline injection port, and emptied it.

The expanding liquid polymer chilled his chest.

He closed his eyes, and when he looked again his blood pressure had stabilized. His head had cleared.

Fred made a short come-here gesture and Kurt groggily rose and went to his comrade.

"There." Fred pointed to far side of the core room. "Three hundred fifty meters. Step up polarization to ninety-five percent, sir, and you'll see them." His voice trembled with rage.

Kurt darkened his faceplate, and then understood the reason for the Covenant's retreat.

Over a hundred fresh Elites massed behind energy-shield generators. Banshee fliers zipped back and forth over them. Plasma cannons were assembled by squads of Grunts. In the very front, Kurt spied a glint of gold armor, their leader—staring back at him.

"They softened us up before the main offensive," Kurt whispered.

"Orders, sir?" Fred asked.

Between the mental shock of losing Holly, Will, and Dante, and the physiological shock his body fought off, Kurt had forgotten he was in charge. His duty to get the alien technology and preserve the entire human race came back with crushing weight.

In truth, there were few options left.

They could fight: advance to meet this new threat before their forces fully crystallized. In the open terrain though, without artillery or armor or air support, even Spartans would be cut down.

They could run: use the slipspace rift in the core. The Covenant force would certainly follow, possibly destroy them, and gain more Forerunner technologies. That was not acceptable. Not when it had cost them so much to get this far.

There was still his last option: the nukes. If he couldn't stop the Covenant, he could deny them their prize. He'd take the warheads to the core and blow it all to hell.

"Keep me posted and stand by," he told Fred, and then limped down to the center.

Dr. Halsey met him. "I'm sorry," she whispered. "Holly and Will—"

She stopped midsyllable and Kurt saw her glasses reflected the jiggling lines of his TEAMBIO signals. He had had no idea she could intercept their encrypted COM channel.

"You're wounded," she stated, and seemed to stare into his body. "Internal bleeding . . . your liver . . . massive laceration . . ." Her gaze came back into focus, and her voice dropped to a whisper. "You're going to bleed out, Kurt, if I don't operate. The only thing holding you together inside is biofoam."

Kurt was lucky that Hunter shield hadn't cut him in half. "I understand." He rechecked his mission timer: 6:32. "I'll hold myself together for a few more minutes. Then you can do whatever you want to me."

He looked past Dr. Halsey to the central rift. The rings here were flattening fastest. The ledges were only an eighth of a meter high and visibly contracting.

Within the rift he caught flashes of golden sunlight. There were other colors: green, blue, and brown, but the distortion was so great, Kurt couldn't focus on what shapes lay beyond.

"Once it closes, this slipspace field will remain intact?"

"I have no reason to believe otherwise," she replied.

"Impenetrable . . ." Kurt whispered.

"To any force in our normal three dimensions, yes."

The Sentinels, the Halo rings, this so-called "shield world," and the clockwork design that the Forerunners had set in motion millennia ago was about to end . . . and it made sense to Kurt.

At least it made sense in terms of him now having a *winning* option.

He unpolarized his faceplate and looked at her. "I think I understand what you were trying to tell me before, Doctor. The

Forerunners built this construct to protect these 'Reclaimers' from the Halo detonations. Like a bomb shelter. But they never got inside. You were going to use it for the Spartans."

"'Behind the sharpened edge of the shield,'" Dr. Halsey quoted. "Safe . . . perhaps from everything."

He locked stares with her and nodded.

"I'm sending Team Saber, Mendez, and you ahead."

She blinked. "I thought you said we stay together."

For the last two decades Kurt had struggled to keep his Spartans alive. But what if Dr. Halsey had been correct and all their battles meant nothing? What if no matter how valiant the fight they could not win this war? Did it make sense to die, or was it better to live to fight another day? . . . Even if that "day" was very far away.

He turned back to the Spartans. "Tom, Lucy, Team Saber," he said over the COM, "set Dante and Will on the pods. Saber will go ahead and scout the core."

Tom and Lucy nodded, and with help from Olivia and Mark, they gathered the fallen Spartans.

Ash jumped into the center and approached. "Sir," he said, "we're not leaving the fight."

"This isn't about a fight," Kurt told him. "You have a mission to accomplish, son. Carry out my orders."

"Understood, sir."

Ash motioned for Olivia and Mark to join him near the rift.

"Go," Ash told them.

Olivia and Mark looked at Kurt and then together jumped into the brilliance.

There were a pair of flares and they vanished.

Ash hesitated, his hand moved up as if to salute, but he stopped, recalling the standing order of "no saluting in combat arenas." He stood straighter, gave Kurt a nod, and jumped after his teammates.

Kurt keyed the COM, "Saber One, you read me?"

"We're goooo . . ." Ash's voice dopplered to the ultrasonic.

"Saber One? Ash?"

Static washed over the channel.

Not even a COM signal made it through—an observation that only strengthened Kurt's conviction that he was doing the right thing. He hoped for the best, hoped Saber and the others would be okay.

"Pods," Kurt said, and motioned toward Tom and Lucy.

His NCOs pushed the cryo pods and the bodies of Will and Dante through. More flashes. Silence.

"Chief. Doctor," Kurt said. "You're next."

Mendez looked to the spatial rift and then to Kurt. He swallowed, and said, "Aye aye, sir. We'll see you on the other side."

For once, Dr. Halsey had nothing to say. Instead she made the traditional Spartan two-finger "smile" gesture over her face. She blinked quickly, and then turned to the fissure.

Mendez took her hand and they stepped—

And were gone.

"They're starting," Fred announced over the COM.

"Guard the opening, you two," Kurt ordered Lucy and Tom.

Kurt then moved back up to the edge of the hill and watched with Fred as 150 Elites moved toward them. This time it was not a slow, careful march with overlapped shields. They charged en masse. Banshees swooped up and over the formation, two high and two low, accelerating ahead of the Covenant infantry and then over the hill.

They ducked behind the towers, and then Linda popped out as the Banshees passed.

"I have them." Linda's sniper rifle was to her shoulder. She stood motionless for a heartbeat, then fired once at the receding fliers, moved her aim slightly, and fired once more.

The rear two Banshee pilots fell. Riderless, the Banshees nosed to the floor, bounced, and sparked to a halt.

Linda dropped the magazine, examined the chamber, cycled the bolt, and then set it down. "I'm out."

Kurt, Kelly, and Fred leveled their assault rifles at the remaining fliers and opened fire. Tracer rounds arced through the air and stitched over the Banshees. Smoke billowed from the leader, and erupted into a ball of flame that smeared through the air.

The last lone Banshee pulled up and circled back.

The advancing horde of Elites and Hunters was only two hundred meters away. A few in their ranks fired, and wild energy bolts streaked overhead.

The towers now lay thirty degrees off the deck, and the "hill" only three meters tall. Kurt knew they'd soon have no cover left.

Fred glanced at the open smoking bolt of his MAB5. "I'm out, too," he said.

Kurt opened up the administrative subdirectory on his heads-up display and accessed SPARTAN-104's file. "As acting CO of Team Blue, I am hereby granting you a field commission to the rank of Lieutenant, Junior Grade," Kurt told Fred. "Congratulations."

Fred shook his head, not understanding.

Kurt uploaded Fred's change of rank, and his IFF icon blinked to the star-and-bar insignia of Lieutenant.

"As an officer, you'll have to keep your eye on the larger picture, Fred. Get your team through that slipspace field. I'll be right behind you."

Linda and Kelly gathered around them.

Kelly whispered, "We lost you once, Kurt. We're not going to leave you again."

Plasma artillery pounded the face of the hill, shattering stone, and superheated convection rolls distorted the air.

"No one's leaving anyone behind," Kurt assured her. "I just have to rig a little welcome present for our friends." He grabbed the pack with the FENRIS warheads, and swung it over his shoulder.

Kelly, Linda, and Fred exchanged glances.

"I'll be right behind you," Kurt told them. "Now, go. The SPARTAN-IIIs are going to need you."

A hail of needler shards arced up and over the top of the slope, impacting the surfaces around them.

The Spartans huddled together, presenting the smallest target surface, their energy shields flaring as the crystal rounds detonated.

The hardened plates of Kurt's SPI armor cracked and the concussion rattled his bones and splintered the hardening biofoam in his abdomen. He tasted fresh blood.

The bombardment ceased.

"Hurry!" Kurt told them.

They all jogged to the center. The rift was fading and was now only a meter across. Deep inside, Kurt caught sight of a ribbon of blue and silver. Water glistening in the sunlight?

Kelly and Linda entered without hesitation; Fred halted, turned, and held out his hand.

Kurt took it and shook.

Fred stepped backward and vanished.

Only Tom and Lucy remained, still standing guard by the rift. Their SPI armor picked up and mimicked the gold sunlight in the fissure.

"Okay, you two—"

"With all due respect, sir," Tom said. "We're not leaving. You'll have to court-martial us."

Lucy said nothing, but made her intention to fight understood as she hefted their last SPNKr missile launcher.

The rift wavered, dimmed, and contracted to a mere half meter.

"There's no time for this," Kurt growled.

Tom took a step closer to Lucy.

Of course, Kurt had been foolish to think Tom and Lucy would leave him after so many years together—orders or not. Perhaps they even knew what he had in mind.

"Okay, you win. How much ammunition do you have?" Kurt moved to Tom. "We'll pool our reserves."

Tom looked down at his rifle—

Kurt hit him, his flattened palm connecting with the underside of Tom's helmet. The impact lifted the Spartan a half meter off the ground, and he landed in a heap.

Kurt wheeled on Lucy and held up a warning finger, indicating that she stay put.

He checked Tom's bio signs. No bones broken. No cerebral swelling. Just coldcocked.

"He'll live," he said. "You're *both* going to live. Now give me a hand."

Shadows crisscrossed the hill, and fifty meters overhead Kurt watched three Banshees streak past.

Lucy dropped the missile launcher and helped Kurt pull Tom up.

Kurt wrapped his limp arm around her shoulder. "You two didn't survive Pegasi Delta to die here," he told her. "There's too much left for you to do."

She shook her head violently back and forth.

"Yes," he said. "Don't make me . . ."

His vision blurred and a wave of dizziness washed over him. His heart struggled, pumping harder and faster. There was a warm trickle in his stomach. He was losing more blood. Slipping into shock.

Plasma blots stitched the stone nearby, shattering them, as Banshees screamed by on a strafing run.

"Please," he whispered.

Lucy reached up to Kurt's faceplate, touching two fingers to his mouth. She struggled to make a sound, but all she could manage was a half-choked cry.

He took her hand, gave it a squeeze, and let go.

Lucy lingered, looked at Kurt one last time, and then slipped into the rift.

"Good-bye," he said.

They were gone. All of them.

Now Kurt could concentrate on what had to be done.

He picked up Tom's MA5K. Its ammo counter indicated half a magazine. It would have to do. He grabbed the last missile launcher, too. He was sure he could find a use for it.

The "hill" around the center was only a meter tall now and shrinking rapidly as the concentric rings eased back to the floor of the room. The finlike towers folded inward, almost flat against the ground.

Elite snipers poked over the top of the hill and fired a tight cluster of plasma.

Kurt was too slow to dodge the shots. His SPI armor heated, cracked, and half of his chest plate shattered away.

Smoldering, Kurt dropped to his knees. Blackness clouded his mind. He struggled to stay conscious—fought his way back by sheer willpower, and his vision cleared.

The snipers backed away, not bothering to finish him off. More Elites appeared on the hill, now only a half meter tall, sinking even faster toward a level topology.

A Hunter pair appeared on the slight rise and assessed Kurt. They snorted, unimpressed.

Almost there, he thought. *Almost done. Almost won.*

Kurt grabbed up the SPNKr launcher and fired from the hip. The missile rocketed toward one Hunter, hit, exploded, and knocked it off the top. Kurt leveled his assault rifle and sprayed the other Hunter, but it turtled behind its shield.

The rifle's bolt clacked—empty.

The Hunter stood and growled. Its mate, bloodied and still smoking from the missile impact, stomped toward Kurt, hands ready to tear him to pieces.

Kurt ventured a glance back. The rift was only a flicker now, and shrinking.

His mission timer read "0:47."

A sharp bark behind the Hunters made them halt in their tracks.

An Elite in golden armor strode toward them, gracing Kurt with a glance that was part disdain . . . and part respect. It jabbered orders at the Hunters and the others.

Kurt's translation software deciphered part of this: *"Damage not the center. Engineers with the slipspace field shunts . . . Reopen the silver gate. Glory is ours!"*

A roar of thunderous triumph burst from the gathered Covenant.

Kurt struggled to rise. There was more pain than he'd ever felt, and his legs had turned to wet sand. His vision tunneled . . . but he got to his feet . . . and raised both hands into a fighting stance.

"You haven't won," Kurt said. "You've still got me to get through."

The Ship Master assessed Kurt and nodded, perhaps understanding him, perhaps not. It gazed upon Kurt as an equal. A fellow warrior.

Around them the concentric rings settled to the floor, and with a whispered hiss, all of the ridges melded into a single smooth surface. The fins touched down silently, thirteen clamping armatures splayed two meters from the center of the room.

His countdown timer blinked at him: "0:00."

He exhaled. The rift was closed.

Kurt opened his team roster—subheading status—and moved Will, SPARTAN-043; Dante, SPARTAN-G188; and Holly, SPARTAN-G003 to the missing-in-action column, adhering to the tradition of never listing a fallen Spartan as "killed in action."

Kurt then highlighted Lieutenant Commandeer Kurt Ambrose . . . and moved that name to the MIA list as well—next to Kurt, SPARTAN-051.

The room started to spin. His mouth went dry. He tried to swallow. Couldn't.

His vision doubled and he thought he saw Tom and Lucy come back to get him . . . but it wasn't them. It was Shane, Robert, and Jane from Team Wolf Pack.

There were hundreds of Spartans with him on the platform— from Alpha and Beta Companies, Dante, Holly, Will, and even Sam . . . all ready to fight and win this last battle with him.

Hallucination? Maybe. It was nonetheless welcome.

The ghostly Spartans nodded, and gave him the thumbs-up "can-do" signal.

Kurt wouldn't let them down. All he had to do was single-handedly stop a Covenant army. One last impossible mission . . . the short definition of any Spartan. It was the least he owed them.

The Fleet Master Elite snarled at Kurt, and the translation filtered through his helmet's speaker: *"One last fight, demon. You will die and we shall reopen the silver path."*

"Die?" Kurt laughed. "Didn't you know?" he told the Elite. ". . . Spartans never die."

Kurt turned his gauntlet face-up and pressed the detonator.

EPILOGUE

SHIELD WORLD

CHAPTER 40

"Sir, something!" Lieutenant Joe Yang hunched over his sensor station, energy spikes dancing on-screen. "Double EMP signature. Subsurface." He shook his head and tugged at one eyebrow nervously. "Multiple energy signatures now. Hundreds. All underground."

Commander Lash and Lieutenant Commander Waters stood over Yang's shoulder and tried to make sense of it.

"Definitely nukes," Waters breathed. "Radiological ratios indicate it's one of ours."

The electromagnetic pulses faded into a roiling sea of larger waveforms.

"That's a lot more energy than two FENRIS warheads," Lash

said. "Something bigger is going on down there." He exhaled, and his breath came out in tremulous shudders. No one noticed.

He opened a SHIPCOM Channel to Cho. "Status of the slipspace capacitors?"

"Seven-three percent," Cho answered, "losing point oh three percent per minute, sir.

"Stand by to jump-heat the reactor," Lash told him, "and shunt all power to the slipspace system."

There was a long pause over the COM, then, "Aye, sir. Cho out."

Jump-heating the rectors would send up a signal flare to the Covenant armada. Lash hoped, though, whatever this planetside activity was would distract them and give the *Dusk* a chance to finally escape.

Lieutenant Bethany Durruno rocked back and forth in her seat, her eyes glued to the three satellite uplinks streaming through her NAV station. She tapped on a trio of microthruster controls, keeping the BLACK WIDOW satellites just hovering at extreme contact range.

She was right on the edge. For that matter, so were Yang and Waters. Even Cho belowdecks was showing classic withdrawal signs that accompanied combat fatigue.

The *Dusk* had survived the destruction of Admiral Patterson's fleet, and then stayed quiet and camouflaged in the dark while the Covenant armada ran right over them.

That had been the hardest on his crew—moving meter by meter toward the moon, drifting through a debris field full of shattered UNSC ship hulls, destroyed escape pods . . . and thousands of bodies of the bravest men and women in the Navy.

They'd made it undetected to the opposite side of the silver moon of Onyx, and gently came to rest in the shadow of a crater.

While the *Dusk* settled to the surface, Lieutenant Commander Cho had released three baseball-sized BLACK WIDOW stealth satellites, so they could monitor the Covenant forces.

"Energy waves spreading across the planet, sir," Yang said, utterly confounded by his readings.

"Put it on-screen," Lash ordered.

The three main viewscreens flickered to life as the feed from their satellites streamed images of Onyx: oceans of lapis and pearl-colored clouds, emerald continents with zigzagging mountain ranges.

In high orbit glided Covenant vessels. They moved in packs, simmering blue against the black of space.

A dot appeared on the planet's surface—a red flare that arced upward, showering molten rock and ash. Three more winked on . . . then a dozen more flashed . . . then hundreds.

Jagged cracks tore between the eruptions and a spiderweb pattern of glowing lava fissures spread over the world. They reached the polar regions and the ice caps detonated into geysers of steam.

"Plasma bombardment," Waters whispered. "The Covenant are glassing the place."

"No plasma detected, sir," Yang said. "All energy originating from *inside* the planet."

A single beam of light pierced the thickening clouds—a blinding gold hue that sliced the upper atmosphere and shot into space.

Wavering spectra flashed on Yang's screen.

"We've seen that before," Lash said. "Combined drone fire."

A second beam joined this first one; then thousands flashed on and radiated from the surface of Onyx—scintillating lances filled space and transformed the world into a sea urchin of pure energy.

Covenant ships caught by the beams vanished, instantly ionized.

Onyx shattered and the surface exploded into space.

Obscured by layers of dust and fire, a blazing pattern emerged beneath: crosses and lines and dots.

"Magnification factor one thousand," Lash ordered.

Yang was frozen.

Waters bent over and tapped in the command.

The view on-screen blinked and stepped closer—past boiling air, clouds, tumbling mountains—zooming to ground level, revealing a lattice of three-meter-long rods and half-meter blazing red spheres that hovered between them, forming a crystalline structure.

"Back it off," Lash said

The view pulled back and showed that this drone-constructed scaffolding stretched over kilometers . . . they had been under every landmass, every ocean . . . under the entire surface—orderly linked rows like the carbon bonds of an infinite polymer chain, or an immense colony of living, interlinked army ants.

The drones were the planet Onyx.

"There are trillions of them," Lieutenant Durruno whispered.

Clusters of drones heated; culminated beams shot forth again, targeting more distant Covenant vessels and vaporizing them.

"They're protecting this place," Waters said. "Why?"

"Shockwave from surface detonation impacting far side of the moon in seven seconds," Durruno said. The blood drained from her face.

The viewscreens filled with static.

"Lost the satellites," Yang cried.

"Cho," Lash said. "Jump-heat the reactor and dump everything into those capacitors. Now! Get us out of here!"

CHAPTER 41

The Spartans and Dr. Halsey gathered about the graves of William and Dante.

It was a fine spot: sunlight dappled the river that flowed past this grove of oak trees. A path of banded onyx curved through the area. They had pried up some of the slabs, scratched in William's and Dante's names, and erected two more to serve as markers for Holly and the Lieutenant Commander.

Senior Chief Petty Officer Mendez read from a small black leather book: "*We have come to a place far from home / Time long passed since we have seen the sun rise / A place where peace can finally come / A place where we can rest and laugh and sing and love once more.*"

He hung his head and closed the volume, *A Soldier's Tale: Rainforest Wars*, the military classic written in 2164.

There was a moment of silence.

"Burial detail dismissed," Fred told them.

Ash set a spent brass casing on each marker, a token of respect for his fellow Spartans. He didn't know what else to do.

It had been a full day and a half since the Lieutenant Commander had ordered them into the rift, and a day and a half since it had sealed, stranding them all here.

The shock of losing him and the others hadn't worn off. They all felt numb and hollow. Spartans usually did not have the luxury of grief; contemplation of the dead was almost always truncated by another mission, a battle, and their focus redirected to the larger strategic picture of saving humanity.

. . . Not this time.

The slipspace rift had been stable when Dr. Halsey and Chief Mendez had first passed through, dropping them three meters onto a grassy hill. The cryo pods and Team Saber had followed shortly thereafter. They watched as the opening then started to collapse.

When Fred, Linda, and Kelly emerged, they immediately tried to return. Tom and Lucy had tumbled through the opening, and by then the rift was too small. They could only watch as it compressed back to a single wavering dot and vanished.

Most of them had thought the slipspace passage would move them to an interior room within the artificial construct known as Onyx.

No one, not even Dr. Halsey, had been prepared for this.

Overhead blazed a golden sun. The sky, if it could be called that, was robin's-egg blue at the horizon but quickly deepened to indigo and black the higher one looked, then warmed again as it neared the sun. There were no stars.

The surface stretched out in all directions—meadows, rivers, lakes, forests, winding paths all perfectly flat. All flat, that is, until Linda sighted through her Oracle scope. She then discovered every horizon sloped upward until these curving surfaces vanished in the extreme distance.

Linda said it felt like being at the bottom of a large bowl.

Dr. Halsey had assured them they most definitely were not in a "bowl."

"A sphere," she said, repeating this for the third time to Chief Mendez, "is where we are."

The Chief sat in the grass. "One more time," he said, "explain it to me, please, Doctor. Slowly."

Dr. Halsey sighed, straightened her skirt, and then sat next to him. "Very well, Chief." She unfolded her laptop, and numbers, charts, and spectroscopic analysis flashed on-screen.

The Spartans gathered as well to listen. In truth, while they understood the scientific principles that led Dr. Halsey to her conclusions, they still didn't quite believe them.

"We start with this so-called sun." She pointed straight up and then gestured to the data on her screen. "Spectra and energy output are consistent with a G2-type dwarf, one of slightly smaller dimensions than Sol.

"Next, you will note the curvature of this world, concave, as seen through Linda's sniper scope." She tabbed to a new screen and it sketched the star and a curve that arced to complete a full circle.

"Extrapolating, I calculate a diameter of one hundred fifty million kilometers—two astronomical units, or a radius equivalent to the distance of the Earth orbiting its sun.

"Conclusion?" She paused for dramatic effect. "We are inside a Micro Dyson sphere."

Ash pulled off his helmet and vigorously scratched his head

with both hands. "That can't be right," he protested. "We stepped through the rift and showed up here instantaneously. Even in Slipstream space it would have taken *some* time to travel to another star."

"Entirely true," Dr. Halsey said, "but we have not left Onyx."

"This is the part I don't get," Kelly muttered.

"The Forerunners' grasp of slipspace technology was far more advanced than ours or the Covenant's," Dr. Halsey explained. "I believe this sphere resides in the center of the planet, encapsulated and protected by a slipspace bubble of compressed dimensionality."

Chief Mendez looked around and shook his head, unable or unwilling to accept her interpretation of the facts.

"If all this is true, Doctor," Fred said, "and the Forerunners built this as a refuge, a bomb shelter to protect them from the Halos or the Flood, then why aren't they here?"

Dr. Halsey shrugged and uttered the words no one thought her capable of: "I do not know." She closed her laptop. "Did something go wrong with their plan? Or did everything go as planned? We may never know. Why the Flood survives today and where the Forerunners went are mysteries we have yet to solve."

They remained there a minute, quiet, pondering the scale of this place, the eon-old Forerunner secrets, and tried to integrate it into the events of the last few weeks.

Fred then grabbed his rifle and said, "Ash, take your team and gather our supplies. We're deploying in five."

"Yes sir." Ash donned his helmet. He and the other SPARTAN-IIIs moved as if jolted by lightning.

"Chief," Fred told Mendez, "I want a count of every round of ammunition we have."

"Sir." Mendez jumped to his feet. "I'm on it."

"With all due respect, Lieutenant," Dr. Halsey said, and remained sitting. "Where exactly do you intend to go? We should rest, think, and heal our wounds. We have lost so many. . . ."

"Yes, we have," Fred replied. "Which is why we are moving out. Dante and Holly gave their lives fighting. Kurt stayed behind and made sure the Covenant wouldn't follow us. Now it's our duty to complete the mission: find Forerunner technologies and get them back to Earth." He lowered his voice and added, "Doing anything less would dishonor their sacrifices."

Linda moved next to him and said, "Suggest we start by finding a way to open Team Katana's cryo pods, sir. Get them up and running."

"Yes!" Kelly said, and joined them. "Crack the slipspace fields on those things, and maybe we'll find some way to bust out of this place, too."

Dr. Halsey stared at them and pushed her glasses farther up the bridge of her nose. "I see. You do understand that while externally, this space may only be a few meters in diameter within the center of Onyx, internally, its compressed dimensionality gives it a surface area"—she cocked her head, calculating—"many times the surface of the Earth."

Fred looked to Kelly and Linda, and he said, "Then we better get started. We've got a lot of ground to cover."

Dr. Halsey stood, sighed deeply, and brushed grass from her lab coat. "Very well, I'll gather my things."

She strode off and the Spartans watched her go.

Kelly whispered, "You think John's still out there? I mean alive?"

"Yes," Linda said.

"He has to be," Fred told her. "He's the only one left to stop the Covenant."

"While we're stuck in here." Kelly kicked the grass. "What's your take on the others? Team Saber?"

"They're kids," Fred said. "But so were we once. I think they're Spartans, like us."

Ash trotted up to them, Olivia and Mark trailing behind, hefting packs.

"All ready, sir," Ash said.

"Good." Fred set a hand on Ash's shoulder, and nodded to the others.

"Welcome to Blue, Spartans," Kelly said. "We're going to make a great team."

ACKNOWLEDGMENTS

First and foremost my wife and fellow writer, Syne Mitchell, and my son, Kai. They lived with a deadline-driven cranky writer for several months. Without their help, love, and understanding no one would be reading anything from me.

Next, the Bungie "Story Four"—Brian Jarrard, Rob McLees, Frank O'Connor, and Joseph Staten—who helped develop the story and checked every nuance of the manuscript more times than I can count.

My agent, Richard Curtis, for his clear thinking and ever-calm character.

Eric Raab and Tom Doherty at Tor Books for their editorial acumen and constant support.

Dana Fos and Matt Whiting at Microsoft Game Studios User Experience.

In the Microsoft Licensing Group: Alicia Brattin, Alicia Hatch, Nancy Figatner, Brian Maeda, Steve Schreck, and Edward Ventura.

Extra special thanks to Mercury Eric, and the many fans who have written to me.

—Eric Nylund
North Bend, Washington
August 2006

ABOUT THE AUTHOR

Eric Nylund is the author of many novels, including the New York Times bestselling works *Halo: The Fall of Reach, Halo: First Strike,* and *Halo: Ghosts of Onyx,* and the World Fantasy nominated *Dry Water.* As a writer for Microsoft Game Studios, Nylund helped develop such game franchises as *Halo* and *Gears of War.* He has also helped shape the intellectual property for some of the world's best videogame developers, including Bioware and Epic Games, and also worked with Amazon's game studios. Nylund lives in the Pacific Northwest with his wife, award-winning science fiction/fantasy writer Syne Mitchell, and their son.

Build Beyond™

MEGACONSTRUX.COM

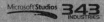